Richard Evans' first book, D... Australian political process t...

Just finished reading *Deceit* and it was gripping; I could not put it down. It was brilliant. I just loved the book and can't wait to read *Duplicity*.' — *FORMER CLERK OF VICTORIAN LEGISLATIVE COUNCIL*

I absolutely loved it, couldn't put it down. I would love to see your book become a movie. – *IAN S., MELBOURNE*

Rich in ideas and provokes much thought about our parliamentary process, abuses of power, corruption, and the need, at times, for ordinary people to step up and take a stand in the name of honour and professional integrity. – *NADINE D., EDITOR*

'The Kill Bill has such a fascinating concept at its heart and you brought the characters to life brilliantly.' – *C.dB, EDITOR*

This is an outstanding debut from Evans, and this terrific read comes highly recommended.' – *GOODREADS*

From former Federal MP Richard Evans comes this exceptional political thriller debut, which serves as the first part of his Democracy trilogy.' *CANBERRA WEEKLY*

I adored Gordon O'Brien. Straight as an arrow amongst those who are only in things for themselves, I couldn't help but cheer him on as he was like a dog with a bone, searching out the truth' *BJ'S BOOK BLOG*

I thoroughly enjoyed the book and did not want to put the book down, but neither did I want the story to end! Congratulations! – *TRINITY MARKETING*

## ALSO BY RICHARD EVANS

**Democracy Trilogy**

Deceit

Duplicity

Doomed

**Referendum Series**

Forgotten People

The Kill Bill

The Mallee

**Stand Alone Books**

Out of my Hands

Selfish Ambitions

**Non-Fiction**

The Australian Franchising Handbook

CAN THE TRUTH OVERCOME THE **ABUSE** OF POLITICAL POWER?

RICHARD EVANS

852 PRESS

852
PRESS

First published in 2018 by Impact Press, an imprint of Ventura Press
PO Box 780, Edgecliff NSW 2027 Australia www.impactpress.com.au

Third Edition published in 2023 by 852 Press,
Suite 12, 12 Eshelby Drive, Airlie Beach Queensland 4802 Australia
www.852Press.com.au

10 9 8 7 6 5 4 3



This book is a work of fiction. The characters and incidents are the products of the writer's imagination and are not to be construed as real.

National Library of Australia Cataloguing-in-Publication entry:

Author: Evans, Richard
Title: Deceit / by Richard Evans
ISBN: 978-0-6452823-1-3 (paperback)
ISBN: 978-0-6452823-2-0 (ebook)
ISBN: 978-0-6452823-3-7 (hardcover)

Australian fiction.
Cover Design: 852 Press

*For Julia*

*Your ideas and good humour have made it fun.*

## The Major Players

**GOVERNMENT:**

| | |
|---|---|
| Andrew Gerrard | Prime Minister |
| Meredith Bruce | Manager of Government Business |
| Zara Bagshaw | Speaker |
| Everett Menzies | Attorney General |

**OPPOSITION**

| | |
|---|---|
| James Harper | Opposition Leader |
| Wilson Campbell | Deputy Opposition Leader |
| Barton Messenger | Manager of Opposition Business |
| Peter Stanley | Member for Curtin |
| Christopher Hughes | Member for Warringah |

**PARLIAMENT OFFICERS**

| | |
|---|---|
| Gordon O'Brien | Clerk of The House of Representatives |
| Nigel Nelson | Black Rod, Senate |

**MEDIA**

| | |
|---|---|
| Anita Devlin | Hancock investigative journalist, Canberra |
| Peter Cleaver | Hancock Chief of Canberra Bureau |
| Cassandra Rogers | Hancock Television |

# PROLOGUE

**EIGHT MONTHS EARLIER ...**

The two ageing politicians sprawled in the leader's soft leather chairs; old friends, comfortable with each other after a slow, four-course dinner in the adjoining dining room. They were enjoying the pungency of expensive cigars, smoke spiralling toward the high ceiling. Both had a tumbler of Irish whiskey, preferring the smooth, refined taste to the harshness of the scotch usually imbibed by the philistines they ruled over.

'I can't do it.' The prime minister stretched his long legs across the heavy coffee table, easing away a pile of books and magazines, his head dropping back onto the green leather. 'It's a generous offer, but I can't.'

'You have nothing to fear, my friend. There will be no trouble for you.' The president blew smoke toward the ceiling. 'It's timing; there's nothing criminal about this.'

'I suspect pocketing a secret commission might be judged criminal.'

'Consider it a gift from me. No-one will ever know.'

'I can't be certain of that – and you can't either.' Prime Minister Gerrard sipped his whiskey and flushed it over his tongue.

'Andrew, you worry far too much. These things happen all the time in my country.'

'To be expected then.

'Exactly.' The president sharpened his tone. 'All I need to make this happen for you is your bank account – Swiss, of course – and your assurance the money will be released by your government to us before March next year.'

'It's way too risky.'

'You should have little fear; trust me. Legislate the money and perhaps tie it to a condition we start construction at once. Transfer the funds, we start site works, and then you let me do the rest. You will not be involved; I can assure you.' Surriento took a small swig of whiskey. 'You get your detention centres, and we provide jobs to many thousands of my people. It's a win-win for our countries – and us.'

'I suppose I could appropriate the money and release it to you before March, but I'll need compelling evidence of your government's approval for the build well before then.'

'It can be done.'

'I would much prefer to see site works begin before we release any money.'

'It is possible.'

Gerrard drew deeply on his cigar, pondering the deal. The president flicked a lump of ash onto the plush woollen carpet.

'What, you can't reach the ashtray?'

'No problem, rub it in, it's good for the carpet, just as this arrangement is good for you and me.' The toothy salesman's grin prompted a sly smirk from the prime minister.

'You dirty bastard.' Gerrard slowly shook his head, considering the offer. 'I can't just let you have four billion dollars with nothing to show for it.'

'Then don't give me the entire amount; we can do it in stages.' The president began reeling in his catch. 'If you are so worried about how this works, then let's do it in four stages. Four hundred million down before March next year, then one billion for each of the next two years, with a final payment of one point six billion on completion. Just think, in four years you could retire on a high.'

'I reckon if I can convince my colleagues to approve the money in the forward estimates next month, that will leave me enough time to get legislation through both houses of parliament later in the year for the first tranche of ten per cent to be paid, possibly enacted by February next year. Is that enough time to begin work on the first centre?'

'Of course, my friend, more than enough time. Once you legislate, we can start ground works, and once we have the money, you will have your money. Simple as that. We can clear it to you within days of each payment.'

The president knew he was close to a deal: 'You know you deserve it; you have worked hard and sacrificed much. This money will help with your retirement.' The president sat forward, sliding his tumbler toward the prime minister for a refill, knowing silence in these moments was a powerful tool for a negotiator.

The prime minister splashed a handsome dram into his friend's tumbler. 'When do you need to know?'

'Now.'

'The parliament is too finely balanced, and a few of my junior colleagues hate your lot. It may be tricky getting the Appropriation Bill through. We're okay for numbers in the senate, but the house of reps may be a struggle given your insistence on murdering some of our finest citizens.'

'Drug traffickers deserve to die.'

'You know that, I know that, but the great unwashed don't like their own facing a firing squad in the jungle.'

The president picked up his glass, rolled it between his hands and pondered for a moment. 'So, you're telling me, if I do a deal on your two citizens, you will approve the money?'

'No, I'm not saying that at all, but it might be helpful.'

'You get state-of-the-art detention centres in my country, and you want me to breach my own laws?'

'Oh, come on, Amir, you know this project will be good for your economy, and it will shut the fucking humanitarians up. We both need this project.'

'Yes, but if we don't get initial funding by next March, we won't be able to do it.' The president had his own deadlines and financial needs.

'You mean if you don't get your money, you won't do it?'

'I have my own troubles, my own projects that need to be funded.' The president took a larger draw of his whiskey, swallowing hard, stifling a small ref lux before the liquid and vapours disappeared. Suddenly, he felt hot and prickly, wiping his brow with his palm as the whiskey coursed through him. 'I won't deny it will help me, as it will you. I just can't release drug traffickers for no reason.'

'Let me give you a reason. I will approve the four-billion-dollar project on the day you grant them clemency. Not a pardon, but clemency from the death penalty. Let the fuckers rot in jail as far as I'm concerned.'

'I can't; I would lose the next election if I were to do that.'

'Okay, so we agree to disagree.' The prime minister could sense a deal was at hand.

'I can't, Andrew!'

'So, this idea of money was just talk – you had no intention of really doing a deal.'

The politicians sat quietly, not knowing who had the upper hand in the negotiations. The prime minister, almost asleep with his eyes closed and breathing heavily; the president smirking ever so slightly in recognition of his friend's efforts to force a winning play.

'Here's an idea,' the president said finally, drawing his friend from his sham slumber. 'What say I allow an appeal on the first payment? This then runs for two years, and if I am re-elected, I recommend clemency when the final payment is made.'

'No, my friend. Just the agreed clemency is no longer on the table. The deal now is – you also agree to release them from that hell hole you call a jail when you receive the final payment, then I will consider your plan to embezzle appropriated funds from the Australian government.'

'Clemency and then a pardon?' the president scoffed. 'So, if I agree to this new outrageous demand, you will get me my money?'

'Our money,' the prime minister said, swinging his legs off the table and leaning forward, his tumbler held out in anticipation of a toast.

The president leaned forward and clinked the proffered glass. 'Best you get yourself a bank account, Mr Prime Minister.'

'To a long and prosperous partnership.'

The president brought his glass to his lips but did not drink. With a barely perceptible smile, he recalled his actions of the morning: he had already decided to grant clemency to the two Australians stopped at Jakarta international airport twelve years earlier with ten kilos of heroin strapped to their bodies. Now he could reverse his decision, leaking it to the media to show he was tough on crime, adding further political gravitas to his re-election campaign in two years' time. He loved his Australian friend like a brother. Their wives were friends from university, and he didn't enjoy taking advantage of him, but this was business – and in his culture, business was never personal.

The prime minister lay back and drew heavily on his cigar,

mouthing smoke rings as he slowly exhaled, reflecting on his newfound wealth. It would be a richly deserved legacy for his years of service and sacrifice. 'I've been in this damn business for nearly forty years, and I still have little to show for it.'

'In my country, it is expected our leaders will be looked after. This is the problem with you Australians – you should embrace the political culture of Asia.' The president smiled; his fat cigar stuck in the side of his mouth. 'It is only a small amount to start with, but it will grow and be ready for when you retire. When will you retire, by the way?'

'I am thinking I might do one more term, maybe two. Margaret still has it in her head to move to France.'

'Perhaps there will be room for us as well. Can you imagine both of us retired in the south of France?'

'That's where the shysters go, I suppose. It's an attractive thought, I must say.'

'Get this deal done on time before March next year, and you will be halfway there, my friend.'

# CHAPTER 1

**MONDAY 4.25 PM**

It wasn't unusual for an October storm to hit the coastal city of Newcastle, but the hammering rain belting the corrugated roof of the makeshift airport office troubled Fred Rocher. He needed to be back in Canberra for meetings, and his pilot seemed nervous about flying in the conditions – the smaller the plane the more nervous the aviator, he supposed.

His parliamentary colleagues had been bunkered down in the small, cosy shed – optimistically called a waiting room by Hunter Air Services – for a little under an hour, with no sign of urgency from the inattentive staff, who were working in a much more salubrious shed next door.

Rocher was obliged to get his colleagues back to the national capital the following day to vote on important legislation. The prime minister had insisted on pushing through legislation-approved seed funding for a state-of-the-art offshore immigration detention centre to be built on the Indonesian island of Ambon, the first of similar centres planned throughout the Indonesian archipelago. He wanted it to pass both houses of parliament before the Christmas break because a four-hundred-million-dollar payment to the Indonesians was required as soon as possible to kick-start the project. The government held only a two-seat majority in the House of Representatives, so every vote was important, and Rocher knew they needed him and his colleagues to make sure the bill passed so they could send it to the senate for ratification.

After a hectic day, the group had stretched themselves out across various rickety chairs and benches. A vending machine provided the only amenity, and a poster of sunny beaches partially stuck to a wall provided the only decoration. Each member of the powerful Environment Committee was working diligently, tapping away on social media, reading a book, or flicking through business papers. They'd been up early, travelling from Canberra at 5.30 am, the sky still brilliant with stars and the lush landscape below shrouded in darkness. The ninety-minute flight took them over the Blue Mountains and on to coastal Newcastle to take evidence for a pivotal inquiry into the establishment of a proposed gas facility, the infrastructure of which would affect the region. If the committee approved the project, after hearing evidence from various stakeholders, then it meant jobs for a region struggling with an economic downturn.

Peter Wilson, the committee's long-term secretary and delegation manager, had arranged a bus to transport the parliamentary group throughout their highly structured day of meetings and formal hearings. The first meeting had been with the mayor to garner intelligence on the local politics of the controversial issue, and then a working breakfast with the mayor and the elected members of the city council had provided more insight into the mood of the community and their views about the proposed facility. After meetings with city engineers to discuss planning issues and the complex infrastructure requirements, the committee was transported to the university to hear from a professor explaining the principles of coal seam gas extraction and rebutting the myths about it, with only one politician falling asleep during the forty- minute PowerPoint presentation. The committee then returned to the city's council offices to formally take submissions from residents concerned about their community's safety and water quality if the proposed facility went ahead, the high-ceilinged room echoing with the amplified voices of concerned and emotional citizens. After a lunch of soggy sandwiches and forgettable, watery fruit juice, the committee took supplementary evidence until three o'clock from mining and engineering experts extolling the economic and social advantages of gas extraction for the region, before leaving for their planned 3.45 pm flight.

Clouds started to roll in across the coast during the early afternoon, darkening as they thickened over the nearby mountains, providing an eerily low canopy of cloud cover from the mountains to the coast, lightning flashing high in the blanket of cloud and illuminating through the darkness. What started as a soaking spring shower so typical for the region increased in such intensity during the last hour to build into a wild storm, with no sign of it easing. Gusting wind rattled the building, and the occasional flashes of lightning breaking through the low cloud and accompanying cracks of thunder suggested the storm was travelling slowly, hemmed in by the mountains. The unseen airline staff were yet to venture out of their office.

'Peter, try to see what's happening will you please.' The delay exasperated Rocher. 'We need to get going if we want to be back tonight.'

'I'll try to get hold of the pilot.'

As Peter stood, the door smashed open, rocking the walls. Pelting rain was driven into the room. A soaking, bedraggled pilot rushed through the doorway and struggled to close the door against the wind. Peeling off his inadequate raincoat, he made his way to the counter, then turned and faced his passengers, raising his voice above the din of the rain smashing on the tin roof.

'We're not likely to take off until the storm passes, I'm afraid. It seems to have set in over the mountains, and we would need to get above it to have any chance of getting to Canberra. I'm not sure my kite can do that.'

'Not acceptable, I'm afraid.' Rocher stood and approached the pilot. 'We need to be back tonight.'

'Hey wait up, Fred.' Mark English put aside his iPad and walked over, keen to join the discussion. 'If the pilot says it's too dangerous, then I'm with him.'

English was a government member and understood the necessity of getting back to Canberra that evening, but his reputation for risk aversion was well established.

'He didn't say it was too dangerous. He said we need to get above the storm to get over the mountains.' Rocher was keen to get going. 'What's the weather like on the other side of the mountains?'

'Perfect.' The pilot conceded.

'Well, there you are then. Taking off in a storm is much easier compared to landing in one, so let's go.'

'What do the others think?' English persisted.

'Not sure they have a vote on this, Mark, but if you insist.' Rocher moved to the centre of the room to address his colleagues, most of whom had paid little attention to the pilot. 'Okay folks, listen up. As most of you probably know, we need to be back in Canberra tonight. Well, we government members do at least. We want to leave now, although it's still raining, but we have a small problem. The storm doesn't seem to be abating, so no doubt we will need to take off over the coast, go out to sea and do a slow climb to get above it, first the cloud bank and then the mountains. It will absolutely be a rough ride, but no worse than some of you have already experienced, I'm sure, and then it's smooth flying until Canberra.'

A crack of thunder rattled the unsecured cupboards, and everyone jumped.

'Christ!' yelped English.

'What are our options?' opposition member Nick Trainer asked, a little louder than he would have liked.

'We can get going now and be back around six. We can wait

until the storm eases and fly with an unknown ETA into Canberra, or we can stay overnight and fly back on a commercial jet tomorrow morning, but I'm not sure the PM would approve because we will miss a vote,' volunteered Rocher.

'It isn't the worst storm I've flown in,' said the pilot, dragging on a cigarette and blowing out a solid stream of smoke. 'But I'm always nervous about taking passengers up in weather like this. I can tell you; it'll be worse than any roller-coaster, and I suspect some of you will find it frightening... and some of you will be sick.'

'I vote we go now,' said Paul Kress, a government member. 'I have an important dinner at the US embassy I can't miss.'

English swayed slowly from side to side. The others looked about their group, waiting for someone to make a decision.

'Don't forget, we have the retirement presentation for the clerk tonight,' added Catherine Kennedy. 'It'd be nice to get there to acknowledge his service.'

'Stuff the clerk. He's never done much for us,' English blurted.

'Ease up Mark, I'm just saying it would be nice to be there.' Kennedy, the deputy speaker of the parliament, gave him a reassuring smile.

'Let's make it easy. Who doesn't want to go?' Rocher impatiently asked the group, who had fallen silent trying to avoid a decision.

'Me,' the pilot said, sucking hard on his cigarette.

Rocher smirked, shaking his head. 'Anyone else? Mark?' The

heavy drumming of the rain filled the room and English bowed his head, defeated. 'Okay, pack up and let's go.'

'I must formally advise you that you are doing so at your own risk, and you'll need to sign a waiver,' the pilot said as he pulled a folded paper from his jacket and passed it to Rocher. 'The airline will not cover any breakages of either equipment or yourselves, is that understood?'

'What about funerals?' Trainer joked, collecting his papers.

No-one laughed.

'Duly noted. Where do I sign? Oh, and Peter, can you record that advice?' Rocher directed as he signed the waiver and passed it back to the pilot. 'Folks, if anyone is uncertain about taking this flight you can stay and take a flight tomorrow morning. Anybody want to stay? Mark?'

English shrugged and no-one else responded as they packed their briefcases and satchels.

'So be it, you're all nuts.' The pilot headed for the plane, rain whipping into the room through the open door. He tossed his sodden cigarette into the wind.

'Come on boys, this'll be fun.' Catherine Kennedy skipped after the pilot into the rain, holding her satchel on her head to protect her stiff bouffant; her signature developed over twenty years of service in the federal parliament.

The others braced themselves against the wild weather, gripping their suit jackets, shrugging their shoulders, then bolting after her through puddles and driving rain to the plane. Rocher lingered by the door, waiting for his secretary, Wilson, to zip his case and join him.

'It never gets any easier, does it? Remember that flight we had in the Kimberley a few months back?' Rocher's broad smile almost convinced Wilson.

'Yes, but I haven't seen rain like this for a long time,' Wilson responded. 'And I'm not so sure this is a good idea.'

'Nothing to fear, Pete. Our man will take us out over the ocean to get us above this lot. Ten minutes of jumping around and then it'll be smooth as silk all the way home. We can crack open a bottle of wine once we're over the mountains.'

'Let's hope so.' Wilson dashed from the room in a wretched attempt to keep dry.

By the time Rocher reached the plane, the single-engine turboprop Cessna was spluttering into action. He climbed aboard, pulling up the steps and sealing the hatch, confirming with the pilot he had done so. He then sank into a leather chair behind the pilot, facing the group, as ground crew in wet weather gear busily secured the plane for take-off and unchocked the wheels.

It was a tight squeeze to get to the back of the plane, the generous leather seats reducing aisle access and movement, but the eight politicians settled in as best they could for a flight, they expected to talk about at future cocktail parties, or when called upon at dinners to recount unusual political experiences. This would be the night they survived potential catastrophe and lived to tell the tale, and the more they told the tale, the more laughs they would get at the expense of their colleagues.

Wet, miserable, and just a little apprehensive, they spread themselves among the fourteen plush seats. The pilot passed back a handful of towels to Wilson, which he distributed to the rest of the group, all keen to wipe themselves down and dry their hands and faces.

Catherine Kennedy seemed the most disordered by the dash to the plane, her trademark bouffant flattened and lopsided, revealing a somewhat sparse patch of scalp. Luckily, she didn't have a mirror; she would not have been pleased if her reputation for perfect grooming was tarnished. Cautiously, she dabbed and prodded at her wet hair, trying to reshape it, while those colleagues sitting behind her smirked and exchanged looks.

Although it was still only late afternoon, the light was grey and ominous under the roof of storm clouds. As the plane moved slowly from the tarmac apron toward the runway, the pilot, visible from the cabin, was working through his pre-flight check, speaking quietly into a microphone attached to oversized headphones. The plane's stability surprised the politicians, feeling only a little buffeting in the gusting wind. Perhaps the anxiety in the cabin was misplaced.

Rocher held up an air sickness bag and asked, 'Anyone want one of these?'

'I've already struggled through those sandwiches once already; I don't want to see them again,' joked Trainer.

'How come you're never this funny in the house?' demanded English.

'The boss always tells me to keep a lid on it, so I behave myself, unlike Harry here.'

'What have I done?'

'Nothing, as usual,' said Trainer.

Harry McMaster, younger than Trainer, squeezed a smile and quipped: 'The trouble with you, Nick, my boy is that you are too predictable. Never a serious word, ever.'

'I'll have some serious words to say about this potential mess, I can tell you.'

'It won't matter,' said English. 'Your team doesn't have the numbers – you'll be in opposition for a long time yet, mate.'

'Oh, I don't know. I reckon Jimmy Harper is the most able man to have entered the parliament since Menzies. He'll take it up to your bloke. Someone has to.' Trainer had reset his political antenna.

'Well, you could be right,' offered McMaster. 'But the PM is not going anywhere, and while he remains in the parliament, you'll never win.'

'You can't be that confident. I'm not so sure your bloke will run at another election. Too old.'

Rocher's phone buzzed, and its shrill alarm startled him. He realised it was the prime minister's call tone.

'Speak of the devil. Hi Andrew.' Rocher had known the prime minister since university and was one of only a few colleagues permitted to call him by name.

'Freddy, where are you?'

'Just about to leave Newcastle. Bad weather has delayed us. It's bucketing down and we're about to take off into it. We should get to Canberra around 6.30.'

'I was just making sure you'll be back for the vote on the Immigration Appropriation Bill tomorrow morning.'

'We'll be there. We understand its importance, and it's the

reason we're all flying back. We couldn't afford to wait here any longer. We should be back in time for your function for the clerk – we're looking forward to it.'

'No big deal. The sooner he's gone the better.'

'Now come on, Andrew, you know he's only doing his job.'

'Bastard, as far as I'm concerned.'

'He'll be gone soon enough, cheer up.' Rocher shifted uncomfortably. 'Look, we're about to take off, so I'll ring you when we land. I need to talk to you about this inquiry in Newcastle and the potential trouble ahead with the local community. It could cost us a seat or two at the next election, which means we could lose government. The opposition is taking a tough line on it.' Rocher winked at the two opposition members listening in to his conversation.

'Sure, do that, old friend. I'll be keen to learn more. Take care,' ended the prime minister.

Rocher dropped his phone into the small upper pocket of his damp Armani jacket and looked over to see an apprehensive Wilson gazing at him from the seat opposite. 'Don't worry, Pete, this bird is one of the safest in the air.'

'We'll see.' Wilson seemed unconvinced.

Facing into the wind, the pilot raised the engine revs to a screaming crescendo, building enough force to propel the plane into the air. The travellers sat silently, feeling the plane wobble as it fought against the brake.

'Okay, this is it boys. Hold on,' Rocher joked to his colleagues.

They all looked past him at the pilot, seeking reassurance but getting none.

Just when the engine seemed about to explode, the pilot released the brakes, jumping the Cessna into a fast sprint along the runway to take off. The plane shook and bumped sharply as it drove hard into the wind, laboriously working to reach the required speed of 150 knots. Rocher squeezed the arm of his chair and gnawed at his bottom lip as the plane's nose lifted. Moments later, with a great shudder and creaking shake, they were airborne – cupboard doors popped open and small, untethered knick-knacks tumbled into the cabin. The politicians sat silently.

The climb seemed dangerously slow amidst all the shuddering, banging, and shaking. Rocher continued gnawing on his lip, glancing at Wilson, who stiffened in his chair. Rocher himself was still gripping the arms of his seat, pushing back hard, resisting the uncontrollable movement of the plane. He was already regretting his decision to take the flight as another thud shook the cabin and he looked out his window, seeing nothing but turbulent, grey cloud.

'Fuck!' shouted Kennedy, as the plane jolted heavily to its left.

'Not likely, Cathy,' joked Trainer, seemingly immune to the unease of his comrades.

'It won't be long now,' Rocher said after a few tense minutes. 'Once we're above the cloud band, it should be smooth sailing to Canberra.'

'I've seen worse,' said Kennedy, trying to regain her composure, her hair slipping further as her head jolted with the turbulence.

Thumps and bangs continued to sound throughout the cabin as the plane shuddered and plunged, fighting to climb through the turbulence, and resisting the furious wind. A sudden eerie silence descended on the cabin, and everyone looked at each other for support, hoping for a little relief.

Bam! A colossal thump shuddered through the entire plane, followed abruptly by a thunderous knocking sound from the front, as if a steel-capped boot was rotating in a clothes drier. An urgent, intermittent warning beep sounded from the cockpit, which glowed with a red flashing light. The plane dropped, shuddered, and jerked, groaning as the pilot fought for control. An automated voice from the cockpit warned, 'Terrain ahead, pull out. Terrain ahead, pull out.'

'Brace for impact,' the unruffled voice of the pilot said.

'Terrain ahead, pull out. Terrain ahead, pull out.'

The politicians assumed the brace position as best they could and waited.

# CHAPTER 2

**MONDAY 5.55 PM**

'Is that a rufous whistler?' Gordon O'Brien said to no-one in particular, staring into a leafy maple from his office window. 'It's a bit early to hear them.'

Standing behind his desk, O'Brien often looked for signs of life within the mighty tree beyond his first-floor window. He loved that maple tree. Ever since he had moved into the office following his promotion to clerk of the Australian parliament, he had watched its changing colours and silhouette throughout the seasons. If he was stressed or worried by his parliamentary duties, he was often calmed by the tree's lush green leaves of summer, or the stark, sculpted boughs of winter. He especially loved the colours of autumn – the golds and amber – and always felt refreshed by the new buds and tiny red blossoms of early spring.

Finding a bird or some other little creature hopping about the branches captivated him, removing him from the demanding daily grind of parliamentary procedure.

Gordon had stared despondently into the tree many, many times over his seventeen-year career as clerk, often wishing he was elsewhere, but in a little over two weeks his career would come to an end as he had finally decided to retire. Paradoxically, he realised he would miss all this, even the stress of managing the daily machinations of the national parliament and thought with dismay about the uncertain loneliness of retirement, and the fear of living a life unfulfilled.

The distinct black, white, and russet markings of the whistler were a delight – it was not unusual to see whistlers in late spring and summer, but still. 'What a little beauty.'

'Who is?' asked Marjorie Earle, Gordon's long-serving personal assistant, as she entered the office and set a pile of papers on his desk. 'What have you seen now?'

Gordon continued to track the bird as it hopped from branch to branch, searching for food. 'I'm going to miss it, Marjorie,' Gordon sighed. 'All of it.'

'You've done enough, Gordon. You can't keep going forever.'

'I suppose so,' Gordon sighed. 'Still, I'm going to miss it.' He drew a deep breath in through his nose, ballooning his chest, and held it slightly before slowly releasing it in a noisy, dejected sigh.

'Don't you dare change your mind.' Marjorie stopped momentarily and studied her boss. 'I've already sold my house, and I'm off in January, so don't expect me to change mine.'

Gordon smiled as the bird fluttered away and he turned from the window. 'You have nothing to worry about.'

'It's almost six. They'll be waiting for you.' The faithful assistant, ever present and confident enough to provide Gordon with advice, even when he didn't want it, straightened the papers.

'Do I have to go?' Gordon dropped into his chair feeling the energy draining from him. The thought of having to mingle with backslapping parliamentary staff and politicians was not one he relished; and he was not looking forward to what he knew he was required to do.

'It's not every day the prime minister throws a party for one of us.' Marjorie slid the first of the files toward him, her bangles hitting the desk.

'I won't miss that one, that's for sure.'

'Come on Gordon, let them celebrate your service. God knows you've sacrificed enough for all of them, so let them thank you.'

'I just want to serve these last two weeks and leave quietly. Frankly, I don't like them that much, and what they've done to this place is disgraceful, so why should I let them celebrate me.'

'Get over yourself, Gordon. Go and enjoy a chardonnay or two and let them fawn over you. You deserve it.'

'What have you got for me?' Gordon carefully scanned each brief for both content and potential errors before signing with his thick fountain pen and sliding it back to Marjorie after blotting his signature. Modern ballpoint pens were yet to touch his much-loved desk.

'Gordon, these things can wait.'

'No, they can't.' Everything had its place and only unimportant items were ever allowed to sit for any length of time awaiting his approval.

Marjorie sighed a little too loudly and bit her lip to stop saying something she might regret. Gordon could flick through a file quickly, scanning the contents, looking for anything out of place, and signing where required. He trained his staff to prepare briefs in plain English on the variety of parliamentary business issues requiring his approval, so there was no confusion with ambiguous language, and clear recommendations for action were set out for him. It made his busy life easier, but he always kept a careful eye on standards.

As Gordon methodically scanned the papers and files, Marjorie stood silently by his side, as she had done for seventeen years. She'd shared his battles with the politicians who had sought to change the protocols and standing orders of the parliament. He often told his staff it was his job to protect the parliament from the political barbarians at the gate.

All parliamentary business crossed Gordon's desk for review and approval. His advice about parliamentary process and procedure was sought by politicians, and he had seen a lot of them come and go. Some were bad, driven by nothing more than self-interest, but most who came to serve their electorates came with good intentions. Gordon knew the rorts, and how to undermine the parliamentary system. He abhorred politicians with a frivolous attitude toward the established historical rules and protocols of the parliament, and often corrected a recalcitrant politician, even the prime minister, when they crossed the line of acceptable parliamentary behaviour. Gordon took it personally if anything untoward happened under his watch and believed that he was the difference between an effective legislative chamber and chaos.

'That's new,' said Marjorie as she admired a small, fluffy object sitting on the brass lamp base.

Gordon paused and picked up his one weakness, a fishing fly. 'Yes, I made it this morning.'

'You really love it, don't you?'

'I'm looking forward to doing more.' Gordon smiled for a moment, twirling the lure in his fingers, studying the orange and green feathers, imagining how a trout might see it, holding it up in the light, his eyes never leaving his creation. 'Could you turn the news on please, Marjorie. I'll listen to the headlines before I go.'

Marjorie moved to the marble coffee table, picked up the remote and flicked on the television. The internal parliamentary telecast from the chamber of the House of Representatives momentarily showed a politician on his feet shouting before she tuned to the local news program. Gordon gently returned his prized possession to the lamp stand and resumed reading a file.

The distinct music of the six o'clock news introduced the headlines, and Gordon listened as he flicked through the final piece of paperwork.

'Prime Minister Gerrard sends a signal to illegal boat people after a meeting with the Indonesian president approving funding for a new immigration detention centre on the Indonesian island of Ambon. Fire disrupts services in the hills, with arson suspected. A teenager struck and killed by a commuter train in Sydney while saving a friend's dog. The Australian cricket team struggles to match England's bowlers in a batting rout in the first test at the Gabba.

'This is National One News, with Sylvia Burns.'

'Good evening. Prime Minister Andrew Gerrard has announced that legislation approving funding for the first offshore detention centre to be built on the Indonesian island of Ambon in the new year will be finalised in the parliament this week. The prime minister made the legislative commitment at a joint press conference after a formal meeting with Indonesian president Doctor Amir Surriento, who is visiting Australia to discuss bilateral foreign policy, intended to reduce the number of illegally smuggled boat people during the summer months. Reporting outside the prime minister's residence is Curtis Jones...'

'You'll miss your old sparring partner, I suspect.'

'I doubt he'll miss me. Turn it down, will you?' Gordon said.

'You really don't like him, do you?'

'If I could leave here and never have to see him again, I would be very grateful. He has upset me so much with his attitude and his changes to standing orders and parliamentary procedure, and the way he mistreats the parliamentary staff is totally unacceptable.' Gordon closed the last file and pushed back from his desk. 'I heard today he's running again at the next election; the man just doesn't know when to give up. You're right, I don't like him.'

'Perhaps you should dismiss him,' Marjorie offered, stifling a laugh.

'If only I could.' Gordon got to his feet. 'Now that I'm going, who will protect the parliament from him?' Just as Marjorie muted the television, the door opened and Paige Alexander, Gordon's diary secretary, entered in a flurry.

'Mr O'Brien, I've just taken a call from the prime minister's office wondering where you are. They're waiting in the speaker's courtyard for you.'

'Yes, okay. I'm coming,' sighed Gordon. Marjorie gathered up the files and papers.

'If I'm not back within forty minutes, please come and get me.'

Gordon collected his jacket, almost identical to the one he'd had on his first day as clerk, and carefully swung it on as he strode from his office.

---

'Where is the pompous goose?'

'He won't be long, Prime Minister. I just spoke to his office. He's on his way.'

'He's a slimy little bastard. I don't know why I even bothered with this.'

'You bother because you are the prime minister.'

'Get me a drink will you. I'll have a beer. I'm going to have a chat to Zara.' Gerrard smirked and watched his principal private secretary slink off to the drinks table, pushing through the mob of politicians and their staff, more interested in the free hospitality than the honoured guest.

Gerrard scanned the room and saw Speaker Bagshaw in a corner talking to someone he didn't recognise, her elegant black frock complementing her brown skin, her pillar-box red lipstick marking her perfect smile. She was oozing charisma as she listened to the conversation, her thick, curly hair adding to her unique allure. As Gerrard headed for her, she saw him coming and whispered a warning to her colleague.

'You look very attractive this evening, Madam Speaker. I love the way you've done your hair,' Gerrard said, ignoring the other women. He towered over Bagshaw, his stature commanding respect, the greying hair marking his sixty-seven years. His suit looked as if it had come from the finest Italian tailor, the subtle pinstripe of the rich dark blue cloth contrasting with a white shirt and striking orange and grey silk tie.

'Prime Minister? How nice to see you.' Bagshaw straightened her frock, cheeks flushing, as her colleague escaped. 'This was a brilliant idea.'

'Well, the old bastard is finally retiring, so why not?' Gerrard almost spat the words. 'It's the very least I can do for the moron, and thankfully the only celebration I'll need to attend for him. Although there is talk of a parliamentary thing, but I won't be going.'

Bagshaw didn't respond. She didn't share the prime minister's view that the clerk was a handicap to the government. 'It's a nice thought anyway. When would you like to speak?'

'I was just thinking,' Gerrard looked about the room and identified the leader of the opposition examining a food tray offered by a waiter. 'Invite Harper to speak first. Don't let him know, though. Put him on the spot and let's watch him squirm.'

'You're rather devious, aren't you?' smiled Bagshaw.

'You, more than anyone else, should know that my dear Zara.'

Bagshaw stopped and looked at her prime minister, and slowly, suspiciously, said, 'Yes?'

Gerrard played the exotic dance of political banter well, his power absolute; he did whatever he liked, and always got what he wanted. 'How's the new husband?'

'He's good,' replied Bagshaw, looking about the room and nodding to various colleagues. She did not want to encourage Gerrard.

'Giving you what you want?'

'All I need.'

'Surely not everything you need?'

'He makes me happy.'

'Does he? Does he make you truly happy, Zara?' Gerrard mocked.

'He does,' Bagshaw snapped.

'I was just thinking, if you ever want what I know you really need,' Gerrard paused, 'then call me. There is never any harm in someone getting what they really want.'

'It's over, Andrew.' Bagshaw anxiously sipped her wine, scanning to see if anyone was listening.

'Hmm,' Gerrard paused for just a moment. 'Are you planning to retire soon?'

'No.'

'Then perhaps you should reflect upon your career choices.'

'You really are a nasty bastard, aren't you?'

'Not really... I just need what we used to have.'

They looked for any glimmer of understanding in each other's eyes, only to be interrupted by Gerrard's private secretary.

'He's here, Prime Minister.' Miles Fisher passed his boss a glass of beer.

'Why, thank you, young man.' Gerrard took the beer and finalised the conversation. 'We can continue to discuss your career in my suite later, Madam Speaker. Say around nine, after dinner, perhaps?'

'Yes, Prime Minister.' Bagshaw regretted saying it, but the prime minister's authority sent a tingle down her spine.

Gerrard moved away to chat with other colleagues and allow the speaker to host the event, now the guest of honour was present.

The speaker's courtyard, with its beautiful garden, catered for the more than fifty politicians and parliamentary colleagues comfortably. It was a secure, enclosed space outside her office suite with large, open, cantilevered, folding glass doors that allowed the garden and office to merge; a glassed walkway between the foyer of the parliamentary chamber and her office doors had been opened to allow even more room for the guests. Six Australian flags hung limply from a row of masts behind the lectern positioned to one side of the folding doors, as formally dressed waiters delivered drinks and cocktail food on silver trays. The guests chatted and laughed, looking forward to hearing O'Brien speak.

Gordon was warmly welcomed by colleagues from the department as he squeezed through the guests toward his host. Bagshaw was his tenth speaker, and Gordon wanted to get to her quickly so the speeches could start, which would allow him to leave earlier than his forty-minute deadline. He had work to do and legislation to approve for the following day's proceedings in the house. He felt uneasy with the backslapping and overly generous remarks; he was only doing his job, that's all, and saw no reason for a servant of the parliament to be honoured in such a way.

'Gordon, welcome.' Bagshaw extended her hand.

'Madam Speaker.' Gordon took her offered hand and limply acknowledged the welcome.

'Thank you for coming. Everyone has been looking forward to seeing you and wishing you well.'

'Thank you.' Gordon dropped her hand. 'Madam Speaker, I have a number of important tasks I must complete before seven, and I wonder if we could get going.'

'Yes, of course. I'll call everyone together. We have a couple of speeches, and a small gift...'

'Thank you.'

'Will you be able to say a few words? I think your friends would like to hear from you.'

'I haven't prepared anything, but I'm sure I could string a few words together.'

'I'm sure you can, Gordon. Would you like a drink?' The speaker summoned a waiter and Gordon took a glass of white wine from the laden tray.

'Thank you.' Gordon sipped his chardonnay and looked about, ending the conversation.

Speaker Bagshaw moved to the lectern on a small wooden podium, switched on the microphone and called for attention, straightening her notes that had been left there by a dutiful assistant. Her husky tones soon quietened the gathering.

'Good evening, colleagues... good evening. I welcome you all here this evening and thank the prime minister for his generosity in supporting this occasion. As you know, we are all here to recognise and celebrate the career of our long-serving clerk Gordon O'Brien, who is sadly about to retire.

'I was in primary school when Gordon first joined the parliament, almost a lifetime ago. He first started as an administrative assistant to the then clerk Sir Angus Levinstan some forty years ago, and quickly progressed to the ranks of management in various departments. Gordon has served as serjeant-at-arms to the house, deputy clerk and now, of course, he has been clerk for the last seventeen years.

'Gordon has the responsibility for overseeing all departments, from catering – ensuring we are all fed and watered—'

'Hear, hear.' The guests expressed their robust appreciation.

'... to transport, ensuring we all get home to our families safely. At the same time, he remains responsible for all legislation and the parliamentary process. During his long career, Gordon has served under just two changes of government, and as clerk he has served ten speakers. I am not sure what that means, but I am sure their length of stay in the chair had nothing at all to do with the unequivocal advice provided by Gordon.' Bagshaw waited for the laughter to subside.

'Speaking personally, I admire his respect for the parliament and its rules. He has been vigilant and is respected by all of us, as is his interpretation of standing orders. I have greatly appreciated his advice as I have settled into my role.' Bagshaw smiled at Gordon, who averted his gaze and shifted his weight uncomfortably.

'While we can often disagree on the interpretation of rules and standing orders, only an ignorant or foolish person would ignore his advice. He has assisted many members of the parliament, and his advice on legislative matters has often been sought. His long career has been outstanding, and his service will long be remembered. We are here tonight to assure him we appreciate the professionalism he has brought to his work, and the support he has provided to us all.'

As spontaneous applause erupted, Gordon shook his head slightly as if to challenge the speaker's assertions, before returning his gaze to his feet.

'We have much to say about you this evening, Gordon, so please allow us to show you our respect for the leadership, guidance and support you have provided to us all. Can I first call upon the leader of the opposition, James Harper, to say a few words?'

Gordon registered that Harper had been taken by surprise – he would not have shoved a hot spring roll into his mouth otherwise, just as he was introduced. He struggled to get the food down as he made his way to the podium, took a moment, and breathed deeply.

'I wasn't expecting to speak, and so I'm afraid I'm not prepared.'

Gerrard smiled, and ever so slightly inclined his head toward

Bagshaw, who returned the gesture with a smirk. 'But I do not need a wad of notes to talk about Gordon O'Brien.'

'Hear, hear,' someone yelled, and there was a smattering of applause. Gerrard frowned.

'Gordon is a rock. For over forty years he has been the very foundation stone of our parliament and he deserves the respect we all, as representatives of the wider Australian community, have for him. More importantly, he will be recorded in the annals of parliamentary history as a bulwark who protected the parliament from politicians with too much power, keen to ignore one of the most important institutions of the land.

'We will miss him. I will miss his counsel and the good cheer he provides, despite his rather stern professionalism.' A few chuckles of agreement came from colleagues. 'We all know Gordon has other plans once he leaves this place – he loves the challenge of fishing in the Snowy – but he will always be welcome back here in the corridors of power. We thank him for his distinguished service, his discipline, and his courage to say no. Gordon, I wish you well, and may your days include a memory or two of the folks you leave behind.'

As Harper moved from the podium to shake hands with Gordon, the appreciative applause lasted an embarrassing long time and Gordon was unsure what to do. He nodded his thanks a few times, pulled a disarming face to try to quell the enthusiasm, and looked at his feet yet again. Harper took his hand and shook it with a warmth Gordon respected, and returned to his place, collecting a glass of wine on the way.

'Thank you, James.' Bagshaw resumed her place before the

microphone and referred to her notes to check if she was missing anything from her running sheet. 'It is now my pleasure to introduce the prime minister. It is fair to say the prime minister and Gordon have had their differences over the years.' A titter or two sounded among the slight murmur from the guests. 'Please welcome, the prime minister.'

Strong applause greeted Gerrard and he waved away the enthusiasm of his supporters, enjoying the moment.

'Thank you – as the cow said to the farmer one winter morning – for the warm hand.' He had used the joke so many times it was almost a cliché, but his minions laughed obligingly. O'Brien and Harper were not amused.

'Friends, we are here this evening to celebrate a career we all admire. We stand before this gentleman – and Gordon is truly a gentle man; a man to be treasured, a man who is almost an institution.' Heads nodded.

'Gordon was here when most of us – well, at least, some of you – were still at school. He has presided over this great parliament with the zeal of a lion looking after his pride. He has protected the parliament from those who would have torn it down, and from those of us who strive for modernity within the standing orders of the parliament. Not for Gordon a modern Australia. Who could forget his stance during the republican debates?'

Certainly not Gordon: it was one of the highlights of his career, foiling the prime minister's plan to change the entire political system in Australia.

'Australians decided it was not yet time to be a fully independent nation, but no doubt one day we will succeed in convincing our fellow Australians to throw off the shackles of British royalty without worrying about who sits in what chair within the parliament.' Gerrard turned and looked grimly at Gordon.

'Yes, Gordon, you played an important role in the republican debate, but hopefully your sage, if somewhat quaint advice – if I may speak candidly – will not survive long beyond your retirement. I trust that when I raise the issue during my next term in office, the good citizens of Australia will see the choice more clearly and vote accordingly.'

Gordon met Gerrard's gaze, feeling a little irritated by his words. He'd expected as much from one of his fiercest critics.

'It is true, Gordon and I rarely see eye to eye on issues of stuffy parliamentary protocol. He has a reputation for being conventional and conservative and, of course, I am a progressive. Yet ironically, for the last seventeen years, we have managed to work together for the enrichment of our nation and achieve many parliamentary reforms. I point to the recent change to the constitution – parliamentary terms have increased from three years to five – as an example of old structures giving way to new ones. Gordon hated that idea, didn't you, Gordon?' Gerrard turned and casually leaned an elbow on the lectern, triumphantly facing O'Brien as he continued. 'Governments can't govern effectively in only three years; they need five to set out their economic plans and get things done rather than focusing on polls and elections.'

'Hear, hear.' Various government politicians dutifully responded. Gerrard straightened and addressed his audience.

'Gordon also supported the idea of ministers coming to question time each and every day, but I was of the view that it was a waste of time and taxpayers' money. The battles we had over that one, eh Gordon? I could write a book. Indeed, such a book would outdo Prince Machiavelli as a work of political instruction on how to get things done within a parliament.'

Gordon put down his glass and seriously considered walking out on the prime minister, then changed his mind. It would be a serious breach of protocol, but he was sorely tempted.

'We now have progressive and modern standing orders. Prime ministers need only be present for an hour once a week. This is as it should be – there is a government to run, and question time is only ever good for the television news cycle. Let the press gallery go and investigate news I say, rather than report the rather dull questions and unseemly behaviour of the opposition at question time. It was a struggle to get those amendments through, but we did, didn't we, Gordon?'

Gordon endured in silence, letting his anger sweep through him.

'However, Gordon has maintained the balance for all of us. We still have the pomp and pageantry of parliament. As you all know, I am a great supporter of the speaker moving back into the robes and ceremonial wig of times past.' Gerrard acknowledged the murmur of amusement, ignoring the glare from Bagshaw.

'Gordon!' Gerrard paused for a moment to ensure he had everyone's attention. 'You have been a terrific servant to – and for – me. No other has served me as well as you have, and I will miss you and your service.' Gerrard quickly looked about him, searching for something. 'Miles, do you have it?'

Fisher stepped forward with a long, thin colourfully wrapped gift.

'Gordon, on behalf of all those colleagues who work within the parliament and beyond, we wish you well in your retirement. As a measure of our hope you do enjoy your retirement, we would like to present you with this gift.

'The government would like to formally bestow upon you a more significant award in the Great Hall early next year. In the meantime, we think you will get immediate joy from our small gift.'

Gordon stepped forward, ignoring the prime minister's outstretched hand, taking the gift, and ripping at the wrapping paper. It was a Lancaster river rod, the best fly-fishing rod on the market, a valued addition to any serious angler's equipment: two thousand dollars of immediate pleasure, and he stood for a few moments admiring his prized gift before moving to the podium. As he did, he flicked the rod a couple of times and the loud swish satisfied him.

'Madam Speaker, Prime Minister Gerrard, James Harper, colleagues, ladies and gentlemen. What can I say? I am speechless. This is the most precious gift, and I look forward to standing in the Snowy and casting for a fish or two.' Clapping broke out from a few colleagues, aware of Gordon's passion for fly fishing. 'You have been so kind with your words and your generous applause, and I feel humbled by it all. I am not entitled to feel anything other than humble, because I was only doing my job, my duty. Certainly, I am proud of the work I have done, as any who labours over their work is entitled to feel. Beyond that, I know I am no more special than the next person who works in this fine building.

'We who work here are privileged to serve. We do so because we know that if we did not, anarchy is close at hand. For if the people of Australia do not have authority over their parliament, then what do they have?

'So, we do our job, and we do it to the best of our ability for the people of Australia. We do it not for ego, as perhaps some in this building may believe.' Gordon allowed himself a quick glance at Gerrard. 'We do it because we are patriots to the cause of democracy and its institutions. We do it because we need to do our duty. So, thank you for your warm applause and this generous gift, I truly appreciate them both.'

A text pinged into a smartphone.

'I thank you for the friendships we have developed over the years.'

Another ping, and then another.

'I thank you for your respect and support.'

Phones were now pinging throughout the gathering. A journalist suddenly appeared at the door to the courtyard.

'And—' Gordon paused, a little distracted by the visitor and the phone tones, clearly something was up. 'I thank you for giving me memories that I will always cherish. I look forward to seeing you all personally before Christmas, as I intend to visit each of you. Thank you, and all the very best.'

Distracted, muted applause broke out, as Fisher whispered into Gerrard's ear the message he'd just received. The prime minister blanched, his mouth dropping open like a fish.

# CHAPTER 3

**MONDAY 6.45 PM**

'A little late this afternoon, Mr Messenger?' The barista at Aussies Cafe tamped the grounds as he prepared another coffee. 'The usual?'

'Thanks, Sam.' Barton Messenger rejected the idea he was a coffee snob; he simply wanted to enjoy his afternoon latte. Melbourne coffee was the world's best in his view, and he never missed an opportunity to remind his parliamentary colleagues. 'Not so hot this time.'

'Busy day?' Sam poured milk into the steel jug and whipped it under the jet of steam.

'Yes, and it doesn't help when the government is yet to set their legislative program. What about you?'

'Ah, you know, always busy, not enough time.'

'You must be a millionaire by now.'

'Ten years I have been working in this place and not one holiday.'

'Didn't you go home to Italy last summer?'

'No holiday for me, family had me working every day.' He slowly poured the heated milk into the glass over a shot of rich espresso coffee, delicately spooning froth to create a rich creme with his signature heart. 'Take me here, Sammy, take me there; no time to put my feet up and enjoy the wine.'

'This is the trouble when you get married, Sam. But, happy wife, happy life.'

'You are so right, Mr Messenger. Enjoy your latte, try and get a little peace for a few moments.'

'Your coffee is almost as good as I get in Melbourne,' Messenger teased. 'Thank you, Sammy.'

'It's the best, Mr Messenger, you know that.' Sam took the offered coins, tossing them into the cash tray. Messenger smiled, collected his coffee, and walked out into the hall, personal papers under his arm.

Squeezing past the scattered tables, he settled into his favourite chair beside the huge window overlooking the garden courtyard to read a speech he had drafted earlier in the afternoon. Later that evening he was due to speak in the chamber for the opposition in response to the newly introduced Immigration Appropriation Bill. It was no noisier here than sitting in his bustling office.

'Hi Barton, mind if I join you?' Anita Devlin mumbled, pen in mouth, pad under arm, her hands occupied with coffee and a sticky tart. 'I'm doing a story about legislation the government is proposing to bring into the house and I need to talk to you about it.'

Messenger glanced up and smiled at the journalist, turned his papers over quickly and glanced about to see who might be watching.

'Sure, welcome to gossip central.' He quickly leaned forward and moved aside a chair for her to sit on. 'Take a seat, I've been meaning to give you a call.'

'What did you want to talk about?' Anita settled herself. 'Ah, that's better. Do you want some?' She offered the pastry to Messenger.

'No thanks, but I wanted to ask you if you're doing a story on the appointment of the new chairman of the Future Fund.

'Why? It seems uncontroversial to me.' Anita took a bite of her tart. 'Harper has said he'll agree. Don't you agree with your leader?'

'I would've thought the process of appointment could have been better. No-one doubts Lyons is experienced, and possibly the right person, but it is the way this government goes about it. No scrutiny. No checks and balances. Gerrard just does what he wants and to hell with the process.'

'I don't see a problem, it's uncontentious and supported by your lot.'

'You don't think a government should be accountable?' Messenger mocked. 'You lefties are all the same.'

'Of course, I do. I just don't think these minor appointments need reporting though. It's a simple decision, why complicate it?'

'Once we stop scrutiny of government decisions, we relinquish power and the unscrupulous take over. Remember the WA Inc. scandals?'

'That was decades ago, things have changed since then.' Anita broke off a small piece of tart and put it into her mouth. 'And FYI, I'm no lefty.'

'Gerrard just does what he wants, so how do you know he isn't doing something shonky?'

Anita shrugged. 'That's why we have you and your conservative mates, Bart. You have a history of seeking out any misappropriation of funds.'

'You truly are a cynic, aren't you?'

'I have much to be cynical about. You lot just keep giving me the self-interest stories. What about that flake from the senate who got caught taking his girlfriend to Broome for a few nights?'

Messenger smiled, looked at Anita and took a small sip of his coffee, washing it back over his tongue. 'When are we catching up for a dinner?'

Anita paused and delicately put another small piece of tart into her mouth as she watched a woman in stilettos march past, heels clacking on the wooden floor. 'I can never understand why my sisters see the need to wear those hideous things.'

'You are tormenting me.' Messenger smiled.

'You know how I feel about all that, Bart. I think we should cool our jets a little.' Anita waited until the woman had passed. 'Christ, I hate those things, such a ridiculous fashion item.'

Messenger was not distracted by Anita's fashion comment. 'You're being rather mean to me.'

'Not really. You're a big boy. You can get over things. It was a mistake, I told you that. Let's just maintain a professional relationship.'

'Ouch.'

'What did you say once? Something about having a hide as thick as a rhino?'

'Yes, but I meant in politics, you need it. I think you should reconsider.'

Anita sipped her coffee. 'Why aren't you at Gordon O'Brien's party?'

'I don't like him. I'm glad to see the back of him.'

'Why? Is it because he gives you a hard time?'

'He gives Gerrard too much latitude, and he doesn't like me,' Messenger said, sipping his coffee. 'It was his fault we have five-year terms.'

'That's harsh; he tried to stop Gerrard.'

'He didn't try hard enough as far as I'm concerned. The prime minister bullied him, and he weakened.'

'You're not saying this because you were tossed out of question time today, are you?' Anita scoffed. 'I reckon his note to the speaker may have had you ejected.'

'Not really,' replied Messenger, reluctantly. 'I had work to do anyway.'

'I would have thought the manager of opposition business would have been a little sharper on the rules.'

'He doesn't like me. I cause the speaker too much trouble.' Messenger shifted in his seat and took another small sip.

'What do you know about the funding for the immigration

detention centres the government is proposing in Indonesia?' Anita took a careful mouthful of tart, to avoid icing sugar falling on her clothes. She worked hard to look professional, but she was always anxious about her choices. It was even harder when black was the only colour she liked.

'We support it.'

'I hear they may be doing something tricky with the funding, bringing a first payment forward to early next year.'

'They tell us nothing.'

'I was told by one of your colleagues you actually do know what's going on.'

Messenger did his look, sip, and smile routine. 'I may have some information.'

'So?'

'Well, it's yet to be confirmed, but I've been advised they will bring it forward this evening for a vote tomorrow morning. They're planning to release funds in four stages with the initial funds as a form of deposit in this first bill. The plan is for the first centre to begin construction in the new year.' Messenger smiled. 'I could disclose more over food. My tongue loosens when food bounces off it. What are you doing for dinner?'

Anita sighed. 'You never give up, do you.'

'No.'

'The government aren't likely to bring it on tonight, given the tragedy.' Anita switched the subject.

'A plane crash is surely not tragic enough to close the parliament. It may be a disaster, but surely not a tragedy. I would have thought a respected journalist and wordsmith like you would know the difference.'

'Christ, you obviously don't know.'

'What?'

'Eight MPs were on the plane.'

'We'll need to make a statement.' Miles Fisher, standing before Gerrard's desk, was working through crisis media management protocol. 'Perhaps we can get a live cross on ABC News. No doubt you can appear on A Current Affair, and the Late News.'

Gerrard didn't respond. He drew long and hard on his cigar, wreathing his face in smoke and sucking it deep into his lungs.

'Boss, we'll need to act soon.' Fisher was more than a little anxious about his lack of direction. 'The nation needs to hear from you.'

'Fuck it.'

'It's a sad day. We've already spoken to the families and arranged for you to speak to them later. Some are in Canberra. I suppose we'll need to have a national day of mourning...'

'Fuck it.'

'We've had calls from the usual suspects, including the president.'

'I lost a great friend today, Miles.'

'We all did, Prime Minister.'

'Fuck it.'

Fisher stood quietly looking down at his boss, waiting for instruction, keen to get moving.

'You know we're stuffed now, don't you?' Gerrard finally said from behind a huge cloud of smoke.

'No. I think this will go well for you in the polls. It's our chance to show leadership.'

'You don't get it, do you?'

'Get what?' Fisher checked his list and flicked a page. 'I think I've covered everything.'

'The numbers change. We lose six votes in the house. That means they now have a majority of two.'

'What do you mean?'

'We can lose government over this – tonight, tomorrow, or whenever the parliament sits again.'

'Oh, shit.'

'Yeah, now you get it, boofhead.'

---

O'Brien was already back in his office calling department heads – grief could wait. He might only have a few days left to serve, but he was needed more now than at any other time in his career. Extremely tragic for the families and those colleagues directly involved, the accident would mean significant operational demands upon the parliament and the electoral system in the immediate future. Work needed to be done despite the dark cloud descending upon most of the parliament.

'Three days I think would be appropriate.' O'Brien was on

the phone to the speaker's office. 'Which means suspension of the parliament for the remainder of the week, then back to work next Monday. A parliamentary memorial service can be arranged for this Friday and perhaps formal state memorials in a few weeks, but this will be up to the prime minister and his department and the leader of the opposition.' O'Brien listened to the response, flicking lint from his trousers.

Marjorie Earle and Paige Alexander, along with Richard Barker the deputy clerk, sat opposite awaiting instructions. 'No, I am yet to speak to either of them.' O'Brien swivelled in his chair and sat upright at his desk, rubbing his temple.

'We should be able to issue writs for the by-elections next week. So that means we can either have the elections next month, if we have time before Christmas, or we wait until February, which is my recommendation. They'll then be sworn in at the first sitting week in March.' He picked up a pen and waited to write something, but nothing came. 'Only if they both agree not to take any votes. If they don't agree, then we could be faced with having a vote of no confidence from the opposition. If the government does not win a no-confidence vote, we can either change government on the floor of the house or be forced immediately into a general election.'

O'Brien listened intently.

'I repeat, only if both the PM and Harper agree not to take any votes. It is only for one more week before the summer recess, so I see no reason why they wouldn't agree. We can assume the numbers will favour the government in the house after the by-elections in March, so it would be a waste of time for the opposition to challenge the current status of the parliament. If we assume the government wins the by-elections, then it would be foolish to change government just for a few weeks.'

O'Brien nodded.

'Okay Madam Speaker, I'll call you back when I have spoken to the leaders and organised events.' He replaced the receiver carefully and sat stroking his chin. 'Paige, the government wants a parliamentary memorial service this Friday in the Great Hall, which will no doubt attract a significant overseas contingent. Gerrard's office has also floated the idea of a religious event in Sydney. I need you to organise the archbishop to make available the cathedral for Friday in, say, four weeks' time.'

'I'll liaise with the government protocol office and ensure we accommodate those dignitaries who want to come to both. What about the funerals?' Paige scribbled into her pad.

'Let's get someone from the PM's office to organise those.' O'Brien suddenly stopped talking. 'God it's terrible, isn't it?'

'The worst, and at the worst time,' said Marjorie, dabbing her eyes with a wad of tissue. 'What do you want me to do about the media? I have already taken a few calls asking about parliamentary procedure.'

'I'll make a statement once I've spoken to the PM and Harper. Are you okay?' O'Brien asked quietly. Marjorie nodded and tears welled again, which she quickly wiped away. 'I see no reason why there should be a parliamentary crisis. The solemness of it all will ensure politics stays out of it.'

'Well, if there was ever a time for Harper, now he has his opportunity,' said Barker.

'He won't do it,' O'Brien said firmly. 'He knows what he must do.'

'Did you want me to get you something to eat?' Paige asked. 'It's getting late and I want to make sure you're not neglecting yourself.'

'No, I couldn't, thanks. I'm too stressed to eat anything right now. Now, please leave me to do my job.' O'Brien picked up the phone to call the leader of the opposition before being connected to the prime minister.

After completing his call to James Harper, Marjorie's voice came through the handset on his desk: 'The prime minister, Gordon, line six.'

'Good evening, Prime Minister,' Gordon said as he stabbed a button on the phone to put the prime minister on speaker, allowing Richard Barker to quietly listen in.

'Gordon, how are you holding up?' Gerrard said. 'Such a tragedy.'

'Prime Minister, I've just spoken to Mr Harper and explained the possible legislative scenarios for him to consider. I put before him a recommendation.'

'And that is?' Gerrard was curious.

'There are two clear scenarios. We can either issue writs for by-elections next week and the status quo remains until the end of parliamentary sittings next week, or the opposition can force the government to a vote of no confidence. If we do that, we are likely to have a change of government.'

'What did he say?'

'I explained it would be likely the parliamentary numbers

would revert to the status quo in March after the by-elections. Therefore, I told him there was little point in achieving a political advantage for so little return by forcing a no-confidence motion in the parliament.'

'And what was your recommendation?'

'I recommended to him to retain the status quo.'

'Good man, Gordon. I knew I could depend on you to do the right thing.'

'Yes, Prime Minister.'

'Is everything else in order?'

'As far as the funerals and memorial services go?'

'No. That's not my priority at the moment. Are we sitting next week? I want to be sure we do.'

'Why is this so important to you, Prime Minister?' Gordon was a little surprised by the request.

'I have government business to complete, and the Immigration Appropriation Bill needs to move through the parliament before the recess. We were going to bring it into the house tonight for a vote tomorrow.'

'This surely can wait until next year, Prime Minister. The money is not due until March, so there is plenty of time.'

'Listen here, Gordon, my government has made promises to the Indonesians, and we need to release funds this year,' Gerrard's voice was louder. 'Do not stop this bill from being passed next week, do you understand?'

'Yes, Prime Minister.'

'Good work. Goodbye Gordon.'

On the second floor of the senate wing, in the Hancock Media offices within the parliamentary press gallery, Anita Devlin worked at her desk, tapping at her computer surrounded by notes and papers. Her filing system was uniquely hers, and she abused anyone who touched anything or disturbed its order. She had her most controversial stories clipped and pinned to the walls like trophy wallpaper. Various coloured sticky notes were stuck to the sides of her computer screen with phone numbers and information that could not be filed.

'Hi,' Messenger stood at her cubicle waggling two wine glasses, tapping an opened bottle on the frame.

'What can I do for you, Barton? I'm just a little busy at the moment.' Anita didn't spend long looking at him and turned back to her computer keyboard. 'Who let you in?'

'I wanted to apologise for storming off, and I thought you might like to share a drink with me.'

'I've got to finish this last piece, I'm on a deadline.'

'I can wait.' He assumed he was welcome and took a chair beside her desk. 'What is it?'

'I've had to do four obituaries.'

'Bummer.' There was no room for glasses and bottle on her desk, so he put them carefully on the floor.

'It's been a little distressing. What do you think will happen?'

'Well, there is a cornucopia of opportunities.'

Anita stopped typing and looked at Messenger with a wry

smile. 'Cornucopia? Not just opportunities, but a cornucopia of opportunities?'

'Yes. Do you forgive me?'

'I need to talk to you anyway. Pour me a drink and I'll send this off.'

'Yes ma'am.'

A flick of a few keys and she was done. 'So, what do you think will happen?'

Messenger poured as he spoke. 'Well, I actually know what will happen. I've already spoken with the leader. Basically, nothing. We have by-elections proposed for next February and we will continue as normal next week. We have the rest of this week off, a memorial service on Friday, and come back for legislation next week.'

'You couldn't expect him to do anything else. I've read the PM's release, and it seems the most appropriate course of action.'

'Cheers.' They both said together as they clinked glasses.

'My only problem with all that is that we have the numbers now, so why not use them?' Messenger took a generous mouthful.

'The government will get them back in March after the by-elections, surely.'

'Not if we prorogue the parliament and call a general election.'

'That's an interesting suggestion, an early election...' Anita sipped and studied the politician at her desk. 'Surely Harper would not allow that. He has already agreed not to take any action that will disturb the current parliament.'

They sat quietly for a moment. Messenger swigged his wine, wrestling with something he wanted to say. 'If we change the leader, then it could be game on.'

'Can I quote you?' Anita picked up her pen and flicked to a new page of her notebook.

'Ease up, Anita, I'm only joking,' Messenger said. 'Not everything I say should be taken literally, politically speaking of course.'

'Of course. You are a politician, after all.'

# CHAPTER 4

## MONDAY 10.55 PM

The prime minister's car rolled into Yarralumla, his official Canberra residence, gravel crunching as it moved slowly to the portico. Gerrard smiled, pleased with what he saw; there had been an extremely negative public reaction to his decision to upgrade the governor-general's residence and move in himself. He used the need to host international dignitaries as the reason for the redevelopment, but many insiders reported it was the loss of the republican vote at the referendum that motivated a vengeful prime minister.

'The president has the White House. The British prime minister has Chequers,' Gerrard explained during an interview. 'We need a similar stately building for our nation's leader, not a rundown shoebox like the Lodge.'

Gerrard wanted the Australian people to know exactly who was running the country, even though they had voted for the retention of the antiquated constitutional monarchy. 'If the governor-general wanted improved living quarters, let the King pay for renovations. She is, after all, his representative.'

The prime minister directed the governor-general to vacate the heritage-listed house and heavily renovated the property, ignoring the public and political outcry. He wanted a grander residence, so he moved the governor to a much smaller residence in an obscure Canberra suburb.

A small administration wing was added to house the estate's management, providing accommodation for the prime minister's staff. He also insisted his wife Margaret had her own staffed office within the wing. Essential house staff lived in separate quarters over the expansive garage. One or two staff had children who were sometimes seen, but never heard, within the main compound.

It was a chilly night. Spring in Canberra was colourful and attracted many thousands of tourists to the renowned Floriade. The weather was normally pleasant at this time of year, but this October day had been unusually chilly, and Gerrard shivered as he left the car. His butler had anticipated his arrival, having received advice from the security gatehouse as the prime minister's car swung into the residence. He opened the large, heavy white door and took the prime minister's briefcase as he entered.

'Thanks, Edmond. Is Mrs Gerrard still up?'

'No sir, she retired around thirty minutes ago. Would you like anything?'

'I'll have a shower and take some brandy to bed. Pour two.

I'm sure madam would like one.'

Gerrard walked through the darkened marble hall to the stairs and padded up the thick woollen carpet to his suite. He had insisted on a separate retreat with a private dressing room and bathroom, so as not to disturb his wife. It was a secure private retreat with a comfortable lounge fitted with all modern communication devices and cable television and served as a soundproof anteroom to the bedroom. This was the area of the house in which he felt most secure. No-one but Edmond ever entered, not even Margaret, his wife.

Gerrard entered the dressing room and kicked off his shoes. He hung up his Zegna jacket and draped his trousers carefully over a chair, tossed his shirt and socks into a cane basket and entered his bathroom, turning on the shower with the pre-set temperature. He walked into the vast marble cubical and stood under the broad stream of water. He insisted on a waterfall stream shower as opposed to the little shower heads so common in hotels; small units were good for small people, but not for him. As he soaked under the warm stream he removed his underpants, soaped them with his imported French body wash, and washed away any evidence – he had learned over the years to be careful.

Ninety minutes earlier, Speaker Bagshaw had not arrived at his office at the agreed time and Gerrard phoned her office insisting she attend an immediate meeting to discuss the tragedy. Bagshaw obeyed and arrived at nine forty-five with Gerrard already two glasses into a bottle of French champagne.

'You can't be serious, Andrew,' Zara said, as he passed her a sparkling flute and resumed his seat with Bagshaw sitting on the other side of the desk. 'This is not a time to celebrate.'

'It has been a trying time for all of us over the last few hours, especially for you and me. I thought we should talk about what to do next, and at the same time have a relaxing drink.' Gerrard raised his glass. 'Cheers, in memory of our sadly departed comrades.'

'Cheers.' Bagshaw took a mouthful. 'I have decided not to reopen parliament until next Monday. We should then have a few days of condolences.'

'Bullshit, we will,' Gerrard almost spat the words as he sat up, slapping the desk with his open hand. 'We open for business as soon as we can. I want a few things through before Christmas, and we only have a week to do them.'

'I can't promise we will not have demands for marks of respect and a need to express that in the parliament.'

'Let them do that crap in the Federation Chamber for the entire week for all I care. We will have the Reps open again on Monday.'

'O'Brien is keen for protocols to be followed. It's his last week, and he wants to ensure the parliament does not carry-on business while the voting numbers are skewed against you.'

'He can get stuffed. We work through. Harper has already agreed not to bring on a division.'

'Prime Minister, are you really sure? This could cause some major challenges for us. Nothing could be that important.' Bagshaw drained her glass. 'The opposition has the numbers so you can't afford any divisions – there is no guarantee the opposition would support us. If they don't support us, they can call a no-confidence motion and we are gone.'

'We must push the Immigration Appropriation Bill through next week. My meeting with Surriento this morning confirmed the government would release the first tranche of funds to Indonesia this year, which would allow work to begin on building the first detention centre. I promised him we would vote on it tomorrow and money would follow immediately after; they are expecting it. Now we have closed the place for a few days, it is absolutely vital that it goes through the parliament next week. We don't need any crap from O'Brien, or Harper for that matter, and we need to sit next week.'

'Why do you need this to go through? Surely it can wait.'

'Never you mind why, just ensure we get it through without any controversy. I certainly don't want any votes taken to a division when we don't have the numbers.'

'What we need is a formal agreement from him not to take a division to count votes.'

'Harper wouldn't do it, he would be stupid to sign a formal agreement, no-one would.' Gerrard retained little respect for the opposition. 'Just make sure we maintain control of the chamber when we are back next week. If there are any problems from Harper, just squash him with parliamentary procedure.' Gerrard drained his glass. 'I am relying on you, Zara. This is an opportunity for you to shine and make sure the government gets its first Indonesian detention centre.'

'I'll do my best.' Bagshaw waggled her empty glass at Gerrard, encouraging a refill. 'I always do.'

'I remember,' smiled Gerrard, as he got up from his desk and walked to the expansive leather lounge, beckoning Bagshaw to follow. She refilled her glass from the bottle in the ice bucket and sank into the soft leather lounge close enough to Gerrard to give him permission.

An hour later, Gerrard was examining his neck and chest for any signs of passion. Satisfied there was no evidence, and smiling at the memory, his long gaze took in his ageing body. He was happy he was still in shape, although when he stood sideways, he slapped his protruding stomach, acknowledging he was getting an oldies' belly. Thin legs, zero arse and a burgeoning belly was the image he'd been fighting against since his days as a talented basketball player. Still, he was pleased with his tanned body – and pleased he was still capable of romancing a woman as he had in his youth.

He wrapped his underpants in a towel and tossed them in the basket, slipped on an overly large silk robe and walked into his suite. As he did, a gentle tap on the door signalled the arrival of his brandy. Edmond's timing was impeccable, as always. He took the tray and moved to the bedroom.

Margaret was propped up among a galaxy of different-shaped pillows, grey hair pinned back off her face and reading glasses positioned on the end of her nose. Age had brought her a mature beauty, and she dressed in a sophisticated style, even to bed. Her long, green satin slip hugged her trim form, the result of constant exercise and care.

She looked up from her book, pleased to see her husband. 'Everything under control, darling?'

'Yes, my sweet. I have a brandy for you. I'm glad you're awake; I need to talk to you.' Gerrard respected his wife's opinion and sought it whenever he had unresolved issues that worried him.

He had been seduced by her when he first heard her laugh and promised he would always keep her happy and laughing. When they first met, he kept her out into the early morning talking about the future and his strategy for the country. She was smitten by his plans and his larger-than-life charismatic nature and knew before she invited him home for dinner with her parents that she would marry him. Three months later he proposed, and they married twelve months after their first meeting. They had been a formidable political team for the forty-five years since.

'How are you feeling?'

'A little upset actually, I insisted Freddy come back to Canberra tonight. I spoke to him when he was in the plane on the tarmac just prior to take-off. I feel responsible ... he was a great mate.'

'Do you want to talk about it?' Margaret took her drink as Andrew sat at her feet.

'I needed them for a vote tomorrow, and now we've lost them, and the vote.'

'I only spoke to Sonja this morning about his retirement at the next election. She was saying they were pleased to be getting out and encouraged us to think about it.'

'It all has to end sometime, I suppose.' Gerrard didn't want to think about his trusted friend and adviser who had entered parliament at the same election he had. 'He only had eighteen months to go.' He took a gulp of brandy to collect himself.

'It got me thinking though, darling. Why don't we take this opportunity to get out now? To step aside so we can go to Paris.' Margaret had been suggesting for many months that it was time to think about retiring. 'This is a great opportunity to do it, you have nothing more left to do and your announcement before Christmas would mean a by-election at the same time as the others.'

'Go easy on the brandy, darling. We'll win the by-elections and then the general election.' Gerrard stretched and dragged a large pillow to prop his head as he lay back across the bed. 'My plan is to do one more term.'

'No, Drew, listen, please darling. If we make a move now, we don't have to face another two years of speculation. What happens if Harper tries to take over? He has the numbers now.'

'He won't do it, the weak bastard. He's already committed to not moving against the government.'

'And you believe him?'

'Harper is a weak prick. He'll do what he's told. He won't want the aggravation.'

'I'm just saying, this is the perfect opportunity. We leave on top and with honour.'

'And go to Paris?' Gerrard mocked.

'You know we've been planning it.'

'You've been planning it, darling. We don't have the money to live in Paris. We live the high life here, but Paris would be very different.'

'I've been thinking about that.'

'And?'

'That could have been you today, darling. You have done enough. You have rewarded your friends and they have a comfortable life. It's now time for us.'

'What are you suggesting?'

'Increase the commission from the Indonesians.'

'You must be kidding.' Gerrard sat up and drained his glass. 'I'm already very nervous about the deal I've done with Amir. This first one was to be a trial.'

'Surriento suggested the deal, so why not ask for more?'

Gerrard didn't speak as he considered the proposition. Surriento was a friend and had counselled him many times on how to personally benefit from the transfer of international funds between governments. Gerrard had not been tempted previously – until this one time over a few too many whiskeys. Still, the secret commission wasn't enough to fund a retirement in Paris.

Finally, Gerrard smiled. 'You have been busy, haven't you?' He loved her assertive nature; she always got what she wanted, or rather she got it most of the time, depending on how he felt. He also knew she was a realist. She understood his flaws and knew of his weaknesses and temptations. He smoked too much, he drank too much, and he shared himself with others too much. But he would always come home to her, and that was why she loved him – and why he loved her.

'I'm just saying, he opened the door for you. Why not take

full advantage and ask for more? Everyone else does, so why not us?'

'You could be right. Let me sleep on it.' Gerrard stood and walked to his side of the bed, slipping off his robe and dropping it to the floor.

'What do you think you're going to do with that?' Margaret purred, tossed her glasses to the side table, and opened her arms as he slipped into bed beside her.

---

Early morning in Canberra is nearly always cold, but Yarralumla's kitchen was warm from the ovens preparing various treats to be consumed throughout the day, including the usual cooked breakfast for the prime minister. Gerrard sat at the stone kitchen bench; his breakfast always formally presented on a stiff cotton napkin with highly polished silver. A three-egg omelette, Earl Grey tea and a small bowl of fruit, cut to spoon-sized pieces. Toast, with a curled tab of butter in a ceramic dish, and a separate one of jam; different every day. Today was his favourite: apricot.

Gerrard was dressed for early media interviews in a blue Italian suit, navy blue silk tie and crisply ironed white shirt. He scanned the Financial Review, flicking past the editorials and obituaries; looking for any political leaks that should worry him. He zeroed in on an article about his meeting with the Indonesian president, then a smiling Margaret joined him, slinging an arm over his shoulder, and kissing his cheek.

'Hello, handsome.'

'Sleep well, gorgeous?'

'Eventually.' She picked at his fruit and smiled.

'I've been thinking about your idea, and I reckon I've worked out a plan.'

'Go on.' Margaret, in her nightgown and silk robe, straddled a stool and joined her husband as Janette, Yarralumla's chef, poured her tea into her favourite over large, colourful china cup.

'Freddy's death has hit me a little bit and maybe you're right, it could be time for me to let go.' Gerrard sipped his tea. 'I was planning to hang around until I hit seventy, and then we could get a job overseas and live comfortably forever.'

'How nice.'

'But now I'm not so sure.'

'I keep asking you to retire, Drew, and this thing with Sonja has sent a shiver through me. I don't know how I feel, but suddenly all of this doesn't seem as important to me anymore.'

'I tend to agree, so I have a plan.'

'Can you tell me, or will it be a secret like some of the other things you do?'

'Well, historically, after significant tragic national events, there is usually a period of community mourning. Don't ask me why, but consumers leave the market for a significant period, leading to an economic downturn. This could be bad news for the retailers during the Christmas trading season. We can't afford to have a consumer-led downturn right now. This could affect the by-elections and the vote could move against us. It may even mean we lose government.'

'Like I said, darling, it might be time to go.'

'You could be right, so I have an idea.'

Margaret turned to the chef. 'Janette, would you mind giving us a few moments.'

The chef wiped her hands and left the kitchen.

'Thank you.'

Gerrard paused for maximum impact. 'We release a Christmas bonus to the punters.'

'How much?'

'I'm thinking six to seven billion.'

'How does that help us?'

'Well, we put an urgent Appropriation Bill into the house. We tie this legislation to the deal with the Indonesians. Not just the first tranche we were planning to vote on today, but the whole lot.'

'Can you do that? How much would it be?'

'The total appropriation would be around ten billion. The media would normally have gone ape-shit over a four-billion-dollar deal with the Indonesians; they've already given me a tough time with the millions in this first lot.'

'Four billion is a lot of money, how can you get it through?'

'Well, if cabinet agree, we tie it to the stimulus package and hopefully it will be lost in the excitement of the announcement. I mean, you would have to be dumb not to see the change, but the politics is so beautiful. Get the punters onside and the Indonesian money will be lost in all the excitement.

'You hope.'

'It will be if it goes through next week.'

'So what?'

'It means paper trails offshore would be harder to follow if we get it done before Christmas. And, anyway, the money would have already gone to Indonesia – too late to get it back.'

'How much more will you add for us?' Margaret took her own selection of fruit from a dish.

'I'll need to talk to Amir.'

'Will he be okay with the changes?'

'I don't know,' Gerrard picked out a piece of rockmelon and slipped it into his mouth, wiping his fingers on his serviette. 'He is such a wheeler and dealer on anything that has a sniff of opportunity for him, but with this idea, I'm not so sure.'

'He wants the money by March, right?'

'It would be difficult to hide, but yes, it would be possible to get the money to him within days of the legislation passing the parliament.'

'What are you really saying?'

'We potentially expose ourselves. I'm concerned about how it will look.'

'It'll be okay, it always is.' Margaret leaned forward and reassuringly stroked her despondent husband's shoulder then eventually said, 'So, if we give him the entire amount, why wouldn't he reward us?'

'I trust him, and it was his idea in the first place, so I'm confident he will agree to increasing our payout.' Gerrard perked up and scooped omelette into his mouth. 'We send the funds to Amir, hopefully, late next week. He then starts developing the first centre on Ambon but skims off a commission to a bank in Switzerland via his normal laundering channels as previously agreed. By my reckoning, if we take one per cent, that should set us up with forty million.'

'Are you serious?'

'No-one will miss one per cent if we do it right.'

'Do you really trust him?'

Gerrard smiled. 'As much as I trust you, gorgeous. So, you'll have to set up the bank account a little earlier than we expected.'

'How much earlier?'

'This week if you can.'

'Will you get it up?' Margaret was staring at her smirking husband. 'The bill, I mean.'

'I'll tell the department to begin work on the roll-out of Christmas stimulus funds today. I'll put it on the agenda for cabinet this morning, and hopefully announce the handout to the punters on Thursday. If Amir comes to the memorial on Friday, I'll confirm the deal. We then put it into the house on Monday and get it into the senate and back to the house by Thursday for final approval. We recess for Christmas Thursday evening, and I could announce my resignation and immediate retirement then in the House, or on Friday.'

'Will you get the numbers to pass it?'

'Harper will be okay. It's O'Brien I'm worried about. I don't need any delays from him, and we can't afford any extra scrutiny by the parliament, so Zara needs to step up and keep him under control.'

'Zara will do what she's advised by O'Brien, surely?' Margaret knew the clerk supervised the legislative program and would determine what was added to the parliamentary notice paper.

'I have her under control, and she will ignore O'Brien. Her parliamentary career relies on her doing what I need her to do next week.' Gerrard took a gulp of tea. Margaret did not miss the momentary hesitation. 'I have lost too many speakers because of O'Brien. She'll be okay, and she'll do what I tell her.'

'O'Brien won't cause much grief. He's out of the parliament in a week,' Margaret said, as she finished picking at the fruit bowl. 'Zara knows what she wants, but just be careful, darling. She may cut you loose if it gets too hot for her.'

Gerrard began quickly tucking into the remains of the omelette; he needed to get moving. He was scheduled to appear on early- morning television.

'I'll keep you advised as I get through it all. Worst-case scenario is we only get the original four million next February, and I don't retire,' Gerrard said before rinsing his mouth with tea. 'Can you begin some research for a bank? Remember, we don't want to leave a paper trail.'

'Leave it to me. I know exactly who I'll talk to.'

'Who?'

'No trails, darling. This is good news, the punters get a Christmas bonus, Immigration gets their offshore detention centres, Indonesia creates jobs for their people, and we retire. It's time. I've just about had enough. I may have been a socialist most of my life, but I can't ignore my own needs.' Margaret rubbed herself against her husband as they stood and kissed him so he would remember. 'I'm so proud of you.'

'Saucy minx. See you tonight. Talk soon.'

Gerrard headed for the waiting car.

# CHAPTER 5

**TUESDAY 8.30 AM**

'Madam Speaker, good morning.' O'Brien entered the office at the appointed time to discuss parliamentary business arrangements following the previous day's events.

'Good morning, Gordon. Such a tragedy, I still can't believe it.' Zara Bagshaw looked drawn and washed out, her face pale without her makeup, her hair pulled back tightly into a bun, her black dress fashionably cut to show off her body.

'It is truly unfortunate and very sad, but we need to work through these priorities we have before us. I have staff waiting.' O'Brien sat at the desk waiting for Zara to put down the newspaper.

'What have you got for me?' Zara asked.

'I've spoken to the government and opposition suggesting we resume next Monday, and after consultation with their respective leadership groups they have agreed, although I suspect the prime minister would not have taken no for an answer – he seems keen for us to resume as quickly as possible. We will need to get the writs for the by-elections notified to the governor-general on Monday, which will allow us to have the elections in February. Based upon current polls they will return the government a majority, although I suspect they could lose a seat or two.' O'Brien flicked through his notes.

'I have spoken to the manager of government parliamentary business and strongly recommended to her that nothing controversial come before the parliament. She agreed and notified there is nothing on the legislative program to be brought forward that is not on the notice paper.'

'What about the Appropriation Bill for funding the first stage of the Indonesian immigration detention centres?'

'She thinks the legislation might be deferred until next year, but she is yet to receive direction from the prime minister. Apparently, there have been some mutterings from a few cabinet ministers about it and the details of the payments. I'm not sure what their concerns are, but they have a further cabinet meeting this morning where I suspect they will discuss it.'

'If they defer the legislation, it will make things a little easier for all of us. But just in case, be aware the bill might come through next week, so allow suitable time for it.'

O'Brien seemed taken aback by the speaker's comment and

took a note. 'Does the opposition propose making the chamber process laborious for the government with suspension motions or other censure debates?' asked Bagshaw.

'I doubt it. Mr Harper understands that the current balance of votes going his way is only temporary, and that the government is likely to retain the numbers in February. He's pragmatic enough to know there's no need to force a change of government on the country for a few weeks.'

Gordon referred to his notes. 'His actual quote was, "We are not a European state, changing government every six months," and he reassured me he will keep his people under control.'

'Nice. When will we do condolences?'

'I have set aside Monday for the prime minister and Mr Harper. The other members are scheduled for the Federation Chamber—' O'Brien stopped abruptly, and the speaker looked up. 'You don't think we should just close the representatives' chamber for the rest of the week and allow members to speak there?'

'I thought about it,' Zara sighed as she slunk back in her chair, rocking it slightly. 'I think the public would expect a period of parliamentary mourning, but then, they are a fickle bunch, and no doubt would like to see their politicians back at work as soon as possible.'

'I suppose we still need to get a number of money bills through, such as finalising the Commonwealth Supply Bill and getting it into the senate, otherwise hard-working public servants may not be paid before Christmas,' O'Brien said.

Bagshaw sat forward in her chair and leaned closer to O'Brien, twirling a pen in her fingers. 'In the unlikely event the opposition passed a motion of no confidence, and we were forced to move to a general election, what would you recommend I do?'

O'Brien considered the point for a moment. 'Stop any motion before it is moved. In other words, if the opposition begins setting the scene for an assault against the government, then refuse to allow them to speak. Worst case scenario, you shut the parliament down.'

Zara sat silently considering O'Brien's advice, then jotted something in her notebook. 'What other legislation is due before we break next week?'

'There is the amendment to the Competition and Consumer Act, the introduction of the Mining Royalties Act, and the government has also listed amendments to the Broadcasting Act to allow the digital media to televise the upcoming visit of the king.'

'Remind me, why do we need the change for his royal highness?'

'The current act prohibits the direct telecast of the royal family unless supervised by a government official.'

'Really?' Zara was staggered.

'I know, it seems antiquated, doesn't it?' O'Brien smiled. 'Apparently when the queen visited soon after her coronation way back when – I think it was late in the 1950s, just after television was introduced to Australia – the Menzies government consented to a clause within the act to prescribe broadcasting of her visit on delayed transmission only. Since the advent of digital media streaming, there is a need to amend the legislation to accommodate the new viewing systems. Under the current legislation, it is illegal for anyone to record and stream a royal event. This amendment to the legislation allows those changes to be enacted and citizens can virtually upload any recording from their phones. Therefore, we may see the king on YouTube during his next official visit as it is happening.'

'He'll probably go viral,' smirked Zara.

'No doubt.'

'Is he coming for the memorial service?'

'Yet to be confirmed.'

'Run me through your plans.'

'We are considering two events, the first, a parliamentary memorial service this Friday, in the Great Hall. We thought it would provide an opportunity for the senators and members to reflect on the tragedy and grieve together. We're expecting international dignitaries, some of whom have already contacted the government.'

'Good word, "reflect",' sighed Zara.

'We then thought we could have a formal memorial service in Sydney in around four weeks if the government decides.' O'Brien referred to his notes. 'Individual funerals could start as early as Friday next week; it depends on the police releasing the bodies.'

They talked for another twenty minutes about the plans for Friday's parliamentary event and the protocols the speaker would need to address during the next few days. O'Brien referred to his notes on issues raised by the speaker, passing her papers for signature as required. Zara felt increasingly confident knowing that, as usual, all details would be well managed by the clerk, who brought the wisdom that came from forty years of dedicated service.

Zara was the only woman O'Brien had served. He considered her tough and formidable when it came to getting her way over process and procedure, and he never took her for granted, as he might have done with some of the other speakers he served. Zara used the power of her position to control the house and ejected any member who did not abide by her standards. She never disciplined or punished the prime minister though – Gerrard was allowed to cajole and berate the opposition, his favourite sport.

Zara learned to look for small gestures – a raised eyebrow, a nod – and listen for verbal clues to ensure the prime minister got what he wanted when he was on his feet at the despatch box. Sometimes she misread him, leading to sharp looks and harsh remarks, but more often than not she read Gerrard right. She had to succumb to him, otherwise she might lose her highly esteemed job.

'Zara? The prime minister is on the phone.' A staff member knocked tentatively on the open door, interrupting, and thus ending her meeting with the clerk.

'I'll have to take that, Gordon,' she said, rising and walking to the door.

O'Brien followed her. 'I was finished anyway. Keep me in the loop if advice from the prime minister's office changes. In the meantime, I will begin communicating with members and senators about Friday and get the invitations out to the embassies.'

Zara left O'Brien as he walked through to the anteroom, returning to her office, and closing the heavy door behind her, skipping back to her desk.

'Hi Andrew, how are you this morning?' Zara said with a big smile.

'Good morning, gorgeous. Thanks for dropping by last night. Always nice to re-engage with you.' Gerrard was polite. 'Can we talk business?'

'Yeah, sure, go ahead.' Zara knew her standing in the relationship with the prime minister. There was no relationship.

'I want to make doubly sure we have the house open for business on Monday. I may be adding an Appropriation Bill.'

'I've already talked with the clerk about the current parliamentary notice paper, and if the government introduces legislation on Monday, we should be able to get it through both houses before we rise on Thursday.' Zara flopped into her chair, sighed slightly, and prepared to take notes. 'What other funding do you need to get through?'

'I'm taking a decision to cabinet this morning to bestow some cash on the punters before Christmas.'

'Why?'

'I think the economy might fall into a funk with the news of the tragedy, especially with the thought that by-elections early next year could lead to a change of government.' Gerrard knew it would be to his advantage to have others sharing his view of potential economic doom and gloom. 'I thought if we provided a substantial stimulus to the punters then they would have a very merry Christmas, and the economy would not suffer as much as we might expect.'

'You are very generous, Prime Minister, but how much do you think the appropriation will be?'

'Does it matter?'

'No, but we will need to ensure we don't scare the other side with any surprises. We wouldn't want them to suddenly not support you and vote against any legislation. It could create chaos in the chamber and could spark a no-confidence motion in the government, which you would lose on the current numbers.'

'This is why you are in the chair, Zara.'

'But I have no chance of stopping a no-confidence motion. A successful vote against you will mean you automatically lose the government benches, and James Harper will be prime minister, God forbid.'

'You will need to assure me you will do all you can to ensure this bill gets through without opposition dissent, and we do not lose a vote.'

'Yes, Prime Minister. I will do my best.'

'Your best is always appreciated, but it will not be enough to save your job if this planned legislation doesn't pass.' Gerrard left no doubt about what he wanted her to do.

---

Gordon closed the door quietly behind him as he left the speaker's office. He passed the framed photographs of the previous speakers displayed along the pale green corridor. As he passed, he looked at them and reflected on those he had served, making a mental note to send each of them a retirement message of thanks; resolving to let them know he was grateful for their support during their term, no matter the length of service.

'Good morning, Gordon.' Barton Messenger had walked up quietly behind him.

'Oh!' Startled, Gordon glanced over his shoulder. 'Good morning, Mr Messenger.'

'I was just coming to see you. I need to discuss procedure for next week. Have you time for a coffee at Aussies?'

'Not right now, I'm afraid.' Gordon was rarely, if ever, seen at Aussies. 'In your role as manager of opposition business, I'd like to discuss various issues with you. Come to my office now if you like.'

'I'll just get my pager and will follow you up.' Messenger veered off into the security entry hall as Gordon began trudging upstairs to his first-floor office.

Messenger greeted the security team and extracted his pager from its numbered position. Only a few units remained, which meant most politicians were in the building. He noted the eight, desolate, unclaimed pagers – a stark reminder of parliament's tragic loss. Clipping the pager to his belt, he followed O'Brien to his office. Always keen to maintain his fitness, he skipped up the stairs rather than wait for the elevator.

Messenger was expected and ushered into Gordon's office. As he entered, Marjorie Earle, who had been taking instructions, finished her notes, collected her papers, and left, politely closing the door behind her.

'Please take a seat, Mr Messenger.' Gordon finalised papers with a signature before carefully placing them in a tray. 'I wanted to talk to you about next week.'

'Yes, I have a few questions.'

'The circumstance in which the parliament finds itself should not provide a political opportunity for you or the government, and I wanted your agreement that nothing will happen to undermine the promise your leader has made to the prime minister.'

'Which is?' queried Messenger.

'Mr Harper has assured the prime minister that there will be no challenges to the authority of the government.'

'We will not bring forward a censure motion if that's what you mean.' Messenger sat further back in his chair and crossed his legs.

'The government will be putting through various pieces of legislation. They are currently on the notice paper, including appropriation bills such as the Supply Bill, and they are all uncontroversial and needed before Christmas.'

'Seems reasonable, I suppose. Of course, we will reserve our rights on calling for a division until we see what is tabled.' Messenger said.

'Of course, this is to be expected and is standard procedure. Are you concerned about anything in particular?' Gordon asked, referring briefly to his notes.

'Nothing in particular. We assume the speaker will follow normal parliamentary process, including motions for debate on various issues. We may pursue some lines of inquiry during question time, which you would agree is to be expected, although I would not think we would be too vocal, given recent tragic circumstances. We are of the view we need to ask the government to continue to explain their actions on mining royalties, for instance.'

'I am sure the speaker will continue to allow these types of questions and motions, so long as they don't threaten the government's standing in the parliament by forcing a vote. Otherwise, she will shut down debate, so be careful and chose your motions carefully.'

'Wise advice, I'm sure.' Messenger slowly nodded his head.

'So, we can count on you and your colleagues to maintain the status quo of the house until the end of next week?'

'Yes, we will agree, so long as there are no surprises.' Messenger was a traditionalist, as most members of parliament were. He believed that community order depended on the nation's elected representatives recognising, and accepting, the rules of parliament. When the Whitlam government was sacked by the governor-general, there was a gossamer thread between stability and revolution, at least that was his view, even though Whitlam had encouraged the community not to overreact by taking to the streets. Demonstrations followed but Whitlam insisted their rage should be shown through the ballot box, not on the streets, and the community had supported this leadership, although they had rejected him at the ballot box.

'If there are changes to the notice paper, I will let you know.' Gordon stood as a sign the meeting was over. 'I wish you well during this troubling week, Mr Messenger. May your sorrow not cloud the important role you play in the parliament.'

Messenger extended his hand. 'It's unfortunate this tragedy has placed a dark cloud over your last two weeks here, but do try and enjoy them, and we will try our best not to create too much grief for you ... so to speak.'

'Indeed.'

# CHAPTER 6

## FRIDAY 9.30 AM

'Are you not going to the memorial service?' Marjorie Earle entered with a cup of peppermint tea for Gordon. For almost ten years, at the same time of day, she had brought the same tea, in the same precious cup. It was white bone-china Wedgewood with navy blue and ochre decoration, rimmed in gold, a gift from his mother. She carefully placed the cup on his desk and waited for a response. Nothing. 'Gordon?'

Finally, Gordon looked up from his papers. 'I have been thinking, we really shouldn't be putting any money bills through the parliament until the by-elections are held. It isn't fair on the opposition if they can't dispute and object to something as important as this, especially such a significant money bill.'

'So, you aren't going to the memorial service?'

'What? Err, no.' Gordon didn't much care for the pomp of parliament, preferring to stay in his office when official events were held in the Great Hall. 'There is far too much to do here. I don't think it would be appropriate for me to attend, they won't miss me. I'll try and get to the funerals though.'

'You won't have to; you'll be finishing up next Friday.'

'I keep forgetting… so much to do.'

'What are you worried about?'

'Do you find it unusual the government wants to rush this Appropriation Bill through the parliament to provide a bonus for the good citizens before Christmas?'

'What's wrong, Gordon?' Marjorie looked at him, waiting for a clue. 'What concerns you?'

'I don't know, it just seems a little strange to me, that's all. It all seems a little hasty.'

'The prime minister announced yesterday why he wanted it done. It sounded fine to me. The extra cash for families will be good for them, especially for Christmas. I know I'll be grateful.'

'I get the politics. I even understand it will be good for the economy. I just don't know why we need to rush it through the parliament when he doesn't have the numbers.' Gordon sat staring at the government announcement before him, unconsciously gnawing at a fingernail.

'Why are you worried? You'll be gone in a week.'

'Doesn't mean I should stop caring today.' Gordon looked up at Marjorie. 'Gerrard is up to something, I know it. I can feel it in my gut. I just don't know what or why.'

'Ours not to reason why.' Marjorie tossed a familiar line back at Gordon. 'A wise old man once told me that.'

Gordon flopped back in his chair, rocking it, and smiled. 'I'm going to miss your gentle prods.'

'Drink your tea while it's still hot, and then get to the service. You should be there.' Marjorie left, thinking how much she would miss him, too.

Gordon took a cautious sip from his cup, testing for heat. It was the little things he'd miss. The tea from Marjorie every morning was a small but important moment of pleasure in a life dedicated to the parliament.

---

The Great Hall of the parliament was an immense room and had hosted many events since its opening by Queen Elizabeth last century. Presidents of the United States of America had been feted in a room full of obsequious guests, as had other world leaders, but without quite as much pomp and ceremony or quite as many guests. The room was often booked for graduation ceremonies by the three universities in Canberra, and many formal dinners had been held when parliament was sitting. It was hired to corporations for events, and even a local dance company held their annual contest in the hall.

The rich red-brown cedar floors shone from their daily polishing, and the enormous tapestry at the opposite end to the entrance was one of the biggest in the world. The renowned Australian artist Arthur Boyd had worked with weavers for over two years to create the stunning depiction of his beloved Australian bush. Boyd wanted to emphasise the importance of the environment and his beautiful work did just that, dominating the hall.

Black, purple, and maroon drapes hung from the first-floor gallery to the floor below, transforming the Great Hall from a cavernous hall into a chamber of reverence. The Canberra Orchestra assembled below the tapestry dressed in black without a speck of colour and began to play Samuel Barber's beautiful Adagio for Strings, adding to the thick air of sadness that hung over the room as mourners assumed their position. It was music that had been chosen for many of the funerals of the great and famous.

The king had sent his eldest son, and the president of the United States of America had sent her secretary of state. China had sent their foreign minister. Distance precluded other world leaders from attending, but ambassadors abounded. The prime ministers of Malaysia, Japan and New Zealand attended as did many of the Pacific Island leaders. President Amir Surriento had returned to Australia for the service, having left the country soon after his meeting with Prime Minister Gerrard on the day of the tragedy.

Gordon took his place in the second row. The prime minister was positioned prominently on the podium, directly in front of him, and he immediately regretted his decision to accept Marjorie's advice to attend. A program of service had been left on his chair and he scanned through it hoping there would be some early respite.

The department had included in the program short biographies of the deceased politicians and Peter Wilson, whom Gordon had originally employed as an intern in his office. He had shown great willingness to learn, and Gordon had little hesitation in recommending him for a position within the parliamentary committee support office.

As he contemplated his former trainee, Gordon became aware of an unexpected welling in his left eye and hoped it was not the start of unwanted emotion. During his early career in the parliament, he was mentored to believe that he was the safety valve of protocol; he needed to show little emotion, going about his duties in a stoical manner. He scorned any evidence of self-pity. As he leaned to his left to pull a handkerchief from his pocket, a tear leaked down his cheek. This prompted Gordon to move a little faster to stop any further embarrassment, and he swiftly swiped the tear and dabbed his eye before folding the handkerchief into the palm of his hand, just in case.

The congregation was solemn as final places were taken. Nigel Nelson, Gordon's friend, and colleague from the senate staff, dressed in his ceremonial black rod uniform, took his place next to him, patting Gordon's knee reassuringly in recognition of the sombre occasion, knowing his friend could be troubled by the emotion.

'Where's your outfit?' Nelson whispered from the side of his mouth. 'I look like a goose.'

Gordon placed his hand in front of his mouth and whispered, 'I wasn't going to come, so I didn't have time to change. You look rather pretty in your ruffled shirt and stockings.'

'You are a wicked man, Gordon O'Brien. Now behave yourself, this is a serious occasion.'

Archbishop Bryan Johnson conducted the service, and Prime Minister Gerrard delivered the eulogy. The congregation listened to the dignified words commemorating the lives of dear friends lost in the tragedy, paying homage to their service to the parliament and the nation. Gordon appreciated Gerrard referring to Pete Wilson sympathetically and respected him for having done so.

All federal members and senators of the national parliament were in attendance, as were state government leaders and representatives. Some family members of the politicians killed had the courage to attend the service, and there were the usual business and social leaders.

The *Adagio* precisely produced the atmosphere the prime minister had intended. He wanted the country to feel deep sorrow for the loss of the members of parliament, and televising the service nationally ensured many Australians would get the message.

The service concluded with a rousing rendition of 'Guide me O thou great redeemer', supported by the Sydney Welsh Choir who were positioned in the gallery above the podium. Gordon watched Gerrard at his distinguished place on the podium singing with gusto and considered him no different from some of the other despots who were in attendance. He couldn't help but think the message of redemption was wasted on Gerrard.

Barton Messenger shared Gordon's lack of enthusiasm, sensing that the service was just another political stunt. Gerrard was out the front, while his leader James Harper was three rows back in the congregation, virtually unseen during the broadcast. Barton knew it was an opportunity for Gerrard to parade as a national leader for the people watching at home. No doubt they were more interested in the money they were about to receive from their leader, who they saw as a caring and progressive man of the people. Little did they know. These were the moments he regretted ever getting involved in politics.

After the ceremony concluded, the distinguished mourners filed from the Great Hall, some lingering in the lavish, marble-floored entrance to murmur condolences and news to colleagues. Others climbed the grand stairs to the refreshment stations in the alcoves on the first floor. Barton followed his colleagues to one of the stations, feeling obliged to publicly grieve but uncomfortable about the pretence; the role of a politician was always to be seen at important events. The scones and cream would be too messy, so he plucked a chocolate biscuit from a carefully arranged basket and moved toward the tall windows overlooking the grassy courtyard below.

'Barton, can I speak to you for a moment.' The voice was familiar. He smiled as he turned to face Anita.

'Sure. What did you think of the ceremony?'

'Proper. Have you read the explanatory memorandum for this Immigration Appropriation Bill proposed by the government?'

'Not yet.' Barton put the remainder of the biscuit in his

mouth and licked his fingers clean, wiping them on a paper napkin. 'Why?'

'It seems a little light on explanation as to where the money is going.' Anita's journalistic sixth sense was never far off.

'I'll have a look at it. What is your concern?'

'President Surriento has a history of never making a decision unless there is something in it for him.'

'That's a bit severe, don't you think?'

'Putting another country's immigration centres on more than one of his islands will not win him many votes at his next election. I suspect there may be other benefits, but I can't find anything in this initial legislation.' Anita put her bag on the floor, between her feet that were, as always, clad in running shoes. She took out a pad and flicked through her notes, searching for a quote.

'There's not much going through. It's only seed money at this stage.'

'Even so, there doesn't seem to be much detail, and no-one knows anything.'

'So, you suspect there's a bit more to the deal?'

'Something like that. Why was he here earlier this week making all those supportive statements? Don't you think it all sounds a little odd?' Anita had built a substantial reputation writing about immigration policy and had been following this one closely since Gerrard announced it in the budget six months earlier. 'I would have thought you guys would be all over it.'

'We'll have a look at it. But this policy is bipartisan. We want these centres to go ahead, and we don't mind initial funding going through. It's only around four hundred million, if I recall.' Barton finished his warm tea. 'Gerrard never includes us in these types of discussions anyway, but we support this, it's part of our policy, and if Gerrard hadn't done it, we probably would have.'

'All I'm saying is, the total funding doesn't add up. This is supposed to be the first of four appropriations, and there's no detail about how it's supposed to work, and no detail about what this first payment will be used for.'

'Okay, I'll check it.'

'Will you get back to me with a comment? I'm on a deadline.'

'I can't promise, but I'll have a look at it.' Barton sounded curt.

'What's up?'

'I'm a little pissed off, actually.' Barton placed his empty cup and saucer on a nearby table.

'How come?'

'O'Brien has told me we'll be operating normally next week. Gerrard is unbelievable. We haven't even buried our mates and he wants us back at work. The government is downgrading the condolences to the Federation Chamber.'

'What does Gerrard want to do now?'

'He wants the community bonus he announced yesterday through both houses of parliament so he can release the funds to the punters before Christmas. He thinks the cash should flow to voters, so they'll remember him at Christmas lunch. The man has no ethics.'

'What are you going to do about it?

'We'll pass it, but that's it. Politically we'd be stupid not to because the punters will hate us if we don't. We won't pass anything else though, which will probably include your immigration centre money for Indonesia.'

'So, you're not expecting the Immigration Bill to hit the house until February, even though it's on the notice paper?'

'If it does, we won't vote for it. We support it, but this is not a time for the government to be ramming legislation through. Jeezus, do they have no respect?' Barton looked out the window. 'We have the numbers now, and they would be mad to try it on when they know it could cost them government if we vote against them.'

'Yes, but surely you can't use your numbers given the circumstances?'

'We are politically obliged not to cause a fuss, so we probably won't if they don't bring anything contentious into the house. But, if we need to use them, we will.' Barton turned and looked at Anita as she pondered her notes. 'I really don't want to be here.'

Finally, Anita looked up and asked, 'Dinner, tonight?'

'Seriously?'

'What?' She smiled demurely. 'Have you lost interest?'

---

Andrew Gerrard had completed his prime ministerial duties and separated himself from the international dignitaries and was standing outside by the entrance of the parliament saying his final goodbyes and thankyous to the guests. Many of the world leaders would promptly head back to their own countries, their planes waiting at Canberra airport for immediate take-off. Others would head to their embassy compound, the short visit a necessary inconvenience. The modern world meant nation states had to be seen to engage with and support one another, especially during times of national mourning. Other leaders would take the opportunity to follow up on various projects under discussion with the Australian government, and perhaps visit expatriate communities, which was always recommended when travelling on taxpayer-funded trips abroad, and good media was always a bonus.

As Amir Surriento held out his soft, bejewelled hand, Gerrard drew him close and thanked him warmly for his support, just days after he had flown back from his official visit. He then quietly put a proposition to him. 'My friend, rather than head back to the embassy, I wonder if you can have your driver bring you to the prime ministerial entrance so we can have a private discussion. I have something to put to you.'

'Ah Andrew, you're not getting cold feet, are you?'

Gerrard nervously looked about to see if anyone was listening. 'No, but I have a proposition for you.'

Surriento tried to read his friend and understood he might have to delay his flight so he could conclude his business with the prime minister. 'I shall be more than happy to spend a few moments with you to discuss affairs of state.'

'I shall see you very soon.'

Gerrard left his friend in the hands of the protocol officers and the Indonesian security team. The Australian protective unit had their own team of beefy federal police officers, distinguishable by a little plastic cord attached to their left ear and a platypus badge – their unit symbol – on the lapels of their bulky jackets.

Gerrard decided to go out onto the forecourt and wave to the crowd that had gathered for the service, which had been broadcast on large digital screens. He had received death threats in the past, and the protection unit had increased their numbers, but they kept their distance, looking like nonchalant parliamentary staff. Although Gerrard believed the community loved him, the election results over the years were getting closer and there was a growing mood for change. While some in the crowd cheered, there were louder boos, and Gerrard quickly withdrew – he knew how quickly crowds could become loathsome if provoked, and he didn't want that on national television.

The prime minister was ushered back through the security point and began his extended walk to his office at the rear of the building. He passed Aussies cafe and stopped to say a brief hello to a table of journalists; they spoke directly to the voters, after all. Gerrard did his fair share of schmoozing with most journos within the Canberra press gallery, knowing his career and the good press he received depended on these relationships and the way he shared stories and exclusives. Likewise, the journalists knew that to maintain their own individual access to the prime minister, and thus the government, they also had to play the schmoozing game, although no-one liked it.

Gerrard quickly crossed the parquetry floors, passing the black marble fountain directly below the towering flagpole, which sat at the highest point of the parliament. It was an impressive space and Parliament House had been designed to allow the glass corridors connecting each chamber to open out into the magnificent atrium, directly behind the Great Hall.

He walked past the newspaper library and into the broad corridor leading to his office suite, the blue-grey carpet softening his approaching footsteps as he passed the heavy security doors. A wave to the security guard behind the thickened glass at the entrance to his office foyer, and he was back in his second home. He crossed to the doors that opened onto the prime minister's courtyard. This space was the most recognisable in parliament: it was where Keating first took questions, and Prime Minister Rudd was drawn to tears as he announced his resignation.

As he stepped outside, Surriento's black limousine drew to a halt and Gerrard opened the back door.

'Welcome, my friend.'

'Andrew, you are the perfect host,' President Surriento said, impressed by Gerrard's timing and his willingness to open the door.

'Come, let's have a brandy, or are you dry today?'

'I am not seeing any of my people, so a brandy would be a welcome treat.'

'This is the problem with some of you, Amir, I can never tell when you are being a devout Muslim and when you are not.' Gerrard draped his arm over his shorter friend's shoulder and led him inside.

The two leaders turned into the prime minister's formal office suite and Gerrard closed the door, urged the president to sit and picked out an Asbach Uralt, his special occasion brandy, pouring two generous splashes into balloons. Gerrard then joined his colleague on the leather lounge.

'Cheers.'

'May your life be full of grace.'

Gerrard rolled the liquid and sniffed deeply from the balloon, the aroma enticing his senses. It helped focus his mind after the solemnity of the previous two hours, which had stifled his usual enthusiasm. 'The Germans sure know their brandies.'

'Yes, but they know little else,' Surriento laughed, and Gerrard heartily joined him.

The biggest diplomatic challenge Australia and Indonesia faced was the smuggling of desperate people seeking new lives: non-Indonesian nationals, engaging non-Indonesian criminals to secure them passage to the Australian mainland or a handy island on flimsy Indonesian fishing boats built for bays not open seas, often sinking with tragic drownings. But neither man was too concerned about this at the moment.

'So, what can I do for you, my friend?' Surriento had a plane to catch and wanted to get beyond the pleasantries.

Gerrard took another sip of brandy to steady his anxiety. 'I have thought about your nation's need for funds for these immigration centres.'

'It is not my need; it is your need to stop the boats. We are willing to help, but you must pay.'

'When do you think we could begin construction?'

'As I have already told you, this will depend on many things.' The president's friend was good company, but he needed to get back to Indonesia for important meetings scheduled for the following morning. 'You have just had a remembrance for your colleagues, so I am not anticipating you getting money to us before the end of the year.'

'I am opening the parliament next week.'

The president shook his head slightly. 'You never cease to amaze me, you and your crazy rituals. Eight dead and you are back to work. If it was in my country, we would be in mourning for weeks.' Surriento sniffed at his swirling brandy. 'This brandy is very good. Now tell me, Andrew, what's on your mind?'

'If I were to approve the money for you next week, how long would it then take to start construction?'

'I should think we could turn soil in February, so long as the money is with us before March.'

'Not good enough.' Gerrard came to the edge of the lounge. 'I need to see site works begin before the end of next week, perhaps even earlier.'

'Anything is possible, but why the rush?'

'Can we get a few signs staked out? Push a tree over perhaps, have your media photograph and interview your works minister digging a hole with my ambassador?'

'I suppose I can manage a sign, but you must tell me why the urgency? We had a plan for February, so why change it? What's the rush?'

'If I release funds to you next week, then I must be able to show my people that you are serious about doing the work on time, and on budget.'

'How much will you be releasing?' Surriento sniffed his brandy again and took a small sip to entice his tastebuds.

'Four billion, the entire amount.'

Surriento began to cough. 'The entire amount, but why are you changing our plan? We agreed on four payments over three years. You now don't expect those drug smugglers to be released as well, do you?'

'I am announcing my intention to retire next week so a by-election can be held in my seat at the same time as the others are scheduled.' Gerrard eased back into the lounge, more relaxed now he had acknowledged his retirement for the first time; there could be no going back now. 'Margaret and I are moving to Europe a little earlier than planned.'

'That is wonderful news, congratulations. You have had a great and worthy career and Australia will always be in your debt.'

'Yeah, well, I want more than just being considered a worthy leader, and I'd rather have no debt owed.' Gerrard knew his friend would appreciate his frankness. 'So, in return for releasing the money next week, I want a larger clip of the ticket.'

'What do you have in mind?'

'I don't want to be greedy, so I think a one per cent clip is fair and reasonable.'

'That is no problem, but of course, with the amount now four billion, you will need to add an additional forty million dollars to the cash transfer to cover your commission.' Surriento placed his brandy on the coffee table before him. 'The problem will be getting such a large amount to you without anyone finding out. I will need to pass it through various accounts if we are to ensure it is not traced to me.'

'I want it transferred to a Swiss bank account the same day

you get it.' Gerrard knew he had to set the rules with Surriento otherwise the whole plan would collapse.

'That is not as easy as you think, my friend.'

'Amir, you know I know this can be done, so stop the bullshit.'

'I will need an Indonesian company to make it happen. So, to set that up for you, I will need twenty per cent of your share.'

'For Christ's sake, Amir, eight million? You are no doubt taking a fair share of the capital, so why do you want part of mine as well?'

'You need a financial stake in the game my friend, and I want you to pay a fair share for the work I will do for you. Of course, I also want to maximise my own personal opportunities. The other money pays for my structures.'

'Twenty per cent? Not ten?' Gerrard knew he would have to pay.

The two sat quietly, looking at each other.

'You either want it, or you don't.' Surriento sniffed his brandy, the exotic aroma intoxicating his senses. 'I don't need the money until March, so if you want it now, make it happen.'

Silence fell between the men, and Gerrard heard a bird call from a tree in the courtyard, a leaf blower buzz somewhere in the distance. Gerrard stood and slowly paced the floor to the large window and gazed out upon his courtyard, glass in hand, gnawing at his lower lip.

'Okay, but I want you to do all the work. I don't want to have any paper trail back to me.'

'You get me the bank account details, and I will set it all up. No-one will ever know you are involved.'

'All right, I'll have the legislation through parliament next week so we can transfer the four billion toward the end of the week, maybe even before. It's then up to you, but you must reassure me that works will begin before the end of next week.'

'Why is this so important to you?'

'The deaths of my colleagues have put the wind up me a bit.' Gerrard sat beside the president. 'I have by-elections in February, and there is no guarantee I can win the seats I need. I could lose government. If that's the case, I'm stuffed, and will retire with nothing except the pension.'

'All will be okay, Andrew. Stop worrying, you are doing the smart thing.'

'I need photographs of the site works for the campaign. Plus, it will help alleviate any media doubt about the money if you can get something to me before Wednesday – that would be very helpful.'

'It will be done, my friend.' Surriento finished his brandy.

'Thanks, Amir.'

'I have a plane to catch.' They stood, shook hands, embraced self-consciously, and the president left to his waiting car, eight million dollars richer.

The prime minister of Australia waved him off and smiled, having secured his own financial future in Europe, with a slightly more generous payout than previous prime ministers on retirement. Gerrard couldn't resist a small fist-pump as he glimpsed his reflection in a window.

# CHAPTER 7

**FRIDAY 8.00 PM**

Gordon O'Brien's office had been busy with parliamentary and government staff coming and going throughout the day as they worked to manage the flow of heads of government and other dignitaries through the parliament. The speaker wanted to ensure all protocols were met and engaged the clerk's resources to manage transport and security. It was vitally important to verify that each head of state left at the appointed time, and in protocol order, so as to not diminish their status among other heads of state. It would have been highly inappropriate for a national leader without very much international standing to leave before a significant world leader. This was enormously stressful for staff as they ensured egos were soothed and traffic was managed smoothly. No international incidents today; not on Gordon's watch.

As the demanding day came to an end and staff began to drift away to their homes for the weekend, Gordon sat talking with his trusted colleagues. The phone rang, and he punched the speaker button.

'Hello, O'Brien speaking.'

'Hi Gordon, it's Zara here. Well done today.'

'Thank you, Speaker, were you satisfied with the day?'

'Yes, very happy. I thought the service was appropriate and solemn enough for the occasion, so well done. Please thank your staff for me, the feedback has been terrific.'

'I will.'

Zara didn't respond immediately, sighed, and then cleared her throat to speak. 'Gordon, I have had the prime minister's office contact me and they want changes to the program next week.'

'Oh yes, like what?'

'They want to add further monies to the Supply Bill.'

'Well, it's already in the parliament and second reading speeches are done; it's about to go to the senate for approval. The public service will need to get their money, so we can't have any further delays if we are to maintain government.'

'The prime minister would like to add the stimulus package he announced yesterday. He wants to be certain the funds get to the electorate before Christmas.'

'Why doesn't he just draw up separate appropriation legislation, so it is not tied to the monies already approved?'

'It seems there are some issues with the prime minister's

office in doing that, so they have requested the additional six billion be added to the current Supply Bill legislation on the notice paper.'

Gordon's staff sat quietly listening and pulled faces of bafflement, shaking heads over what they were hearing.

'Speaker, I have to say it seems highly irregular, not to mention cumbersome. The government Supply Bill has completed debate and is ready to go to the senate; we really should not be amending it.' Gordon gnawed his lip before adding, 'The prime minister announced the stimulus funds only yesterday, so it really should go through the parliament on its own merits, and then it can be properly considered by the parliament. This is not an appropriate way to manage such huge amounts of public money.'

'The prime minister would like the stimulus cash for the electorate made available as soon as possible, and he has suggested he may add other funds. The prime minister's office has asked if we could accommodate their request within the Supply Bill so as not to make a fuss.'

'What other funds?' Gordon sat forward on his chair and looked quizzically at his surprised staff.

'I am not at liberty to say at this point.'

'The opposition has already agreed in principle to the stimulus cash splash for the community, so I'm not sure they will agree to adding more funds to the Supply Bill. The second reading has been completed and is due for a third reading in the house on Monday morning, so unless the government withdraws it, it will have to go to the senate as it is.'

'The prime minister wants the stimulus package through parliament before the end of the week.'

'He can still get it through in a totally separate Appropriation Bill, why does he need to add it to the current Supply Bill? It makes no sense.'

Zara raised her voice. 'Gordon, it seems you are not listening to me. The prime minister wants to have the amended bill through the parliament with the added expenditure without withdrawing it.'

'Not possible, I'm afraid. It's against parliamentary practice and wouldn't hold up if challenged.'

'What's it got to do with parliamentary practice?'

'Practice clearly states that Supply Bills are used to provide monies from the Consolidated Revenue Fund to pay public servants and so on.'

'I know that.'

'An Appropriation Bill is used for the purposes of funding special projects, such as was announced by the prime minister yesterday, therefore the stimulus funding would need its own specific legislation.'

'Is there no other way we can ensure it happens?'

'Speaker, all we need to do is prepare separate legislation setting out the six billion in payments.'

'Well, as I said, it could be more than that figure. Can it be done in time for Monday?'

'If the drafting office works on it over the weekend, we can have it in parliament on Monday for a first and second reading. It then goes to the senate, perhaps Tuesday at the latest, and then back in the house on Wednesday or Thursday for final assent.' Gordon paused. 'How much extra money does the government want to put through?'

Zara ignored the question. 'Will there be a problem getting it through both houses before the end of next week?'

'The government needs the support of the opposition, and I am not sure they will take kindly to further expenditure at this late stage of the process.'

'We have to get the stimulus package through the parliament next week; an awful lot depends on it,' Zara said, her voice quivering ever so slightly. Everyone listening noticed the tremor.

Gordon lowered his voice, leaning closer to the phone, 'Why the late change, Speaker?' Process and parliamentary protocol were always his concern, but he sensed his colleague was troubled. Marjorie quickly stood and ushered the others out as Gordon picked up the handpiece. 'The government has already identified six billion for the handout, so how much extra are we talking?'

'Four billion, but tell no-one,' Bagshaw quickly whispered.

'For what?' Gordon was startled by the amount.

'It's to build the offshore immigration centres in Indonesia. The government wants them to begin construction immediately, and therefore the Indonesians have said they need the entire forecasted amount brought forward. Some deal has been done with the president earlier today, apparently.'

'Speaker, this is highly inappropriate; it does not please me to hear this news.'

'I suppose there are valid reasons, Gordon.'

'The government already has four hundred million in the

parliament on the notice paper as a part payment, the first of four. What will happen to that legislation?'

'It will be withdrawn.'

'I cannot allow this to happen, Speaker.'

'Why would you be concerned? The immigration centre money was in the forward estimates when the federal budget was approved by the parliament last May, so the idea of the funding should not be an issue. The stimulus package has been announced and agreed to by the opposition, so what is your problem with this, Gordon?'

'Timing, and the rush to get things through during a period of parliamentary uncertainty.'

'Can the senate amend the Supply Bill to make it easier for everyone?'

'Not really. They have amended money bills in the past, but these have all been rejected when they came back to the house.' Gordon ran his fingers through his hair and scratched the nape of his neck. 'As you know, the senate is all about reviewing legislation; it cannot initiate money bills and, for that matter, rarely amends government money bills.' Gordon paused, waiting for the speaker to respond. He could hear her breathing into the mouthpiece, but she did not answer.

'This is a little inappropriate wouldn't you say, Speaker? The initial four hundred million was only for seed funding to commence one centre on Ambon, with a further three payments made annually. Now the government wants the whole lot to go through, linked to a dubious stimulus package?' Gordon surmised he wasn't being told everything. 'Why can't they just amend the initial immigration expenditure legislation enacting the centres, which is on the current notice paper?'

'The prime minister wants to combine the two funds into one bill and has asked me to make it happen this way before Christmas, so we are obliged to meet the government's need.'

'Why now? It seems a little hasty, don't you think, given we only have a week before the summer break of parliament? The government doesn't have the numbers, and work is not scheduled to begin on any site by the Indonesians until early next year.' Gordon waited, but there was no response. 'What's this all about, Speaker?'

'The PM wants the Christmas bonus for the punters to hit bank accounts in two weeks, and he wants his promise to build immigration centres acted on before the by-elections in February.' Zara said. 'It's not unreasonable, given he has been promising action on this policy for some time.'

'Has treasury approved it?'

'The prime minister didn't say. He only said to ensure I make it happen. This means I am directing you to make it happen.'

'This is highly irregular, and I want it recorded that I am against this un-parliamentary procedure.'

'So recorded.'

'Send the legislation over when it's done, and I shall look at it.'

'Good night, Gordon.'

Gordon softly replaced the receiver, and fell back into his chair, rocking and thinking. Marjorie entered, closing the door behind her, and taking her seat in front of Gordon, waiting for direction.

'You look as if that was bad news,' Marjorie said, breaking the silence.

'I'm annoyed with what I've just been told, to be perfectly honest with you.' Gordon sat up, swung his chair into the desk and looked at his confidante. 'Not sure why, but I think something untoward may be happening that could compromise the parliament.'

'What is it?'

'The government wants to bulldoze the stimulus package through next week, and at the same time, they want to increase the proposed funding for the Indonesian immigration detention centres, apparently to accommodate the Indonesians, so work can start immediately. This would not normally cause a problem for anyone, given the Indonesian funding is already approved and it is a bipartisan agreement, but the funds are significant.'

'I'm sure they wouldn't be doing it unless the government funds were needed to begin construction.'

'I'm not so sure about that. It appears hurried to me. Why the sudden rush by the Indonesians less than a week after they agreed to a four-payment deal? I wonder if treasury has looked at it.'

'What has changed this week?'

Gordon didn't have an answer but wondered aloud. 'Of course, there was the tragedy, and there is no actual guarantee that the government will win their seats again at the by-elections. Who knows how the electors will vote? If they don't get them back, they'll lose government.'

'Why should you worry?'

'If I don't, Marjorie, who will?' Gordon pushed back in his chair and placed his hands behind his head.

'Don't the politicians run the parliament?'

Gordon humphed and sat back into his desk. 'These folks come to this place inspired to do good work, but they always get seduced by self-interest. They don't care about this money. It means nothing to them, only votes.'

'Surely, they care.'

'They only care about what their voters think. If voters want a problem solved, then politicians will spend as much taxpayer money as they need to, to get it done. Millions or billions of dollars are only words to these people.'

Marjorie studied the anguished look on her boss's face for a moment. 'You only have a week to go before all of this is behind you. Stop worrying.'

'You are my rock sometimes, Marjorie.'

'Go home and enjoy the weekend.'

'I will once I speak to Messenger. Can you track him down for me please?

---

'You look gorgeous.'

'And hello to you to.' Anita offered her cheek as Barton bent to kiss her.

'Sorry I'm late.' Barton sat opposite and unravelled his

napkin, draping it across his lap. 'I had a few things to tidy up and I got stuck on a media call – you know how it is.'

'Yes, I do know how it is.' Anita continued with their game. 'This is why I don't think getting into a friendship with you is a good idea.'

'Well, I was hoping for a little more than friendship.'

'Yes, I bet you were.' Anita studied her menu. 'I believe the duck is good.'

'The what is good?' Barton asked, provoking a smile from across the table.

'The duck.'

'Oh, I must have misheard you.'

'Yes, of course you did.' She didn't raise her eyes; a smiling Barton Messenger was irresistible.

Anita had suggested they meet at the Ottoman, a high-class restaurant that catered for the politically powerful. She didn't want to be seen with Messenger in a secluded romantic bistro, even though she might have preferred it, or the gossips would have the meeting on twitter by morning and her links to her many confidantes would be threatened. Journalists need to work both sides of the political fence, and jeopardising trust was the first law of ineffective journalism. She knew that having dinner with Messenger, the opposition's manager of parliamentary business, in Canberra's most political restaurant was a good idea.

The clatter of plates and the rich background music masked hushed political conversations. Many schemes and political coups had been formulated on the trendy stiffened paper that protected the expensive Turkish linen tablecloths from wine and food stains.

Several politicians were scattered around the eatery, some enjoying what seemed to be a wake for lost colleagues, while others were in quiet conversation, checking over their shoulders for eavesdroppers. One or two media gallery members were also engaged in these quiet conversations, and Anita was optimistic her ruse of dinner with Messenger would not be uncovered.

'Would you like a wine?' Barton was keen to engage in conversation but seemed nervous.

'A dry white would be nice, perhaps a sauvignon blanc. You choose. What are you going to eat?'

'I think I might go with some lentils... or perhaps the rabbit.' A waiter appeared at his side, and he ordered a Marlborough sauvignon blanc with Turkish bread and a variety of dips for starters.

His dinner date seemed impressed with his choice, put her menu aside and leaned into the table. 'Barton, I wanted to talk to you further about this immigration detention centre funding.'

Barton interrupted and waved his hand. 'I thought we'd be having a quiet dinner together, as so-called friends, and all you want to do is talk about work. I wish you'd warned me.'

'That's totally not fair. You know this place has ears as big as Dumbo the elephant. I'm hoping to get them focused elsewhere.' Anita responded. 'You just sat down. We have lots of eyes on us, no doubt trying to lip-read what we are talking about. So, Einstein, do you think we start with a little work before we move on?'

'Move on to where?' Barton wanted an answer but was not getting one. 'Cat got your tongue?'

'Don't make this harder than it should be.' Anita picked up her glass of water and Barton saw that her hand was trembling slightly.

'Okay, what do you want to know?'

'Bart, I'm sorry. I'm nervous about being here with you. I don't want to start any gossip about us.'

'Why would you care? You're just here doing your job, aren't you?'

'No.'

The waiter arrived with the wine, but the couple did not avert their eyes from each other. Barton waved the waiter on, who then carefully poured wine into the glasses, placing the bottle into a nearby ice bucket and left. Barton lifted his glass for a toast and Anita responded by softly clinking his glass with her own, their eyes still locked.

'If I live to be a hundred, I will never forget this moment,' Barton said.

'You are such a politician.' Anita smiled, sipped her wine, and returned to the menu. 'I think I may have the duck.'

Suddenly, Messenger's phone buzzed. He reached into his jacket and withdrew it to check if it was an important call. Anita looked up as he realised, he would have to take it.

'I won't be a moment.' Barton quickly got up and answered as he hurried toward the front door to escape the noise. 'Hello, Barton Messenger.'

Gordon O'Brien apologised for the lateness of the hour but

asked if Barton would have the patience to return to the parliament for a meeting. He understood if this could not happen, but he would not be asking unless it was important.

'I'll be there in twenty minutes. Can you send a car to the Ottoman?'

Messenger looked through the restaurant window as he put his phone back into his jacket, wishing the call had never arrived. He would have time for a glass of wine and some dips, which had been delivered to the table. He watched Anita as she gazed about the room. Her long dark hair was flowing over her bare shoulders, free from its usual restraints. Her red dress complemented her dark Mediterranean complexion, and her tanned legs were graced with perfect black stilettos, such a contrast to the sneakers she was never out of around the parliament. She had provided him with so much pleasure, and now he was squashing it before it could develop further.

'That was O'Brien, he needs to see me.' Barton sat and sipped his wine before tearing off some bread to taste the dips.

'Well, you must go,' Anita announced immediately. 'We can do this another time... hopefully in another place.'

'You are wonderful. I feel dreadful about leaving you.'

'Barton, get over yourself, will you. O'Brien needs to see you. He would never call unless it was important.' Anita seemed to know she needed to help him. 'Just make sure I get the exclusive on whatever story he wants to discuss with you.'

'I need to get back to Melbourne early tomorrow for meetings in my electorate, but can I see you next week?'

'You'll see me.'

'No, I mean, can I see you?'

'And, as I just told you, you will definitely see me.'

'Should we kiss goodbye?' Messenger drained his glass.

'Are you serious?' Messenger stood to leave. 'No, but you can kiss me hello next week... maybe.' Anita smiled broadly as she watched him shrug, softly wave, then leave.

---

Gordon sat at his desk; his office dimly lit by his ornate desk lamp. Messenger knocked and Gordon beckoned him in to sit.

'The service was very good today, Gordon, thank you for your efforts.'

'Not just my efforts, Mr Messenger, the team performed very well during a very difficult and stressful time. The loss of the deputy speaker has hit the team hard, as has losing the others, of course.'

'What is so urgent that you needed to talk to me tonight?' Barton still harboured some resentment about being called from his dinner.

'I have been advised by the government that they want to add more money to the government Supply Bill, to allow for the stimulus package they announced.'

'What?' Messenger was confused. 'They can't do that; we've completed second reading speeches.'

'That's what I advised the government. I have suggested a separate Appropriation Bill for the stimulus package.'

'That idea makes sense, and it would be our preferred process. We can talk to the funding in detail.'

'They also want to add more funds, other than the stimulus cash.'

'Why, for what?'

'It seems they want the entire allocated funding for the offshore detention centres to be transferred to the Indonesians, which was agreed in the budget, to allow construction to begin immediately.'

'I would have thought that could be covered by an amendment to the Immigration Appropriation Bill. It's on the notice paper, but it's not due now until early next year, given the state of the parliamentary numbers. Our team still want to debate it.'

'The government are asking for a little more than the four hundred million, I'm afraid.'

'How much is a little more?'

'The prime minister wants the project's fully allocated four billion dollars to be transferred in one transaction and wants it all approved within a new Appropriation Bill that will come before the parliament next week. He tried to get it into the Supply Bill but that wasn't possible, so now they will bring a new money bill in on Monday, to be approved by both houses of parliament before week's end.'

Messenger sat quietly, slowly nodding his head as he thought through the various options open to the opposition. 'We will vote it down.'

'Mr Harper has already committed the opposition to agree to the cash stimulus being provided to the community before

Christmas, and these immigration detention centre funds will be added to that figure, taking it to ten billion.'

'I understand that, but we will not be voting for it.'

'The prime minister has given a direction that this will need to happen next week, and I have been advised by the drafting office that they are already preparing legislation with the increased funds for tabling on Monday.'

'I question the validity of the entire proposal.' Messenger was now considering the politics associated with the request.

'The opposition leader has provided support for the stimulus payments, and he has agreed on not forcing any votes. So, I am not sure what the problem is.' Gordon was just as concerned as Messenger about the process, but he was required to do what had been requested of him.

'The problem is, Mr O'Brien, we do not approve of the legislative process for this funding, nor the poor timing, ramming it through the parliament without sufficient scrutiny or debate. There is no need for a sudden rush. We will approve the stimulus, but we will not approve the Indonesian funds. What are they doing with the current bill on the notice paper for the initial four hundred million in funding they wanted approved before the accident changed everything?'

'They will be withdrawing it.'

'It would have been much easier for the government to amend the Immigration Appropriation Bill, which would then separate the stimulus money into its own Appropriation Bill. It makes no sense to rush it.'

'If you have already agreed on the budgeted figure of four

billion, then I see you have little objection to what they want to do,' Gordon prodded him further for a response. 'Plus, they are already drafting a bill.'

'So what?' Messenger gazed at O'Brien for a moment, gnawing at his lip. 'We want the two funding proposals in separate legislation, that's what makes better sense.'

'Maybe they don't want the scrutiny of the parliament.' Gordon tested Messenger further with a hint that the proposed funds were being transferred under some cloud of secrecy.

'What, if the government consolidated it with the stimulus package, do you mean?'

'Yes, it seems there is a story we are not aware of, and I agree with you that the full amount for the project should be in the Immigration Appropriation Bill that is on the notice paper.' Gordon sat quietly studying the manager of opposition business, whose job it was to work in partnership with the clerk to reduce any controversy in the house. 'Although, I must admit, it would be very hard for you to justify a backflip on this approval.'

'Backflip or not, we will not be supporting a consolidated money bill.' Messenger pushed himself out of his chair, ready to leave. 'We will insist the government isolate the payments to the Indonesians. We will support the stimulus payments to the electorate but, I can absolutely assure you, we won't be supporting any payments now, or indeed in the future, to the Indonesians, unless there is an opportunity for proper parliamentary scrutiny.'

'You will have to agree, otherwise there is a chance you could bring down the government if it loses a vote.' Gordon pushed a little harder.

'So be it.' It was time for Barton to leave – he needed to speak to his colleagues – so he walked to the door before turning to look at O'Brien. 'We will not be agreeing to this, Gordon.'

'If they consolidate it into one bill and you reject it, this could potentially harm your chances at the by-elections, as the community is expecting their money before Christmas.' Gordon also stood and courteously followed him.

'I think what the community is expecting, Mr O'Brien, is good government – not a Gerrard cash splash,' Messenger said over his shoulder as he left. 'We won't support a consolidated bill.'

Gordon watched him go, and as he heard the outer office door close, he smiled. 'Good for you, Mr Messenger, good for you.'

# CHAPTER 8

## SUNDAY

Zara Bagshaw returned home to her country in far north Queensland over the weekend, seeking to soothe away the stress of the previous week and grieve the loss of her colleagues, especially her deputy, Catherine Kennedy. The tragedy thrust major issues before the parliament, especially now the prime minister wanted her to drive the passage of contentious legislation, and the clerk such a stickler for propriety. She needed to be home on her land, to breathe again.

Zara spent Saturday walking through her favourite part of the rainforest, the coolness of the shade and the dampness in the air bringing her closer to her ancestors who had walked these hidden tracks. She breathed in the history of her sacred place and contemplated those who had gone before her. The lush undergrowth and tall trees filtered the sun, and she began to feel cold as her damp shirt clung to her. She brushed past a small tree and a leech dropped onto her neck seeking fresh blood. She flicked it off, flipping up her collar and buttoning up her shirt to the top to protect her neck – she hadn't brought insect repellent.

Zara had been prowling through the forest for more than 30 minutes when she suddenly emerged at her waterhole – an oasis in the middle of nowhere with shafts of sunlight sparkling on the water like glittering diamonds. Water purled from the undergrowth, creating a small waterfall that flowed into the pool.

Zara kicked off her boots, stripped off her clothes and tentatively entered the water. She pushed off and floated on her back for a short time, eyes closed, enjoying the warmth of the sun and the crisp chill of the water. She stroked over to the small waterfall and thrust her head under it, as if she could wash away the white world, she had tried so hard to join.

Her husband had stayed in Canberra, knowing Zara needed time with her family and the spirit of her country. Their marriage was new, and they were still working out their boundaries, but John Reid had quickly learned a Kuku Yalanji woman needed time in her country. He didn't understand it, but he wanted to support her in any way he could.

Before Zara embarked on her long trek back to Canberra, she sought out her father for a private chat. She wanted to discuss the challenges that lay ahead for her. Her father was respected in the district, active in the land rights campaigns where he had sometimes ended up on the wrong end of a police truncheon during demonstrations in the early days. He was tireless in his attempts to explain to recalcitrant Europeans that Indigenous culture was different from their own; not inferior.

Zara carried a tray of refreshments to the verandah where her father had perched himself in a wicker chair to escape the increasing heat of the day. She placed the iced lemonade and plates of salad and dip on the glass-topped wicker side table and slumped on the couch beside him, grabbing and dipping a carrot stick before she did. Her father had left the family home when she was very young and established another family, so relations between father and daughter were often tense. Visits had been sparse during her teen years but as she matured, she had come to realise the wisdom in his teachings.

'This is nice, thank you, darling.'

'It's a pleasure, treasure.'

Jeremy Bagshaw picked up a glass of lemonade and took a refreshing mouthful. 'So, what do you plan to do?'

'I don't have any options at all. I need to protect Gerrard.'

'Surely he doesn't need your help. He's the prime minister.'

'It's a little tricky with the numbers in the house at the moment. Basically, after the deaths, the majority is now with the opposition. They could bring the government down by voting against any money bill.'

'That sounds like bullshit to me.'

'The parliament must retain confidence in the government's ability to run the country successfully, so if it loses a confidence vote, or can't get a money bill through, then the parliament has no option but to go to the people for an election.'

'If I know Andrew Gerrard, he will never let that happen.'

'Not sure he has too much choice.' Zara leaned forward and took a few more carrot sticks and dip. 'He hasn't got the numbers and you can never guarantee an election result. We could lose government if the by-elections don't go our way.'

'Pass me a bit of that, will you please, darling.' Bagshaw sat forward pointing to the dip. 'So why are you so worried?'

'Gerrard has flagged extra money to be added to the punters' stimulus bill, which he wants passed next week, and he's rather insistent that it goes through without any trouble.' Zara poured her father a refill from the glass jug and settled back with her own glass. 'Damn it.' Condensation dropped onto her silk shirt, and she flicked her legs off the couch, sitting up to brush away the excess water.

'And this is a problem? I thought I saw on the news that Harper has agreed to pass it?'

'He has, but the PM wants to add more money to the bill, which the opposition has not agreed to.'

'How much are we talking?'

'I'm told a little over four billion.'

Bagshaw whistled slowly and sat up straighter in his chair. 'So, if the opposition vote against the bill, then they could bring down the government and force it to an immediate general election?'

'Exactly!'

'I see your problem.'

'It gets worse still. Gerrard has, in no uncertain terms, threatened me with not only losing my job, but ensuring the party immediately disendorses me.'

'He can't do that! You're the first Indigenous politician to hold such a senior parliamentary role.' Bagshaw almost spat the words. 'He not only can't do that, but I'll make sure he doesn't.'

'Dad, he can, and he will if I don't help him next week.' Zara looked out into the garden. 'He's even threatened to end the funding for your school.'

The silence between them was interrupted by the screech of a pair of white cockatoos flying overhead.

'This is what concerns me. Gerrard wants this money bill to pass, and I must admit, it is against parliamentary procedure. It looks dodgy, but who am I to question it when Prime Minister Gerrard wants it? If Harper changes his mind, then it will apparently be my fault, thus ending my career.'

'So don't allow Harper to change his mind.'

'How is that possible?'

'You control the parliament. Let them play by your rules. Don't let them call for a division.'

'But they need to vote on the Appropriation Bill.'

'Yes, but they don't need to have a division to count the vote, you can pass it on voices, surely.'

'That's true, but they can call for a division.'

'So don't let them.'

'Dad, of course they will call for a division. If they don't approve the expenditure, they will ask for a count, believe me, and then that will trigger an election.'

'Two things to consider. Firstly, they would be mad to.'

'Why?'

'Because the population would be annoyed and never forgive

them for not getting their money, especially after they were promised it for Christmas. How much is it?'

'Around a thousand dollars per household.'

'Significant, so if the opposition went to an election breaking their promise, they'd be smashed.'

'Your second point?'

'They could be bound by agreement not to force a division to count the votes.' Bagshaw placed his glass on the tray and wiped his hand on his shorts. 'Why don't you get Harper to sign an agreement that he won't challenge the numbers in the house, before he sees the bill.'

'He won't do that. He's not stupid.'

'It's not about stupidity, it's about protocol. James Harper is a decent man and will comply with parliamentary protocol.'

'What happens if he finds out about the extra money? He'll never agree to ten billion going through when he's only expecting six billion.'

'So don't put it in the initial bill, get the senate to amend it.'

'Constitutionally, the senate can't initiate money bills.'

'They aren't initiating, they're amending.'

'They really can't amend money legislation either.'

'They can if it comes back to the house for approval.'

Zara studied her father. 'Maybe.'

'You get the initial Appropriation Bill through the house, amend it in the senate and have the house approve it when it all becomes too late for the opposition to act.'

'Nice one, but is it legal?'

'Is the money being fraudulently taken through the parliament?'

'Not really.'

'Has it been approved by the government and the opposition?'

'The money has been agreed to by the opposition during the budget sessions, back in May.'

'Then you have nothing to worry about.'

'You are joking, aren't you?'

'Just don't let them call a division. Everything will be fine, trust me.' Bagshaw smiled at his daughter and chewed on a carrot stick.

'Stuff Gerrard, I can't understand why this Indonesian money is suddenly so important to him.'

'The PM has his reasons; those brothers up north know how to get blood from a stone.'

'Yes, but why all the pressure on me?'

'Honey, the prime minister wants it done, so you are under an obligation to ensure it passes the parliament. Do it so it doesn't create conflict in the chamber.'

'So, if I get Harper to agree to zero divisions to count votes, then we won't have any disruption, and we can all go and have a happy Christmas. The parliament won't be back until February, after the by-elections, and the status quo will prevail, fingers crossed.'

'Now sweetheart, that wasn't too hard, was it?'

'I suspect it isn't going to be as easy as that.' Zara shifted deeper into her cushions. 'I still have O'Brien to contend with.'

'Zara, you are the Speaker of the House of Representatives of the Commonwealth Parliament, and you hold the fourth highest office in the land, so be proud of who you are and the position you hold, on behalf of your people. It is your house, so rule it and ensure they march to the beat of your drum. Even the prime minister should respect your decisions.' Bagshaw dabbed perspiration off his face with a paper napkin. 'How is the old bloke, still treating you well?'

'He always treats me well, Daddy.'

Zara stood and hugged her father. It was time to think about leaving for the airport. She lingered in a tight embrace, drawing as much energy from him as she could, never wanting him to know what she had been doing to maintain her authority. Gerrard had a hold on her that no other man had, and she couldn't give it up.

---

'Fancy a wine, Gordon?' The next-door neighbour was at the door waving a bottle of chilled white wine. 'You sound as if you've had a bad time at work.'

'How do you know?'

'You always play Mozart way, way too loud when you're stressed. So, I figure it's wine time.'

'Well, since you're here, I suppose you'd better come in.' Gordon unsnibbed the security door and let Jon Pettifer brush past him into his lounge.

'You work too hard; I've always said that. You need to stop occasionally.'

Gordon went to the sideboard and withdrew two wine glasses and turned down his music. 'How's your day been, Jon?'

'I'm a little hungover from last night. A few of us went off to a club. They missed you.'

'I'm a little too old for such carry on.'

'You're never too old, Gordon, not for me at least.' Jon cracked the seal and filled the two glasses held before him, took one from his host and sat on the couch taking a generous mouthful. 'Ah that's better. So, have you got much planned for your last week? A few parties?'

'No, not really. They did a presentation last Monday, and then I've been worried about managing the place ever since.'

'Such a tragedy, and I heard on the news today it didn't have to happen; the pilot should have waited for the storm to pass, apparently.'

'Yes, tragic.'

'So, what's the news? Any gossip? Anything thrilling? Titillating?'

'You can't help yourself, can you?' Gordon smiled and took another sip of his wine.

'Gordon, come on, you know I live for scandal and if you don't give it to me, I have to rely on boring Kevin on the other side, and he is useless.'

'I have nothing for you.'

'Then why do you look as if you've aged ten years since I last saw you? Come on, let yourself be free and get rid of the stress. Speak.'

'You wouldn't understand.'

'Try me. Just imagine I'm your therapist and you've come to see me.' Jon drained his glass, refilled his and splashed a touch into Gordon's. 'Mr O'Brien, thanks for coming in, now tell me what's troubling you?'

'I'm worried about some of the things happening at the parliament.'

'Yes, good, go on.'

'It's nothing, really.'

'Gordon O'Brien, judging by your sad little face and the enormous bags under your eyes, this thing that is worrying you is a little more than nothing. Now tell me, I'm a doctor, you can trust me.'

'There's a lot of taxpayer dollars going through the parliament this week and I'm not sure it's all above board.'

'Now that wasn't too hard, was it. Tell me more. Why don't you think it's appropriate?'

Gordon drained his glass and flicked it at Jon to refill it. He recoiled, protecting the bottle. 'Don't worry, I have another in the fridge.'

'Of course, you do, dear, probably muscat or hock or some other old thing.' Jon filled Gordon's glass and splashed some into his own. 'So, you think this money shouldn't be going through parliament, but aren't we getting a government handout shortly?'

'Yes, that's part of it.'

'So, what's wrong with that?'

'Oh, I don't know, maybe I'm quibbling over nothing.'

'Listen, my friend, I've known you since you were this high to a grasshopper,' Jon held out his hand. 'And if you say you are uncertain about something then more often than not there is something wrong, so what is it?'

'The prime minister—'

'That bastard!' Jon shrieked.

'... the prime minister wants to change legislation to get a project funded ahead of the agreed time.'

'So, the money is paid early, so what?'

'Well, on its own absolutely nothing, but when he is doing it the way he is, then I become suspicious of his motives.'

'So, what should he have done?'

'There is legislation already on the notice paper he could have amended.'

'OK, strike one. Could amend existing legislation. What else?'

'He could have drafted separate legislation.'

'Perhaps there is a timing issue, and he didn't want a delay.'

'Then why not amend the original legislation?'

'Good point, what else?

'He tries to dump it into legislation that has already passed the house.'

'You're lucky I know what you're talking about, you know. Do you ever think of that?'

'I know, and that's a good point.' Gordon reflected on the innocent comment.

'It's working in the members dining room. I pick up all sorts of things.'

'The fact is, no-one actually knows what's going on with legislation, so the money gets lost in translation.'

'How much are we talking?'

'Four billion.'

'Four billion bucks, for what?'

'Indonesian immigration detention centres. They were approved in the budget and were to be paid over the four years of the project. Now they want all the money up-front.'

'You know something? I could believe that. Do you remember that cute little Balinese fellow at the club? He's always asking me for money.'

Gordon ignored the interjection. 'So why is the government trying to do something shifty?'

'Oh, I don't know, Gordon. Go and get the other bottle will you, and make sure it's not muscat,' Jon said as he emptied his bottle into the two glasses, overfilling both.

'It's chardonnay, you know that's all I drink.'

'Even when you go fishing?'

'Even then.'

'So, when do you think you'll be out casting a rod again? I have a week off after the parliament closes, so perhaps we can go camping.'

'That'd be great, maybe next weekend,' said Gordon, returning from the kitchen with a freshly opened bottle in his hand. 'This is a nice Western Australian number from a small winery near Pemberton – I bought a case.'

'Of course, you did, dear, nothing else to spend your money on, so you may as well.' Jon joked. 'So is the moron going to get the deal done, or will he have to do what Gordon tells him?'

'Well, if he puts it with the Christmas stimulus package he'll be in trouble because the opposition have said they'll reject it.'

Gordon fetched fresh glasses from the sideboard. 'So, I'm not sure what Gerrard will do; that's what worries me.'

'What, that useless Harper said no? Good on him.'

'No, it was Messenger.'

'I quite fancy him, you know – such a handsome fellow.'

'I haven't noticed.'

'Rubbish!'

Their raucous laughter was interrupted by Gordon's mobile phone buzzing. 'Gordon O'Brien.'

'Mr O'Brien, it's George here, just letting you know she has redirected a car to take her to the parliament.'

'Thanks, George, good man. Keep me advised.' Gordon pushed the end call button and slipped it into his trouser pocket.

'Who was that?'

'George from security. He's keeping tabs on a few people for me.'

'You sneaky so-and-so.'

'Maybe so, but I need to make sure nothing is happening that I'm not aware of.'

'Well, nothing is happening here, so let's go eat somewhere.'

'I have a casserole in the fridge.'

'You're kidding me. Thursdays are your casserole night, and it's usually a beef curry, am I right?' Jon rushed to the fridge to check. 'Thought so. I'm not eating three-day-old curry. Let's go to the club.'

'Okay, but I'll drive. I want to get home early – I have a big week ahead.'

'Stuff that, we'll take a cab and be home by nine, I'm not having you not drinking.'

'Jon, seriously, I need rest. I haven't had much sleep over the last week.'

'You'll be in bed by 10.30, I promise. Now drink up, pour me another, and I'll call a cab.'

---

The flight back from Cairns to Canberra seemed to be longer than usual, touching down at 6.30 pm after travelling via Brisbane. As the plane taxied to the terminal, Zara received a text message.

urgent u cum asap

Zara recognised it was from the prime minister's personal phone, the one he kept for their private communication. Although she didn't want to have a late night, she directed her driver to the parliament, and asked her to wait for her in the basement carpark. She promised she wouldn't be terribly long.

Zara entered the house through the representatives' entrance, passed security and walked to her office. She waited anxiously for five minutes just in case any interested person wondered what she was doing in the house so late on a Sunday. It was not unusual for politicians to labour hard in their offices late into the night, returning early the next morning.

When she considered she had waited long enough, she slipped

out of her office and silently moved through the darkened corridors to the prime minister's suite. The office had been converted to two levels from the original plans, forcing the ministerial suites above the prime minister's office to be relocated. This increased floor space for staffing and provided a private suite for the prime minister on the first floor. The internal stairwell was added at great cost, and its grand sweeping staircase added pomp to the entrance from the prime minister's courtyard. Upstairs was the prime minister's private office, meeting rooms, staff offices, a lounge, dining room and personal suite.

Zara had been given a key to a fire door on the first floor. She checked the dimly lit corridors for movement, and seeing no-one she entered quietly, closing the heavy door softly behind her, entering the personal suite of the prime minister. She never heard the click of a camera shutter.

Gerrard sat on a soft leather lounge watching a sports program with the ubiquitous cigar in one hand and brandy balloon in the other.

'Zara, there you are. Come in and put your feet up, you must have had a long day.'

'I have a car waiting.' She wanted to get home and not linger.

'Never mind that, do you want a drink?'

'Andrew, I need to get home. Can we get this done? Why do you want to see me at this time of night?'

'I want to discuss the legislation I'm tabling tomorrow.'

'Can't we do that in the morning.'

'No, we can't.'

'Come on then, let's get to it.'

'So, do you want a drink?'

'Champagne, please.' Zara relented slightly, knowing when to ease up. Andrew Gerrard may have been her occasional lover, but he was also the prime minister. 'What do you want to talk about?'

Gerrard had opened a bottle of Dom Perignon in anticipation of Zara joining him and poured a chilled glass, handing it to her and moving to a leather chair, leaving the lounge for her. 'Take a seat, this won't take long.' Suddenly serious he added, 'I took a call from the clerk this afternoon.'

'Oh yes, what did he want?' Zara sat opposite on another chair, avoiding the lounge.

'I can't believe that guy has only five fucking days left, and he still thinks he is the keeper of the flame.'

'What did he say?' The champagne was chilled perfectly, and the bubbles were working their magic.

'He thinks we should defer the Appropriation Bill, or at the very least drop the immigration centres' funding.'

'I spoke to him on Friday and told him what was happening. What's got into him?'

'Fucking treasury. They told him they haven't reviewed it. Mind you the treasurer has said it's all right, but because some bureaucratic wanker in treasury said he hadn't seen it, O'Brien wants to stop it.'

'So, what's the problem? Get the money for the punters through and defer the Indonesians until next year.'

'Nope. No good.' Gerrard sucked on his cigar and blew the smoke toward her.

'Why?'

'They're beginning site works as we speak.'

'On a Sunday?'

'The Muslims don't rest on Sundays, Zara. It's only lazy Christians who do that.'

'That's a potential problem,' Zara said.

'I knew you'd understand.'

Zara understood all right, something dodgy was going on with Gerrard, hence the late meeting. She swigged some champagne and looked at Gerrard, searching for something to help her.

'There are two things I want you to do.' Gerrard ashed his cigar then took a large draught of brandy. 'The first is, we must ensure the stimulus and the Indonesian legislation gets tabled in the parliament tomorrow, and we have to get it out into the senate by Wednesday morning at the very latest.'

'We can't afford to have a call for a division on it. Given the numbers, you will lose government if we do. How is Harper holding up to his agreement?' Zara asked.

'I'm not so worried about him, it's O'Brien I'm concerned about. It wouldn't take much effort on his part to get the drafting office to delay it on a technicality, then we're all stuffed.'

'I know you've had your problems in the past with him, but he doesn't call for a division, the opposition does.'

'O'Brien can lean on Harper if he thinks the bill is suspicious.' Gerrard drained his glass.

'Is it?'

'No, of course not.' Gerrard stood and moved to his liquor sideboard to refill his glass. 'The fucking Indonesians have changed their minds at the very last moment, asking for the entire amount allocated in the budget, so I'm trying to facilitate that when we don't have the damn numbers.'

'So why not wait?'

'The Indonesians have told me in no uncertain terms that if the money is not released to them before Christmas, the deal is off. I can't afford to look as if I can't control those rat fuckers. Plus, they'll now go ahead with the executions if we don't do as they ask.'

'But Andy, it's only a couple of months.' Zara pointed at her glass and Gerrard took the champagne from the ice bucket. 'Surely they can wait?'

'It needs to be done and dusted this week without any delay. That's what I want to happen and that's what I want you to make sure happens.'

'We need to lock Harper away first, before we worry about what the clerk may do.'

'Do you have a suggestion as to how that might happen?' Gerrard asked as he slowly poured the champagne.

'Invite him to your office tomorrow morning for a joint press conference. You and he can announce the formal signing of an agreement between the government and the opposition that is effective for one week only, where no divisions will be called for on the floor of the house. Sweeten the deal by saying to him he can call a formal vote on any money bill, which means he won't suspect anything.' Gerrard replaced the bottle in the bucket and sprawled in his chair. 'This then allows Harper to feel as if he is in control and not giving too much away with the agreement, which of course he isn't.'

'I'm listening.' Gerrard blew smoke high into the fug above his head.

'You then table your stimulus package legislation for the first and second readings tomorrow morning, after prayers. And here is the most important point,' Zara sat forward, looking at Gerrard to ensure he was paying attention to what she was about to say, 'the legislation does not include the funding for Indonesia.'

'How is that any good?' Gerrard straightened up. 'That's crap, I just told you we need to get the fucking money through this week.'

'Wait.'

'For what? That is a ridiculous plan. If we can't get it into this new Appropriation Bill, then how are we to get it through the fucking house this week?'

'It gets the legislation through the house without controversy and up into the senate without having to take a formal vote. Then it is amended by the senate to add the funding for Indonesia.'

'You of all people should know the senate can't initiate money bills. For fuck's sake,' Gerrard sneered.

'True, not unless it then comes back to the house for approval.'

Gerrard stopped his carping and looked at Zara. 'You're suggesting we send the stimulus package to the senate without the immigration centre money.'

'That's right.'

'We then amend it in the senate to add the four billion.'

'Now you're getting it.'

'I see, so we get it through the house without controversy

from the opposition or the media, and then bring it back amended, which we then approve.'

'This allows you to sweet-talk the media before it comes back to the house, highlighting the pressure from the Indonesians, blah blah blah. You've already had Harper agree not to take any formal votes, and his mob has already approved the stimulus package. When the legislation comes back amended, he can't then vote against it. He would look like a goose denying the punters their Christmas treat, and during the process we can sideline O'Brien.' Zara took a generous mouthful of champagne and sat back in her chair.

'That could work.'

'The most important part, Andrew, is Harper. You have to blindside him tomorrow morning before prayers with some sort of signing of a formal agreement.'

'I get it. I can get the governor-general along and maybe one or two others to witness it, then we announce it on morning television.' Gerrard smiled slowly. 'This will shut down any debate, and finally O'Brien will be out of my hair. I like it.'

'You like it?'

'You bet, but what happens if the opposition gets restless in the chamber?'

'That's when I will shut them down. They would have agreed not to take a division in a formal agreement. If they try anything or even get close to calling a division, I will just leave the chamber, automatically closing proceedings.'

'Harper retains the authority to reject money bills, but by the time it comes back from the senate, he'll have already approved it once, and won't reject it again – brilliant.'

'As I suggested, he would lose too much credibility with the punters if he stopped their payments after already voting for the stimulus package.'

'This is fantastic. Is this your own work or did dear old Dad have a say in it?'

'He says hello.'

'Okay, so I get Harper on side. We table the legislation, and we wait for it to come back amended from the senate. By the end of the week the punters will have their money, and the Indonesians their cash, O'Brien retires, and we all go off for a very merry Christmas. Brilliant.'

'You just need to get the legislation redrafted quickly, which shouldn't be a problem.'

'I'll make a few calls tonight and get some lazy fucking bureaucrats out of bed.' Gerrard smiled widely.

'What's the second thing you want done?'

'What? What do you mean?' Gerrard tossed his cigar into the ashtray.

'You said you wanted me to do two things?'

'Oh yes. One was to ensure the money got through,' Gerrard began to unbutton his shirt, pulling it from his trousers and dropping to his knees before her, tenderly placing his clammy hands on her knees and gently easing them apart. 'The other thing I wanted done, is you.'

# CHAPTER 9

## MONDAY 8.45 AM

Gordon O'Brien had been waiting almost an hour for his allotted meeting with the speaker. It was nearing 9.00 am, he was yet to hear from her, and he had other urgent duties to attend to – the parliament was reopening and there were instructions to be given to managers and staff. No-one in her office knew her whereabouts and she was yet to come in for the day. He sat patiently in the lobby of the speaker's suite, knowing he had plenty to do elsewhere, but his meeting with the speaker was the most important.

'Mr O'Brien? Speaker Bagshaw will see you now.' A personal assistant appeared from the speaker's office and seemed apologetic, although offered no actual apology.

Gordon followed the staffer into the speaker's office, where she sat behind an enormous desk covered with files and papers in no discernible order. The full-length windows overlooking a grotto of ferns and water features did not allow in much light until the sun rose higher, and a desk lamp shone brightly as the speaker worked on her notes.

'Ah, Gordon, nice to see you, good morning. Did you have a good weekend?

'Yes, Speaker.' Gordon had risen early, with a slight headache and dry mouth, unable to remember much from his previous evening with Jon.

'Please sit down. You wanted to see me?' No apology was forthcoming, and Gordon sat, placing his files on his knees.

'Yes, I thought we had confirmed eight o'clock, but it seems I must have got the time wrong.'

'No issue, Gordon, what is the problem? I have important work to attend to.'

Bagshaw did not make it easy for him. 'This appropriation legislation the government wants to enact this week – I have issues with it.'

'Namely?'

'Well, there are a number. It is too rushed. It hasn't been vetted by treasury. It does not have the endorsement of the opposition. The parliament has skewed numbers and...'

'There's more?'

'I believe there may be some unethical activity associated with it.'

'You had better explain yourself.' The speaker stopped

doodling and looked at Gordon. 'Who do you think is responsible for this unethical activity?

'I'm not sure, Speaker. I'm not even sure what it is.'

She raised an eyebrow quizzically.

'Speaker, you are going to have to trust me on this, but no-one at treasury has approved the draft.'

'That's an alarming allegation to make, Gordon.' Bagshaw sat back in her chair seemingly surprised by O'Brien's take on the legislation. 'Who do you think is doing this con job you are suggesting, and why?'

'I have a suspicion the government is attempting to release taxpayers' funds without the authority of treasury. I am unclear as to the government's reason for this unseemly rush to get the stimulus package and the immigration detention centres' appropriation through the parliament this week.'

'The prime minister has now publicly explained why he needs the funds passed this week.' Bagshaw looked down to refer to her notes. 'He believes the tragedy last week will impede the economy, and he wants a cash stimulus for all Australians to ensure the Christmas trading period has the best chance of meeting forecasts.'

'I get that, Speaker, and while I don't agree with it, I understand the prime minister's need to pander to the electorate.'

'Nice word, pander, but entirely inappropriate here.' Bagshaw referred to her notes again. 'The prime minister is concerned about the economy and its impact on retail sales during December. Given the uncertainty of a virtual caretaker government until the February by-elections, the prime minister wants to ensure economic stability during this period. No pandering.'

'And the four billion for the Indonesians?'

'It was in the budget last May.' Bagshaw reached for her tea and took a sip, then replaced the elegant cup in the saucer. 'No-one had an issue with it then, and indeed I recall even you thought it was good government policy.'

'Tied to an immigration policy with legislation currently before the parliament I do, yes.' Gordon wiped his brow, pushing at his hair. 'It's not due to come into effect until the middle of next year; there are a further three annual payments to the Indonesians, so why is the money suddenly so urgent?'

'Who knows, Gordon. It is not our job to question what the government does.'

'The parliament is the final arbiter on all these policy matters, and we have a responsibility to ensure legislation is in the best possible form before it goes to the chamber. Given treasury has not given the nod to the legislation, I suspect something is going on.'

'A conspiracy, Gordon? Surely not.' Bagshaw took another draught of tea, peering at him above her cup. 'You're not suggesting the government is putting one over the parliament are you, Gordon?'

'They've done it before.'

'Gordon, you're overthinking this. The government wants the punters to have the stimulus money before Christmas, and maybe they are tying in the Indonesian funds so work can start as soon as possible.' Bagshaw replaced her cup. 'They are Muslims after all, so they won't stop work over the festive season, as we do here.'

Gordon knew the speaker supported what Gerrard wanted to do and sat silently looking at her.

'So now what happens?' Bagshaw interrupted the uncomfortable silence.

'I have spoken with the opposition, and they will not vote for an amended stimulus package Appropriation Bill with the Indonesian immigration money in it.'

'Really?' The speaker was genuinely surprised.

'Confirmed on Friday with their manager of business before I spoke to treasury.'

'You have been busy, haven't you, Gordon.'

'Just doing my job.'

'A job that has only five days left.' The speaker glanced at the clock.

'I've been at this for almost forty years, Speaker, and it's part of my job description to ensure the parliament is protected.' Gordon felt a prickly flush move through him and shakily wiped his upper lip of perspiration. 'I will continue to work hard no matter how much time I have.'

'Well, you had better take a look at the television and watch how I do my job.' Bagshaw pointed a remote at the television and flicked it on. Gordon turned to the television, which was tuned to Sky News, and saw the prime minister enter the courtyard outside his office, flanked by James Harper, and stand behind a lectern and arrange his notes before adjusting the microphones.

'Ladies and gentlemen, thank you for coming. With the

tragedy of last week still fresh in our minds, and its sadness still embedded in our hearts, we must nevertheless continue the work of government.

'You all know we will be moving to by-elections at the very earliest opportunity, and I would like to announce now that they will be held on Saturday the seventh of February next year. It is important to realise that government must continue to function until that time, despite holding a minority of seats in the parliament. Clearly, we are hamstrung in what we can do, but nevertheless, we have bills to bring before the parliament this week and questions of importance to answer.

'This morning, I have had a protracted meeting with my colleague Mr James Harper, the leader of the opposition, to discuss what should be done during this stressful and uncertain period. He has agreed with me that for the sake of stability, we should allow the government to run its course until the results of the by-elections are known in February. In other words, there will be no change to the government until the results of the elections are known.

'I wish to thank Mr Harper for his very honourable response, and I will be delivering that message to the governor-general this morning. To ensure the stability of the government, the market, and other institutions, I wish to make several announcements.

'I have discussed with James a number of policy issues and we have agreed to make these announcements together. This is what a cooperative and inclusive government does at a time like this, when ill-considered actions could unsettle the economy and the markets. We have put aside our partisan disagreements and we will work together for the betterment of our nation.

'Today we will be tabling in the parliament legislation foreshadowed last week concerning an economic stimulus package that will allow the distribution of significant benefits to all Australian households before Christmas. On average, every taxpaying Australian will receive nine hundred dollars. For those Australians who do not pay tax, they will receive five hundred dollars. There is no cut-off point, no cap, no discrimination: this will apply to all Australians.

'We estimate the amount of six billion dollars will be released into the economy over the next few months. Our hope is that Australians will spend their cash bonus, ensuring retail sales over Christmas and early next year will be sustained. The quid pro quo for this release of funds into the economy is that those who receive it, should spend it. Yes, that's right, we want all Australians to have a very merry Christmas this year.' Gerrard and Harper exchanged smiles.

'To ensure we have stability of government, I have discussed with James the passage of this legislation through both houses of parliament this week, and he has assured me that if all things are equal in the drawing up of the legislation, then the bill will move through both houses and be passed without objection this week. To this end, the government and opposition have drawn up an agreement to ensure the stability of the parliament this week, which we will sign before you today.

'Before signing the agreement, are there any questions?' A gaggle of voices erupted from the assembled media. 'Paul?'

'Prime Minister, will the money be guaranteed to be in taxpayer bank accounts before Christmas?'

'The answer is yes. With the agreement of Mr Harper, I have instructed treasury to begin the task of releasing funds for transfer by the middle of next week. It is therefore important we get this legislation through this week, which is why we are working together to ensure it happens. Michael?'

'Will there be dispute over who is eligible?'

'Those Australians who completed a tax return on time this year, and those Australians who are currently on welfare will receive the funds. One more, Anita?'

'Prime Minister, there has been a lot of work done with the Indonesians regarding the announced offshore detention centres, and indeed legislation with the initial allocation of four hundred million dollars was drawn up for tabling in the parliament last week—'

'Is this a statement or a question?' Gerrard interrupted.

'Why did you initially have it listed on the notice paper and now it is no longer listed? There is a rumour you originally wanted the entire budgeted amount of four billion dollars for the project to be coupled to this stimulus package Appropriation Bill. Are you now saying it is not required? And is it just the punters who are getting this cash splash or do you have plans to pay the Indonesians?'

'The answers to these questions can be found in the budget papers. We announced an agreement with Indonesia and confirmed last week when their president was here that the project was going ahead. I held further discussions with the

Indonesian president last Friday, after the memorial service. Our intention is to clear funds for construction works as soon as possible. As you may not know, the Indonesians have already commenced preliminary site works. We are also looking forward to resolving the moral dilemma of the execution of the drug smugglers, which has outraged the Australian public for many years.

'I know I can speak for James when I say that we are working together to rid ourselves of the scourge of people smugglers. We believe the bipartisan approach taken to the issue so far has been very helpful. Funding is not an issue, as it has already been forecasted and budgeted. So, whether it happens today, next week, next month, or even next year, it will have no bearing on our commitment to establish centres in Indonesia.

'Okay, let's sign the agreement so I can take it to the governor-general.' Gerrard flipped open a leather compendium on the lectern and held out a pen to Harper, cameras firing to capture the moment. Harper hesitated before stepping forward with a smile to sign the document.

O'Brien turned back to the speaker and reflected for a moment about what he had just witnessed.

'Well Gordon, it seems your fears were unfounded. The prime minister doesn't intend to have the Indonesian funding in the legislation after all, so your conspiracy is without foundation. And even if he did include it, as he explained, it is fully accounted for, so no conspiracy. Stop worrying.' Bagshaw softly smiled.

'And Gordon, in just five more days it will all be over for you. You can go fishing then, literally.'

Gordon, still uncertain, lingered. 'Anything else, Gordon?'

'No, Madam Speaker.'

---

'Mr Messenger, this is the clerk.' Barton was at his desk reading the morning papers when he took the call. 'Are you able to help me?'

'If I can, I will, Mr O'Brien, what is it?'

'This agreement Mr Harper has just signed, is it something that was discussed with you over the weekend?'

'What agreement?'

'The agreement signed between the government and the opposition not to call, or force, any formal votes in the parliament this week. Is that something you have thought through?'

'What are you talking about, Gordon?'

'Go see your boss, laddie.'

Barton replaced the receiver after the sudden click and, as he did, it instantaneously rang. 'Hello?'

'What the heck has that dickhead done?' It was the deputy leader of the opposition, Wilson Campbell – his vocabulary was unmistakable.

'I'm not sure I know. What's he done?'

'He's gone and screwed us, that's what. You don't know?'

'Christ, will someone just tell me.'

'Fucking Harper has agreed we will all be good girls and boys this week, and not take a division.'

'On what?'

'On everything!'

'He's what?' Barton shoved back his chair and stood.

'Tell me you at least knew. Tell me he hasn't done this on his own. Tell me he is not a megalomaniacal dropkick!'

'Wilson, I can't tell you a thing. Look, let's get over to Jim's office and sort it out. Grab Pete on the way will you, and I'll grab Christopher.'

'See you in ten.'

Barton hung up, but before he could move it rang again. 'Hello?'

'Bart, what's going on?' Anita seemed more concerned than perplexed. 'Are you okay?'

'I don't know. I have to go. I'll talk to you later.'

As Barton prepared to leave his office he stopped to speak to his staffer, who was eating a toasted sandwich. 'Trust no-one, Julia. Sadly, that's the number one rule of politics. I'm off to the leader's office for a powwow with the leadership team. I'll let you know if I get held up. Hey, nice hair, looks great.'

'Thanks,' Julia mumbled around a mouthful of food.

Barton scuttled down the nearest stairwell and hurried along a green-carpeted corridor. He burst through the office door of Christopher Hughes, the shadow minister for industry, and strode through the anteroom into his office. 'Chris, what's going on?'

'Not sure. I just saw it on Sky, not sure what he's thinking.'

'What happened?'

'The boss just signed an agreement with Gerrard not to have any formal votes in the house for the week. The government has moved into caretaker mode, and it seems we will pass the Appropriation Bill for the stimulus package, sight unseen.'

'Did he talk to you about it?'

'He never talks to me; the bastard always thinks I want his job.' Hughes was first elected to the parliament seventeen years ago, identified then as a future leader. His seat of Warringah on the prosperous north shore of Sydney was normally reserved for future leaders.

'We're meeting with Will and Pete in his office now, let's go.' Barton was the junior member of the leadership group, which consisted of the leader, James Harper; his deputy, Wilson Campbell; Christopher Hughes; and Peter Stanley, the long-time member for Curtin, in Western Australia. Together they formed a tight collective of senior opposition MPs developing strategy and determining policy. Added to this group was their senate leader, Joe Anthony, from Queensland. 'I didn't see the stunt. Did he say anything?'

'No, he just stood there, sort of smiling that goofy smile of his.'

The pair almost ran along the corridor past the entrance to the House of Representatives and the speaker's office suite, turned right into a long corridor past the whip's office, and finally around two corners to the entrance to the opposition leader's office suite. A staffer sat at the front desk. Without any pleasantries or courtesies, the two opened the door and stepped into

Harper's empty office. The staffer followed them in and advised them that the leader was on his way from the ministerial wing. As the staffer left, Campbell and Stanley arrived.

They stood before Harper's desk dumbfounded, feeling a mix of incredulity, disappointment, and wonder, but mostly anger. They waited, knowing that if one spoke, they all would.

It wasn't long before Harper arrived. After what he had just been through with the prime minister, he seemed to be expecting them. 'I thought I'd see you here. Morning, chaps. Is Joe joining us?'

'He could.' Campbell, the senior and Harper's deputy spoke first. 'What do you think you are fucking doing?'

'Would anyone like a cup of tea? I'm going to have one.' He looked toward the staffer at the door. 'Could you also manage a biscuit please, Michael. Anyone else?' They remained silent and the staffer left with the order.

'Please sit down, you're making me feel uncomfortable standing there like that.' Harper took his seat beside the lounge and beckoned the others to follow. They didn't. 'Now, what seems to be so important for all of you to be here?'

'I can't believe you,' Campbell began calmly, keeping his volatile temperament in check. 'We are either part of team, or we aren't. Why are you making agreements with Gerrard, without first consulting your fucking leadership group?'

'Anyone else have a comment, before I answer?'

'Jim, we are either in this together or we are not,' Stanley, the respected sage among them, said. Mooted as the rising star when he first entered the parliament twenty-nine years ago, he served for a short time in the ministry, in a junior portfolio, before the election that brought Gerrard to power. Now he provided guidance and advice to those with the enthusiasm and energy he no longer possessed. 'It seems you have made an announcement that is contrary to the protocols within our group, the very protocols you insisted upon having, I might add. We are here for an explanation, which I am sure will be worthy. And we seek your reassurance that we are not now running a leader-only system of decision-making.'

Barton and Hughes remained mute, satisfied with the opening statements. One angry, one balanced.

'Christopher? Want to say anything?'

'Leader, we are here to support you, but we need to know why you have taken us down this route.'

'Christ almighty, Jimmy, what the fuck were you thinking?' Campbell expressed himself with his usual vivid turn of phrase.

'Well, it's very simple really, I had no alternative. Please, sit down.'

Barton and Hughes took a seat on the lounge and Stanley wandered behind; arms crossed. Campbell paced the floor behind Harper. 'Gerrard rang me at six this morning and asked me to see him at seven for a brief meeting.'

'So, what was discussed?' demanded Campbell.

Harper ignored him. 'Not thinking much of it, I went to see him, and he had breakfast prepared for me, with his other guests – the governor-general; the speaker; Sheldon, the head of prime minister and cabinet; and Tony Hancock had come in from

Sydney on his private jet. When I saw them, I knew something was up.'

'Why was Hancock even there?' Barton asked.

'A witness from the media,' responded Stanley. 'Plus, he's a mate of Gerrard's.'

'Well, fuck me.' Campbell could not contain himself.

'That's exactly how I felt, Wilson, and sure enough I was.' Harper guffawed until he coughed.

'What did they want?' Stanley asked.

'It was more what Gerrard wanted. I'm fairly sure the others were not in on the purpose of the meeting before they arrived, although I am not so sure about Hancock.'

'Well, he is the biggest media proprietor. He would have been there to provide the illusion of transparency, I suppose,' suggested Hughes.

'Exactly.' Harper was calm as he explained the morning's events. 'Gerrard outlined the plans for a minority government until the by-elections, which basically meant he agreed to virtual caretaker mode, doing nothing controversial until we see the result of the by-elections. Anyway, the governor-general approved of this arrangement – she told us she had sought advice from the crown solicitor and the chief justice last week when it became apparent the parliament would sit this week. The advice from those eminent folks was basically that the government was in a weakened state due to its loss of numbers caused by the recent tragic deaths, and that by-elections may or may not change the state of the parliament. Therefore, to ensure propriety and allow government to continue to do its work, we should move into caretaker mode.'

'Seems reasonable,' Stanley said.

'There was only one catch,' Harper replied.

'You had to agree,' Hughes said.

'Not only that, but I also had to agree that censure motions, or other destabilising votes, would not be taken in the parliament this week – there would be no calls for a formal count of votes at all.'

'Why are we even sitting?' Hughes asked.

'Exactly. You should have told them to go fuck themselves.' Campbell was a clever politician, but sometimes engaged his mouth before his brain.

'I considered it, but that was when I understood why Hancock was there. Gerrard needed his support in the media – and if he had it, the media groups would follow. Mind you, if I didn't comply to this idea of a caretaker government then we would have been pilloried.'

'What were his conditions?' Hughes asked.

'As I said, to not have any divisions, other than on the Appropriation Bill, which he said we could reject if we wanted to.'

'But Gerrard said you have already agreed,' said Hughes.

'I assume we are not going to block a cash handout pre-Christmas, and before crucial by-elections, when we could possibly finally win government. We can't not approve it, otherwise it will kill us in the polls and at the election,' Harper said.

'So, what happened to the funds they were talking about for the Indonesians?' Barton asked.

'I'm not sure. Your briefing on Saturday morning helped me a little, so when I raised it, Gerrard said he had changed his mind, and would put it through after the elections in February.'

'Why?' Barton asked.

'I didn't even consider it to be honest. We have already agreed to it in a bipartisan sense, in the budget, so funding it next year will no doubt be part of our policy. I see no issue around when it gets paid. Although it's better that we control it if we get into government.'

'So why publicly sign an agreement? asked Hughes.

'And why didn't you refer to us before you did?' Campbell added.

'Well, we were all sitting around discussing the events of last week enjoying breakfast when the speaker says her goodbyes, it's getting on to nine o'clock and she has a meeting apparently, and the whole tone of the meeting changed.'

'How do you mean?' asked Stanley.

'Gerrard suddenly gets serious and asks Sheldon for a file. Not only was there a reason for Hancock to be there as a witness, Sheldon from PM and C was also there for a reason. He tabled the agreement for all of us to consider.'

'Now I understand,' Stanley said. 'You were set up, beautifully.'

'How do you mean?' asked Hughes.

'If James had agreed, which he had no choice about, given the governor-general's comment, then no matter what the agreement said, he was bound by his agreement to sign it. Classic Gerrard.'

'It gets worse.' Harper now had his tea and biscuit, slipped to him surreptitiously by his staffer, and he took a quick sip. 'As we were breaking up, after I had signed the initial first document, Gerrard quietly asked me to follow him for a quick chat in his courtyard. What do you think I was thinking when we walked out into a press conference?'

'Fuck me.' Campbell expressed it for all of them.

'Exactly.'

# CHAPTER 10

## MONDAY 9.30 AM

Gordon thought it unusual for the speaker to be so chirpy, and so correct, so early in the morning. How did she know about the announcement, and why had the legislation been changed? Did it have anything to do with her late-night meeting at parliament? These were questions that perplexed him as Marjorie entered his office with his peppermint tea.

'How was your weekend, Gordon? Tell me you got away.' Marjorie placed the cup and its saucer before him.

'Unfortunately, not. I worked on a project or two. I have too much to do, and too little time I'm afraid. Although, I must admit, I am a little hazy after last night.' Gordon was thankful for the interlude, and sat back in his chair, beckoning his faithful assistant to sit. 'My neighbour dragged me out for a quick bite, and perhaps I had too many chardonnays.'

'Well, your tea may help, if I understand you correctly. How's the head?'

'A bit tender I'm afraid, but I had a Berocca before leaving this morning and I think I'm slowly coming good.'

'It's a rare thing to see you enjoying yourself, Gordon. I'm pleased you were able to get out with a friend, even if was just for a few hours.'

'It's been a tough week, so let's hope this next week is different.'

'Well, there are only a few days left. Let's try and keep the workload down and concentrate on enjoying what time we have together.'

'Ah, Marjorie, you are so good for me, and that's what I'm trying to do, but these political dills around here are making it hard for me.'

'No, they're not. It's you who's making it hard for yourself.'

'There is just one last nagging issue with the government's stimulus package.'

'Why should you care what they do this week? The department can look after things. Richard is on top of everything.'

'As you know, I spoke to the speaker late Friday, and she advised me the government wanted to add the stimulus funds to the Supply Bill. I told her they couldn't do it, of course.'

'Didn't you suggest a separate bill?'

'Yes, I did, so I spoke to treasury and their response was that there was no problem with them agreeing to it so long as they see the legislation prior to it being tabled.' Gordon sipped his tea. 'But remember the money for the immigration centres was also being forced through by the government? Anyway, I rang the drafting office on Saturday, to determine if the government had decided to put the two money bills in together, and they advised me they had, and they were drafting legislation for around ten billion.'

'What's the problem? That was your original suggestion.'

'I'm not sure. The speaker just advised me this morning that the immigration money was no longer in the Appropriation Bill that was being drafted.'

'That's a good thing then, isn't it? That's what you wanted, so you win again.' Marjorie smiled broadly, and silently clapped her hands.

'I suppose so, but the prime minister also asked James Harper not to cause any disruption in the house this week, and that concerns me because he formalised it with a signed agreement. Unheard of, really.'

'Gordon, these are all good things I would have thought. You need to relax and stop thinking something is going on, when clearly there is nothing untoward happening.'

Gordon's mobile shrilled. 'Hello, Gordon O'Brien.'

'Mr O'Brien, it's George.'

'Yes, George.'

'She visited the PM's private suite at 7.25 and left at around 11.45. I have photos.'

'Thanks, I'll chat later.' Gordon slipped his phone back inside his jacket pocket. 'Well, thanks for the chat, Marjorie. You're quite right about Richard, he'll be a great clerk, probably better than me.'

'Sooner or later, you will come to realise that your service to the parliament has been significant,' Marjorie said. 'But now, it's almost over, and this week should be a relaxing time for you. Enjoy the moment, it's almost time to move on.'

'To what exactly?' Gordon looked at his assistant, his mind racing with George's news.

'You have your fishing.'

'Yes, I do love the thrill of the catch, but I doubt it will excite me quite like the daily challenges I've faced here over the years.'

'Write a book then. You must know all the secrets of this place, so it's sure to be a bestseller.'

'Too many secrets I'm afraid, and they will have to stay secret, although I have thought about writing another edition of *Parliamentary Practice*.'

'Boring! Can there be anything as boring as that book?' Marjorie began to move off, obviously not a fan of books on parliamentary procedure.

'Cheeky possum.'

'Gordon, can I ask that you just deal with that pile of papers, and I'll pass all the rest on to Richard. I've been doing that sort of thing for the past month, anyway. You should even consider not going into the house at all this week and leave it to Richard, although I suspect they have valedictories planned for you on Thursday.'

'You're right, as always, Marjorie.' Gordon smiled. 'I should just float about the place and do nothing.'

'Now you're talking. Enjoy your tea while it's hot, and I'll hold calls for an hour.'

Gordon sipped his tea and reflected upon the activities of the last week. It would have been easier to close the parliament and wait until the by-election results were in to determine if there was to be a new government. He wondered why it was necessary to even have this week of extended sittings. The government could have passed the Supply Bill and their stimulus package today, and had it rushed through the senate, then deferred the rest of the parliamentary business until February.

Gordon leaned back in his chair and pulled his tea closer, closing his eyes for a restful moment.

---

'Excuse me, Gordon.' Marjorie had returned after an hour, which to Gordon seemed but a moment. 'Meredith Bruce is here to see you about the notice paper for the week. She wants to discuss timing.'

Gordon quickly collected himself and sat straighter in his chair; his tea remained untouched. 'Please ask her in.' He stood to greet the manager of government business, exchanging pleasantries before offering her a seat on his lounge as he sat nearby.

'Gordon, I have just met with the parliament's selection committee, and we have come up with a draft program for the week. We are seeking your advice.'

'There should be nothing controversial, given we aren't

taking divisions.' Gordon took the document Bruce had proffered and scanned the program.

'That's true, but there is plenty of work to get through.' Bruce had been appointed just six months ago, having been elevated to the ministry in a Gerrard reshuffle. Gordon originally considered her a favourite of Gerrard's, being groomed by him as he had groomed other female colleagues only to discard them later when they failed to meet his exacting standards. But as the months passed, she showed she was a very capable parliamentary performer in getting through the government's program on her own terms. As a former criminal lawyer, she'd no doubt had plenty of experience with similar shady types, Gordon thought wryly. 'As previously agreed, we will move the Condolence Motion to the Federation Chamber to allow as many of those who wish to speak to do so. We consider the speeches important, but we should not tie up the main chamber.'

'What legislation do you plan to work on for the rest of the week?'

'We plan to have the appropriation legislation back into the house on Thursday, about an hour before question time, for formal assent. We have allocated one hour.'

'Why an hour? Surely if it's coming back from the senate and it's previously been approved, then there's no need to have time allocated. Isn't it just a procedural reading?'

'Just in case.' Bruce shifted in her chair.

'In case of what? It's a money bill and the senate can't amend it. In case of what, Meredith?' Gordon saw that Bruce was a little uncomfortable with the question.

'The prime minister has asked me to allocate the time, and Messenger has agreed, so we have it in the program.'

'Why does the prime minister feel the need to have time allocated to a procedural matter?'

'Maybe he wants to talk to the legislation again. The point is this: the prime minister wants it, the opposition agreed, so we scheduled it.'

Gordon didn't like the answer and stared at Bruce. She averted her eyes, looked back, and quickly averted them again.

'What's going on, Meredith?'

'Nothing.' Bruce fell back in the leather lounge, crossed her legs, and then her arms tightly across her chest. 'What do you mean?'

'Forgive me for questioning you and perhaps being a little overly vigilant, but I want to ensure we follow procedure.' Gordon stood, walked behind his desk, and sat, putting distance between himself and Bruce so she could relax. 'We have had an unbelievable tragedy, which has led to a minority government until by-elections can be held next year. Rather than close the parliament out of respect for the dead, we stay operating to get a cash splash approved for the community. We then have the opposition publicly agreeing not to call for a vote or take a division, which is unprecedented in itself, and now you are putting it to me that there could be further debate on an Appropriation Bill at assent, after it has already been agreed to by the senate. I am a little confused.'

'Gordon, relax, there is no ruse, nothing dodgy going on. We are just managing the parliament and allowing for potential timing issues.'

'Timing issues? The senate cannot add to or amend a money bill, yet you are putting into the program time to address any amendments, and therefore suggesting the possibility that the senate might amend the bill.'

'No, that's not true.'

'Not true?' Gordon stood up and returned to Bruce. 'How is it that, until this morning's announcements by the prime minister, four billion dollars for funding detention centres in Indonesia was included in the original drafting of the bill, which has now magically vanished.'

'I don't know what you're talking about, and I don't like your tone.' Bruce seemed genuinely ignorant about the four billion. 'The only draft I have received was for six billion for the stimulus package. What detention-centre funding?'

'On Saturday I was advised by a drafting clerk that he was asked to prepare legislation that appropriated six billion for the stimulus cash splash, and four billion for the Indonesians for their immigration centres.'

'News to me.'

'Are you playing me, Meredith?' O'Brien stared at her, and she shifted uncomfortably in her seat.

'I can assure you, Gordon, the only advice I have received from the PM and C, and the drafting office, is for the six billion Appropriation Bill. I don't know what you are talking about.'

'Then, I respectfully suggest you investigate the matter,

because it seems to me there is indeed something going on, and we may all be being played.'

'I can only put to you what I know, and what I have received from the drafting office.' Bruce seemed confused.

'Why all the secrecy with regards to this bill?'

'What secrecy?' Bruce sat forward, collected her papers, and slipped her glasses back on. 'Yet another conspiracy, Gordon?'

'It seems there's a bipartisan agreement about the funds to the Indonesians – one minute we're giving them the entire amount, the next minute we're not.' Gordon sat down near Bruce. 'So, again I ask, what is going on, Meredith?'

'Gordon, I suspect you are overreaching yourself. There is little, or indeed no evidence for any political conspiracy.' Bruce made a few notes to prompt herself later. 'And you're probably right, the Indonesian money has already been approved anyway and will no doubt be paid early next year. So why this drama now? It makes no sense and I doubt anyone has drafted the legislation as you suggest.'

'Let's check, shall we?' Gordon moved back to his desk, picked up the phone and punched in a number. As he waited for the connection he stared at Meredith, looking for any sign of uncertainty. 'Hello, it's Gordon O'Brien here, could I speak to Robert Haworth please?' Nothing, he saw nothing at all in Meredith's response to his phone call. 'He what? When? When is he due back?' When he got his answer, Gordon hung up. 'That's very odd.'

'What?'

'Robert Haworth is on some sort of approved leave until next week – overseas apparently.'

'What's odd about that?'

'I approve all leave and travel arrangements for all members, their families and parliamentary staff, and I haven't signed, nor even sighted for that matter, his request for leave.'

'Maybe you overlooked it.'

'Don't you think it strange that the person charged with writing this appropriation legislation is conveniently on leave this week and virtually uncontactable? He specifically told me it was being drafted for ten billion dollars, and now he's disappeared.'

When the parliamentary bells stopped ringing, the speaker was in her place in the chamber of the House of Representatives. The large teak chair and desk on the platform was more like a throne than a place from which parliamentary proceedings were managed. Her desk was set up so that she could access parliamentary papers digitally and read them when required. Before her lay the daily proceedings list. To open the parliament, she recited the Lord's Prayer, as she did on every sitting day, and everyone settled into their places. She called the prime minister, standing at the despatch box, who moved a condolence motion about the untimely and tragic deaths of eight members of the parliament. Prime Minister Gerrard spoke eloquently and reminded the house of the achievements of each of the parliamentarians killed the previous week, only stumbling a little when he spoke at last of his long-time friend, Fred Rocher. He reminisced about their time together in their first term of parliament, the practical jokes they used to play, once dressing in a chicken suit, and being judged unparliamentary. Gerrard's speech was full of pathos mixed with humour. It was the speech of a statesman and Gordon was impressed with the emotion Gerrard evoked.

James Harper spoke in similar terms, only stumbling when he spoke of his young colleague Martin Downer – a first-term parliamentarian – whose wife had given birth to their first child just two months earlier, and the tragedy of his young daughter Nadia growing up without her father.

When Harper finished his speech, Meredith Bruce stood at the despatch box to ask that debate on the motion be adjourned and further debate on the Condolence Motion be allowed to be made in the Federation Chamber. The speaker put the question, issuing the first call for a vote, and it was passed on the voices, without anyone paying attention.

'Clerk.' Speaker Bagshaw called upon Gordon to introduce private members' business.

Gordon stood, and said in his usual deliberate style, 'Private members' business: a motion calling upon the government to establish protection orders for amphibians.'

The speaker took her cue and called upon the member for Cowan to begin her motion. Shirley Edwards stood and began setting out the details of a report that described the alarming drop in frog numbers in the wetlands in her electorate north of Perth. There was now growing evidence of serious ecological destruction which, added to climate change, was leading to dwindling numbers of amphibians which in turn impacted other species, such as native birds. Gordon regretted it was time for him to leave the chamber to return to his office as the topic interested him, so he slowly straightened his papers and called upon Richard Barker to take his place at the large table of the house below the speaker's podium.

Gordon approached the speaker. 'Speaker, may I have a word?'

'Yes, of course,' Bagshaw replied. 'I'll be right behind you. I'll see you in my office.' As the Member for Cowan continued her animated address about the lack of frogs in her electorate, the speaker vacated the chair to one of the members of the speaker's panel and withdrew from the chamber, her black ceremonial robe billowing behind her.

Gordon walked out of the chamber and up the half dozen steps to the speaker's concourse. To the left was the government whip's office, and to the right of the foyer the opposition whip's. He entered the government whip's office and said, 'Good afternoon, Rosie, do you have any requests for leave or travel from your members?'

'Not yet, Mr O'Brien, but if I do, I'll get them straight up to you.' Rosie Cameron had formerly worked for Gordon in the clerk's office but found the cut and thrust of organising politicians more stimulating than the tedium of double-checking other people's work.

'Thank you so much. Let me know if you do.'

Gordon retreated and headed for the speaker's suite. Speaker Bagshaw had already returned and flung her robe across a chair.

She was flicking through papers on her desk while her assistant waited patiently by her side. Bagshaw passed the papers to her assistant who quietly removed herself, closing the door behind her.

'What can I do for you, Gordon?' Bagshaw motioned him to sit, but Gordon preferred to stand.

'I am concerned about the program this week. The government seems to be anticipating something that could not possibly happen.'

'How perceptive of them, what is it?' Bagshaw rocked back in her desk chair.

'They have allowed time for further debate on the Appropriation Bill when it comes back from the senate, and I wonder if you knew anything about it?'

'Not a word.'

'You seem to have been across the issues this morning. Why not this one?'

'Mind your tone, Gordon.'

'My apologies,' Gordon bowed his head at the rebuff. 'But, if you knew about the government backflip on the stimulus package, then how is it you are not aware of the government requiring further time to be allocated on a bill yet to be passed by the senate?'

'What specifically is your concern?'

'The leader of the house met with me earlier and she has allocated sixty minutes for the stimulus package when it comes back from the senate.'

'And the problem is?'

'It is an assent process and doesn't require speeches. It normally takes ten minutes at most, you know that.' Gordon breathed deeply. 'The question I have is this: do you know why the government wants sixty minutes to do something they can do in ten?'

'You are correct in assuming I know something about the arrangements this week. The prime minister had me in on the meeting this morning with the governor-general and James Harper. We sorted out protocols for the week, and as you know the two leaders agreed in principle to a caretaker government, but also allowing this final money bill through the parliament this week.'

'I respectfully remind you that you insisted the Indonesian money was to be linked to the stimulus package last Friday, so why the change of heart to the amendments you said I was to expect? I don't understand.' Gordon moved from one foot to the other.

'I have no idea why they changed their minds. I told the PM's office of your concerns on Friday after speaking with you, and I suppose they responded positively to your suggestions by dropping any proposed amendments.'

'I am suspicious of the government's motives here.'

'What are you suggesting?' Bagshaw sat forward in her chair.

'I would hope the speaker's office is not embroiled in some covert manipulation of the parliament.' Gordon almost choked on the words.

'I find that suggestion reprehensible.' Bagshaw stood, strode to the door, and opened it, implying it was time for Gordon to leave. 'Gordon, you have four days left; do not spoil them by forcing me to take action against you. Keep to the parliamentary program that has been agreed by the parties and everyone will be happy.'

'I'm sure they will,' Gordon said as he swept from the office, ignoring the startled staff. As he reached the parliamentary entrance, he thought through what he already knew, trying to piece together a pattern. Then he changed direction and headed toward Barton Messenger's office.

'Could I see Mr Messenger if he is available, please?' Gordon waited as a male staffer knocked and entered Barton's office, closing the thick soundproof door quietly behind him. After a few moments the staffer returned saying, 'He's just finishing up a phone call, he won't be long.'

As the staffer resumed his seat, the door opened. 'Gordon, nice to see you, please come in.' Barton stood back and allowed the clerk to enter.

All offices in the parliament, other than in the ministerial wing, were exactly alike: timber furniture, modern green leather lounges and green patterned carpet for the representatives, red for the senators, in accordance with Westminster protocols – same size and shape for all. Gordon sat in a visitor's chair at the desk and Barton, following his lead, sat opposite.

'What is your view about the program this week?' Gordon asked.

Barton seemed surprised by the question, 'Other than having to be here, when I would argue we should not be out of respect for our dead colleagues, nothing much. It seems benign to me.'

'I have a few concerns and I wonder if I could share these with you.' Gordon leaned into Messenger.

'Namely?'

'I am wondering why there is time allocated for debate on the return from the senate of the Appropriation Bill on Thursday.'

'Meredith Bruce explained it to me. The prime minister wants to be able to have a final say on wishing folks a merry Christmas before it is passed.'

'She did not suggest that to me when I saw her earlier. Do you believe her?'

'I have no reason not to. She's a good egg, among those other rotten ones, and I believe her. What are you seeing that I'm not?'

'Maybe I'm overreacting.' Gordon hesitated. 'When I met with you on Friday, I was certain the government was planning to bring an amendment to the appropriation legislation and add the Indonesian funding to the bill. Indeed, I was absolutely positive that was going to happen, as I had every indication from people, I was talking to that that was the case. The speaker confirmed it, treasury had advised they had no problems with the funding, and the drafting office even told me the next day they were following government direction in drawing up legislation, and this is what I expected was to be done.'

'You told me there were two money issues to be drawn up in a new bill: the stimulus package and the immigration centres. I told you flat out we would not vote for it.'

'But now things have changed for no apparent reason.'

'That's a good thing, Gordon, surely,' smiled Messenger.

'I suppose so, but I discovered this morning that Robert

Haworth, the drafting clerk who did the original combined funding bill, has gone on unannounced leave. Don't you think that is strange?'

'Gordon, I suspect the funding for the immigration centres would have been approved anyway, seeing as it was in the budget, and our side have already agreed to it. We just would not have voted for it in a combined Appropriation Bill this week. It doesn't really matter, does it? I mean, we are now voting on it in February, apparently.'

'It does matter if there is no scrutiny of the money transfer, and that can only ever happen before the parliament.'

'How so?'

'Most money bills are approved by treasury, yet treasury have not been asked to approve the Indonesian money. They don't like signing a cheque unless it has been scrutinised by the parliament, and proper examination and appropriate checks made. But if any money is approved by the parliament prior to going to treasury, then treasury must do its duty and meet the deadlines set by the parliament and transfer monies. It's too late for any checks then.'

'Yes, but if we approve funding then surely the money is transferred with conditions.'

'It's too late to ask for money back when it has already gone, and that was my concern over the weekend.'

'But where would it go?'

'This is what I'm worried about. Money is never rushed through the parliament when it is going overseas, never. And yet, we saw an attempt by the prime minister to do just that only a few days ago.'

'Gordon, the government is not planning to pass any money to Indonesia now though, is it? They have obviously changed their mind, and we would never have voted for it.'

'Have they?' Gordon could do no more than raise his doubts with Messenger, it was up to him as the opposition to find out more and do his own investigations. 'Check the program and keep an eye open for any sudden changes.'

'Gordon, I think you worry too much, but I will raise it with my colleagues.'

'That's all I ask.' Gordon left, and Barton shouted to his assistant.

'Charles, get me the leader's office on the phone will you.'

Gordon was pleased with Messenger's response but concerned about his lack of enthusiasm for taking on the government. He hoped he could rely on them to act if they were called upon to do so. He strolled back to his office, walked through to Marjorie's workstation to check if any messages had come in while he was in parliament, but there were none. A large envelope stamped 'Confidential' had arrived from security for him, which he took into his office and dropped on his desk as he moved to the window and stood looking out onto his tree.

Marjorie followed him and said, 'Thought you might like a nice cup of tea and a chocolate biscuit – your favourite.'

'Thanks so much, Marjorie. Would you care to join me?'

'Can't right now. Richard wants some files completed before he's back from the chamber, so I best get it done.'

'He really is onto it, isn't he?'

'He's a good man and he'll be a worthy replacement.'

'Well, I haven't gone just yet.' Gordon smiled as he sat down and began tearing at the confidential envelope, revealing a single sheet of paper, headed Cabinet Briefing Notes, dated the previous Tuesday. He sipped his tea as he read the contents, unsure why someone would send him minutes of a meeting between the prime minister and his ministers, discussing the tragedy and plans for a memorial. What did pique his interest was the reference the prime minister had made to including the funds for the immigration detention centres in legislation before the meeting with the Indonesian president on Friday, after agreeing the previous day to monies being paid in four tranches. He noted with interest that the prime minister also insisted that all ministers should be in attendance on the last day of sittings prior to question time, which had now been allocated for finalising the stimulus package.

Marjorie returned to the office and placed several files in the large basket on Gordon's desk.

'I thought you wanted me to wind down. Those files don't look as if I'm winding down at all.'

'They only need a signature. Richard has already dealt with them.'

'What is your opinion on this here?' Gordon was pointing to the paragraph advising the ministers to be in the chamber on Thursday. 'What did the prime minister have in mind a week ago, before it had even been agreed that parliament open this week?'

Marjorie studied the paper, 'Perhaps he's making time for you.'

'I doubt it.'

'It does seem odd that he was talking about these matters last week. Maybe he has something planned for the last day – valedictories perhaps?' Marjorie handed the sheet back to Gordon. 'Where did you get this from?'

'Someone was concerned enough to send it to me.'

'Who might that be?'

'Someone in the cabinet who perhaps shares my concerns. I don't really know.'

'What are you going to do with it now?'

After a long pause, Gordon picked up the phone, punched numbers and waited for an answer. 'Hello, George. Can you pop by, please? I have a delivery for you to make.'

# CHAPTER 11

## MONDAY 2.15 PM

Manuka is a small leafy suburb of Canberra, almost in the parliamentary precinct, renowned for its oval that hosts the annual prime minister's XI cricket match against a touring international team, and one or two Australian Rules football games during the winter. Manuka is also a popular locale for politicians to relax and enjoy themselves in the restaurants and bars, a short, chauffeur-driven trip from parliament house. It allows politicians and their hangers-on to enjoy the games that stimulate those with power and provides social access to politicians and decision-makers, away from the cavernous parliament.

Manuka also has a cinema complex with three theatres. Anita Devlin sat in one, nibbling popcorn out of habit rather than hunger. She had already seen the movie and pecked at her popcorn waiting for further instructions, convinced another remake of A Star Is Born should never have been produced. She had not recognised the number with the bizarre text message suggesting she buy a ticket for this session of the movie if she wanted information about the prime minister. She'd checked the message with her editor, who thought it was a waste of time but encouraged her to go, with a colleague as sentinel.

Third row from the back, three seats into the left of the aisle. She had been promised information and like any investigative journalist she was tempted to believe her anonymous messenger might have something important for her, although her colleague sat further down the aisle, prepared for anything untoward. A few dark shapes littered the cinema and she looked anxiously about her whenever someone came in or she detected movement. Anita had been told to be there within twenty minutes; it'd been a rush, especially with the time it took to find a carpark, but she had taken her seat in time, and now waited, one sneakered foot dangling over the seat in front of her, a little anxious about what would happen next.

Her phone flashed a text.

> check under your seat. follow the money.

Anita looked around the cinema but could not see anyone behaving oddly. She leaned forward and her fingers touched paper. She snatched out the envelope and checked once more for any movement or illuminated phones, then she texted her colleague:

I've got it, let's go.

---

'They left me this.' Anita held out the yellow A4 envelope by one corner as she stood before the desk of her editor, Peter Cleaver. 'What should I do?'

'Get some gloves, and let's open it.'

Anita left the office and went back to her desk. A colleague, Craig, had his oversized ski gloves waiting for her, but she hesitated. 'Aren't there any latex ones?'

'This ain't no hospital, honey. Come on, open it up.'

Anita placed the envelope carefully on her desk, put on the gloves, and fumbled open the flap. She emptied the contents onto her desk – a single sheet of paper. She scanned it then reread it more carefully, trying to understand what it meant, and why the secrecy about its release.

'What is it?' Cleaver had joined her at her desk.

'It's a cabinet brief from last week. It seems Gerrard had an unscheduled meeting on Tuesday and sought approval for the release of funds, first for the punters, then a second amount for the detention centres in Indonesia. There was general discussion about the proposal within the cabinet and it was agreed to reconvene on Thursday once a few questions were placed on notice to be resolved by the prime minister. It seems they were happy to approve the stimulus package but were reluctant to change funding arrangements for the Indonesians, which had already been agreed to the previous day.'

'Does it list the questions?' Cleaver asked.

'How much, and if there was a chance of more funds being required. It also asked if President Surriento was involved directly – apparently there had been a suggestion of impropriety with the president in the past. They also sought clarification about why all the funds were required before Christmas, instead of the planned first tranche released in March.'

'Big deal. There's nothing in it. Why all the secrecy? The funds have been approved in the budget – so what?' Cleaver could see no story in the cabinet note. 'The Indonesians will build the detention centres and the people smugglers will lose their customers, game over and everyone is a winner.'

'I don't know, maybe it means something, but I'm not sure what. My mystery caller said I should follow the money.'

'What money? Only the stimulus package has gone into the parliament and Gerrard told you this morning the Indonesian money has been deferred until February. Someone is having a laugh.'

Anita kept studying the brief. 'There is something here that's a little strange.'

'What is it?'

'Gerrard has denied all travel this week and wants the cabinet in the parliament for a speech on Thursday. How did he know the parliament would be open then?'

'It's a waste of time. It obviously refers to O'Brien's retirement.'

'He hates O'Brien.'

'Why else would he want them all in the chamber?'

'If I know Gerrard, he'd prefer a five-minute valedictory for O'Brien with no-one in the chamber.' Anita was working through some creative options. 'No, I think it's something else.'

'Forget it, this is crap. Why didn't the wanker just put it in the mail?' Cleaver left Anita still contemplating the note.

'Any idea who sent it to you?' Craig asked.

'Nope, none. I'm not so sure I share Cleaver's lack of enthusiasm; although it does seem like it could be a bit of a beat-up.' Her phone buzzed with a message.

Fancy a coffee?

When she arrived at Aussies Cafe there was already a crowd after question time. She saw Barton, smiled, and went to order a coffee. The baristas were moving through the queue quickly, and within moments she was sitting with her coffee waiting for Barton to speak.

'You look different somehow. What have you been up to?'

'You know I'm chasing this immigration detention story.' Anita took a sip of her coffee. 'Well, I've had some strange information fall into my lap.'

'Ah, another leak, eh? This place is like a sieve. What have you got?'

'A cabinet minute document.' Anita spooned froth into her mouth.

Barton jumped, glanced over his shoulder to check who might be listening. 'You have what? From when? What does it say?'

'Last week, and not much.'

'Can I have a look at it?'

Anita slowly shook her head.

'Okay, can you at least tell me about it?'

'No. I think I have a story, but I don't know what it is.'

'How did you get it?'

'That's the strange part. I got it at the movies, stuck under a seat in the cinema where A Star Is Born is playing. Hey, I wonder if that's a clue?'

'Sounds a little weird to me. Why not just mail it to you?'

'Maybe it's urgent. You know how unreliable the mail is in the press gallery. But the secrecy has got me thinking I may be missing something, and it could be bigger than I imagine.' Anita sipped her coffee. 'How was question time? Anything exciting happen?'

'The house is all a bit too solemn at the moment, plus we've been bound by an agreement to behave.'

'I was going to ask you about that. How come?'

'Harper was stitched up by Gerrard this morning at a breakfast. It seems he wants us all to be on our best behaviour this week.'

'Gerrard doesn't do anything for the common good; he wants you compliant for a reason.'

'I know he's a self-interested twat, but this week there's only the stimulus package and a couple of other pieces of bipartisan legislation going through the house. There's nothing controversial happening at all.'

'My source says I should follow the money.'

'What money? The only money is the stimulus package going to the taxpayers. How're you going to spend yours?'

'On getting fatter, I suppose.' Anita laughed. 'Or I might get a new pair of sneakers.'

'I'll spend mine on a case of good wine. Shall I get white or red?' Barton smiled and cocked his eyebrow hopefully.

'Nice try.' Anita replied playfully. 'Why would I be asked to follow the money if there's none to follow?'

'O'Brien thinks there is,' Barton offered.

'What do you mean?'

'O'Brien thinks there's something brewing in the government. He's worried about the extra time scheduled for the bill when it comes back to the house on Thursday. Thinks it's unnecessary, and he could be right – it's a simple matter of assent. He thinks it might mean the government's being shifty. I spoke to Meredith Bruce about it, and she assured me there's nothing to be concerned about. She had a request from the prime minister apparently, so he could speak again and tell us how generous he is.'

'According to my source document, he wants the entire ministry in the house on Thursday.'

'Why?' Messenger spooned himself froth from his coffee. 'I would have thought he'd let them go early, since it's only valedictories.'

'But why would he insist on you blokes behaving this week?'

'He doesn't have the numbers, so it can't have anything to do with a vote. It wouldn't be about the clerk, and it's not valedictories, so it has to be an announcement of some kind.'

They sat and sipped their coffee, pondering what it might mean.

'O'Brien suspects there could be an amendment to the money bill to add more funds for the Indonesians.' Barton broke the silence.

'What?'

'The immigration detention money, which is now scheduled for February. O'Brien is of the view there was a push to have it approved by the parliament this week.'

'Is that even possible?'

'We've already approved it. It was in the budget and it's due next year anyway, so it's not controversial. Even if it did come in, we really wouldn't have trouble with it.' Barton finished his coffee. 'I told him we would need to consider it in detail and if it was pushed through this week by the government, we would reject it.'

'You can't force any divisions, remember.' Anita flicked open her note pad, pulled a pen from her ponytail, and began to take notes. 'So, why is O'Brien concerned?'

'He thinks if it was in the legislation with the stimulus package it wouldn't have been scrutinised as it should be. I told him to stop worrying and enjoy his last few days because it's not in the stimulus legislation. Anyway, the senate can't amend a money bill.'

'Who says so?' Anita asked.

'The constitution.'

'Really?'

'Yep, Section 53. So, O'Brien is silly to think the senate would amend the bill.'

'But O'Brien thinks if the government does amend it, there may not be the usual scrutiny and review.' Anita scribbled a few notes on her pad.

'Crumbs, you look gorgeous when you're intense like this.'

'Barton, this issue of the Indonesian funding could be very serious. I've been told to follow the money, and now you're telling me there could be some dodgy parliamentary business concerning money.'

'I am yet to see a link, but I take your point,' Barton said.

'Thank you.' Anita flopped back in her chair. 'Now get me another coffee, please, there's a good boy.'

'I'd rather get you dinner,' Barton said, as he rose to buy more coffee.

---

Gerrard found his wife sunning herself out by the pool. She looked tanned and taut, and he felt a fondness mixed with his normal carnal urges as he approached her. She looked up as she heard his footsteps, shading her eyes.

'How was it?'

'Exhausting, but it's all finally under control. The bill is in its second reading and passes the house tomorrow with the opposition totally under control and none the wiser. If all goes according to plan, the senate will send it back for amendment on

Wednesday night, and it's back in the house on Thursday first thing.'

'She's a smart girl, that Zara.'

'Yes. Little does she realise she has just cost the nation forty million dollars.'

'You have played her beautifully, darling. It seems those late nights with her have been useful after all.'

'I've decided to take the rest of the day off,' he said, neatly redirecting the discussion away from the speaker.

'Great, get into your trunks and have a swim, the water's gorgeous.' She lay back to enjoy more sun.

'I will, but I wanted to talk to you first.'

'Why, what are you worried about?'

'You know me, always worried about things not in my direct control.'

'For a politician with such confidence, you really do suffer from self-doubt, don't you?'

'Has the banking been finalised?'

'I had a little trouble with my reasons for establishing the account and providing an identity that was acceptable, but I resolved them. Your department wants you to declare it on your parliamentary interests' statement, but that's no issue I'm told. I didn't quite appreciate how hard it has become to open a bank account, especially overseas, but I've had wonderful support from a few friends in France who I've spoken with, all hush hush of course.'

'We tightened the laws to stop the illicit transferring of funds from crooks and fraudsters.'

'I must say it works a treat. It was damn near impossible to do, but I found a way – best you don't know, darling.'

'Quite. What are your plans for the remainder of the week?' Gerrard began loosening his tie.

'I fly to Zurich on Thursday afternoon to complete the banking arrangements, although I may have a stop-off somewhere – apparently they need a personal meeting to finalise the account details and verify identity. All being equal we should be able to deposit money into the new account by the following Monday or Tuesday at the latest. It just needs Amir to do his part. When do you release the funds?'

'Thursday night if all goes well in the parliament. Amir will formally request the funds from the government before 5.00 pm his time, which means treasury will transfer them overnight from Australia. He should have them first thing Friday, and then he can begin to wash it. He says Monday, but sometimes I don't trust the smarmy little prick.'

'When do you think you can come over?'

'I'll need to clear my commitments here, but I reckon before Christmas.'

'Christmas in Paris would be delightful.'

'I'd expect we'll come back in January for the by-elections and the swearing in of the new prime minister.'

'Who's that likely to be?'

'It depends on the by-election results, but I suspect Jonathan will win the vote.'

'When will you announce your retirement?'

'I'm a little unsure if I should do it in the parliament on Thursday or wait until Friday.'

'Have you suggested anything to anyone?'

'No, only you and I know what I'm planning.'

'Oh dear, thank goodness we're moving to Europe.'

'You do realise, if this blows up in our face, we may never be able to come back.'

'Yes, darling, I know. But it won't blow up. It's all under control, so stop worrying and go for a swim, and get your handsome body out in the sun. There's nothing better than a tan on a man in Paris.'

Gerrard began pulling his shirt from his trousers. 'I never thought it would be this easy to give it all up, but I must admit, since we started talking about this last week I'm pleased to be going, quite frankly, especially after losing Fred. I find I'm rather tired of it all.'

'You've done your time and sacrificed many things for the nation, my daring. The people of Australia will miss you, but I doubt we will miss them.'

# CHAPTER 12

## WEDNESDAY 7.35 AM

'Good morning, Mr O'Brien, sir.'

'Good morning, George.' Gordon placed his briefcase on the conveyor as he always did, with the assistance of George Nikolaos, the senior security officer at the entrance to the House of Representatives.

'Just two more sitting days, sir, then you can kiss this place goodbye. We'll miss you.'

'Thank you, George, and I'll miss you.' Gordon passed through the security scanner without any intrusive beeps emanating from it, collected his briefcase and began to leave the security room. 'Have a good day.'

'I will, thank you, Mr O'Brien.'

Gordon was tempted to visit the speaker's office as he had done every morning for the last seventeen years when he arrived at parliament, to check on any overnight instructions and receive any briefings, but this morning he'd decided he didn't want to be bothered with any of that. Richard could look after it all. He'd listen to Marjorie's sage advice about stepping back from the work. He smiled as he passed the office.

Instead, he decided to have an early morning coffee at Aussies Cafe, a place he rarely frequented, preferring his own company to mingling with the other employees. When parliament was sitting, the population of parliament house increased to roughly five thousand. It was just too many people to cope with at any one time, so he steered clear of places that attracted large groups of people such as the staff dining room or the cafe. But today was different. It was still early, and since the plane crash many staff had left for home. Besides, he didn't have much to do. He decided to read his newspaper and see if this cafe was as good as everyone in his office said.

He walked the long corridor past the many backbenchers' offices, the soft green carpet muting his footsteps, noticing the names embossed on glass plates beside each white gloss door, many festooned with Christmas cheer, most carrying political posters or commentary. Partisan politics was hard to ignore.

He noticed how quiet the building was, a silence that contrasted with the power and political scheming that flowed through the place. He could hear nothing other than the swishing of the suit trousers he'd purchased a year after he was promoted to clerk.

He turned left at the second junction and headed for the central building. The carpet gave way to highly polished jarrah floorboards and then black marble as he walked through the glass passage connecting the two buildings: the House of Representatives and the central core with its ministerial wing. His footsteps echoed in the hall as he walked across to the security door and entered the front foyer. No expense had been spared on this fine building, and he was reminded of when Queen Elizabeth II had opened it in 1988. He crossed the empty foyer and entered another security alcove, flashed his identity card against a recording device and entered yet another corridor that led eventually to Aussies Cafe. It had taken him five minutes of brisk walking to reach the cafe, only a fraction of the five kilometres of carpeted walkways throughout these buildings.

The cafe was quiet and there were plenty of tables. He dropped his briefcase on a chair before moving off to order an Earl Grey tea instead of coffee. He hardly ever drank the stuff and smiled at the thought he might have suddenly ordered one. Life must be changing.

He balanced the cup and teapot on its little wooden paddle, collected a newspaper and headed to his table. Pouring a refreshing cup – no sugar, nor milk – he took a sip then opened the newspaper. Splashed across the front page was an article on the money about to hit every Australian's bank account from a generous government, legislation having passed the House of Representatives late on Tuesday. Little did they realise it was their money they were receiving. As he read the article by Anita Devlin, he reflected on his initial concerns about the stimulus package, smiling sheepishly at his suggestion that the speaker might be implicated in an unethical manipulation of the parliament. He still didn't trust Gerrard – and still hadn't received an adequate response to his question about why the extra time was required for the bill once it was back in the house on Thursday.

'Hello, Mr O'Brien, mind if I join you?' Anita had a cup in her hand and an intoxicating smile on her face.

'I was just reading your story on the stimulus package.' Gordon couldn't refuse and beckoned her to sit as he folded his newspaper. 'Please, it would be a pleasure.'

'I've been asked to do a story on the last few weeks of the parliament, and I wanted to get your insights, if I may.'

'It's been a stinker, hasn't it?'

Anita smiled at his candour. 'Can I quote you?'

'I think not. It's not for me to be quoted on such things.' Gordon suddenly felt a little uneasy and straightened in his chair.

'I think it would be nice to add a human element to your highly respected but rather stoic image.' Anita settled in at the table.

'Do you have anything specific you want to ask me?' He suddenly wished he could return to his newspaper.

'I just have a couple of questions about process if you don't mind.' Anita knew not to push her luck. 'The Appropriation Bill is due for a quick vote in the senate today, and then will likely be back to the house tomorrow. Why is there extended time allocated for speakers when it returns, if the stimulus package is not controversial?'

'The prime minister has requested an allocation so that he

may speak to it. It's unusual, but not a problem. These types of requests are not unheard of.' Gordon began to relax.

'Why has the prime minister insisted that all his cabinet, and indeed the entire ministry, attend the house at this time?'

'Has he? I'm not sure I knew that. I suspect it has something to do with valedictories, since the house is not taking votes.'

'Yours?'

'Given the prime minister and I, ah, do not see eye to eye on many issues, I suspect not.'

'Why do you think the Indonesian detention centre money was not included, as planned, in this bill?'

'It had previously been approved when the government's budget was passed by both houses. I suspect the government wanted greater parliamentary scrutiny and is deferring it until after the by-elections in February.'

'Is it true you suspect there may have been some covert scheme developing regarding this funding allocation for the Indonesians, and if so, have you changed your mind since the legislation is now already through the parliament?'

'I have no such suspicions. I thought you were going to ask me to speak about the last two weeks?' Gordon unfolded his newspaper.

'Just one last question, if you don't mind?' Anita pushed her luck.

'One last one.'

'If the prime minister were to retire tomorrow, how does that affect the caretaker government?'

Gordon carefully took a sip of tea, considering the question.

Anita sat quietly waiting for his response. Knowing when to wait and say nothing was a crucial skill for a journalist – silence sometimes drew out information that otherwise would not have appeared, and this might be one of those times.

'I'm not sure how to respond to that.' Gordon hadn't even considered this intriguing proposition. 'I suspect it would have little impact, as the bureaucracy is now commissioned to maintain the government until after the by-elections, so it matters not who is leading the government. It would have little impact, quite frankly, and maybe it would be a good thing. Certainly, I'd be happier.' He allowed himself a small smile.

'Thank you, Mr O'Brien, you have been very generous with your time, I appreciate it.' Anita stood to leave, and Gordon, ever the gentleman, also stood to wish her farewell and courteously shook her hand. 'I wish you well in your retirement.'

'Thank you so much, Miss Devlin.' Gordon resumed his seat, flicked open his newspaper and tried to concentrate on the articles of national importance. The idea of a prime ministerial resignation kept popping into his head; it required further consideration. Considering the time Gerrard had allocated, it just might indicate he was about to announce his retirement. If he did it before the valedictories, then the session would be all about him. That would be typical of the man, always chasing the spotlight.

Gordon dismissed the idea – Gerrard would never retire so soon after the plane tragedy. Although, what if Gerrard lost the by-elections? Could he ever accept not being prime minister?

Perhaps not, but would he retire before he knew the results of the by-elections and be branded a quitter?

He finished his tea, neatly folded the newspaper, picked up his case and moved off toward the ministerial wing. He wanted to pass the waterfall one last time. The Greens Party, when they had six senators many years previously, periodically linked hands and encircled the pool to chant, whatever it was those strange idealists chanted.

On this occasion Gordon barely stopped before moving through the glassed tunnel leading to the chamber of the house. The original design of the building had allowed for the speaker to have an uninterrupted view of the senate, and for the president of the senate to overlook the house through the glass doors. Tradition dictated that the two presiding officers should see each other so each knew if the other chamber was sitting. Modern ways and modern design meant that sometimes tradition disappeared into history, tossed aside by those wanting to make their own mark. Throughout his career Gordon had tried to remind elected politicians that their service was for a short time only in comparison to the history of the parliament – they were custodians of its traditions. That was why he was so continually frustrated with Gerrard, a prime minister who had nothing but contempt for the traditions of the parliament.

The chamber's door was locked so he took the route through the members' lounge. It must have seemed like a good idea at the time when architects planned for greater social interaction around the chamber, compared to the cramped quarters of the former parliament house, but unfortunately politicians were rarely seen outside their offices.

Gordon was now approaching the government whip's office, the place where party discipline was distributed, and legislative business managed for the government. He popped in to have a quick chat with the whip's clerk Rosie Cameron.

'Are you giving leave or pairing with the opposition for any of your members who may be missing for the last two days, Rosie?'

'No, not allowed to Mr O'Brien, although plenty have asked over the last few days.'

Gordon thought this unusual, given a few former colleagues' funerals had been originally arranged for Thursday and Friday. 'Thank you, enjoy your day.'

As Gordon took the fire escape stairs to his office rather than the lift in the next lobby, he began playfully scheming. Perhaps Gerrard was about to retire after all.

'Good morning, Mr O'Brien.' Paige Alexander was her usual chirpy early-morning self. 'A Mr Forde from prime minister and cabinet would like you to call him urgently, the number is on your desk.'

'Thank you, Paige, and good morning to you. When is Marjorie expected?'

'She's already here. She's over at the travel office regarding a query on travel requests from the PM's office.'

The clerk had the authority to approve all travel during sitting weeks because politicians were the responsibility of the house while working in Canberra, not the department of administrative affairs, which looked after them when they were back in their electorates. He didn't want the responsibility, but it was foisted onto his department many years ago when a travel scandal embroiled several ministers and members who were found to be dishonestly rorting the system. Gerrard bumped the responsibility back to the clerk and let him take the media heat instead of the politicians.

Gordon dropped his case on the leather lounge and took his position behind his desk, turning on his ornate brass desk lamp as he sat. He didn't know this Forde chap, so picked up the phone to call him, punching the numbers from the note before him.

'Gordon O'Brien here, how can I help?'

'Mr O'Brien, I have had a request from foreign affairs to confirm details of the parliamentary program for the remainder of the week.'

'Why would you have such a request?'

'I am not at liberty to say, sir. Suffice to say, it is a procedural matter concerning a member establishing an overseas finance investment account. Before the account can be opened, we are required to add the details to the member's disclosure statements before adjournment this week. So, when might that be?'

'We expect the house to adjourn before 4.00 pm on Thursday. Does that help you?'

'Yes, it does, thank you.'

Gordon was a little unsure of what to make of the call as the government bureaucracy was forever trying to justify itself. Why would the department want to know a parliamentary program for a member's disclosure statement?

Gordon was more interested in his new theory on what might

be going on in the government than any wayward politician trying to open an international bank account before the end of the parliamentary term. He pushed the hands-free call button and punched in the numbers to connect him with his colleague, the black rod of the senate Nigel Nelson, much younger than Gordon and, he sometimes hoped, more than just a colleague.

'Gobby, how are you? Nice to hear from you.' Nelson was loud and rambunctious, but Gordon was never offended by his nickname. 'How's your last week progressing?'

'Not bad, Nigel. Listen, I was talking to a journalist this morning who suggested to me the prime minister might resign tomorrow. Have you heard any gossip?'

'You are kidding me, right? I haven't heard a damn thing. No-one ever tells me anything. What weight do you place on it?'

'Did you hear the PM speak on the condolences the other day? He was almost brought to tears when he talked of Fred Rocher. He seemed to suggest life meant much more than hanging around this place.'

'Is that all you've got?' scoffed Nelson.

'I have it on good authority the government has cancelled all leave, and the PM insists on all ministers being present in the chamber tomorrow prior to valedictories and question time.'

'Your idea is starting to sound a little more interesting.'

'And the strangest thing just happened. Someone rang me from PM and C, asking me about this week's program, apparently to have a member's disclosure statement adjusted. It seems a member wants to open an international bank account and to do so, they have to disclose it before it is approved.'

'Gerrard's wife has always been a Francophile – I read it in some women's magazine.' Nigel was always a great source of information about pop culture. 'I think it was in September, I was at the dentist, and surprised they had an up-to-date magazine instead of those tatty things they normally leave in the waiting room.'

'So, the Gerrards could be retiring and going off to Europe on an extended stay,' Gordon sighed. 'Gosh, I hope so.'

'I don't think you have much hard evidence in among that lot, Gordon,' Nelson chortled. 'But I like the idea of them rushing off overseas if he does retire.'

'So, you're not convinced?'

'No, but I'm happy to start a rumour.'

'Will the senate have my stimulus package legislation done and back to the house this afternoon?'

'Afraid not, ol' boy. The government has moved it into committee, and we won't get onto it until this evening. They've scheduled a late night.'

'Why are they doing that? It's straightforward, surely they can see that.'

'It's to do with extra allowances for sitting late. It's the old ploy to draw out more bonus pay for their staff, who no doubt will sit around until late.'

'Unbelievable. Let me know if you get any further information about it, please.' Gordon smiled, leaned forward, and said quietly, 'No need to mention the retirement thing to anyone.'

'Right you are. Let's have lunch on Friday if you're free of course.'

'That would be nice, thanks Nigel.'

Marjorie Earle walked in with files and papers to sign as Gordon pushed the disconnect button. 'Sorry, Gordon, but Richard has referred these to you, given you are still the senior officer. He'd like you to sign them – he sees no trouble with the applications.'

Marjorie had international travel requests with her. There were some thirty requests for the clerk to formally consider and approve, which Gordon's assistant had already scrutinised.

Gordon flicked open the first file: 'Callaghan, off to Europe and Ireland, probably to see his family.' He signed and then went to the next file and the next. 'Kelly, going to Brazil for a green-house conference – now that's a waste of time and money.' He continued going through the files and signing where he was required. Smith, off to India for bilateral meetings. Butler, visiting Canada; Sierowkoski, meeting his wife in Japan; the Morans off to Africa; Gerrard to Zurich; Baldwin, off to China like Ronald-son; Cartwright to Norway for a parliamentary meeting of members to the International Parliamentary Union.

Gordon suddenly stopped signing and flicked back to a request for Mrs Margaret Gerrard to fly to Zurich on Thursday. 'Marjorie, did Richard check this trip?'

'Which one? I think he checked the veracity of all of them.'

'Mrs Gerrard is travelling on Thursday, on a private trip to Zurich.'

'She can't do that?' Marjorie queried, surprised by Gordon's tone, as if the travel request were unusual. 'Doesn't the prime minister's wife have a personal allowance to travel internationally?' Marjorie was now looking over Gordon's shoulder trying to see the previously unseen.

'She does, but I still need to approve it, and this seems unusual, given it has an open return.'

'Richard phoned the prime minister's office and apparently she's undecided as to whether she should go to Paris before she returns.'

'Good for her, Francophile indeed.' Gordon closed the file and passed it on and signed off the remaining files. 'Can you get me Anita Devlin, please. I'll speak to her when I finish these.'

'That's the girl from Hancock Media?'

'Yes, and I suspect she'd be most pleased to hear you calling her a girl.' Gordon smiled.

'You know what I mean. At our age everyone is a girl, or a boy for that matter.' Marjorie laughed.

Gordon finished the last file, leaving Marjorie to scoop them up and set up his call from her office. It didn't take long before Gordon was speaking with Anita.

'Miss Devlin, I want to apologise for snapping at you this morning. I should have been more willing to discuss your rumour about the prime minister, but I wanted to reassure you, I do not expect the prime minister to announce his retirement tomorrow as you implied.'

'Why do you say that? How can you be so certain?'

'His wife is off to Europe tomorrow. I wouldn't expect her to be doing that if her husband was pulling the pin as leader, so to speak.'

'I suppose so. Where's she off to?'

'I didn't tell you this, but she's travelling to Zurich.' Gordon didn't have a chance to say goodbye before Anita hung up. 'Now, perhaps you can piece something together and call yourself an investigative journalist,' Gordon said to himself.

# CHAPTER 13

**WEDNESDAY 11.30 AM**

Barton Messenger was waiting patiently for his shadow cabinet colleagues to arrive for the daily strategy meeting to discuss question time. This was the theatre of the parliament and television news grabs were always taken from this hour-long session. All members of the parliament attended, and the prime minister would no doubt be keen to shove the political knife into the opposition – as he had done almost every day he was in the chamber since being elected prime minister.

The media's forensic review of every question time meant it was vital for the opposition to prepare a coordinated assault on the government. The strategy team met each day to consider prominent political issues, write questions, determine who would ask them, and discuss parliamentary tactics before the usually combative sessions in the parliament. Not for the faint-hearted, these sessions were nevertheless a political stage for the ambitious.

By signing the no-vote agreement with Prime Minister Gerrard, James Harper had foregone any opportunity to use opposition numbers against the government. It meant the opposition could not move any censure motions or seek a vote of no confidence, tools they had used effectively during question time before.

Harper had asked his colleagues for a moratorium on attack questions, preferring to respect the solemnity of the house as it struggled with the loss of their colleagues. Barton was a little keener for a fight than his colleagues; he preferred to confront the government on issues that were important in the electorate and would shed a positive light on the opposition in the media.

Messenger had previously requested more questions on the illegal refugees, especially the boats from Indonesia, which seemed to be arriving in national waters more regularly, and summer was the season when people smugglers increased their activity. He remained unconvinced that the detention centre strategy with Indonesia would stop the smugglers, and believed it provided little impetus for the government to take control of the borders. He also wanted to attack the government on the failure of the education scholarship scheme in India, exposed by Anita Devlin as a scam; questions needed to be asked.

The opposition had not asked a question on the economy all week. Consumer spending was tightening, which would justify the stimulus package, but was it enough? Would the cash splash stimulate the economy? He considered the opposition was wasting a perfect parliamentary opportunity to position themselves as the alternate government prior to the campaigns for the eight by-elections.

Barton sat alone, waiting in the shadow cabinet room, an extension to the opposition party meeting room, tucked down at the end of a corridor in the house of representatives. The government's party room was in the same corridor, but way down the other end of the building more than two hundred metres away. The government of course had its own meeting rooms for its cabinet, in the ministerial wing. It was a demonstration of the little importance the parliament placed on those not in government. A polished wooden table filled the sectioned-off space, with twenty wooden chairs arranged around its perimeter. The leader's chair was always at the centre of the table on one side, so as not to be too far from the shadow ministers. The distant ends of the table were left for juniors.

Barton was considering tactics and what approach to take with his colleagues in the meeting when his phone buzzed.

Can you talk?

I need to tell you something.

Are you coming to dinner after all?

Call me asap.

I have something for you … maybe

Is that maybe for dinner, or maybe
you have something for me?

Call me when you can.

A few Barton's colleagues began to wander into the room and take their allocated positions, some with takeaway coffee cups, others pouring a glass of water, so he decided he had enough time to remove himself and call Anita.

'Hello gorgeous, what's up?'

'You recall my spy caper from Monday, when I was given an envelope containing a cabinet minute?'

'Yes, why?'

'The message when I picked up the envelope was "Follow the money".'

'Have you found it? If you have, are you buying dinner?'

'Smart-arse, there's no money yet, but if I was going to hide cash, where in the world would I go?'

'Umm, Nigeria? Or maybe Switzerland?'

'Guess where Mrs Gerrard is travelling to tomorrow?'

'Lagos?'

'She has a ticket to Zurich, scheduled for tomorrow afternoon.'

'Well, that ends the prime minister's retirement-speech theory.'

'Why?'

'She wouldn't be going anywhere if he was about to resign.'

Anita hesitated. 'I think this is part of a plan. I still have a hunch Gerrard is about to announce his retirement and they are setting up their European adventure.'

'That's a long bow, Anita. She could be going there for a whole variety of reasons.'

'True, but why now?'

'I have no idea. Let's talk about it over dinner.'

'Raincheck, I'm working tonight. The senate is sitting late.'

'Your loss. Catch you later.' Barton slipped his phone back into his jacket and returned to the meeting room. As he resumed his seat he asked, 'Does anyone know why the senate is sitting late tonight?' A couple of shrugs and shakes of the head – it was going to be another riveting tactics meeting.

Harper glided into the room and took his place, calling the meeting to order. The whip took notes, and the discussion followed the recent benign form of previous days.

Barton sat opposite the leader, which meant he was in the leadership group but on neither his right hand or left hand; those chairs were left for deputy leader Wilson Campbell and Peter Stanley, the shadow minister for health. Even in the party room, everyone sat in the same seat for every meeting, as if they were part of some psychological experiment.

However, Barton was pleased just to be at the table. Almost thirty minutes into the meeting he asked again, 'Why is the senate sitting late tonight? Is there anything we should know about?'

'It has referred the Appropriation Bill to committee, and they'll vote later this evening.' Harper had been briefed by his senate leader, Joe Anthony.

'Does that not seem strange to you? Why is the senate sending straightforward legislation to committee, and voting on it after the house has adjourned and we've left for the evening?' Barton didn't believe in conspiracies, but his question piqued the interest of some of the others. 'I think we should ask a question about it.'

'If you think it's a big deal, we'll give you number nine,' said Harper. 'What about the last one, question ten – anybody?'

'Can we leave the last question to the chamber? I suspect we'll want a follow-up from question nine,' Stanley said. Harper agreed, and that was the end of strategy for another day.

'I'll get them typed and distributed,' said Barton as he arranged his notes, nodding agreement with the whip.

As they were leaving, Christopher Hughes, the rakish and ambitious member for Warringah, pulled Barton aside. 'Another waste of time. What are you thinking about the referral of the stimulus bill to a committee in the senate?'

'It seems unusual procedure to me, as if they're trying to hide something by delaying it coming back to the house until tomorrow. They could vote on it now, so why wait until we close the house this evening before they vote on it? What's the big deal?'

'Maybe they want to add an amendment,' Hughes suggested.

'The senate very rarely amends money bills, Christopher, you know that. Even so, if they did amend it, surely we are not stupid enough to stop the stimulus package?'

'We'll just have to wait and see.'

Anita Devlin sat in Peter Cleaver's office, sneakered feet on his desk waiting for the answer to her question.

'Are you sure you want to run this? It is pure speculation on your part. It's a big call and it may well jeopardise your career, at least with us. You've already been linked to the opposition and the government will no doubt come down hard on you.'

'I'm not linked to the opposition in any way, Cleave. You know that.'

'What about your mate, Messenger?'

'He's just a source.'

'If you run this the prime minister's office will be down on you like a ton of bricks. At best you only have a guess, you've got no solid evidence to go on.'

'Of course, they'll come down on me, but it's their fault, they won't respond to my questions. Something fishy is going on, I can feel it, and my story might flush out a reason why these apparently unrelated things are happening. If a big stink is what we need to flush out the story, then so be it.'

'Hancock will go off his rocker about this.'

'Since when has that ever affected your decisions?' Anita dropped her shoes from the desk and sat forward. 'She's going to Zurich by herself for Christ's sake – I tell you, there's something going on.'

Cleaver looked at Anita, picked up a crumpled packet of cigarettes from the front of his desk and slowly pulled out a survivor, placing the bent tobacco stick in his mouth. He lit it, drawing the smoke deep into his lungs before exhaling across the desk and coughing.

'Okay, let's do it.' He smiled. 'I don't believe I just said that. Put a short rumour piece up on the afternoon digital edition, and work on a more substantial column for the paper tomorrow. If we publish it online, the opposition might raise it in the house at question time, and we might get more material, or at least a direct denial from the PM.'

'You're a saint, Cleave.' Anita kicked out of the chair and returned to her desk to write a story based upon pure supposition – that the prime minister of Australia was about to announce his retirement.

'Let's hope you still have a job tomorrow,' Cleaver yelled after her.

Anita filed the story to her sub-editor and within thirty minutes it was online; five minutes later she received a call from Barton.

'What are you doing, are you crazy?'

'I haven't had a call from the PM's office yet, so maybe I'm not.'

'Have you found out why the prime minister's wife is going to Zurich?'

'Not yet. I thought this story might help,' Anita said.

'Get to question time, I may have a question on it.'

'See you there.'

---

'Gordon, your Miss Devlin is causing a bit of a stir,' Marjorie said as he prepared himself for question time.

'How so?' He straightened his lace neckpiece in the mirror making sure everything was perfect. Traditionally, the clerk and his assistant wore black robes and white lace neckpieces. He rued the day his horse-hair wig was consigned to the rubbish bin of history – such a pity.

'She has published a short editorial online implying the prime minister is about to resign.'

'A very courageous thing to do, I would suggest.' Gordon finished fussing with his neckpiece and began to comb his hair. 'If you follow the sequence of events, it's a reasonable guess, I suppose. Except for Mrs Gerrard, leaving for Zurich tomorrow.'

'Maybe she's off to close her accounts,' Marjorie joked. 'Or maybe she's about to open one.'

Gordon stopped combing his hair, struck by the innocence of Marjorie's comment. It sparked an idea linking trivial scraps of information. He moved to his desk and sat down, reaching for a sheet of paper, and taking up his fountain pen. He began listing the things he knew, to try and order his thinking.

*Mrs Gerrard to Zurich*

*Loss of majority in the house*

*Agreement for no votes in the house*

*Loss of government possible, maybe in February*

*Indonesian president has now requested all funds*

*Speaker misled on Indonesian money*

*Funding for Indonesia proposed and then deferred*

*Drafting clerk disappears on holiday*

*Request for an addition to a member's interest declaration statement before opening an overseas account.*

*Overseas account? Switzerland?*

*All government members in the house on last day*

*Bill for stimulus delayed in Senate – why?*

*Prime minister retiring?*

*Tax haven account?*

*What and where is the money?*

Gordon carefully folded the paper and slipped it into the inside pocket of his jacket. He made his way to the chamber, mentally working through the issues on the list. Could the prime minister possibly be considering somehow swindling the government with the Indonesians and then resigning to cover his tracks? It was a preposterous idea.

He wandered into the speaker's office for the usual briefing before question time. The speaker was robing herself as the clerk entered. 'Have you seen the latest from Hancock Media?' Gordon inquired. 'It seems the prime minister is about to announce his retirement.'

'Rubbish,' Bagshaw sniffed. 'He has never even suggested anything remotely like that to me.'

'And you would know, of course,' Gordon said, but the speaker didn't respond. 'Has the government made any changes to the program today?' Gordon was trying to get any clues to add to his list.

'Just another day I suspect, Gordon. Today and tomorrow and you're all done with the politicians, so Friday should be a relaxing last day for you. Are you looking forward to it?'

'Yes.' Gordon surprised himself with his answer. 'If there are any questions based on the story from Hancock's, how do you want to play it?'

'The prime minister has not advised me, so I suspect I will allow them.' Bagshaw was now adjusting her robe. 'The story is out there in the public domain. No doubt the prime minister can look after himself and give the evening news a good grab or two – he normally does – and he doesn't need my protection.'

'Best we go then,' Gordon suggested.

The speaker moved toward her door, where the serjeant-at-arms was already waiting to lead her to the chamber. Tradition has its place, and the procession was one tradition the politicians wanted to keep. Gordon stepped back and allowed the speaker to leave the office and then followed, a half-dozen steps behind. Speaker Bagshaw stepped out after the serjeant-at-arms who was resting a thin gold staff, about a metre and a half long, on his left shoulder. He was dressed in the traditional garb of the serjeant of the parliament, a black tunic with long tails, black breeches, white stockings, lace jabot and black shoes. Gordon followed, also in step, and the three walked in single file through the glass tunnel, across the black marbled alcove, down six carpeted steps and waited at the door for the precise moment to enter the chamber. A security officer stood waiting for the serjeant's nod to open. The serjeant stood looking at the clock above the door and as the second hand clipped to 1.59.59, he nodded and the officer opened the door so the three could move off as one into the chamber.

'Honourable members, the speaker.'

# CHAPTER 14

## WEDNESDAY 2.00 PM

The speaker entered the chamber and resumed the chair, mounting the three wooden steps to the podium as the speaker panellist vacated the chair for her. Bagshaw composed herself, straightening her robes as she sat, and looked about the chamber. 'Order, it being 2.00 pm, debate is interrupted in accordance with standing orders to be resumed at a later time. It is now time for parliamentary questions. Are there any questions?'

James Harper stood at the despatch box on the opposition side of the parliamentary table.

'The leader of the opposition.'

'My question is directed to the prime minister, in what may be, according to the very latest news reports from Hancock media, his last question time.'

'Hear, hear.' The opposition members cheered.

'Order, the leader will ask his question,' Bagshaw said.

'Yes, of course, Madam Speaker.' Harper bowed slightly to the speaker. 'Can the prime minister reassure the house that the Indonesian detention centre policy his government is implementing over the next few years will eventually stop the people smugglers' boats and bring order to our nation's borders? Can he explain to the house why the boats keep coming?'

As Harper asked his question, Gordon looked through the questions the party whips had delivered to his staff to check for intended or unintended controversy. Nothing problematic on the government list, which was to be expected; they were all easy questions to allow a minister to speak in glowing terms about the achievements of the government, while at the same time verbally kicking the opposition and highlighting their inadequacies. Surprisingly, nothing listed on the opposition questions was anywhere near provocative, other than question nine asking about the progress of the stimulus package through the senate, and there was nothing listed for question ten.

'The prime minister.'

'Thank you, Madam Speaker, and might I say it's a pleasure to see you, as always.' Gerrard smiled rather too long at the speaker.

Bagshaw paid no attention. The prime minister flouted protocol, saying and doing whatever he wanted, and ignored political correctness, but Gordon knew from long experience that this compliment was Gerrard's way of asking the speaker to provide protection if the opposition got too lively during his answers today.

'Madam Speaker, I first want to address the spurious claim by the leader of the opposition that this may be my last question time and address the recent article in the Hancock Media on its digital news site today.'

Opposition backbenchers hooted and heckled.

'Order, the prime minister will be heard in silence.' Bagshaw had taken her cue.

'It seems the opposition are overly eager for me to retire. They would rather have their own leader compete with someone with less experience than test their policies on me.' Gerrard was never modest when talking about himself.

Messenger jumped quickly to the despatch box.

'The prime minister will resume his seat. The manager of opposition business?'

'Point of order, Madam Speaker, on relevance. The prime minister was asked about illegal boats arriving continuously on our shores, and about his policy for stopping them. He is now talking about the opposition, and I request he be brought to order.'

'The prime minister has barely begun his answer, there is no point of order. I call the prime minister.'

Gerrard resumed his position. 'Thank you, Madam Speaker. As I was saying, the opposition has no-one worthy of leading our great nation, and they would like me to retire to increase their puny chances of winning government at the next election. I can assure them and the good people of Australia, Madam Speaker, that I have no plans to satisfy them by retiring any time soon.

'To the question of the honourable gentleman, we face serious challenges associated with people smugglers, the very worst of human beings, and their trade in human misery for profit. These pirates leave Australia to pick up the dead bodies when their rickety boats sink, and the lives of innocents are lost. Who could forget the recent images of one of Australia's finest, a navy officer, cradling the body of a dead toddler? It was a terrible image and one we should never accept or allow to happen again. We understand the pain this despicable trade brings, we understand the desperation of people seeking sanctuary, we condemn their exploitation by profiteering people smugglers, and we intend to stop it.

'We have initiated a policy in partnership with Indonesia that includes the building of offshore detention centres in Indonesia. As you no doubt know, Madam Speaker, the president of Indonesia, a very good friend of Australia's, and for many years a personal friend of mine, has agreed to build and operate detention centres in his great country. Indeed, you may recall, Madam Speaker, the president's and my government jointly announced the funding for the centres and the immediate commencement of construction of the first of these new centres on the island of Ambon. It is hoped that, with the opening of this and other detention centres, we will be able to stop the scourge of people smuggling and maintain the sovereignty of the borders of both nations. Just in the last few days our Indonesian friends have begun preparing for construction on Ambon, which I am sure you will agree is a sign of tremendous goodwill. They began work when we agreed to release government funds to them.

'The government has received a formal request from our friends in Indonesia as late as last Friday to provide all the agreed funds immediately to help with the work they have commenced, and we have agreed and will transfer them as quickly as we can, although I am saddened that our initial plans to get funds through this week were prevented by other tragic circumstances. We will now need to wait, perhaps until next year, unless we can think of other ways to get the money to our friends without further delay. The Australian people have told us they want action to end people smuggling, and we say to the community we are doing our best, if only the opposition would work harder to save lives and secure Australia's borders.'

The prime minister concluded his answer and sat as the speaker called a government backbencher to ask a question of a minister. Gerrard leaned back in his chair oblivious to the question and smirked at Harper. 'You'd love me to retire, but that'll never happen while you're leader,' he called across the table.

Harper ignored him and watched as the health minister approached the despatch box to answer a government question about the growing waiting lists for elective surgery in public hospitals, and what the government had planned to cope with demand.

Messenger heard Gerrard's comment and scooted across to the chair beside Harper, engaging him in whispered conversation. 'He's too smug today, Jim, let's bring forward question nine.'

'Why, and have Gerrard belt us around the ears about the Christmas bonus? No thank you.'

Messenger withdrew and confided in Stanley, who sat beside him on the long green padded frontbench. 'Pete, I think we should bring question nine forward.'

'What did the boss say?'

'No.'

'Then no it is.'

Harper had again received the speaker's call as the health minister completed her answer. He asked the prime minister a follow-up question on health policy, which Gerrard had anticipated.

'Is this the best you can do? Is this it? Is this the type of question we can expect from the alternate government? This question is unworthy of the attention of any government minister, let alone the prime minister. It's weak and without any basis in fact, yet the opposition leader thinks he should ask it. Whenever the leader of the opposition stands at the despatch box he is always carping and complaining. You may recall, Madam Speaker, the great servants of this house who have stood behind that very despatch box and worked with government for the betterment of the nation, but no longer, not this miserable example of a leader.'

Messenger was again on his feet asking for the prime minister to answer the question, and again he was dismissed by the speaker.

'Time and time again, as that mob try and get themselves in order, they come into this honourable place humbled by their dearth of ideas. Politics, Madam Speaker, is about ideas, and as we know, ideas win the hearts and minds of Australians. Ideas grow a nation, and we need ideas from our politicians no matter who they are. Instead, we have a simpering, whimpering, complaining Negative Nancy, who we reluctantly call the leader of the opposition.'

Messenger was again on his feet at the despatch box asking for support from the speaker, and again receiving none.

'Just look at them, Madam Speaker. Their party attracts the ragged and the wretched. They attract the dregs of university coffee shops and miserable failed corporate lawyers. The latte sippers and the champagne plonkers. The only bright spark they had was tragically killed last week.'

Gerrard's comment sparked an immediate uproar from the opposition benches. Messenger scrambled to the despatch box, but before he could make the call, Gerrard apologised. 'I withdraw, I withdraw. I understand the sensitivity around comparing this opposition leader with colleagues dead or alive, for there is no comparison.'

The noise in the chamber did not dissipate and the speaker stood, attempting to silence the house. Gerrard on cue, promptly resumed his seat, for when the speaker was on her feet, everyone must immediately be seated and silent. It took a little time for the cacophony to subside, but eventually protocol was reinstated. Bagshaw waited until there was an extended period of silence.

'I know some of you want to leave early, and you may wish to test my patience today, but I ask the house to retain its dignity and decorum as we work to the end of a rather horrid fortnight.' Bagshaw resumed her seat. 'I call the prime minister.'

Gerrard continued his answer, but this time carefully explaining the many achievements of his government in health, while at the same time highlighting the weaknesses of the opposition.

Only three questions into the usual twenty, and the chamber echoed with abusive interjections and commentary from the opposition benches. Gordon was concerned about the increasingly unruly behaviour, and as the prime minister began his fifth minute, he quietly left his chair and approached the speaker.

'Speaker, I believe you are in for a difficult time today. Best you take firmer control of the prime minister. He is obviously being provocative and misusing the no-vote agreement with the opposition.'

'I will control them the way I believe they need to be controlled, thank you, Gordon.' Gordon was dismissed.

Messenger again turned to Stanley. 'We're getting murdered here, Peter, can we move question nine forward to change tack a bit?'

'Let's wait to hear from the boss.'

Gerrard finished his answer and resumed his seat, looking across at Harper. 'Had enough yet?' he said. 'Maybe it's time to give someone else a go?'

A government question was asked of the trade minister regarding the negotiations with South Africa on the soon-to-be-signed free trade agreement and the house quietened. Gordon looked at Messenger and could see he seemed annoyed and frustrated with his senior colleagues. He withdrew his list from his inside jacket pocket and spread it out in front of him. He looked at the smug Gerrard and considered whether today's aggressive posturing had anything to do with his list. He wrote a quick note and pushed a button to summon a chamber steward to deliver the message. Stewards delivered various messages during question time as members sent information, suggestions or even jokes to one another. Sometimes it was just a request for water, but mostly it was to deliver a note to another member.

The clerk, as an independent officer of the parliament, usually did not need to write directly to a member unless it was about parliamentary procedure. On this occasion, it was an idea about process, and Gordon slipped the note to the steward. He then watched as the steward made his way to another steward sitting behind the government, who delivered the note to another steward on the other side of the chamber, sitting behind the opposition, who then passed it to Messenger's adviser sitting in the adviser's box, who was surprised to receive it.

The staffer saw that it was addressed to Messenger but had no way of getting his attention. She could not engage with a member of parliament sitting over the low wooden barrier across an aisle next to her. So close, and yet too far away to contact. She would have to wait until she could attract Messenger's attention.

The trade minister had finished his answer and Harper was again on his feet at the despatch box. 'My question is to the prime minister, and it follows on from a previous question and his subsequent answer. Is the prime minister aware of news reports today advising that Indonesia has begun breaking ground for the proposed new detention centres? How is this possible, given they are yet to receive any funding from Australia?'

'What the Indonesians do is entirely a matter for them,' Gerrard said and resumed his seat, ignoring the opportunity to give the opposition a metaphorical kick as he had done with his previous answers, which caught the speaker by surprise.

'Ah, yes, the member for Hindmarsh.' Bagshaw smiled as she called the member.

Messenger looked at Gerrard, wondering why he hadn't bothered to respond at length as he had with his other answers. He seemed relaxed, smirking, and swivelling in his chair, but Messenger knew he was always planning something.

The member for Hindmarsh asked a question of the small business minister. Minister Puopolo was now waxing lyrical about the government's new business enterprise programs, developed to help small businesses overcome the increased administration costs due to the change from annual to quarterly reporting; small business owners hated the idea of having to report more regularly.

A frustrated Messenger jumped up, and Puopolo saw that he was coming to the despatch box to interrupt him by calling for a point of order, so he stopped talking and stepped back from the despatch box in anticipation. Messenger feigned a stop while the minister waited nervously for his interruption, but then smiled and walked past his colleagues toward his staffer, Julia Dusting, to ask a question about the detention centres. 'Have the Indonesians actually started site works? Has that been confirmed?'

'By our embassy, yes today. And I have a note for you.'

Messenger took the note and resumed his seat before opening it. The small business minister was showing no signs of finishing his answer. He flicked open the note and looked around the chamber to see who might be looking at him so he could identify who had sent it, but he saw no-one seeking his attention, so he looked down and read:

*Ask the prime minister why he is required to add to the register of members' personal interests before the end of this parliamentary sitting.*

*Is he opening an overseas account?*

Messenger immediately looked up, scanning faces, yet again saw no-one. He didn't recognise the handwriting. He caught Meredith Bruce's eye and flicked his head to indicate he wanted to talk to her. She got up, as he did, and they both walked toward the speaker's chair so they could talk privately behind it, a secluded place away from the activity of the chamber. The speaker's chair, its high back decorated with the Australian Coat of Arms outlined in gold leaf, was only a metre from the back wall, providing a shadowy recess for any discussions between the two managers of parliamentary business or any political combatants seeking to secure agreement on procedure during robust debate on the floor.

'Meredith, your boss is a little over the top today. Can we tone him down a bit?'

'I'll try, but if you keep asking lame questions, it's no wonder he whacks you.'

'I can't guarantee we'll hold our peace if he keeps attacking us.'

'You'll have to, as we don't have any voting procedures, remember? Another crazy decision by you guys.' She withdrew.

'I call the leader of the opposition.' An audible groan came from the government backbenchers as they laughed and mocked Harper as he stood at the despatch box.

'My question is to the prime minister. I direct his attention to recent media reports regarding the daily delivery of excessive amounts of flowers to the prime minister's residence at Yarralumla and ask what the finer things in your life are costing the Australian taxpayer?'

Messenger winced; he had not agreed to the question when Harper proposed it earlier, and now it sounded even worse. There was no reason to ask such a question, but Harper wanted to try and charge the prime minister with wasting taxpayer funds on trivial daily expenses, to provide a negative about Gerrard before the by-elections.

'Prime minister.'

Gerrard rose to the despatch box, slowly shaking his head, a mocking smirk on his face. He leaned on the box and looked back at his team, who were hooting and laughing. 'Madam speaker, the economy is strong. We have full employment. The kids will enjoy a good Christmas this year thanks to my government's stimulus package that will pay a bonus to every household, and yet we get this type of question, a question from a dill about a few bunches of flowers.'

Messenger jumped to the despatch box, 'Point of order, Madam Speaker.'

'The prime minister will resume his seat, the member for Gellibrand on a point of order.'

'Madam Speaker, the chamber today is out of control and the prime minister has been the chief culprit...'

'You will come to your point of order.'

'It is a disgrace that we have to endure this nonsense. My point is, Madam Speaker, the prime minister used an unparliamentary term when referring to the leader of the opposition and I ask that he withdraw.'

'The prime minister will withdraw.'

'Withdraw what, Madam Speaker?'

'You will withdraw the unparliamentary term.'

'What, dill? Oh yes, how silly of me to use a term that described the leader of the opposition as a herb, when we are talking about flowers. I should have used daisy, or better yet, pansy. If it will assist the house...'

'It will.'

'...then I withdraw my insensitive comment.' Gerrard was leaning over the microphone and smirking at Harper. 'What a sad, sad example of leadership here in the parliament of Australia where we are charged by the Australian people with providing leadership on important issues. I must say, Madam Speaker, there are plenty of important issues before us, which I could list.'

'List them! List them!' shouted his backbench.

'My colleagues want the list, which I like to call the leadership list. This is the list of a government doing the right thing for the Australian people and shows my government getting on with the job. So let me list just a few: we have a financial stimulus going to the people of Australia to help them at Christmas time and provide an economic lift to the many retail small businesses in Australia which will have a strong flow on effect; we have new developments in our health system to help the Australian people and those less fortunate than many of us; we have a new trade agreement with South Africa being negotiated that will add jobs and growth to our economy; we have an agreement with the Indonesians to build detention centres and protect the sovereignty of our borders ... I could go on and on, but these important issues are ignored by the leader of the opposition. Does he ask me important policy questions?'

'No!' responded his backbench in unison.

'Does he ask questions on the economy?' Gerrard asked, enjoying the theatre.

'Nooo!'

'The house will come to order,' the speaker tried to reduce the noise level.

'Does he show any leadership at all, on any policy?'

'Nooo!'

'Order!'

'Apparently there is nothing better to discuss than floral arrangements. Well, petal, perhaps I can provide you with a botany lesson.'

Messenger was immediately on his feet seeking the call and getting it. 'Madam Speaker, I rise on a point of relevance. The question was about the misuse of taxpayers' funds, which the prime minister ...'

'Order, there is no point of order. I warn the manager of opposition business and ask him to withdraw the inference.'

'What inference?'

'You know very well, and I ask you to withdraw.'

'Please help me, Madam Speaker, I am at a loss to understand the inference you seem to have thought I had made.'

'You know full well what I am referring to, and I ask you to withdraw. Otherwise, I will be forced to deal with you.'

'If it pleases the house, I withdraw any inference the prime minister may be using taxpayers' funds for his own benefit.' Messenger pushed the speaker, and the government backbench erupted. Bruce was immediately on her feet to complain but was waved down by the speaker.

'Order! You will withdraw, unequivocally.'

'I withdraw.' Messenger bowed.

'I call the prime minister.'

Messenger resumed his seat and Harper turned to him, damning his byplay. 'This session is bad enough without you having to antagonise them further.'

'I told you it was a dumb question.'

'Madam Speaker, we have just witnessed the opposition's smears and innuendoes. Not only do they have a dud leader incapable of running a national government, but they also have a henchman, a political thug, to smear and diminish the role of the prime minister. A henchman who will play with language to imply that the highest officeholder in the land would consider defrauding hard-working Australians of their taxes. Mind you,

Madam Speaker, they have not sat on this side of parliament for such a long time, they may have forgotten what it is like to be a respected leader. And I must say, Madam Speaker, they will never be on this side of the house while lightweights like that trumped-up little piece of Hogwarts' refuse they call the member for Gellibrand consider themselves as leadership material.

'Their leadership group is full of flakes and fakes; they are not leaders, they're losers, Madam Speaker.' Gerrard panned across the frontbench with a pointing finger and on cue the opposition politicians erupted, shouting, and pointing back at Gerrard. The prime minister stood back feigning shocked indignation and smiled, waiting for the speaker to bring them to order.

The speaker moved on cue. 'Order! Order! The house will come to order.'

Many respected her position and stopped shouting, but others were so fired up by the prime minister's comments that they ignored her plea. The frontbench didn't respond, disheartened by the verbal attack they had endured, or perhaps agreeing with the prime minister that they were weak on leadership.

The government members sat silent, knowing it was best to stay quiet during such dramatic moments in question time so the media grabs would be all about opposition rowdiness. Gerrard often performed this routine when an election was in the offing so that he could portray the opposition as unworthy to lead the country.

'Order, the prime minister will be heard in silence.'

'Thank you, Madam Speaker. No amount of discipline can be used to contain the wild beasts in the opposition. They do not deserve to be in this place working with my government for the betterment of the Australian people.' Gerrard was not letting up and the opposition members again broke out in a chorus of shouting as Messenger again sought the call.

'The prime minister will resume his seat.'

'Go on, sit down.' Messenger waved Gerrard down.

'The manager of opposition business on a point of order?'

'Yes please, Madam Speaker.'

'Your point is? Make it swift.'

'Relevance, Madam Speaker. While it is a privilege to listen to the prime minister's rhetorical flourishes, none of them is relevant, and I ask you to either bring him to order or sit him down.' Messenger had rousing support from his backbench.

'The prime minister will remain relevant to the question.'

'My apologies, Madam Speaker,' Gerrard nodded to Bagshaw. 'As I was saying, they are not beasts. Even beasts are worthy of respect.' The opposition erupted again. Messenger was on his feet seeking the call, and Gerrard was enjoying himself.

'Speaker, Madam Speaker.'

Bagshaw looked at Messenger and waved him away. He didn't move and called her again. Harper tugged at Messenger's jacket encouraging him to sit. Messenger ignored him.

'The prime minister will resume his seat. The manager of opposition business is seeking the call. I warn the member against any more spurious points of order.'

'Madam Speaker, relevance, I—'

'There is no point of order, the prime minister.'

Harper muttered to Messenger, imploring him to sit, and he

eventually obeyed his leader, as Gerrard continued the assault. Messenger glanced at the press gallery high above the speaker's chair hoping for a familiar face among the hundred seats but could not see one.

Gerrard chided the opposition and Harper for another few minutes, while Messenger and his colleagues sat in stony silence taking it all. Suddenly, Gerrard sat down, and no-one knew whether he had answered the question or not. Certainly, no-one in the opposition cared – they just wanted him to stop.

'The member for Richmond.'

While the government member asked a question of the education minister Meredith Bruce about government funding for preschool children, Gerrard went to his advisers in their box to speak with Miles Fisher. 'I think we should go for the jugular now, what do you reckon?' he said.

'Give it a couple more questions and allow us to ask it, so it gives you greater credibility. I'll give it to Michael to ask.'

'Are you sure? They look a little sore and sorry right now.'

'Let them ask two more, bat them away quickly, and let us ask the climate change question and then your question so that you can reveal your coup de grace. The media should be ready for it by then.'

'You're a good man, Miles.' Gerrard took his advice.

As he returned to his place he stopped at the speaker's elbow and leaned in. 'Is there any chance you can come to my suite after question time? I feel a little aroused and I need you,' Gerrard whispered and moved on with a leer. The speaker did not respond other than to nod, but she looked a little flushed and distracted.

Messenger was rostered on for the next opposition question about road transport, and began to mull it over, trying to think of a verbal whack he could deliver the government, yet the anonymous note still lingered in his mind.

Meredith Bruce finished her answer and Messenger sprang to his feet seeking the call from the speaker, which he received. He took his place at the despatch box shuffling his papers, looking for the question.

'My question is to the prime minister.' Messenger paused for a moment to think through his options.

'Come on son, what's keeping you?' Gerrard smiled at Messenger's hesitation.

'Ask your question.' Bagshaw directed.

'Yes, thank you, Madam Speaker.' Messenger shuffled his papers and took the question he had covertly received. 'Can the prime minister confirm if he is required to add to the parliamentary register of members' interests, and if so, under what circumstances is he required to do so?'

The chamber fell silent for a moment as politicians tried to grasp the relevance and intent of the question.

The speaker looked to Gerrard who quickly drew his finger across his neck on the pretext of adjusting his collar to indicate she should reject the question.

'Before I call the prime minister, I will seek advice.' The speaker leaned forward in her chair and beckoned the clerk to come forward. Gordon moved promptly to her side, and they whispered together.

'What's this about, Gordon? Is it relevant and within practice?'

'Yes, it could be interpreted so – the parliamentary register of interests is a matter for the parliament – but it is not government business, so it is up to you to allow it.' Gordon stepped away and resumed his seat.

The speaker moved further forward in her seat to address the chamber. 'The question goes to the issue of personal interests and the parliamentary register of members' interests which is publicly accessible to those who may be interested in such things and has nothing to do with the issue of government. I rule the question out of order.'

Messenger was quickly back at the despatch box, and the chamber quietened.

'On indulgence and addressing your ruling, Madam Speaker. Many times, in its history the parliament has sought information from particular members about gifts they have received and investments they may have. This is no different. It is a question of clarification about whether the prime minister is required under parliamentary rules to add information to the parliamentary register of members' interests prior to the house rising later this week, and if so, for what reason he is required to do so, as is required of all members of this parliament.'

Bruce came quickly back to the despatch box.

'In response to the honourable member's comments, can I

add that it is not common practice to discuss the personal interests of members, and we agree with your ruling.'

'I have already ruled on this matter; the question is out of order. The member for Banks.'

'Madam Speaker, can I speak to your ruling?' Messenger asked.

'No, I have already ruled.'

'Can I seek leave to move a motion of dissent in your ruling?'

'The member for Gellibrand would know there has been a bipartisan agreement to not move motions of the type he is suggesting, so leave is not granted.'

'On a point of order, Madam Speaker, I wish to move a motion and the standing orders of this parliament allow for motions to be moved.'

'The member will realise that his protestations have been recorded in Hansard and his rejection of my ruling will be recorded formally within this discussion. We are not proceeding with any further debate on this matter, and I call the member for Banks to ask her question.'

Messenger withdrew and sought a brief huddled whispered consultation with the leadership group.

'What the hell was that all about?' Messenger asked, perplexed. 'A simple question got that reaction from the speaker!'

'Why are you asking it anyway?' hissed Harper. 'You're supposed to keep to tactics for chrissakes.'

'Got him in the goolies though, didn't it?' Campbell said, quite chuffed. 'I asked it because it was given to me,' Messenger responded. 'He obviously didn't like it.'

'At least it stopped his rants,' Stanley said.

'That may be so, but while I am leader, we stick to the plan. Agreed?'

The environment minister was finishing her answer about the cost of relocation of wind turbines and the impact on the government's climate change policy, but before Stanley could get to the despatch box to ask his rostered question, Gerrard stood at the despatch box microphone.

'I ask that all further questions be placed on the notice paper.' This immediately closed question time and Gerrard stormed from the chamber like a man on a mission.

The opposition sat momentarily stunned by the prime minister's response. They couldn't understand what had just happened in the chamber and no-one else watching did either. The parliament slowly returned to itself, and members sauntered from the chamber leaving Meredith Bruce tabling papers, including the program for Thursday's notice paper. It was then the turn of the clerk to table petitions. Gordon read out various petitions from member constituents concerned about a particular local issue – having petitions signed by hordes of citizens and subsequently ignored by everyone was an integral part of the political process.

As Gordon read the petitions robotically, as he had done for many years, he pondered his question and the subsequent reaction from the prime minister in closing down further questions. His list now took on deeper meaning as he added Gerrard's reaction to it.

# CHAPTER 15

**WEDNESDAY 2.55 PM**

'What was all that about?' Wilson Campbell asked the leadership group as they came together for a quick debrief in the opposition members' lounge outside the chamber. 'Gerrard was unbelievably confrontational today.'

'We were smashed, quite frankly,' Messenger said.

'Don't overstate it,' said Harper. 'Sure, he was over the top, but the media understands the difficulty we have.'

'You are kidding me, James, aren't you?' Messenger said. 'We were dreadful in there. We were smashed, and I suspect some folks, especially those in the media, are beginning to believe his rubbish.'

'Ease up, Bart.' Stanley tried to change the tone and focus.

'Hey, what twigged Gerrard? He certainly didn't like the disclosure question. How come you asked it, Bart?'

'I received an anonymous note from someone in the chamber soon after we started. I assume it was from the government – who else would send me such information? He was a little touchy on the issue though, wasn't he?'

'It means nothing,' said Harper, moving away from the group and ending the conversation. 'I'll be in my office.' The others lingered, watching him go.

'He's a little bruised, I suspect.' Stanley observed. 'He needs some downtime, alone.'

'If we keep him as leader, we'll have more downtime than we can handle,' said Hughes after a short pause. 'He should not have agreed to that stupid no-vote deal with Gerrard. We could have moved a motion, and we should have done it, no matter what the deal is with the government.'

'I'm with you, Hughsie,' Campbell said. 'Shove it up 'em, I say.'

'It doesn't matter, we only have one day left,' Stanley sighed.

'Yes, it does matter,' objected Hughes. 'We have an opportunity to push for a general election, not just the by-elections in February.'

'How do you mean?' Campbell asked.

'If we move a no-confidence motion against Gerrard, either today or tomorrow, and we win the vote, then there's no option other than to prorogue the parliament,' Hughes said. 'We then run a general election instead of the by-elections, and campaign about overturning all the changes Gerrard has made in the last few years. We beat them in an election, and we take government, finally.'

'Sounds great, Chris, but I suspect it might be too much for us to get organised in a day,' Stanley added. 'Jimmy wouldn't agree to it anyway.'

'We don't need him,' Messenger said. 'Maybe it's a little harsh to think about it right now, but it's an option we may have to consider at some point. Gerrard could be right; we may never win an election under the current leadership.'

No-one spoke as the significance of Messenger's suggestion slowly sank in.

'It's not something we should be talking about,' Stanley said finally, moving off.

'Not yet,' said Hughes. 'Let's chat about it another time.'

'What say we have dinner together and discuss tomorrow's tactics, Bart?' Stanley said. 'What about you, Willy, want to join us? Let's meet at the Wild Duck, I feel like a Chinese feed.'

'Count me in,' said Campbell. 'I love that place.'

They moved off, and Messenger headed for a coffee, texting Anita as he walked, asking her to join him.

Already here. Will wait for you.

'How come you weren't at question time?' Messenger said as he sat down with his latte. 'Are you working on something more important?' He shook sugar into his glass, stirred, and licked the froth from the spoon.

Anita smiled. 'As I understand it, you were smashed anyway.'

'Yeah. Gerrard had his knife out and wanted our blood today. I suspect he may have drawn a drop or two.'

'What does that mean?'

'He may end up with Harper's scalp on his belt.'

'What?!' Anita checked herself at once, regretting her outburst. Leaning forward she whispered, 'What are you saying?'

'We won't win government while Harper is leader. I think it's time for him to go – by the way, this is off the record.' Messenger trusted Anita, but not fully – she was a political journalist after all. 'Have you had much feedback since your retirement story?'

'You can't change the subject like that, Bart, and expect to fob me off. What are you planning?'

'Nothing, I can absolutely guarantee you that. I have a dinner later tonight to talk about the by-elections. We have nothing else planned, I promise.'

Anita sat quietly, looking at Barton, who stared into his coffee to avoid her gaze, knowing she wanted more information from him.

'Anita, it's been a stressful few days, and I suspect we are jumping at shadows at the moment.' Messenger tried to ease the tension. 'Gerrard got us today, and it just highlighted the leader's weaknesses, that's all.'

She continued to study Bart and said finally, 'Strangely, no-one has called me about the resignation piece.' Now Anita wanted to change the subject. 'But did you know the prime minister's wife is off to Zurich tomorrow?'

This information meant nothing to Messenger. 'You mentioned that before, so what?'

'Well, my cynical friend, my spy told me to follow the money, and the fact that the prime minister's wife is off to the private money capital of the world must mean something.'

'What money?'

'That's my problem at the moment. I don't know what money there is floating about to take advantage of unless there's something going on with the funding for the immigration centres.'

'The government have deferred any consideration of that money until February next year, after the by-elections. Anyway, it's been approved by our side, so it really is no big deal. We'll need to scrutinise the legislation when it finally makes an appearance to make sure the funds are being dispersed properly.' Messenger seemed uninterested in Anita's story. 'If you want to follow a conspiracy, why not question Gerrard over his response to a question today.'

'I thought he did you over?'

'He did, but he cut off question time when he was well and truly kicking us in the head.' Messenger sipped his coffee. 'I asked him about being required to add to his member's interests' disclosure.'

'Why would that worry him?'

'It normally wouldn't – we all have to do it. What was strange though, was that I was sent a note by someone from the other side to ask him the question, and once I did, he shut down questions.'

'Who sent you the note?' Anita scribbled something in her notebook.

'I don't know.'

'Interesting a government member would think that question was important enough to ask the prime minister, and then get you to ask it. I wonder who it could be?'

'You really are seeing conspiracy in every little thing these days, aren't you? How's your story going for you?'

'Since you've asked, let me tell you what I know.' Anita was keen to share. 'I've learnt the Indonesians have started work on the first immigration centre on Ambon. This is not unusual, but what is strange is that they haven't got the money from the Australian government yet.'

'Yeah, we asked a question about that.'

'What was the response?' Anita again scribbled notes.

'They didn't care, and said the Indonesians could do whatever they wanted,' Messenger said. 'Gerrard implied it was an act of goodwill.'

'They have never started anything in the past without funding.' Anita took a mouthful of coffee. 'Indeed, the president said at the very start of negotiations he would not touch a blade of grass until he received the money or legislation was passed guaranteeing prescribed payments, something to do with capital investment and cash flow.'

'Yet he starts capital works last Sunday without any money. Go figure.' Messenger drained his coffee.

'Do you think he already has the money?'

'No,' Messenger laughed. 'They're not likely to have any funds until at least February. The house is not due to approve it until we return next year.'

'Unless he's on a promise, it seems to me they're acting as if they already have it,' Anita said.

'You know the Indonesians. When it comes to money, never stand between them and a bag of cash.'

'You can't say that.'

'Why?'

'It's racist and out of character for you to say such a thing.'

Messenger dropped his head, a little embarrassed. 'Sorry, I meant it as a joke.'

The silence between them was uncomfortable.

'What normally needs to go on a member's disclosure?' Anita finally asked.

'Literally anything that comes our way. We have to list all gifts, like tickets to the football, or the theatre,' Messenger replied. 'We have to immediately list any changes to our financial position, all our bank accounts, even credit cards. It's so cumbersome to keep track of it all, and I'm not sure why they need the details.'

'So, if you open a bank account, you need to disclose.'

'Yeah, sure. Absolutely.'

'If you were married, and your wife or children opened an account?'

'Yep, it all has to be declared, sometimes beforehand.'

'Even if they were in Switzerland?' Anita flirted with the idea.

Messenger's phone buzzed a message.

PM is working on a scheme.

'Do you recognise this number?' He showed Anita his phone,

slightly baffled by the message. 'Now someone else seems to be pushing a conspiracy.'

Anita squinted at the number on the screen. 'No. What does it say?'

'It suggests the prime minister is up to something.'

Gordon O'Brien had been waiting for more than twenty minutes in the speaker's office for her return. He'd been told she'd slipped out to visit the prime minister after question time and would return shortly. He gave up waiting for her after thirty minutes and returned to his office, having instructed Bagshaw's staff to call him when she returned.

He was frustrated by the behaviour and events in question time and wondered about the prime minister's reaction to the question he had sent Messenger. He took out the phone George Nikolaos had dropped off earlier and contemplated it. After a few moments, he sat forward and took his official phone from his pocket and searched his contact list, finding the number he was searching for, and began tapping a message into the new phone. He pushed send, taking the first step on a regrettable journey he hoped he would not have to finish.

PM is working on a scheme.

It was another ninety minutes before Gordon was advised the

speaker had returned, so he immediately walked to her office to speak to her in person, rather than use the phone.

'Speaker, I wish to counsel you on a most serious breach of protocol in question time today.'

'What's the problem, Gordon? It's all politics, no-one cares.'

'I do.'

'Well, you only have one day left, so I suspect no-one really cares what you think.'

Gordon watched Bagshaw reach for her glass of water. She almost toppled from her chair. 'Are you drunk?'

'I may have had a glass of wine at lunch, but of course I am not drunk. What are you suggesting?'

'I am suggesting, Madam Speaker, that you do your job and manage the parliament as it should be managed, and not allow the prime minister to bully you as he did today.'

Bagshaw smiled. 'I can assure you; the prime minister is not bullying me. In fact, we have been meeting together just now to discuss arrangements for tomorrow's adjournment of parliament.'

'Although we only have one day remaining, you must remain impartial, especially if it gets challenging in the chamber as it did today.'

'How do you mean?'

'It is important that the parliament and its processes are not compromised.' Gordon hesitated. 'I remain suspicious that there may be a challenge to the parliament's protocols and perhaps your authority tomorrow. It is vital you protect the dignity of the parliament.'

'I will do the right thing, and all will be as I determine,' Bagshaw said, then lowering her voice she added in a menacing tone, 'You must remember, Gordon, I am speaker, and you are the clerk, therefore you will take my direction at all times, not the other way around.'

'Speaker, it is my role to protect the parliament, and the institution that provides a voice for the people of Australia.' Gordon stood before her. 'The parliament is not owned by the government, nor by you, and certainly not by the prime minister. I will do what I can to do my duty and ensure that there is no breach to the standing orders.'

'Are you threatening me, Gordon?'

'Not at all. I am advising you as I am obliged to do.' Gordon straightened and stiffened. 'So, I am formally advising you, I will do my duty.'

'Goodbye, Gordon.' Bagshaw sat back in her chair and waved him away.

Gordon stood before her desk, thinking through what to do. Without another word he turned and marched from the office, leaving the door open and gliding past staff without returning the usual pleasantries.

'Get me the prime minister!' The speaker's voice followed him.

Gordon strode to his office, keen to think further about his list. The speaker seemed ignorant of any government plan other than the need to protect her friend, the PM. He knew he was missing an important piece of the puzzle and needed to talk with his colleague.

'Marjorie, could you see if Nigel Nelson is available for a phone call, please, in, say, ten minutes?'

'Sure, Gordon, what's up?'

Gordon merely shook his head and walked into his office. He sat down, flicked open his pad, pulled his list out from his jacket pocket and began considering the information he already had. He doodled as he thought through his information:

*Follow the money.*
*Zurich.*
*Member disclosure.*

'What's the matter, Zara?' Gerrard asked the speaker.

'Don't fuck with me, Andy. When I ring, it's normally urgent. I don't expect to be left waiting for twenty minutes.'

'Ease up, Zara. What's the matter?'

'O'Brien has just threatened me.' Bagshaw was pacing her office.

'What did the prick want?'

'He's demanded I follow protocol and not disrupt the process of the parliament, reminding me my role is to stay impartial. Me!'

'So what? He only has a day left, don't worry about him,' Gerrard soothed her. 'We only have a day left to get it done, and then he's gone forever.'

'What do you mean?'

Gerrard quickly switched course, 'Oh, I mean, we only have a day left before we rise for Christmas, that's all.'

'Will it be okay tomorrow? Are you sure it's okay to be doing what we're planning to do with the amendments to the stimulus package?'

'Zara, relax.' Gerrard didn't need her getting nervous. 'Everything is fine. We're not breaking any rules. Just ensure O'Brien doesn't become a problem in the process tomorrow.'

'Can I come and see you later?'

'Not tonight. I'm a little busy right now, I still need to run a government.'

'Yes, of course. I'll see you tomorrow then.'

'Take care.' Gerrard replaced the receiver, raised his glass of brandy, and said, 'Now, where were we?'

'You were about to offer me the role of deputy prime minister when the parliament resumes next year,' Meredith Bruce smiled.

'You really are ambitious, aren't you? All in good time, gorgeous. Here, have another drink.'

---

'Pete, can I come and see you?' Messenger was seeking counsel. 'I have a couple of theories I want to run past you.'

'I'm just having a quiet drink with Christopher, so come on over.'

Messenger had spent the hours since question time reflecting on Anita's story, and the weird text he had received from the unknown source. He needed help with his scheme, and Stanley was his mentor and role model. He was confident Stanley would help him get to the bottom of whatever was going on.

Peter Stanley was from Perth, holding the seat of Curtin for almost thirty years. He had seen off five attempts to oust him through the preselection process, and he always had the numbers. He was fond of telling his colleagues that politics is nothing but arithmetic, and to be a long-serving politician you only needed one skill: how to count.

'Pete, I don't want to be an alarmist, but I suspect we could have a serious political issue before us.' Messenger began to raise his concerns once he was seated with a glass of beer in hand.

'Do tell, old boy.'

'Everyone loves a political conspiracy, so share, old son,' added Hughes.

'I think the prime minister is about to announce his retirement, and he could be building a retirement nest egg with government funds.'

The older politicians continued to gaze at Messenger without changing their expressions, and he began to feel uneasy. 'Gentlemen, I hope one day to master your admirable control of facial expression, but in the meantime, do you have nothing to say?'

The politicians glanced at each other and then came back at Messenger, who continued, 'I'm not sure how, or when, he proposes to do it, but I suspect it may have something to do with the bill coming through the senate tonight and tomorrow's sitting day. There are just too many irregular coincidences.'

'The stimulus package?' asked Hughes. 'What do you think is going to happen?'

'I don't know exactly, but I suspect the prime minister is crafting a retirement package.'

'Another beer, Chris?' Stanley asked nonchalantly, after a short period of silence.

'I wouldn't say no,' Hughes said as Stanley went to his bar fridge and returned, handing him a can. The silence lengthened, broken only by the gas release from two beer cans being opened.

'Nothing? You listen to what could potentially be a huge political announcement and you leave me hanging?' Messenger said, frustrated.

'It's an interesting idea,' Stanley finally offered.

'Yes, interesting,' agreed Hughes.

'What have you got to support this interesting idea?' Stanley asked.

'I have a text message.'

'Oh, a text message. Who from?' asked Hughes.

'I don't know.' Messenger began to understand his colleagues' lack of enthusiasm for the proposition.

'You don't know who sent you the message?'

'What did it say?' asked Hughes.

'It suggested the PM is working on a scheme.'

The three politicians sipped their beer in silence.

'You know, of course, that ripping off money from the government is fraud,' Hughes finally said. 'So, you can only do it fraudulently.'

'Your point is?' Messenger had no idea where the conversation was going.

'Just trying to help with your phraseology, son.'

'What evidence other than the text do you have?' Stanley asked.

'Look, I know this sounds... umm... unlikely, but it's the only conclusion I can draw,' Messenger was not convincing. 'I wanted your view before going to see the leader to raise it with him.'

'What have you got?' persisted Stanley.

'Just follow me on this one boys, please. Okay, we have a destabilised parliament, but the opposition has the majority.' Messenger counted off on his fingers. 'We have the agreement for no divisions forced upon us by the prime minister, which protects the government.'

'That was a mistake right there,' said Hughes.

'We have deferred legislation for the Indonesian money until next year yet, get this, they started construction last Sunday.' Messenger took a swig of his beer. 'We have the Appropriation Bill for the stimulus package getting pushed through the parliament and now delayed in committee in the senate for some unknown reason. We have the prime minister shutting down question time today, when he was smashing us, after my question on his member's interests.'

'This is not evidence,' Stanley said, 'just observations. I would have expected more from a smart kid like you.'

'No wait, there's more. We have Margaret Gerrard travelling to Zurich tomorrow – why? We have no media from the prime minister's office on the Hancock story about his rumoured retirement. We have the cancellation of all leave and pairs...'

'So what?' asked Hughes.

'Why cancel leave and pairs if we are required to not take a vote? He knows we can't call for a division, so why does he need the numbers in the house? Why is he insisting on all his team being in attendance unless he is going to retire, sensationally announcing it to the parliament where his colleagues will swamp him with kudos?'

'So, you reckon he's going to retire, skimming some money to take with him?' said Stanley.

'He can't get any money from the Appropriation Bill, it's fully allocated to the punters,' Hughes said. 'Where is he getting this so-called fraudulent money from?'

'I reckon he's getting it from the Indonesians,' Messenger said.

'That's crap, son. No way Gerrard would do that,' Stanley chided.

'How?' asked Hughes. 'How do you reckon he'll get the money from them, when we haven't even seen any legislation yet? They even stopped their first payment legislation from last week, so how would he do it?'

# CHAPTER 16

**WEDNESDAY 5.15 PM**

'Nigel, got time for a catch-up?'

'Sure, Gobby, when and where?' Nelson knew his friend didn't like informality and enjoyed stirring him up.

'I don't want to go anywhere crowded, and I'd rather not meet at your office.'

'Why the mystery, old friend? What's going on?'

'I need to talk to you about a few things, a few concerns I have about parliamentary process.'

'I'll meet you in the meditation room.'

'I'd rather get out of the parliament. Can you get out for an hour or so?'

'Not sure when we are finishing tonight, but now would be good.'

'Okay, see you soon out front, I'll pick you up.' Gordon took pleasure in his younger colleague's fellowship sometimes. At other times, it was a bit too much. Nigel drank heavily, and when he did, he grew loud and indiscreet and often disclosed things he later regretted. He'd been known to pass judgement on many senators publicly over the years, which created the occasional public-relations problem for his department.

Gordon didn't have to wait too long outside the senate entrance before Nelson jumped into the Ford. Twenty minutes later they had ordered and were halfway through their lavish cocktails as they waited for tapas to help soothe their early evening hunger, resigned to the idea of having a very late dinner.

'What's troubling you, Gobby? You look very stiff and serious this evening.'

'I am really concerned about what's going on in the house,' Gordon said.

'Shame, man. Tell me all about it.'

'Over the last few days, I have made a list of some extraordinary circumstances, which by themselves mean absolutely nothing, but together could mean something quite serious.'

'Like what?'

'Well, for example, why has the Appropriation Bill been deferred to a senate committee, with a vote not due until later this evening?'

'Why should that be an issue?'

'That's the point, by itself it means nothing. Yet, why vote in the senate after the house has adjourned?'

'Is that it?' Nelson drained his glass and called the waiter for another. 'Is that what's upsetting you, just a few days before you retire?'

Gordon drew his list from his jacket. 'Why is the first lady going to Zurich tomorrow?'

'Skiing?'

'Why has foreign affairs asked that a member add an account to the members' interests before they allow an international account to be opened?'

'Who has been required to do that?'

'I don't have that information, but the prime minister's office rang about the register yesterday.'

'Perhaps, if it's for the prime minister, he wants to add a gift he received from the president of Indonesia during his visit last week.'

'Yes, of course, I didn't think of that.' Gordon now felt a little silly. 'As I said, on their own, they mean absolutely nothing, but together they are an enigma.'

'And what code do you see, Gordon?' Nelson chuckled at his joke. When he got no response from Gordon he added. 'Enigma code, get it?'

'I'm not in the mood for jokes right now, Nige.'

'You never are, that's the whole point. Perhaps you should lighten up.'

The tapas arrived, Italian sausage in one dish and sautéed prawns in the other, and the friends prepared to eat. Nelson picked up a prawn by the tail and bit off the peeled flesh. 'Christ, that's hot.'

'I think the prime minister is planning something. I'm not sure what, but I can feel it.'

Nelson rolled the scorching prawn about his mouth, sucking in air. 'You what?'

'Mind you, I can't prove a thing, and I admit, nothing seems out of place.' Gordon eyed the sausage. 'I know it sounds crazy, but I think Gerrard is doing a dubious deal with the Indonesians and the immigration detention funding.'

'That's not due until February. Why the concern now?'

'That's what I don't understand.'

'These are serious accusations, my old mate. Are you sure you want to raise them?'

'Last Friday, the Indonesian money was combined with the stimulus legislation that's before the senate right now. I talked to Robert in the drafting office, and he confirmed he was asked to consolidate it. Now he is conveniently incommunicado and the money he drafted into the bill has strangely been dropped from the legislation.'

'So, you think they're going to try and add an amendment to the legislation when it comes back from the senate?' Nigel tried another prawn, this time blowing on it first.

'That doesn't make sense either because if they were able to do that, then it would need to go back to the senate again for approval.' Gordon fiddled with his fork. 'Unless they amend it first in the senate.'

'It seems to me you're trying to see something that just isn't there,' said Nigel, biting off the prawn tail and dropping it on the plate.

'There are just too many strange circumstances ...'

'Are you sure you want to rake up trouble, Gordon, when you're out of here in a few days? The PM wouldn't be trying to shaft the government now, would he?'

'That's why I wanted to talk to you.' O'Brien scooped up some sausage and pushed it into his mouth.

'Have you spoken to anyone else?' Nelson said.

'No, of course not.' Gordon kept chewing. 'This is only my thinking, I have no evidence to support it, I'm just guessing at this stage.'

'You had better be careful who you talk to, or this could come back and bite you – in a big, big way,' Nelson said, his mouth full of food.

'I have sent a note to a journalist with a cabinet minute file, but there has been no action from her other than a story she wrote about Gerrard retiring.'

'Is that likely?'

'Not with his wife leaving for overseas on the same day, no, I wouldn't have thought so.'

'Anybody else?'

'Well, I may be encouraging a politician.'

'Sneaky little bugger, getting others to do your work for you.'

'Look, Nigel, something is going on, I can feel it. There are just too many strange coincidences happening. I know I could be imagining things, but I remain concerned and, as I said, I have this strange feeling. My intuition is suggesting something unethical is underway and when I listen to it, I am hardly ever wrong.'

'Mate, you need to stop thinking about Gerrard, and get a life. You'll have a life from the end of the week – hallelujah.'

'This has nothing to do with Gerrard,' Gordon snapped. 'I mean it has, but it has nothing to do with the way he has treated me in the past.'

'I think there may be a possibility you're being blinkered on this, ol' son.'

Gordon began to doubt himself. 'I know he wanted that money in the Appropriation Bill, I just know it. Robert suddenly going on leave without telling us, doesn't that seem strange to you?'

'Maybe it wasn't sudden and it's just a coincidence.'

'I approve all leave, you know that, and I never got an application from him. I tried his phone, but it's switched off.'

'Well, he's on holiday after all.'

Gordon sipped at his drink. 'I know something's up, but I just can't prove it.'

'You have nothing to worry about, the bill doesn't have the immigration money in it.'

'Would it make a difference to your opinion if it did?'

'It could. I'm not saying it would, but if the money was in the current legislation, then you could have a valid point.'

'Why has Gerrard allowed extra time for it when it comes back to the house tomorrow?'

'Look, I don't know Gordon, maybe he wants to do a speech about you, you are retiring after all.' Nelson was losing patience with his friend and indicated to the waiter he wanted another drink. 'Knowing him, he'll use the occasion to talk about how good his government has been and why the punters should be grateful to get their Christmas bonus.'

'Just imagine, for a moment, I am right. What could be done?' Gordon asked idly.

'Nothing.' Nelson had finished his food and was picking at his teeth.

'The funding couldn't be delayed?'

'Look, the only way to stop money going out of the country would be to stop the appropriation when the legislation hits the parliament. Where's the waiter?' Nigel was getting restless. 'Mind you, we don't have to worry about that, do we? Because the current bill before the senate hasn't got the Indonesian money in it.' Nigel said almost sarcastically. 'So, stop worrying about nothing and let's have some coffee. I need to get back to the parliament.'

Gordon was now thinking about potential delaying options, should he need to act.

---

The bells adjourning the house for the evening were ringing when James Harper took a call from Peter Stanley and was told the leadership group wanted to meet with him. They wanted to discuss 'matters of concern'. The very fact that Stanley had rung was in itself concerning, as he'd never rung in the past. Stanley and Harper were friends, and Peter had his full confidence. Harper relied on him for advice and to protect his numbers in the party room, but when a group of politicians established a delegation to visit their leader, then there was always potential for trouble.

Being the alternate prime minister was a burden Harper struggled to carry. Leadership can be lonely, especially in politics where there are few friends, only colleagues – self-interested colleagues who could change their view on any subject at any time to suit themselves and could never be trusted.

'James, thanks for agreeing to see us,' Stanley walked in with a smile, trying to alleviate the tension he immediately felt in Harper's stiff posture. 'We have a proposition for you.'

'Take a seat, boys. How can I help you?' Harper ignored a drinks offer – it was not the time for social conviviality when confronted with a leadership group delegation.

'Barton here has an idea that the prime minister is about to commit fraud on the Australian taxpayer.' Stanley wasted no time and gestured to Messenger to take up the story.

'Jim, I've had a number of things come to me throughout today that could indicate the prime minister is about to announce his retirement and is possibly doing a deal with Indonesia for a pension payout.' Messenger was nervous delivering his pitch, given the evidence was so flimsy.

'You have got to be kidding, right? How does he propose to do that?' Harper sounded incredulous.

'I think he will announce his retirement in the house tomorrow, and I suspect he has done a deal with the president of Indonesia. That's why we're putting the entire amount for the immigration centres into new legislation next year, rather than the agreed four payments.'

'So, he is retiring tomorrow and getting paid by the Indonesians in February for monies that aren't in any form of legislation before the house?'

'I know that sounds weird, but I have thought he could be using the Appropriation Bill for the stimulus package, and he may well add money to it tomorrow when it comes back into the house.'

'That's crap, he would never do it.' Harper couldn't believe what he was hearing.

'Listen to the boy, Jimmy, please,' Stanley advised.

'Okay, but this better be good.' Harper sat back in his chair and relaxed a little; it wasn't the discussion about leadership he had been expecting all afternoon.

Messenger then set out his fraud theory, covering the information as he knew it, and the links to the various other pieces of news, including the anonymous text message, which he showed to his colleagues. None of them recognised the number.

'By themselves they mean nothing, but together they are more meaningful, don't you think?' Messenger asked.

'And what would you like me to do about it?' Harper asked.

'Go to the media?' Messenger suggested with a grimace.

'Do I look stupid to you?' Harper was getting annoyed. 'Do I?' Messenger gave a slight shrug of the shoulders, so he continued. 'You come in here with an unbelievably harebrained idea, and you expect me to believe that the prime minister of Australia is about to commit fraud in an alliance with the president of Indonesia, and you want me to go to the media? You have got to be kidding me.'

'We just wanted to get your view on it; there's no need to get snarky.' Hughes came in to save Messenger.

Harper stood and began pacing behind his desk. 'You think the prime minister of Australia and the Indonesian president are criminals, and you want me to go on national television to expose them, is that right?'

'Jim, calm down,' Stanley counselled.

'Calm down?' Harper stopped pacing. 'Calm down? Let's see, I am forced to sign an agreement not to cause any dissent within a parliament in which we hold a majority, I am pilloried in the media for doing it, my party in Queensland have suggested I lose my preselection, such is the respect I have in my own fucking home state. I then get humiliated in the parliament and can't do a thing about it, and journalists are already predicting I'll lose the leadership after the by-elections if we don't win, and now I'm presented with this theory about the prime minister ripping off the country because one of you received a text, and you want me to calm down?' Harper had rested his fists on his desk and leaned into his colleagues. 'You want me to go to the media and accuse the most popular prime minister for the last fifty years of being a thief, without one whiff of evidence, and you want me to calm down?'

'Yes, I do.' Stanley said quietly.

'Just say for one daft moment that I agree with your dumb analysis and the PM is ripping off the country, what the fuck do you think I should do about it?'

'Vote it down,' Hughes said.

'Vote it down? Vote it down?' Harper was winding himself

up again. 'How do you expect me to vote it down when we have signed an agreement with the government, which is virtually in caretaker mode until the elections, and which the fucking governor-general witnessed for chrissake? We cannot vote anything down.'

'We don't need to keep to it,' Stanley said.

Harper was surprised by his friend's view. 'There is just one thing missing from your unbelievable plan.'

'What's that?' asked Messenger.

'Where is he getting the money from?'

'The Indonesians.'

'The Indonesian money is not in the fucking parliament until February, you moron!'

'And, if it were?' asked Stanley.

'We still wouldn't vote it down, and I'll tell you why.' Harper straightened up. 'We have already agreed to the funds being released to the Indonesians, and if they put it into the stimulus package and we vote it down, what the hell do you think will happen?' The group remained silent. 'No ideas? We vote down the Christmas money for all Australians, and if we do that then we are fucked.'

'That's why he's going to do it,' Messenger said.

'Bullshit!'

'Come on, we're wasting our time.' Hughes got up and left. Messenger followed, while Stanley lingered.

Harper sat down and put his head in his hands, giving himself a vigorous massage in an attempt to release the tension knotting up his head and neck.

'Are you okay, Jim?'

'It's been a bad day, and Shirley has received threats over my signing the agreement. I mean threats, Peter!'

'Is she okay?'

'Not really, but she'll get over it. She just wants me home.' Harper took a few deep breaths and looked up at his friend. 'Do you really believe this conspiracy crap?'

'I don't know, but I thought we should talk to you about it. I wouldn't put it past Gerrard to try it on.'

'Maybe that's why he got me to sign that fucking agreement. He's at the top of his game; why would he need to do anything like this?'

'I watched him during the condolences the other day, and he appeared to be very upset. Maybe he thinks it's time to go?' Stanley regarded his friend. 'Money can be a great seductress, and you know very well there's not much in our pension plans any more. Gerrard may just think he's owed something. It's happened before. Maybe there's a retirement project going on we don't know about. Anyway, do you want to join us for dinner?'

'No thanks, mate.'

'Would you like me to stay?'

'No, Pete, you go. Thanks for your support, though.'

---

The others had waited for Stanley in the corridor outside the leader's office. 'He's just under a bit of pressure, that's all,' Stanley said with a shrug as he joined his colleagues.

'Let's go and get pissed,' said Hughes, walking off toward the representatives' entrance where a waiting commonwealth car would take them wherever they wanted to go, just one of their parliamentary perks.

'That was stressful,' Messenger finally offered, as the car ferried them to their favourite Chinese restaurant in Kingston.

'He's under a bit of pressure. His wife has had threats,' Stanley said.

'That's rubbish, he knows what he should be doing,' Hughes interrupted.

'And what's that?' Stanley asked.

'He has to fight Gerrard all the way, all the time, and never give in. He gave in with the signing of that ridiculous agreement.'

'Look, maybe I'm overstating the case against Gerrard,' suggested Messenger.

'Maybe you are,' Stanley said, looking out at the darkened streetscape.

Many politicians preferred the Chairman and Yip in the centre of the city for Chinese, but these MPs thought the Wild Duck in Kingston far superior. When they arrived, Wilson was already waiting for them with a waiter pouring the last of four beers.

'Cheers, queers,' said Campbell, glass raised as they settled at the table. 'Where have you been? What's taken you so long?'

'We stopped by to see the leader,' Stanley said, clinking his glass. 'Oh yeah, what about?'

'His attitude to winning the next election,' said Hughes before taking a good long draught.

'We will never win with him as leader. I keep saying it, but no-one believes me,' Campbell said.

'Wilson, I think you've said it too often for anyone to take you seriously,' said Stanley.

'Have you ordered, Will?' asked Messenger.

'Not yet, let's go the banquet.'

The men laughed and chiacked each other through four rounds of beer, three bottles of wine and a one-for-the-road brandy when Stanley took a call from Joe Anthony, the leader of the opposition in the senate. He asked the others to quieten down so he could hear what Anthony was saying. Once he understood the message, he ended the call and looked at his colleagues.

'What's up, Pete?' Messenger was the first to speak.

'You may have been right.'

'Tell us, will you?' Hughes was losing patience.

'That was Joe. It seems the government have moved an amendment to the Appropriation Bill. They've added the Indonesian money, suggesting to the Greens that it was required before the end of the cyclone season, so they've voted with the government.'

'And those morons bought that?' asked Hughes.

'It seems so. The total spend is now ten billion plus.'

'They can't do that,' Campbell said.

'They just did.' Stanley said.

'When does it go to the vote?' Messenger asked.

'It's already passed, and our boys voted for it.'

'Say what? Why would they do that?' Messenger asked.

'We support it,' Stanley confirmed.

'But that will mean we can't fight it in the house,' Messenger said. 'What a dumb move.'

'Fuck, now what?' Hughes asked.

'Let's get the troops back. We need to discuss this in the party room before tomorrow. Jimmy needs to consider his position,' Stanley said.

Campbell had become focused very quickly. 'I'll call the whip and get him onto it.'

As Messenger left the restaurant, he felt a text buzz on his phone.

Now is the time to act. Vote down the money.

Who is this?

A concerned citizen. Vote it down.

We can't.

Ignore the agreement. Vote it down.

Complex. Leader doesn't agree.

It's fraud.

Can you share evidence?

Messenger slipped his phone back into his jacket pocket as he got into the commonwealth car waiting to take him back to the house. There was no response to his question.

Gerrard had retired to Yarralumla to wait for a call from his man in the senate. It came just after ten, with the news he expected.

'Well done, Kevin. I owe you.'

He replaced the phone and moved to his liquor tray for a solid dram of his favourite Irish whiskey. He splashed it into two glasses and returned to his private lounge, where he made a quick call. 'Congratulations, darling, your plan is in place. I have a whiskey for you, I won't be long.'

He took a swig of his drink and punched in another number; this time international. When he was finally connected, he was pleased to tell his fellow conspirator the news.

'Mr President, your country is now funded for the immigration centres. Now get me my money, and I will pay you yours.' He waited for the response.

'If I have my money by Monday, you will have your commission on Tuesday. Good night, my friend.'

# CHAPTER 17

## WEDNESDAY 10.18 PM

'Gordon? The worst thing that could happen, has happened. You had better take a seat.' Nigel Nelson had phoned his friend as soon as he was out of the senate chamber. 'The senate has amended the Appropriation Bill.'

'You are kidding me.'

'I wish I was, Gobby,' Nigel replied. 'They were about to approve the legislation as it was when the government suddenly moved an amendment to add the Indonesian money we've already spoken about.'

'How much?'

'A little over four billion.'

'The full amount for the entire project?'

'Yes, although a little more was added, some forty million,

explained as additional site costs.' O'Brien said nothing as he lay back in his chair resting his face on his right hand, rocking ever so slightly back and forth, listening. 'Are you there, Gordon?'

'Yes, I'm here.'

'What do you think?'

'I'm not sure I want to think about anything at the moment.' Gordon sat forward, picked up a pen and hovered it over his note pad. 'You know what this means, don't you?'

'The senate overstepped its authority?'

'There's that, but it's much worse than the senate spending taxpayers' funds without any authority to do so.'

'What could be worse than that?'

'It means there will be no parliamentary scrutiny, which might unfortunately mean my conspiracy theory is right.'

'Big call that, Gordon.'

'I know it is, and I feel ashamed even thinking about it, but what else could be happening? There is no need to put this money through while the government is in caretaker mode – where's the scrutiny of the parliament?'

'That's true, but the money was always going to be spent, it was clearly in this year's budget.'

'Yes, but spent over a period of three years, not all in one payment like it is proposed now.'

'The opposition has no issue with it – it's also their policy.'

'Did they vote against it in the senate?'

'No,' Nigel responded, surprising Gordon.

'Then they are ignorant of what could be going on. What a stupid and careless thing to do.'

'They really didn't have any option. If they voted against the bill they would be hurt politically because the punters are now expecting their money from the government before Christmas.'

Gordon dropped his pen and fell back into his chair. 'Greed knows no boundaries when it comes to self-interest.'

'Do you honestly believe the government is doing a job on us?'

'There's just too many coincidences, too many questions.'

'Why would Gerrard want to do it? What's in it for him?' Nigel queried.

'Maybe he has a deal with the Indonesians for some personal benefit, maybe it's money.' Gordon was yet to make a mark on the pad. 'Why is Mrs Gerrard travelling abroad? Why does he want everyone in the parliament tomorrow?'

'Why do you think?'

'Well, if my fantastic conspiracy theory is correct, Gerrard is about to announce his retirement as prime minister and scurry off to some exotic place with funds made possible by the president of Indonesia.'

'Preposterous!' Nelson exploded. 'I would advise you to be very careful who you discuss that ridiculous idea with.'

'I suggested it to Messenger. Now after this amendment, maybe he might finally share the idea with his colleagues and actually do something.'

'What do you expect him to do?'

'Convince his leadership group to vote against it, I suppose.' Gordon did not have high hopes.

'The opposition signed an agreement not to initiate a formal vote, so the money will go through the house tomorrow on voices and that will be that,' Nigel said. 'How can they vote against it in the house when they voted for it in the senate?

'I can't allow this swindle to happen, Nigel,' Gordon whispered, feeling defeated. 'Not on my watch.'

'What can you do?'

'The opposition can block it, and they should. I also provided background to the media.'

'You are a servant of the parliament, Gordon, you can't be playing with the political process like this; it's against everything you stand for.'

'I'm ultimately a servant of the Australian people, and I must protect their democratic institutions by stopping those who would take advantage for their own benefit. If I don't do something about this, then my years here will have been wasted and I will have achieved nothing. I will be nothing.'

'That's a little extreme, Gordon, don't you think? Anything I can do?'

'No.' Gordon paused for a moment. 'Ultimately, it is the speaker who will need to act, so if you could discuss your concerns with the president of the senate, maybe he will speak to her.'

'I don't have any concerns,' Nigel responded forcefully. 'It seems you may be seeing things others do not, and I remain troubled you are sheeting this home to Gerrard virtually on your last day.'

'My attitude toward Gerrard has nothing to do with it,' Gordon snapped

Nigel looked askew. 'Are you sure?' Gordon did not respond.

'He has given you hell over the years, and like a trooper you have stood and taken it all. Are you absolutely sure you are not seeking retribution on him in this unbelievable scheme you seem to have plotted?'

'Maybe.' Gordon closed his eyes and searched for any doubt. 'There is something wrong, I just know it.'

'Have you any evidence *at all*?' Nigel demanded.

Gordon paused as he wrote the word evidence on his pad. 'No, not really.'

'Mate, if I were you, I would let it go,' Nigel counselled. 'Sure, the process of the bill is strange, and yes there are some quirky things happening around the parliament, but these funds for Indonesia have been approved by both sides of the parliament, and now it is just a timing issue, that's all. Let it go.'

'Thanks Nigel, but I can't.' Gordon replaced his handset without saying goodbye, thinking about his friend's advice. He sat doodling on his pad, his head resting on his hand, thinking through possibilities. He reached into his desk drawer and retrieved a phone, punching in a message.

Now is the time to act. Vote down the money.

'Anita? Sorry, did I wake you?' Messenger was keen to share his news. 'You may have stumbled upon something. The senate has amended the money bill.'

'You're kidding me. Oh shit, the paper is already printed!'

'Look, I just rang to let you know we are going into a party meeting. In fact, I'm just walking in now.' Messenger was holding the door open for colleagues as the stragglers wandered in, some looking a bit worse for wear at such late notice, and from perhaps a little too much wine. 'Can I call you later? You may want to know what we decide.'

'Of course. Let me know any news, no matter how late.'

The whips had advised that the party meeting would be convened for midnight. Harper was already at the leader's table at the front of the room, with Wilson Campbell, his deputy, beside him. Senators and members had slowly assembled in their usual places.

As the clock indicated midnight, the leader stood to outline the issues before the meeting.

'Colleagues, tonight in the senate, if you have not already heard, the government, with the support of the Greens, amended the Appropriation Bill to include the budget allocation for the immigration centres in Indonesia, and in accordance with our agreement with the government we did not vote against the amended legislation.' Harper then asked Joe Anthony to explain the process that was followed in the senate earlier.

Senator Anthony stood at his place and explained that the moving of the amendment had come as a total surprise to him. He explained that they used procedural motions to try and gag debate, but the Greens were supporting the government. 'When the motion was finally moved, the Greens supported it, and it took less than five minutes to get it passed. No debate. No questions.' Anthony looked tense and angry. 'When the legislation was called to a final vote, we did not vote against it in accordance with the agreement Jim had signed with the government, but I feel as if we have been set up. The government told me they wanted to move it to committee, but once it was past eight o'clock, their tactics suddenly changed.'

There were no questions of Anthony, but an incredulous ripple of whispering passed through the room among his colleagues.

'We now have to determine what our stance will be on the legislation when it returns to the house tomorrow.' Harper was on his feet. 'As you know, I agreed to allow all legislation through the parliament on the voices without the need for a division.'

'That was a mistake.' A voice, Tilley's, came thundering from the back. A third-generation politician of a northern Queensland rural family who had served the federal and state parliaments for more than ninety years, Bob Tilley III was loud and often rambunctious in his views – and no different from his father or grandfather, or even his highly respected great grandfather. The family's passion and their politics always put the electorate of Kennedy first – stuff the rest of the nation – but Tilley's comment did draw a few nods of agreement, which were not lost on Harper.

'Hindsight is a marvellous thing, junior,' remarked Harper. 'Now we are in a very different political position to the conditions we faced at the start of the week. We have to make a decision to either approve or reject the legislation when it hits the house tomorrow.'

'Why are we doing this so late at night, couldn't we meet in the morning?' asked Charlie Edmunds, the member for Ryan.

As leader of opposition business, Messenger stood to answer the question. 'Tomorrow morning will be too late. I cannot guarantee when the government will bring it on, no matter what the notice paper says.' Messenger paused and looked to Harper. 'And we need to decide what we are planning to do in the parliament so the leader can face the early morning media with confidence.'

'Peter Stanley.' Harper called on his friend to speak first. Hands immediately shot up from all over the room, indicating a wish to speak. Harper noted the names on a pad in order. He would then mark each name either for or against the intention to approve the legislation. The party rarely took a vote among its members on any issue other than leadership positions. It was the leader's prerogative to read the mood of the meeting and decide on behalf of the party. And so, the business of listening to all the members and senators speak began.

'Thank you, leader.' Stanley needed to nail this speech to ensure the room would support Harper. 'Colleagues, at first this news was overwhelming. I cannot understand what compelled the government to pass this legislation. Their haste and timing, ignoring the protocols of the parliament, leads me to think that there is more to this legislation than meets the eye. My first reaction is to vote against it.'

'Hear, hear.' A strong response from the room followed his statement.

'But... with my political strategy hat on, I am wary of the outcome if we do reject the bill.'

'Such as?' Tilley, never silent, demanded.

'If we reject this legislation, we reject the stimulus money, which the punters are expecting for Christmas. We say to the electorate that we don't care about them and their needs. We say to the electorate that we don't want them to have a happy Christmas. We say to the electorate that when it comes to the by-elections in February, we do not care what they think, and we are taking them for granted. If we do that, we say to our supporters that they can wait a few more years before we win government.

'The tragic deaths of our colleagues have placed us in an invidious position. If we retain our own seats and win two of the government's, we can take government without having to face a general election. Is that not an outcome we would want? Colleagues, we are so close, I can smell the scent of victory, and government is the prize.

'But, if we were to vote against this legislation, then I contend we will not win the hearts and minds of those voters who need to change their votes to support us at those by-elections. I suspect we will be relegated to second place once again, and we will have to face Gerrard's sanctimonious pronouncements for two more years. I, for one, do not look forward to that prospect.

'If we are to reject the amended legislation, then let us do it knowing the dire consequences to our support in the electorate. I therefore vote for agreeing to the legislation.' Stanley received enough applause to suggest he had achieved what Harper had asked of him.

'Christopher Hughes,' Harper said as he added more colleagues to the expanding list of speakers.

'Thank you, leader.' Hughes was ready for this opportunity to mount a strong argument to change the dynamics of the party. 'I hate Gerrard. I truly hate him. Hate can be a wasted emotion in politics, but nevertheless, if there is one person that I loathe it is Andrew bloody Gerrard.'

'Hear, hear.'

'I smell a rat. I smell a stinking rat, which means there is something afoot with Gerrard and his band of crooks and we do not yet know the full details. What is even worse, that rat Gerrard has used the death of our friends to put us on the back foot.'

'Hear, hear.'

'I have many questions over this legislation. Why did they deliberately mislead us by taking the funding for the immigration centres out of the legislative program last week? Why then did they sneak it back in during the senate debate away from the scrutiny of a second reading in the house? Why has the senate broken with convention by amending a money bill? Barton Messenger believes there is skullduggery afoot, and I agree with him.

'Barton thinks Gerrard is about to resign and skip the country with funds syphoned off from these Indonesian funds, and I tend to agree with this outrageous idea. I wouldn't put it past Gerrard to have concocted some deal with his mate from Indonesia. Why the secrecy and this manoeuvre in the senate unless there was something going on? Apparently, Margaret Gerrard is off to Zurich in the morning. What for? Is it to do some banking?

'For these reasons alone, we must reject the legislation. I agree with Barton, I think there is double dealing going on and if there is doubt on issues like this, then we must remain true to our liberal beliefs and values. Let us take the hit in the electorate, and vote against this legislation. We cannot be seen to be weak, and now is the time to stand up to the government. We have the numbers, let's use them.'

'Wilson Campbell.'

'Thank you, leader.' Campbell wanted to vote against the legislation but valued his role as deputy leader too much to speak against Harper. 'Colleagues, we must remember the funding for the immigration centres is part of our policy. We have agreed to fund them. We have committed to that policy. Should we be elected to government next February, then our government would continue to fund the centres, so to suggest we now vote against them is just plain silly, and we will be pilloried in the media for this policy backflip.

'The punters are looking forward to their cash handout, especially so close to Christmas, and they will punish us everywhere if we do not allow them their money – not just at the by-elections. I can tell you this; they will never forget it or forgive us. We may never see the government benches again for at least another election cycle, maybe more, if we reject this bill.

'I hate Gerrard, but I am also pragmatic. We have agreed to the Indonesian funding, the punters deserve a boost at Christmas, and it will only hurt us if we challenge this. I will, therefore, vote for supporting the amended legislation.'

Over the next ninety minutes, member after member stood to express their feelings and opinions about tactics and strategy. Arguments were put that Gerrard was disliked by the electorate, and now was the time to politically strike. Others observed they had no option but to support the amended legislation otherwise the media would blame them for cancelling the Christmas bonus. A level of tension over the opposing views grew as the party room was split in its opinion. It would come down to the leader's call.

When the last speaker listed had submitted her view, it was two o'clock.

'Colleagues, thank you all for your contributions.' Harper had considered the mood of the room. 'I must say, there were strong arguments for and against agreeing to the government's legislation. I am of the view that we have committed to three fundamental things.

'We have already agreed to the stimulus money for the electorate, and therefore we are obliged to pass the legislation tomorrow so they can get it before Christmas. Second, we have also put into our policy the funding for the Indonesian immigration detention centres, and we would be treated very harshly by the media, and no doubt the electorate, if we were now to say we didn't support the funding. Illegal immigration is one of the hottest topics in the electorate right now, so if we say no, then I am absolutely positive we will live to regret it.

'Third, we agreed earlier this week not to go to a division to force a vote, and although this was unexpectedly imposed upon us by the government, I would consider breaking that agreement. No matter how shonky the legislation may be, it would result in political damage, possibly for many years to come.

'I have determined the mood of the party room, which is

never easy because you all have valid views. With all those things in mind, I therefore declare that we will support the legislation.'

The politicians had been expecting this announcement from the leader and some had begun to saunter toward the door.

'Vote!'

'What?' Harper was bewildered by the demand.

'According to party rules, if a vote is called for, then a vote must be taken.' Tilley was now on his feet. 'And, as I am requesting the vote, I also request a secret ballot.'

'You have got to be kidding, Bob.' Stanley was on his feet immediately, understanding the political implications of a vote. 'You understand what you are asking?'

'Yes, of course I do, I want a ballot.'

Stanley quickly marched to the leader's table and Messenger joined them.

'Don't do it,' Stanley said. 'Stick to your guns.'

'What harm would it do if we were to have a vote?' Harper replied.

'If you agree to a ballot, and lose it, then you lose your leadership. This is virtually a vote on your leadership, don't do it.' Harper drew back thinking about the implications of Stanley's advice. 'Jim, if you lose the vote now, you lose everything.'

Stanley had quickly grasped the politics – Harper had announced the party's strategy to vote for the amended appropriation legislation with the added Indonesian money, if the party room, then voted against his decision, he had no option other than to resign his position as leader, as the party would clearly have lost confidence in its leader.

'Look, by my reckoning the vote was close, but it favoured supporting the legislation,' Harper said.

'My advice is not to do it,' said Messenger. 'I suspect Tilley doesn't fully understand the implications of a vote, so let me talk to him and explain the implications if we vote on this. Call a short adjournment so I can explain.'

'Hmm, it seems we have a little problem.' Harper was steely in his response. 'The trouble with many leaders of today is that they have to lead. They can only ever lead if they have followers, so now I am faced with a leader's paradox ... take a vote and perhaps kill my leadership, or not take a vote and lose the perception of leadership in the electorate anyway. If I say no to a ballot, then I'm finished anyway, so let's do it.'

'Courageous, but stupid, Jim,' said Messenger. Stanley had already moved away.

'Whips, prepare a ballot,' Messenger announced. 'Simple question: do you support the leader's decision? If so, write yes on your ballot paper. Write no if you do not support the leader.'

The whips quickly set about distributing the yellow ballot papers and preparing the wooden boxes for members and senators to cast their ballot. The chief whip scurried off to his office to put a message on the parliamentary pager system to ensure all members and senators, including those who might have left the party room, knew there was a vote taking place with closure of the ballot in five minutes.

'So, what do we do if he loses?' Messenger asked Stanley.

'He has no alternative other than to step down, and we elect a new leader,' Stanley replied. 'This is very risky for him, but we should be okay.'

'Who steps up if he loses?' Messenger asked.

'I suspect Wilson would be the obvious choice.'

'Let's hope Jim gets up.'

'Go and scout for comments and try to remind them of the importance of their vote. Tell them not to be frivolous, as we may have to change the leader if they are, and it's not a good look.'

Messenger went first to Hughes.

'Although I remain firmly against the idea of voting for the legislation, I know what to do. There is no way I am voting for a change of leader, so I will put a yes vote in,' confirmed Hughes.

Messenger then moved around the room talking to individuals and groups, asking for the views of his colleagues. To obfuscate when asked about one's voting intention would consign a politician to the *do not trust file*, and no politician ever wanted to be sidelined. This brought a sense of control to the political process.

'It'll be close,' Messenger reported to Stanley. 'If it goes the other way, we should talk about tactics to get the leader we want.'

'We'll call for nominations as usual and take the vote. No dramas,' Stanley said.

'Yes, but who will nominate? We don't need Wilson as leader. Nice bloke and all, but he won't win us an election.'

'Let's hope we don't have that dilemma. If we do have to vote for a new leader, why don't you put your hand up for deputy?'

Messenger was astounded by the comment and didn't know if Stanley was serious or joking. He occasionally considered leading the party, as most politicians in safe seats do, but he never seriously contemplated his career ever being good enough to result in his being elected leader by his colleagues.

'I could never do it,' Messenger finally offered.

'Well, you may have to consider it, if someone nominates you.'

Messenger sat back in his chair to wait for the close of the ballot and the count, pondering what he had just been told by his mentor. He resolved to reject any nomination if it came to him.

The chief whip closed the ballot then retired to an office opposite the party room with the other whips to count the vote. It was fifteen minutes after two in the morning.

After a further ten minutes, the chief whip Hayden Charlton made his way to the front of the room. A former air force squadron leader, he retained his military bearing as he stood before his colleagues, his expression giving nothing away. 'In the vote to determine if we support the leader's decision to support the Appropriation Bill, the results were ... Ayes: fifty-one.'

Messenger breathed a sigh of relief. He knew it would be close, but not that close. There would have been a couple of abstentions and informal votes, and perhaps a member or two would not have returned to the party room. There was never an even vote on the numbers, so that was a good result for the leader. Not a strong supportive vote, but fifty-one votes was good enough. Harper had scraped through.

'Noes: fifty-two.'

'Christ, what's happened? Quickly, come in.'

Messenger didn't look well, tie askew, shirt partly untucked, hair dishevelled, in fact he looked on the brink of an emotional collapse.

'I just need someone to hug right now.' He fell into her arms.

Anita welcomed it, not a romantic embrace, more a healing hug for this troubled man. He said nothing, did nothing. He just needed a hug. 'Bart, tell me, what's happened?' Anita pulled back and cupped his face.

'What have we done?' A tear spilled from his eye.

'Tell me, what's happened?'

'I'm the new deputy leader.'

# CHAPTER 18

## THURSDAY 6.35 AM

'For those just waking to the news of the hour, we have a new leader of the opposition.' Distinguished journalist Cassandra Rogers introduced the next segment on the Hancock Broadcasting Network's Breakfast Show. 'In what can only be described as the night of the long knives, James Harper was dumped as leader of the opposition early this morning in a hastily arranged party meeting that went late into the night. Harper had lost the confidence of his party after a dreadful day in the parliament yesterday. Sources suggest there was a late-night meeting called to debate the government's Christmas bonus legislation, which was amended and subsequently passed by the senate late last night. The opposition had taken a vote to determine their position on the Christmas bonus for every Australian, and Mr

Harper's position was rejected by one vote. A new leader was then called upon.' Rogers was speaking straight to camera without a teleprompter. 'We have the new opposition leader in our Canberra studio. Good morning, Mr Stanley.'

'Good morning.'

'*Do* you still have blood on your hands this morning?'

'That's an outrageous thing to say. Of course, I don't have blood on my hands. I would have thought a respected journalist like yourself would not stoop to tabloid hashtags.'

'Then tell us, how it is that you are the new leader of the opposition?'

---

The prime minister was flicking through the national newspaper as he picked slowly through his fruit, carefully cut into bite-sized pieces by his chef, Janette. The television attached to the wall behind him was switched to the Breakfast Show, which he usually ignored, but today Cassandra Rogers introduced Peter Stanley, and he swivelled on his stool to pay closer attention.

'A new opposition leader, Janette, what do you have to say about that?'

'I didn't know we had one to replace.'

'Exactly, and this one will be even worse; he needs a charisma transplant to get some warmth and character into him.'

---

'My colleagues, last night, determined that I am the best person to lead them into the next election. Politics can be bruising sometimes, and last night was one such time. James Harper is a respected politician. He has served the party very well, and through his efforts we are now in a position to be a credible opposition and the alternate government. We have solid policies, and we have a dynamic frontbench. We are looking forward to the privilege of serving our fellow Australians in government, if the people give us that opportunity.'

'If James Harper is as good as you say, why was he knifed by you in a leadership coup?' Rogers' fierce reputation for asking tough questions during her days at Hancock Media was well-earned.

'There was no coup, Cassandra.' Stanley shifted in his seat ever so slightly. 'You are using very provocative language this morning. Sometimes, as politicians, we must stand by our principles. James Harper has always been a man of principle, and when asked to put his convictions to a vote, he had no hesitation in agreeing.'

'Yes, but you didn't support him, did you, Mr Stanley?'

'The party voted on a decision to either support the appropriation legislation, due back in the house today, or not. The senate had amended legislation to add extra funding to the bill, and although that funding had previously been allocated in the government's budget, it has yet to be scrutinised by the parliament. The party chose not to support the legislation, preferring to ensure the money added at the last hour by the senate should be scrutinised in the usual way and included in separate legislation next year.'

'So, your party chose to deny money to the needy just before Christmas, is that what you're saying?'

'It's not our party that linked the Christmas bonus to this huge lump-sum payment—'

'So, what you're saying is that neglected children can forget about finding presents under the tree, or the poor enjoying a hearty meal with their family at Christmas?'

Stanley winced slightly and rushed his answer. 'The party decided not to support the amended Appropriation Bill, which we must remember was rushed through the senate late last night.'

'The kids won't care about amendments – they just want to have a good Christmas. Isn't that what you and your colleagues want?'

'Cass, this is the first time the senate has amended a money bill for some time. It is a parliamentary convention our party feels very strongly about, and we reject the idea that the senate can amend money bills.'

'Isn't this just a reason for the conservatives in your party to play scrooge at Christmas time? You just don't like giving taxpayers back any of their money, do you?'

'No, that's not right. The issue is rushing through a huge amount of money for Indonesia, which we do not support until the usual parliamentary checks and balances have been completed. If the government chooses today to amend the legislation once more and remove the funds they added last night for the immigration detention centres, we will then support the

Christmas bonus legislation, and the people of Australia will have their money before Christmas.'

'So, you're holding hard-working families to ransom over parliamentary procedure, is that it? Aren't you and your colleagues a little out of touch?'

---

Barton Messenger twitched as he watched the interview from Anita's couch, beneath a comforting doona. He had hidden under it for a few hours, and now he was slowly returning to the land of the living. His phone buzzed a message.

Congratulations. Your country thanks you.

Who are you?

It doesn't matter now. You did well, thanks.

'How did you sleep?' Anita was yawning as she strolled into the room with a pale blue satin gown over her short summer pyjamas.

'Fine. Hey, thanks for letting me stay. I didn't want to go back to the hotel last night.'

'I'm glad you called. Are you feeling better? Can I get you a coffee, or a tea?'

'No, thanks.' Barton sat up, wrapping the doona around him,

allowing Anita to perch on the lounge. 'It seems Pete Stanley is getting some stick from Rogers.'

'That old biddy should just retire. I only ever watch to see if Donnie will do something stupid.' Co-host Donnie Maguire was renowned for putting his foot in it.

'She is ripping Peter apart. I'd better get moving. I suspect it will be a long and hectic day.' Bart got up, quickly pulled on his trousers, slipped on his shoes, grabbed his jacket, and headed for the door.

'Do you want a shower or anything?'

'No, I'll do that at the office. I'll walk up, it'll do me good to get some fresh air.'

'I suppose I should get moving as well. As you say, it may be a hectic day for us as well.'

'I reckon your "follow the money" story is dead, buried and cremated, given we're not approving the legislation today.'

'It'll be interesting to see what Gerrard does now. But anyway, you are the story today.'

'No doubt.' Barton turned back to Anita as he got to the front door. 'Hey, thanks again for letting me stay over, I really appreciate it.'

Anita was close, so Bart slipped his hand into the small of her back and drew her closer. She fell against him, and the kiss was even better than the last time, lingering a little longer, soft, and warm. It was clear she wanted more.

'See ya.'

'Yeah, okay, see you.' Anita was a little confused as she

watched him leave. This politician was going to be trouble for her.

---

'No, I don't think we are out of touch. What I think the people of Australia want is certainty in government.' Stanley's voice became stronger as he spoke. 'Certainty that we will do the right thing by all Australians. Certainty that they are never taken for granted by my party, and certainty that their leaders will do the right thing by the institutions they entrust to politicians. We do not want cowboys in government, playing fast and loose with the taxpayers' hard-earned funds. The community expects its leaders to be truthful and transparent and not to rush through deals with foreign countries in the senate late at night.'

'Didn't you do a deal late at night?'

'I didn't go to that meeting thinking I would be leader by its end. No-one went to that meeting thinking there would be a change of leadership, that's just the way it panned out. No-one is more surprised by these events than me. But, having said that, I am proud to be leading my party. I have been its loyal servant for almost thirty years in the parliament. I have been humbled by the faith and trust my colleagues have placed in me.'

Rogers was about to interrupt, but Stanley raised a hand. 'I am not here to say the events of last night were not disappointing, they were, for everyone involved and certainly for the many supporters of our party. But we, as members of the party, have a duty to ensure we represent its ideals and prove ourselves worthy of the trust the community has placed in us to lead them.'

'What does this say about honesty and loyalty?'

'Cass, politicians are servants of the community. Our job is to serve by doing the right thing all the time, as we did last night in voting to stop the senate amending money bills, which is highly inappropriate for the government to force it to do. Sometimes we have to be less pragmatic and do the right thing when it is required of us. Last night we chose to protect Australian taxpayers' precious funds.'

'Let me get this right, your leader asks his party to follow him, they say no, and you tell me that's not pragmatism? You tell me that changing leaders through rebellion in the ranks is doing the right thing? I think the Australian people will see this as a cynical grab for power.'

'There was no rebellion. What we were focused on was the issue of forcing money through parliament without proper scrutiny. We have to face several by-elections in February, and then a general election the following year. Our policies are in place, our leadership is in place, and we stand ready to be judged by the electorate. What we won't countenance, Cassandra, is a prime minister ignoring the protocols of the parliament and amending legislation to suit his own crass political needs. Doing this grubby little deal last night betrays the trust of the Australian people. I think that trust, which we all must earn, is more important than any baubles the prime minister may wish to dangle before the Australian people to buy him votes. I think the Australian people are more intelligent than the prime minister, and perhaps you, Cass, give them credit for.'

'Well, it's not about me, but it is about the internal struggles that have marked your party and kept you in opposition for many years. Thanks for joining us. That was Peter Stanley, the new leader of the opposition.'

'You go girl,' co-host Donnie Maguire said, when he was back in frame. 'Some tough questions asked, and answered, I think.' He was reading from the teleprompter.

'Yes. I often wonder what goes through our politicians' heads when what they should be focused on is the voters,' Rogers said in response, looking straight at the camera and ignoring her colleague.

'Now it's off to Hollywood for the more interesting news of the day, with our reporter Stu Whitecross. How are you, Stuie? What's going on?'

---

Gordon O'Brien had been waiting in reception outside the speaker's office for forty minutes, since seven o'clock, after texting her earlier to confirm what time she would be in. She was late, very late, but he was not moving until he saw her. His last days in the parliament would not be spoilt by the poor behaviour of those who should know better.

When the speaker arrived, she asked him to follow her into her office.

'May I close the door please, Speaker.'

'If you must.' Bagshaw sighed.

'Speaker, I have very serious concerns about the events overnight.'

'Oh, yes? Not just "serious", but "very serious".' Bagshaw flopped into her chair. 'What could they be? Let me guess.'

'This is not a time for flippancy.'

'Nor is it a time for you to be rude and disrespectful, especially with only two more days to serve.'

'You have misled me, and by implication, the prime minister has lied, not only to me, but to the house.'

Bagshaw didn't move, the words stunned her, and she sat motionless as she thought through her options. 'That is an outrageous thing to suggest. These are very serious charges. On what basis do you suggest such a disgraceful thing?'

'The fact is, Speaker, you assured me that the Appropriation Bill was only for the payment of government funds to taxpayers. When I challenged information about the initial drafting, you assured me the funding for the immigration detention centres would be deferred until next year to be properly scrutinised by the parliament.' Gordon stood rock solid before her desk. 'Now, this is not the case, as the government has amended the legislation in the senate, violating convention. You have misled me.'

'Are you calling me a liar?'

'Yes.' O'Brien could not control himself; he was angry. He was a servant to the parliament, but he felt obliged to ensure propriety and standards were maintained, no matter who threatened them.

'That is an abhorrent suggestion. I must formally warn you,

Mr O'Brien, that your behaviour is unacceptable.' Bagshaw prodded a finger at Gordon. 'Remember who you're talking to.'

'My behaviour is entirely honourable, and it is you who should search your conscience and remind yourself of the standards that must be retained in this institution.' Gordon could feel his mouth drying and his throat tightening. 'It is you who should be apologising to the parliament for misleading it, and it is you who should not allow this abuse of parliamentary process by the prime minister. It is you who should do what is right.'

'Be careful, O'Brien.' Bagshaw stood and walked to the door, motioning Gordon to leave.

Gordon did not move, 'I have no need to be careful. You must understand there is strong evidence to support a case of fraud against the commonwealth, and your actions have implicated you.'

'What fraud?' Bagshaw experienced a sudden small stab of doubt.

'It is my solemn belief, now confirmed by the actions of the senate last night, that the prime minister is doing a dishonest deal through an arrangement with the Indonesian government. I also believe he is about to resign his commission today.'

The enormity of the charge drove Bagshaw to sit. 'You are kidding me? What proof do you have?'

O'Brien stalled.

'So, you have nothing,' Bagshaw snarled.

'Well...'

'Yeah, right! You puffed up, pompous bureaucrat.' Bagshaw stood and reached for the doorhandle. 'How dare you wander into my office, call me a liar, and accuse the prime minister of dishonest dealing with another country and outrageously suggest he is embezzling funds. Get out, while you still can.' Gordon did not move. 'Get out!'

'The opposition is likely to call votes today, and you will comply.'

'How dare you,' Bagshaw hissed, struggling to control her breathing.

'They have changed their leader, making the agreement with the government void.' Gordon smiled, ever so slightly. 'They now have a majority in the parliament, and they will take a vote on the legislation, voting it down. So, the little scheme you and the prime minister have cooked up will fail.'

Now Bagshaw was bellowing. 'How dare you threaten me. How dare you think you can tell me how to do my job.'

'You have a duty to the Australian people.'

'Get out!' Bagshaw flung open the door.

O'Brien paused for a moment before striding from the office, crashing through the doorway, and alarming the staff.

---

'It's Zara, Prime Minister. Good morning.' Bagshaw had phoned Gerrard immediately, struggling to control her voice. 'I need to talk to you, can I come over?'

'Sure, Zara. Come now, before the day gets started.'

The parliament was scheduled to start at noon and the prime minister was at his desk, editing his resignation speech that he planned to deliver as soon as the amended legislation was passed by parliament. Gerrard had earlier waved goodbye to his wife as she set off for Sydney, where she'd catch the plane to Zurich. As he waited for the speaker, he cleared his desk, moving precious ornaments to the safety of the bookcase.

'Come in, Zara, come in,' Gerrard moved to greet her with the corporate kiss to both cheeks. 'You look very alluring today.'

Bagshaw brushed off the advance by avoiding him. 'There is no time for that shit today, we may have trouble with O'Brien in the chamber today.'

'Fuck that wanker!' Gerrard waved one hand dismissively. 'What does the moron want now?'

'He has just called me a liar.'

'The bastard!' Gerrard flung himself onto the lounge.

'Worse than that, he seems to think you are doing some deal with the Indonesians and making some fast cash out of the immigration- funding deal.'

'Unbelievable.' Gerrard was instantly alert, consciously avoiding any sign of uncertainty or anxiety that Bagshaw might pick up on.

'He has demanded I allow votes today.'

'And what did you say?'

'I told him to fuck off, and not tell me how to do my job.'

'Good girl. What do you think he might do?'

'I don't suppose there's much he can do, I mean he has no authority in the parliament, he's just the clerk after all.' Bagshaw sat at a chair near the desk. 'But it's not him I'm worried about, it's Stanley. Will he abide by the agreement

Harper signed, or will he force a formal vote on the amended legislation?'

Gerrard stood abruptly and walked behind his desk, falling into his chair where he rocked to and fro considering the point. 'It's unfortunate the opposition has changed leaders, but there's no reason why we should change our plan.' Gerrard sat forward. 'If Stanley wants a vote, shut him down.'

'How?'

'Either rule his request invalid, referring to the agreement signed this week, or ignore him.'

'I can't do that if he's standing at the despatch box.'

'You can if you vacate the chair,' Gerrard asserted. 'Mind you, that would shut down the entire parliament, and we can't do that permanently until we have the money legislation passed.'

'Are you resigning today?'

'No,' Gerrard tried to sound credible. 'What makes you say that?'

'O'Brien is convinced you are.'

'That moron is working his last day in the chamber. He hates me, and no doubt wants to make it tough for me today, so he'll say and do anything.'

'So, what's in it for me?' Bagshaw suddenly changed the subject.

'What do you mean?' Gerrard had been waiting for the question for a few days now and was surprised it had taken so long for her to get to it.

'I want a promotion to your frontbench.'

'Speaker not good enough for you?' Gerrard responded.

'I've had it being your puppet, I want a policy job.'

'You're being a little ambitious, aren't you, Zara dear?'

'If you want me to do this for you today, and it seems all hell may be about to break loose, then I want more than this miserable job as my payment.'

'We'll see.'

'What the hell does that mean? "We'll see?"' Bagshaw stood before Gerrard's desk, leaning over him. 'You either have a job for me or you don't. If you don't, then I will consider my position.'

'Your position!' Gerrard's eyes narrowed and his voice dropped. 'You have no position without me, and indeed, your position is lying under me, whenever I demand it.' Bagshaw stepped back from the desk. 'Your position is to do and say exactly what I want, whenever I want it. Your position, dear Zara, is to do as you are told. If you do not, not only will your new husband be advised about his adulterous wife, but you will also lose your preselection, and you will never ever have a career again dealing with anything remotely political. This will mean your family in Cairns will lose access to funding from their land council. Your relatives will lose their jobs, all of them, and you will be disgraced. So, you have choices, my dear, and I suggest you choose wisely.'

Bagshaw, surprised by the outburst, stepped further back, nervous, and afraid. Gerrard had a reputation for political brutality, but she had never been on the receiving end of it, until now. She made her way to the door and stood there, shaken by the attack. 'I only want my due.'

'And you shall have it, dear Zara, but when it is offered, and never ever when it is asked for.'

Bagshaw turned to leave.

'Stay focused today, give me what I want, and we will talk about your generous reward tomorrow.'

# CHAPTER 19

**THURSDAY 9.35 AM**

'O'Brien, this is the prime minister.'

'Good morning, Prime Minister. How can I help?' Gordon stood at his chair, almost at attention.

'I've just had the speaker in my office, a little distressed, reporting on a meeting she had with you earlier.'

Gordon grunted.

'I must say, I suspect she is overreacting, but is there any reason for me to be concerned about your abuse?'

'I was not abusive.'

'A woman does not claim abuse unless there is abuse, and you called her a liar, did you not?'

'What do you want, Prime Minister?'

'It's been a long journey for you, O'Brien, and today is your last day in the chamber before you retire tomorrow, so don't spoil it by doing something stupid.'

'I am not in a position to comment.'

'Let me make it clear to you, so you understand perfectly.' Gerrard slowed and deepened his voice. 'If you do anything that inhibits the smooth operation of the parliament today, you will live to regret it.'

'Are you threatening me?' Gordon struggled to swallow.

'Let me repeat, if you want a long and safe retirement then stay out of the chamber today.'

Gordon could almost feel Gerrard's breath. 'If you do take your place, then ensure you do nothing to disrupt the duties of the speaker.'

'Anything else?'

'No. Have a nice day.' Gerrard cut the call.

Marjorie entered with a cup of tea and a piece of fruit cake, followed by his office staff. 'Are you okay, Gordon? You look as if you've seen a ghost.'

'I'm fine.' Gordon gave her a sickly smile.

'Is there anything we can do to help?' Marjorie asked.

'I think Richard should open, and I shall come to question time. I would prefer to stay out of the chamber today if I can.'

'Are you sure about that?' Marjorie asked.

'Yes, I am sure. Thank you, Marjorie.' Gordon was suddenly focused. 'Richard, I want you to ensure the standing orders and parliamentary protocols are followed in the chamber. I am expecting a torrid time today.'

'Will do, Gordon.'

'Paige, I expect there will be media hanging about the office today, so be sure to curtail their enthusiasm. I would prefer to do no media until tomorrow.'

'Rightio, I'll make sure they don't bother you.'

'George, I want extra security on today, especially inside, and around the chamber.'

'Expecting fireworks, sir?'

'No, but I feel we should be prepared for anything.' Gordon had no idea how the day would pan out and what passions might be stirred. 'This amended legislation has so far caused one change of leader, and if it doesn't get through the parliament today, the mob could get excited.'

'I'll talk to the federal police and ask them for an increased presence for the day.' George made a note on his pad.

'Marjorie, could you arrange a meeting for me with the chief justice?'

'When were you thinking?'

'It's urgent, so as soon as he can come to the parliament. Tell him I need his advice on definitions of parliamentary practice, and I need it before ten thirty.'

'Are you sure about all this, Gordon?'

'Relax, all's well.' Gordon tried to reassure her. 'Just get him here as quickly as you can. That's all folks.'

The team dispersed and Gordon sat quietly looking out his window into his maple tree. He sighed and searched for any wildlife among the leaves, but there wasn't any. He was anxious about what might happen during the day – and the very real possibility that his beloved parliament would be trashed when the opposition voted against the amended legislation.

Gordon opened the second drawer of his desk, prodded aside the tissue box, and took out the phone.

Keep your phone close.

He pushed the send button and was surprised to receive an immediate reply.

Who is this?

Gordon thought about responding and disclosing who he was, but sent instead:

A friend who wants you to do the right thing.

What's that?

You'll know if you keep your phone close.

Chief Justice Benjamin Hopetoun arrived at the clerk's office at 10.00 am, bemused by the urgency of the request, and concerned about the covert nature of his entry into the house via the underground carpark staff entrance, below the public entrance.

'Hello Gordon, care to tell me what's going on?'

'Hi Ben, thanks for coming at such short notice. I have a

dilemma and I need your advice. Please take a seat. Would you like tea?'

'Yes, please.'

Paige Alexander had waited at the door for the affirmative, and she quickly arranged the tea, which she served on the low marble table as Gordon joined the chief justice on the lounge.

'Milk and sugar?' Gordon asked, as he poured milk into his own cup. 'Yes, and two, thanks.'

'Ben, I want to know your view on what might, or might not, happen in the chamber today.'

'You have my attention.'

'We have a money bill before the house that was amended by the senate last night, contrary to normal parliamentary practice and convention.'

'Is this the Indonesian deal that was finally signed off last week by the prime minister and the president?'

'Yes.'

'I did hear you were promoting a story about it.'

'Well, it is a significant amount of money, and it allows funds to be transferred offshore without the normal checks and balances within parliament. I am concerned about the way it has been dealt with, and I suspect there may be questionable behaviour behind the haste in getting it through the parliament.'

'Any evidence of that?'

'No, not really, just a hunch based on a number of disparate events.' Gordon fidgeted with his jacket. 'It has been linked to legislation for the release of stimulus funds to taxpayers, prior to Christmas. Nothing controversial about that part of it, especially given the national tragedy of last week. It's always political, this type of expenditure. These things happen all the time, especially when elections are so close.'

Hopetoun slowly stirred his tea. 'Why are you concerned, Gordon? I thought the opposition have already included the funding for the Indonesians in their policy.'

'As I said, I have no evidence to support my theory, so I prefer not to canvas my reasons right now. Suffice to say, I have grave doubts about the process.' Gordon lowered his voice. 'The opposition was forced into agreeing not to call a division on any issue. They signed a deal with the government, and indeed, the governor-general witnessed the document, thus making it almost rock solid.'

'I would suggest there is nothing to stop the opposition from rejecting that agreement.' Hopetoun picked up his cup and saucer and relaxed on the lounge. 'It holds no legal status, after all, only a piece of paper, it certainly has no authenticity in the parliament. It's only a political document to impress the media and the electorate.'

'Yes, that's true, and with their change of leadership overnight, I suspect they may try to vote the amended legislation down. They have the numbers to do so.'

'So, what is the problem?'

'I don't know what to do if the speaker refuses to allow a vote.'

'Would she do that?' Hopetoun sipped his tea.

'I have a suspicion she is under riding orders from the prime minister.' Gordon patted a large envelope on the coffee table. 'I have confirmation of poor judgement made recently in partnership with the prime minister.'

'And because of this so-called evidence, you think she will ignore parliamentary practice and do what she is told by the prime minister?'

'I would be very surprised if she didn't. I have had a heated exchange with her this morning, and she seems determined not to heed my advice.'

'What happens if there is a formal vote?'

'The government will lose.'

'Would that be a loss of confidence in the government?'

'Yes.' Gordon sipped his tea again.

'So, the government could fall if they lose the vote...' Hopetoun gently stroked his beard. 'Do we then go to a general election, or would the opposition just assume the government benches?'

'They could win the government benches anyway after the by-elections in February, but there is no guarantee. I would think if the government lost a vote today, the opposition would ask the governor-general to go to an immediate general election. There is still time to have one prior to Christmas, if the writs are issued today.'

'So, why do you need me? It is the governor-general's call.'

'I need you to confirm, or at least provide a view, on the removal of the speaker.'

The chief justice sipped his tea, once, twice, before returning the cup to the table. 'My understanding of parliamentary practice is that the speaker can be removed for any number of breaches of the conduct codes – has she breached any?'

'You are right, but this is usually done in the house. I need to know if it can be done outside the chamber?' Gordon had exposed the reason why he needed the chief justice's advice, and now he seemed committed to a course of action that could be based on very flimsy evidence.

'What are you thinking the charge would be?'

'Back last century, in 1955, Speaker Cameron had a motion moved against him that stated he was biased toward the opposition, was making arbitrary and unjust decisions, and that he was breaching standing orders.'

'His behaviour and decisions must have been very poor to have had a motion moved against him,' Hopetoun said.

'Apparently, he was really disagreeable, but he survived the parliamentary manoeuvre.'

'If the opposition were to move that type of motion, they could remove the speaker legitimately, is that not an option?' Hopetoun asked.

'The problem I have with this type of motion is that the government will shut the parliament down before a vote is taken.'

'How?'

'The speaker can adjourn the house, by leaving the chair, and not return. This means parliament is closed until she determines when to take the chair again, virtually stopping any attempt by the opposition to force a vote.'

'So, if you say the parliament is under significant threat by the actions of the speaker, then she needs to be removed outside the chamber. If that is the case, then I consider there are only two options – either she resigns or she dies.'

'Heaven forbid she suddenly has a heart attack or gets run over by a bus.' Gordon's attempt at levity failed.

'What happens if she does resign, and the parliament is without a speaker?'

'A new speaker needs to be elected by the house. That process is lengthy, and it would give me enough time to have the appropriation legislation deferred until next year after the by-elections for proper scrutiny by the parliament. This is what should happen, rather than this rush through the parliament.' Gordon sighed. 'That is my preferred outcome.'

'The electorate would not be happy about it, Gordon. What about their Christmas cheer?'

'This is not about doling out money for Christmas gifts, Ben, it is about protecting our institutions. The parliament is under threat when the senate starts amending money bills, especially one that is so irregular. What would you do if your court were under threat?'

'I would protect it with all my power.'

'That is exactly what I am trying to do.'

'You'll need a good reason to force her to resign.'

'I think I have one.'

---

At noon, the speaker's procession opened the parliament while Gordon settled into his lounge with a salad sandwich and a glass of water, picking up the remote and flicking on the television to watch the proceedings in the house. As he took a cautious bite of his sandwich, careful not to drop any beetroot juice or carrot on his tie or white shirt, he imagined how the speaker would handle the new opposition leadership group, confident his assistant Richard Barker would provide the advice he had instructed him to give when asked. This was now the moment he had been looking forward to, although he would have preferred it had there been no change to the leadership of the opposition. He would be delighted to see the prime minister fail to achieve whatever it was he had planned, now he was certain the opposition would vote the Appropriation Bill down.

As the speaker took the chair, the gold mace was placed on the table and Bagshaw bowed to both sides, who in turn bowed back. She began the lord's prayer, then called for the clerk to begin the order of proceedings.

The parliamentary day had begun no differently from any other day in parliament – politicians with a strong religious faith were lifting their heads after the prayer, and most of the opposition were in attendance; a good sign they were committed to action.

Richard Barker stood. 'Third reading, Appropriation Bill number seven, as amended, for the purposes of funding of immigration centres and disbursement of funds to the Australian population.'

'The question is that the bill be read a third time with incorporated amendments,' declared Bagshaw.

Stanley rose from his chair and stood at the despatch box waiting for acknowledgement. 'I call the member for Curtin.'

'On indulgence, Madam Speaker, and for the benefit of the house, I wish to advise changes to the leadership and management of opposition business.'

'Proceed.'

'Thank you, Speaker. I wish to announce my elevation to the position of leader of the opposition, and with good grace, I hope this appointment will be accepted by the house.' Stanley momentarily bowed his head to the speaker.

'Hear, hear.' The opposition members expressed support for their decision.

'I would also announce the appointment of the member for Gellibrand as the new deputy leader, replacing the member for Brand, who replaces the member for Gellibrand in the position of manager of opposition business. I thank the house.'

'Also on indulgence, Madam Speaker,' Meredith Bruce had taken a position at the government's despatch box. 'The government congratulates the Member for Curtin on his appointment to leader and wishes him well in his new position. We also acknowledge the leadership potential of the member for Gellibrand,' Bruce smiled and nodded toward Messenger. 'And of course, we welcome the circumspect and often erratic member for Brand to his new role as manager of opposition business, and I look forward to our further discussions on process and procedure for this parliament.' Bruce resumed her seat. 'Game on.' She mouthed to Messenger, who smiled with menace and tapped his forefinger to his lips.

Stanley sprang to his feet and stood at the despatch box seeking the speaker's call. 'The leader of the opposition.'

'Thank you, Speaker.' Stanley referred to notes. 'I move that so much of sessional and standing orders be suspended to allow the following motion, that the House of Representatives expresses its great concern about the procedural matters contravened by the senate in amending Appropriation Bill number seven, that the senate conflicted with—'

'Order. The leader of the opposition is out of order, and I ask him to withdraw.'

'Madam Speaker, I have the call and I am calling forward a motion.'

'You had the call, and I have asked you to withdraw.'

'Speaker, I am moving a motion.'

'Leader of the opposition, I have asked you to withdraw, now withdraw.'

'I will not withdraw, Speaker, I am moving a motion.'

'I have asked you to withdraw, now I am telling you to withdraw or suffer the consequences.'

'I will not withdraw, Madam Speaker, I have the call and I am moving a motion.'

'It's a pity you ignore the ruling of the speaker. Under Standing Order 94A, I suspend the leader of the opposition from the chamber for one hour.'

The opposition benches erupted with many members bouncing to their feet shouting at the speaker, pointing to her and Stanley, trying to make the point that the decision was out of order. The cacophony drowned out the speaker's attempts to bring order and she stood, seeking silence in the house, but getting none. It wasn't until Stanley turned to face his colleagues, gesturing with his hands to quieten them, that members resumed their seats and stopped shouting. Stanley then plonked himself into his chair.

'The house will come to order. The leader of the opposition will withdraw himself from the chamber for one hour.'

Stanley had no choice. If he did not leave the chamber as directed, he would have been escorted out by the serjeant-at-arms. Being forcibly removed from the chamber would not have been a good look for him or his party on any news broadcast; and his first day as leader would have been irretrievably tarnished. As he left, the opposition benches erupted again with a cacophony of noise as voices shouted to be heard.

'Order, order.' The speaker tried in vain to quieten the baying members on her left.

Messenger sprang to the despatch box waiting for the call, but the noise behind him did not subside. To gain control the speaker again stood at her place, but it had little impact. The house seemed out of control. Bagshaw then switched tactics and stormed from the chamber, immediately suspending further parliamentary proceedings, and automatically adjourning the house until a time she chose to reopen.

Gordon was astonished at what had just happened in the chamber, but very concerned the Appropriation Bill had been read a third time and was now available for a vote without debate. It could be decided only on voices at any time the speaker chose, clearly a distinct advantage for Gerrard and his suspect scheme.

He abandoned his lunch and strode quickly to his desk to call Hopetoun to make sure the prime minister could not have his way, worried about the possible motives behind Bagshaw closing the parliament within minutes of it opening.

'Ben, it's Gordon. The parliament has suddenly been closed by the speaker after the third reading to accept the amendments of the contentious Appropriation Bill. I expect this might be government tactic to stop any further action by the opposition to force a vote.'

'I should have a legal opinion to you within the hour, but you will need solid evidence for this dismissal to be valid.'

'I only have wild guesses at the moment, but I expect some hard evidence of collusion to be with me shortly.'

'Like what?'

'Photographs of clandestine meetings.'

'That could be enough, but her actions in the house should also be enough to support intended action.'

'I look forward to receiving it, as quickly as you can.'

---

As the noise quickly subsided, members began drifting out of the chamber to discuss what to do next. Messenger walked across the chamber and confronted Bruce.

'What was all that about?'

'I have no idea. I'll go and see her and find out when she is planning to reopen the parliament.'

'Are you shafting us, Meredith?' Messenger asked.

'Come on, you know me better than that. I have no idea what that was all about.'

'We were not planning on asking for a vote, just a debate on the propriety of the senate amending a money bill.'

Bruce raised her hands in frustration and shook her head. 'Maybe you should have squared it away with me first.'

'Let me know when the speaker plans to reopen the chamber, will you please?'

'I thought Wilson was the manager of opposition business and now my go-to man? You swapped roles, didn't you?'

'He is, but on this matter, I would prefer you to continue to deal with me.'

'No worries, comrade.' Bruce smiled.

Messenger walked off looking for Chief Whip Charlton, wanting to call an immediate meeting of members to discuss tactics and process for what looked like being an extremely long day.

---

Anita Devlin was sitting at Aussies with a latte, scrolling through media reports on her iPad, nibbling a sesame-seed bar, oblivious to the start of the parliament. She normally paid little attention to the early procedures in the house, but the sudden eruption of noise disturbed her research and she looked up to check one of the three televisions broadcasting the house. She watched as Stanley was ejected, and then saw the speaker withdraw from the chamber, adjourning the parliament. Anita quickly phoned her editor.

'Cleaver, did you just see what happened in the house?'

'Yeah, animals behaving like animals, so what?'

'I suspect it might be more than that. I think our idea about the additional money in the legislation being a secret commission could have weight. My theory about a plan to misappropriate money from the government may still be on, and I think the speaker may be colluding with the prime minister in the scheme.'

'Evidence? Where is your evidence?'

'I bet you she'll prevent the opposition taking a vote today, and she'll ram the bill through.'

'That's crazy stuff, Anita.'

'What?' Anita stood, preparing to leave. 'You don't think the amendments made by the senate aren't provocative enough?'

'Look, it could be adding weight to your speculation, but I can't see where the connection is, you have nothing other than gossip and parliamentary chatter – I need more.'

'I am going to write the story, and if you print it, you print it.' Anita was ready to leave for her office. 'Either way, I am going to write it.'

'If I print it, Hancock will have my balls. Your retirement piece yesterday didn't go down well with him.'

'Nice to hear you have some. Why don't you use them, Cleave?'

'Listen here sweetheart, you need confirmed facts linking all these ideas together, not gossip!' Cleaver yelled, forcing Anita to move the phone away from her ear. 'I will print facts, not fanciful chatter from a creepy clerk on his last day in the parliament, and conspiracy theories from some loser lover from the opposition.'

'If I am wrong then sack me, but I know there is something going on.'

'I am not saying I will print it but get me a story with a bit more grunt and a lot more evidence. If you give me more facts, then I may be more open to your literary charms, but I want facts.'

'How long have I got?'

'Two hours.'

'Not much time, but I'm on it.'

As Anita pushed cancel, a text message buzzed her phone.

You must follow the money. Check the new amount – why different?

Who is this?

Ask questions. Stop this fraud.

Anita didn't recognise the number and quickly scrolled through her favourites list and tapped a number.

'Hi Bart, listen, last night you mentioned Senator Anthony had said there was a question about the funding and the exact amount being added. What was it?'

Messenger, distracted and focused on the game of politics said, 'He mentioned the final figure put into the legislation was only slightly different from the original budgeted amount.'

'By how much?'

'Forty million dollars more than the budget announcements.'

'Did he say why?'

'Additional administration costs, extra site costs – apparently the Indonesians have incurred further costs.'

'Thanks, and good luck today. You look as if you might need it.'

'Yeah thanks, and thanks for last night as well.'

'No worries, what about dinner tonight?' Anita offered.

'Serious?'

'Yeah, why not. You've slept with me once, so why not dinner?'

'Cheeky.' Messenger smiled. 'Okay, it's a date, but no expectations.'

'You're on, good luck today.'

Anita rang off, now focusing on the research she needed to do, and where to begin. She already had a few clues and considered going to the prime minister's office to get a statement from an adviser about why the additional funds were being added to the legislation but surmised this would be pointless as thy would tell her nothing she could use, so why give them the idea she was tracking them. She decided to visit the parliamentary library, the place to go for all quality research and the repository of all knowledge, if you were assisted by the right librarian. She collected her things, shoving them into her tattered shoulder bag, and began the trek to the library to research the budget papers and try to piece together a money trail.

# CHAPTER 20

**THURSDAY 12.37 PM**

'Hi Gobby, what's going on?' Nigel Nelson burst into the office and collapsed onto the lounge, picking up the uneaten half sandwich. 'Do you mind?'

'We have a situation, Nige, that requires your Machiavellian mind.' Gordon walked over to the lounge and joined his colleague.

Nelson, mouth full of bread and salad, mumbled, 'Anything for you, my friend.'

'The speaker is going to ram this appropriation legislation through the house. She has ejected the leader of the opposition for an hour and closed the parliament, but only after ensuring the third reading was introduced in the chamber so it can now be moved by the government at any time for approval.'

'Seems like she may be trying to even up the numbers before a vote and started by throwing out Stanley.' Nelson popped the last piece of sandwich into his mouth as he spoke. 'The easiest way for the government to resist a potential vote is to get the numbers in the house to favour the government. How many does she need to toss out?'

'Three.'

'There you go, she'll either toss out two more opposition members or try not to have a vote.'

'So, what do you think I should do?'

'Nothing.'

'I can't,' Gordon hesitated. 'I know this legislation is wrong and I have to stop it.'

'What can you do? You are only the clerk, you cannot dismiss the speaker, only the parliament can do that, and that will never happen.'

'But it's wrong, and if it passes, Gerrard wins again.'

'You mean the people of Australia will win, Gobby, surely.' Nelson sat forward on the lounge and placed his hand on Gordon's shoulder. 'Mate, listen, you have to let it go. If you keep trying to stop this money going through today, you will be pilloried for it.'

'Gerrard has already threatened me.'

'What? How? When?'

'He called me earlier and told me to keep out of the chamber and not cause a fuss.'

'Then heed his advice. He's not the type of man you want to upset today.' Nelson squeezed Gordon's shoulder. 'Mate, this is your last day in the house after a fine career, you deserve to be praised. Don't do anything that could destroy your legacy.'

Gordon brushed him off and stood, beginning to pace. 'I can't allow this money to go through unscrutinised, I just can't.'

'The opposition have approved it for heaven's sake, there is nothing wrong with it, let it go, Gordon, let it go.'

'What would you do if you were me?'

'Well, I'd be out to a boozy lunch,' Nelson cackled. 'But if I were you, I reckon the only folks who can take action are the opposition, and they have to remove the speaker.'

'That's what I was thinking.'

'Promise me this, Gordon,' Nelson stood to leave. 'If they do not take action, then you have to let it go.'

'I can't do that, Nigel, I love this place too much to see its conventions trashed like they were in the senate last night.'

'I understand that my friend. Give me a hug will you, I think you need it,' Nelson stepped around the marble table and walked into Gordon's open arms. The friends grabbed each other and slapped each other's backs. 'You take care, and let's catch up tomorrow at the club for lunch.'

Gordon stepped back, head bowed, and a forced smile. 'Thanks, Nige, I appreciate your support. If you think of anything else, let me know.'

'No worries mate, and thanks for the sandwich. More mayo next time, eh?'

As Nelson left, Gordon walked to his desk and opened his second drawer.

Messenger's phone buzzed as he sat waiting for his colleagues to assemble in the party room.

You will need to remove the speaker.

Too difficult.

It's the only way to defer legislation until next year.

How?

Bias toward the government. Check 1955 Cameron case.

She won't let us move a motion of dissent.

She is evening up the numbers. Be careful.

Peter Stanley called the meeting to order. 'Colleagues, we are now in a parliament that, for the first time in history, seems to be at the beck and call of the prime minister, and his speaker.' The party room was full, all seats taken, with a few members choosing to stand at the back, checking their phones, texting, and swiping though messages. 'I am very concerned parliamentary process has been trashed today within the first few moments of the session opening, before the house even had its full complement of members, and for no obvious reason other than to stop process. The question then becomes, what are we to do?'

Tilley bounded to his feet first with an opinion, as he almost always did. 'Leader, I think we should go on strike, and not attend the chamber for the remainder of the day.' There were a few titters of disbelief toward the back of the room.

'Thanks, junior, but I suspect the government would welcome our non-appearance in parliament, as it would allow them to pass the appropriation legislation without dissent. They run the house. They are responsible for a quorum. They don't need us in the house to have it operate. Anyone else with a suggestion?'

'I think we should gain control of the chamber.' Charlie Edmunds was on his feet two rows back from the front. 'If we are serious about stopping this legislation, then we have to bring down the government – and that will take some backbone; and it will take cooperation from all of us.'

'How do you mean, Charlie?' Stanley quizzed.

'Look, the speaker will act to get rid of any one of us for any reason.'

'She wants to even up the numbers,' interjected Messenger.

'Exactly, she has already shown what her tactics will be by expelling the leader for nothing more than moving a motion. I reckon she wants to even up the numbers in the house before she puts the appropriation legislation to a vote. So, if we stay mute, then she has no reason to expel anyone, and the only option is to bring on the legislation. When she puts it to a vote, we dissent, and force a formal vote.'

'Terrific idea, Charlie, thank you.' Stanley smiled. 'I suspect you are right about the speaker ejecting anyone from the house who plays up, so let's not give her any reason to eject us. We will need to be on our best behaviour. Any other comments?'

'I agree with Charlie.' Wilson Campbell said, surprisingly supportive, given his colleagues had sacked him just ten hours earlier. 'I don't think Bagshaw will allow a vote. I think she will ram the bill through on voices, and not call a division if she has that opportunity. From her actions this morning, I suspect she is under instructions from the government.'

'You mean Gerrard, don't you?' shouted Tilley.

'Then how are we to get what we want? If we are to stop this Indonesian funding going through, what can we do?' Stanley asked.

'We get rid of the speaker,' Messenger said firmly.

'How? We can't call a vote of dissent against her, she won't allow it,' Stanley said.

'We formally ask her to resign in her chambers, right now.' An immediate buzz of conversation burst out among the politicians at this audacious suggestion, some wondering aloud if the idea had merit, should even be considered.

'That's a fairly drastic step,' Christopher Hughes said.

Messenger moved to the front of the room, allowing all his colleagues to see him. 'If we write a formal letter setting out our concerns, quoting the unprecedented action against the leader, pointing out that she walked out of the house, deliberately shutting it down, thus intentionally denying the opposition the right to move a motion, then she needs to consider her position as the parliament's highest officer. If she retains any respect at all for the parliament, she may just agree and then resign. It seems to me that we have a case, and if we ask her to resign, who knows, she may be persuaded. If we are serious about stopping the legislation, it might just work.'

'Not if no-one knows about it and she doesn't feel any pressure,' Hughes added.

'Then we brief the media. We send a copy to the governor-general, and we advise the clerk,' Messenger said.

'Bagshaw won't do it, and even if she does, what happens then?' Stanley said, slowly shaking his head, looking around the room for a contrary view.

'If she does comply with our request, we are then required to elect another speaker. We have the numbers in the house, and we can put one of ours in the chair.'

'With the media in a sudden panic and the pressure that would generate, and if the governor-general gets involved, it might just work,' Hughes said.

'She won't do it,' Stanley repeated. 'And how can we bring pressure to bear quickly enough?'

'Let's try; we've got nothing to lose.' James Harper added his support.

Peter Stanley sat silently for a moment, tapping his fingertips in front of his face at the leader's table. 'Okay, let's do it. Chris, use your legal language in a nicely worded letter for us. Hayden, formally request a meeting with the speaker before the house reopens for business.' Stanley distributed tasks to his leadership group. 'Everyone else, make sure you remain so quiet in the house that we can hear a pin drop. I know it will be hard, but no matter the provocation from the speaker or the government, we need to remain quiet. Do not, under any circumstances, do anything that will get you ejected for any reason. Especially if Gerrard says anything outrageous; stay silent. We need the numbers.'

Everyone left in a rush, but Messenger took a seat as the others left. He withdrew his phone and tapped:

We are formally asking the speaker to resign.

Excellent. Use the Cameron case.

Anything else?

Invite the clerk as a witness.

Who are you?

Not important at the moment.

Gordon O'Brien put the phone back in his shirt pocket and waited for a visit from Messenger. It wasn't long before Paige Alexander announced Barton Messenger and Christopher Hughes.

'Gentlemen, come in. Please sit down.' Gordon ushered them to sit. 'Can I get you a drink of something? Tea, perhaps?'

'Thanks, but no thanks, Gordon,' Hughes said, as the two politicians took a seat before Gordon's desk. 'We are here to talk to you about a matter vitally important to the preservation of the parliament.'

'Not more retirement joy? Surely not.' Gordon wanted to

seem as unaware as possible of the political dance that was going on behind closed doors.

'Gordon, you are no doubt aware of what happened in the chamber earlier,' Hughes began.

'Yes, it was very disturbing. I am not sure what the speaker was thinking.'

'We remain very concerned about the correctness of parliamentary practice and standing orders not being applied so that the parliament operates appropriately, and we think what the government did in the senate last night is unacceptable.' Hughes set out the case. 'We firmly believe the appropriation legislation, specifically the new money added by the senate, should be subject to greater scrutiny by the parliament than has been the case so far, and we believe we should vote it down today.'

'Fair call,' O'Brien said. 'The entire legislation or just the amended version?'

Messenger jumped in. 'We only want the Indonesian money taken out; the stimulus package can go through.'

Hughes continued. 'We don't believe the speaker will allow us to debate the legislation, or indeed allow a formal vote on it. We consider her actions in expelling the leader when he had the call to move a motion was reprehensible, and contrary to the standing orders of the parliament. Therefore, she is not acting in the best interests of Australian citizens, and it is not appropriate for her to continue as speaker.'

'I must refresh your memory about the agreement with the government that you signed on Monday, and there is not much you can do about that,' Gordon offered. 'You have agreed not to take a vote, so the speaker is within her rights to withhold any vote.'

'Yes, that may be so, but the scene has changed now. What was once is no more,' Hughes said. 'We have a newly elected leader, and it is our view that all bets are now off. The agreement does not mean diddly-squat anymore.'

'I'm not so sure the prime minister would agree with your view.' Gordon swiveled in his chair.

'Yes, agreed. The prime minister no doubt wants us to allow the amended legislation through the parliament and we unfortunately believe the speaker is acting under his instructions.' Hughes wiped a hand across his face. 'She is normally a reasonable and fair chair, but she has been a little too ruthless with us in recent days and loose with procedure this week. Gerrard's fingerprints seem to be all over her closing down the parliament.'

Messenger added, 'We have therefore made the decision to ask her to resign, effective immediately. We are presenting a letter to her at 1.15 pm, prior to her reopening the chamber.'

'This will be unprecedented.' Gordon, pleased with the announcement, remained deadpan.

'We are aware of how important this action is and that it is regrettable,' Hughes said. 'But it is clear to us that we cannot have Speaker Bagshaw impeding proper parliamentary process if we are to be allowed to vote on the legislation.'

'So, why are you telling me this?'

'You are the parliament's most senior officer other than the elected representatives, and we would like you to attend our meeting with the speaker, as a witness to the proceedings,' Hughes said.

'You really need a legal officer. Have you considered the chief justice?' Messenger and Hughes sat mute and looked at each other. 'What you are about to do is very grave and Hopetoun should be there.'

'We probably would prefer not to engage him at this time.' Messenger sounded a little unsure about the suggestion. 'What do you recommend the procedure should be if she does resign?'

'You will need to immediately elect a new speaker. Parliamentary practice states that if the speaker were to vacate the chair, then the deputy speaker would need to be appointed, but given the tragedy, and the unfortunate death of Catherine Kennedy last week, that obviously is no longer possible.' A replacement has not been nominated by the government.

'Why can't we just ask the chair of committees to stand in as speaker?' Hughes asked.

'If the speaker were absent, that would be fine, but if she resigns, then the parliament virtually closes until we have a new speaker,' Gordon explained.

'Who is the chair of committees?' Hughes asked Messenger.

'Charlie Edmunds.'

'If she doesn't resign, why don't we just have parliamentary officers detain her in her office and have Charlie take the chair?' Messenger asked.

'A very creative idea, Mr Messenger,' said Gordon. 'I suspect Zara Bagshaw is not the type of person who could be detained.'

'Well, it's something to consider if the meeting with her

doesn't work out.' Messenger was out of his chair. 'So, we'll see you there at one-fifteen then, Gordon? Thank you for seeing us.'

'Jeezus, they are kidding me.' Peter Cleaver was responding to an email from the leader of the opposition. 'Anita! Get the hell in here.' Anita Devlin was not at her desk as Cleaver burst from his office; she was in the parliamentary library.

'We have a mutiny on our hands, folks!' Cleaver shouted to the office so everyone could hear. 'The opposition have suddenly grown big hairy balls, and they are about to go to war.' Heads started bobbing above cubicles. 'It seems the opposition is calling for the speaker to resign and they have cited the Cameron case from the fifties as their reference.' Cleaver was looking for volunteers. 'Who wants to handle this page-one story?'

Heads started disappearing, but a few intrepid souls, the hard news nuts, were keen.

'Okay, Denis, Margot and Laurie, get what you can from the opposition, and seek a view from Gerrard's office – should be interesting, although most of it will likely be unprintable. Let's get it up online before the meeting at one-fifteen. Depending on what happens, we may run it on the front-page tomorrow.'

The parliamentary library, on the second floor of the ministerial wing in the centre of the parliament, was bright with sunlight from the window wall and quiet with researchers and librarians capable of putting together a research paper in a few hours. Anita Devlin had sifted through the budget papers and discovered the estimate for the immigration detention centres was four billion, payable in four lots over three years – four hundred million next February, and the rest in three allocations over the following two years. She also confirmed that the amended appropriation legislation now contained an extra forty million added to the budget estimates, without any explanation about what the money would be used for. She searched the papers but found no references to contingency funding. This was the first point she identified that added weight to the potential scam she thought was being cooked up by the prime minister, an administrative cost that had no connection to anything previously planned and conveniently equaling one per cent of the total project.

Anita was now scanning Indonesian newspapers to find any references to construction plans for the immigration centres and was not having much luck. A researcher was sitting nearby studying a book and taking notes.

'Excuse me, sorry to disturb you,' Anita crept up to her. 'Do you find it curious that there have been no announcements in the Indonesian press about the money Australia is providing their government? I do.'

'Perhaps they haven't announced it yet. Maybe they want to keep it a secret until they are ready to announce it.'

'A secret?'

'Maybe they don't want anyone to know their government is getting the money.' The researcher went back to her book.

As Anita scanned *Bisnis Indonesia*, the national daily business newspaper. She was interested to see several photographs of President Amir Surriento pictured with various business entrepreneurs, confirming his reputation as a politician keen to encourage serious property development and a supporter of business in his country. It suggested the president was too close to many of the developers, implying that he benefited from this association and approved questionable projects, although there was little evidence of corruption.

She found a reference in a profile piece on the president of an allegation from years earlier about a residential tower in Bandung being approved under suspicious circumstances – the appropriate approvals had not been given by the Regional People's Representative Council, and the mayor of the city was Amir Surriento. Nothing unlawful had been found against the council or the mayor, but there was a suggestion of corruption within the article.

As she scanned through back copies of the newspaper looking for any news about the president, she noticed that in most photos, there was an unidentified man lurking near the president. She first thought the man must have been his bodyguard, but she noticed he didn't have the protective services insignia on his lapel, nor the standard plastic cord attached to his ear, so she kept looking, trying to find a connection between the two men, but without any luck.

Anita checked the time on her phone and realised she was running out of it. She was about to call it quits when she flicked onto the Bintel Indonesia website, the television tabloid, to search through the social pages. It was in an edition dated January of that year that she spotted a familiar face from the business photographs. Mr Tombi Wawason was enjoying the largess of television executives at the start of his advertising campaign for a luxury apartment complex in central Java. Mr Wawason was the managing director of the Javanese construction company, Yogyakarta.

The construction company name struck Anita as familiar, so she flicked back through her pad, searching her notes, finding her scribblings about Yogyakarta. It was a significant construction company specialising in residential and commercial towers, and was a major tenderer for the immigration centres, although the winning bid was kept a secret. It was a gossamer thread of evidence linking the president with the managing director of a construction company that could have successfully tendered for the project, but it was still a link. If the president could be linked with Yogyakarta, then it might link back to the Australian funding, maybe. She just needed a little more evidence.

'Where the hell have you been? The shit is about to hit the fan in the house, and I need you here.'

'Cleave, I have a possible lead on the money and its feasible connection to the legislation. I want to follow it up, can I get more time?' Anita pleaded.

'What is it?'

'I'm not sure. I think I know the winning bidder for the detention centres, and I might have a link to the president, but I need more. If I could find something linking Surriento, then maybe I could get Gerrard embroiled in it.'

'Are you sure? I need you here.'

'No, I'm not sure, but I am close.'

'Okay, I'll give you until 1.30, but then I need you back in here.'

'Why, what's happened?'

'Stanley is demanding that Speaker Bagshaw resign.'

Anita was staggered by the news, but instinctively knew her story would be bigger. If she could link the president to Yogyakarta and any of its real-estate developments or identify a strong business association between Surriento and Wawason, then maybe there was a reason why the funds were being pushed through with the extra money. Photographs of the two together were helpful, but not good enough on their own to assume a solid evidentiary link; there needed to be another stronger link between the two.

She returned to her desk with the Indonesian Parliamentary Handbook, flicked open President Surriento's biography and looked for anything that might trigger a line of inquiry. Among the many achievements listed were his education qualifications; the Indonesian Institute of the Arts was listed as his principal college. Anita suddenly became animated, bouncing in her chair, resisting a squeal when she read that Surriento's principal college was based in Yogyakarta – the name of the construction company.

Andrew Gerrard had stretched out on the leather lounge in his parliamentary office after watching the shenanigans in the chamber, admiring the work of his comrade, sipping on an Earl Grey tea prepared for him by Miles Fisher. A warm beef and mustard sandwich waited for him on the table beside him. Soon after the speaker fled the chamber, Miles's voice broke the silence: Zara Bagshaw wanted to speak with the prime minister. Gerrard struggled to his feet, sauntered over to his desk, and took up the phone with a sweep of his hand as he flopped into his chair.

'Hello Zara, what a good job you are doing.'

'You have what you want, now tell me what to do?'

'Stay calm for starters would be my advice.' Gerrard sharpened his tone to reassure the speaker, needing her to be on her best political game to withstand the pressure that might come in the chamber later. 'When are you planning to reopen the house?'

'I haven't had time to consider that yet. How many times do you want me to shut down debate today?'

'We already have the amended legislation as next business item before the house, and we only need to formally move the third reading motion that it be agreed to, and you call the result.' Gerrard smiled, relaxed. 'Only shut it down again if they look as if they're likely to start moving motions.'

'I thought if I began to bounce them from the chamber, we could get the numbers back to favour you. So, I'll call a vote when you have the numbers.'

'Brilliant idea, I knew you were clever.'

'When will you be in the chamber?'

'I'll come in after you reopen so I can speak to the bill. We should try and get this legislation through before question time is due. Once we have it approved and I have spoken again, you can adjourn the house until next year, after the elections.'

'Do you still want to speak after the legislation is passed?'

'Yes. Once the legislation is enacted, call me to make an address to the house.' Gerrard leaned back in his chair and put his feet on the desk. 'This will be over in a few hours, gorgeous, so stay strong. Use whatever methods you can, but ensure the legislation gets through today.'

'I don't like this Andrew,' Bagshaw said softly.

Gerrard picked up a partially smoked cigar from his ashtray, flicked open his lighter, and drew the flame into his cigar, blowing out a cloud of smoke. 'Zara, you'll get what you want, just stay focused and don't let those conservative morons from the other side take advantage of you. I'm relying on you.'

---

Gerrard had been little help to Zara, and she replaced her phone feeling a little queasy. She imagined a lump of stress building in her stomach – she hadn't eaten at all, yet she felt enormously full. Zara wanted comfort and support from Gerrard but got nothing and now she felt abandoned. She knew the media would hound her after the outcome today, and her family would be disappointed in her. She promised herself her family would never know she'd breached parliamentary practice to save them from hardship. She hoped her father would understand that her actions were necessary to protect him and their mob, given it was his idea in the first place to send her on this hazardous political path.

Zara stood and crossed to her window, closing the thick green curtains, and shutting out the day, then doing the same across the glass corridor that led to the chamber, allowing just enough light for her to fumble to her desk and sit quietly for a few moments, taking a tissue from a box on her credenza. In the darkness, she melted into tears.

She was not surprised when the opposition leader requested a formal meeting with her at one-fifteen. She had been expecting a delegation from the opposition seeking an explanation and asking about parliamentary procedure for the remainder of the day. She was very surprised to be advised that the clerk would also be at the meeting. She made a call to a colleague, asking him to come to the meeting as well to support her.

# CHAPTER 21

## THURSDAY 1.15 PM

Gordon waited by the glass corridor leading to the speaker's suite, looking out into the small adjourning courtyard where he had been presented with his Lancaster fishing rod, pondering whether he would use it as intended next Sunday, or if unfolding events would stymie his plans.

The idea that a speaker would resign on the demand of the opposition was far-fetched, but Gordon hoped the plan would work and save him from taking a more egregious step to ensure the amended legislation was stopped from passing through the parliament. He was only assuming the prime minister was colluding with the Indonesian government – he didn't have time to investigate a more substantial link – but the small coincidences raised serious doubts in his mind.

Gordon checked his watch and could hear the noise of the delegation approaching with what seemed to be a buzz of journalists asking questions. He turned to meet the politicians.

When the delegation had left their leader's office, they had not expected the crush of media cameras and lights. Journalists stood behind the cameras bellowing questions at the men as they squeezed past the throng of flashing cameras. The five-strong delegation refused to answer questions as they marched in single file toward the speaker's office. As they reached the whip's foyer and turned, they were greeted by Gordon. He stood aside and allowed them to pass without comment and followed the group as they entered the speaker's chambers, journalists still shouting their final questions but receiving no response.

Speaker Bagshaw was not alone. She had asked a parliamentary colleague to join her for what she guessed would be a stressful meeting. Everett Menzies, the highly regarded and distinguished attorney-general, the first law officer of the land, had joined the speaker to listen quietly to the protestations from the delegation, and provide legal advice if required.

The delegation formed in front of her desk, with Stanley front and centre. Harper and Campbell stood to his right with Messenger and Hughes to his left. Gordon moved to one side, standing in front of the windows, which were now bright with sunshine.

'Speaker, it gives us no joy to meet with you like this, especially under these circumstances,' Stanley said.

'I too am concerned about the circumstances in which we are

meeting,' Bagshaw replied, and Menzies stepped in to stand close behind her. 'This afternoon you sought to move a motion that obviously would have required a vote, thus breaching your agreement that no formal votes would be taken on any issue within the chamber. An agreement Mr Harper signed just four days ago.'

'That agreement between the opposition and the government, to which you refer, was made on two understandings,' Stanley said confidently. 'Firstly, the agreement was made with the knowledge that the Appropriation Bill was only for the disbursement of funds to the electorate in the form of an economic stimulus package. Secondly, the agreement was made with James Harper, the previous leader of the opposition, and as I did not co-sign such an agreement, I have little regard for it.'

'Technically, you must, Peter,' Menzies interrupted. 'The wording of the agreement implies that his majesty's opposition will comply with the request not to ask for a division for the purpose of counting votes. The recent tragedy has meant that the numbers in the house have changed, and to ensure secure control for the government your party agreed to the status quo. This has nothing to do with who was leading your party at the time.'

'Everett, this is not a simple case of one in all in. Jimmy didn't have shadow cabinet approval to sign such an agreement, and he has explained that he was pressured, indeed virtually forced to sign the agreement before it could be vetted by us.'

'You may say that, but I say the agreement is binding upon the opposition and you were about to blatantly breach it in the chamber,' Bagshaw said.

'So, what are you going to do? Send us to the naughty corner if we breach it again?' Campbell couldn't contain himself and Harper placed a reassuring hand quietly on his arm to hush him.

'Madam Speaker, we believe you have failed in your duty to manage the chamber in an unbiased manner.' Stanley formalised his position. 'We believe you wilfully breached the protocols and practice of the House of Representatives. We also believe there is evidence to support a claim of your breach of standing orders, as we believe you are acting under the instructions of the government to withhold fairness, rather than following established parliamentary procedures. You are therefore threatening the institution of the parliament. For these reasons, regrettably, we formally ask for your resignation as speaker, effective immediately.'

No-one moved. This moment in history slowly sank into those in the room as they attempted to grasp the significance of the request and waited for the speaker to respond. Bagshaw stood silently, staring at the men before her, rage building within her as she clenched her fists.

'You can all go and fuck yourselves,' Bagshaw snarled.

Menzies stepped forward to divert attention from the speaker's loss of control and stop a tirade that would later be regretted.

Bagshaw reflected for a moment, staring at the delegation before collapsing into her chair and pulling it closer to the desk.

Stanley withdrew a crisp white sheet of paper from his inside jacket pocket, unfolded it, and began to read. 'Furthermore, we charge that you made an arbitrary and unjust decision in expelling the leader of the opposition from the chamber and adjourning the house without sufficient reason or notice of motion. We also contend you failed to interpret the standing orders in a fair and just manner today. And for these reasons, we again ask for your resignation.' Stanley stepped forward and placed the notated request silently before Bagshaw. 'Speaker, we again formally request you consider this submission and provide an answer before the resumption of the house at 1.30.'

Menzies stretched over the desk and picked up the document, quickly scanning it and replacing it. 'Peter, this is a very long bow you are drawing without much consideration for the history or process of the parliament. Your formal petition is potentially a disruptive instrument to the entire parliamentary process and could have serious ramifications if the speaker cedes to your request. Certainly, at the very least, it is politically provocative, and I ask you to reconsider your actions and withdraw your letter of request.'

Menzies opened his hands like a priest about to deliver the Sunday sermon. 'Come on, boys, this can only end badly for you. The press will murder you, and you won't be applauded by the electorate after you reject the stimulus package, as I assume this is what your prank is all about. Please reconsider, I beg of you.'

'Is it any wonder you morons are stuck in opposition?' Bagshaw abruptly stood with her fists resting on the desk. 'Who the hell do you think you are? How dare you come in here with your pompous demands for my resignation?' She thumped the desk, then took a breath. 'You know something, Stanley, I don't like you. I don't like your party's born-to-rule attitudes, the pompous manner with which you all swagger around the parliament as if you own the place. Who the hell do you think you are?' Bagshaw snatched up the document, screwed it up and tossed it back at Stanley. 'You will not have my resignation – you can shove it up your arse for all I care. You will not have a chance to overrule my decision, and believe me when I say, you will not be calling for any divisions today.' Bagshaw pointed to the door and growled, 'Now get out, the lot of you.'

'Speaker, if I may,' Gordon attempted to intervene. 'Perhaps, I can offer some advice.'

Bagshaw rounded on Gordon, her face contorted with anger. 'What?!'

'There may be a compromise. Why not let the chair of committees take the chair for the remainder of the day, thus alleviating the need for you to attend, on the proviso the opposition does not call for a vote?'

'It seems a reasonable compromise,' Menzies suggested. 'What do you think, Peter?'

Gordon was struggling to keep his breathing under control, hoping his discomfort could not be seen and his dishonesty detected, for he had no intention of the legislation being passed in the chamber today. The speaker vacating her chair would be the best result and would stop him from having to act. He hoped she would see sense. He took a deep breath, silently blowing away his nerves.

Before Stanley could speak, Bagshaw's face resolved into a sneer. 'You have got to be kidding me, O'Brien. I am not giving up my job so some conservative moron can come in with his own interpretations of the rules.' Bagshaw shoved back her chair and began to advance on the men. 'We already had Stanley breach a signed agreement. What makes you think he will keep his word now?'

'Pompous gentlemen always do.' Stanley tried to break the tension with a little humour.

'No, I will not agree. Now get out.'

With her final words Stanley, Messenger, Campbell, Hughes, and Harper turned and retired from the office. Gordon and Menzies replaced them in front of the desk.

'Speaker, the compromise may have resolved the obvious tension we shall have for the rest of the day. Do you think it wise for you now to call on the Appropriation Bill?' Gordon tried again.

'I tend to agree with Gordon, Zara. Do we really need another confrontation in the parliament today? We must think how this will be played out in the media.'

'The bill will go through today, of that I am sure,' Bagshaw snapped. 'We will stick to the notice paper, and it will proceed before question time.'

'As you wish, Speaker.' Gordon nodded and withdrew.

Bagshaw watched O'Brien leave, took a huge breath, and sat as she tried to release the adrenalin coursing through her.

'That was fairly ballsy, Zara, well done,' Menzies offered after O'Brien closed the door. 'I don't think I could have handled it as well as you did.'

'That's because you're one of them, Everett.'

'One of them, how do you mean?'

'One of the squattocracy.'

---

The bells rang at 1.25, indicating the house would resume in five minutes. Gerrard finished his now cold beef sandwich and began the trek to the chamber, knowing that this could be the final time he would ever walk that route, feeling good and enjoying the four-minute walk. He met ministerial colleagues along the way and shared the latest joke, the Christmas holiday banter, all of them oblivious to what had happened ten minutes earlier in the speaker's office. When Gerrard saw Menzies, he sidled up to him for a private briefing as they walked to the chamber.

'She did really well, Prime Minister.'

'I would have expected nothing less from my girl.'

'The clerk mentioned something about the chair of committees taking over and the opposition agreeing not to vote.'

'Moron, Christ, it's his last day. Why does he have to spoil it with rubbish like that?'

'Zara saw him off in no uncertain terms, so I think we'll be fine for the rest of the day. How are you feeling?'

'I feel great,' Gerrard smiled. 'It's a great day, isn't it?'

They walked into the chamber together and assumed their places on the frontbench, the prime minister sitting at the table beside the despatch box. The opposition was already in place, subdued, but ready for a fight. The press gallery, high above the speaker's chair, was unusually full of journalists, presumably following on from the opposition leader's press release, keen to witness the parliamentary proceedings and record any disruptive action. Some of them would have been surprised to see the prime minister looking so cheery as he waved to them with a broad smile. Even the public galleries were fuller than usual. Perhaps the word had got about, and staff and other visitors anticipated interesting times in this next session.

At precisely 1.30 the bells stopped, and the serjeant-at-arms announced the speaker. She took her place, first bowing to the government benches and then to the opposition benches.

'Before continuing with the business of the day, I would like to make a statement.' Bagshaw picked up a paper and read the words prepared for her by the prime minister's office. 'Members will be aware that this is the last day of sitting for the year. It is my intention to not allow unparliamentary behaviour to continue, and I provide a general warning to all members. I will remove any member creating a disturbance and not following my rulings, under Standing Order 94A. They will be asked to leave the chamber immediately.'

A smiling Gerrard scanned the opposition, pursed his lips in a silent kiss and gave a knowing wink to Stanley.

'It has been agreed by the leaders of both parliamentary parties that there will be no divisions or votes, out of respect to our fallen colleagues, tragically killed last week. I remind members that we should honour their memories by not allowing the parliament to fall into disarray with poor disruptive behaviour during this day. Clerk.'

Stanley rose to get the call before the clerk could respond. 'Leader of the opposition.'

'Madam Speaker, I seek leave to table a letter addressed to you from the opposition seeking your resignation from your position. The letter cites our reasons, and I think it should be made public.'

'Is leave granted?' Bagshaw looked to Meredith Bruce for direction, who was shaking her head in the negative. 'Leave is not granted.'

Gordon, watching the proceedings on his television, quickly pulled his phone from his jacket pocket and tapped a message.

Move a no-confidence motion on the speaker.

'Madam Speaker, on a point of order.'

'Leader of the opposition, on a point of order.'

Messenger felt his phone buzz and read the message.

'Speaker, we would like to know when you will respond to the house on the matters contained in the letter.'

'There is no point of order.'

'Rubbish!'

'The Member of Brand will remove himself from the chamber for one hour, under Standing Order 94A.'

Wilson Campbell remained firmly seated; he had no intention of moving. 'Serjeant, please escort the honourable member from the chamber.'

The serjeant, seated by the front door to the chamber

leading to the ministerial wing and directly opposite the speaker, rose in his place and began walking toward Campbell to escort him out.

'Don't bother, I'm going.' Campbell stood and moved past the despatch box, shaking his finger at Gerrard. 'You'll get yours one day, we know all about you.'

Gerrard was fairly sure they knew nothing, and it was all bluster and bluff. He gave the victory sign to Stanley, 'Two more, keep going.'

'Madam Speaker, on indulgence. I would like to know—' Stanley continued as Campbell moved past him.

'The leader of the opposition will resume his seat,' Bagshaw interrupted Stanley.

'... why you believe I have no point of order to this—'

'The leader of the opposition will resume his seat.' Bagshaw stood, immediately stopping Stanley, and he sat waiting for the call. As he sat, Messenger quickly moved into the vacant seat beside him.

'Move a motion of no confidence,' Messenger urged.

'We can't vote. They won't let us.'

'It doesn't matter, at least it will be on the record.'

The speaker resumed her seat. 'On the matter raised by the leader of the opposition, I can advise him I shall seek legal counsel and formerly write to him with my response.'

Stanley snapped to the despatch box, 'On indulgence, Madam Speaker.'

'No indulgence given, resume your seat.' Bagshaw was out of her chair again silencing potential dissent. Gerrard leaned back in his chair, rocking back and forth, following the proceedings with an admiring smirk.

Still standing, the speaker said, 'This is a house for the consideration of bills that come before it. I have a bill at the third reading stage, which I would like to have passed by the house before we move to question time. It is time the leader of the opposition stopped his political game-playing and allowed me to get on with the business of the house.'

As she resumed her seat, Stanley stood waiting for the call, prompting groans of contempt from the government backbench.

'The leader of the opposition,' Bagshaw sighed.

'I seek leave to move a motion that the house has lost confidence in the speaker and in the manner in which she is discharging her duties.'

'Is leave granted?'

Bruce shook her head.

'Leave is not granted.'

'I therefore move for the suspension of standing orders and the order of the day, so that the following motion can be moved: that this house has lost confidence in the speaker and in the manner in which she is discharging her duties.' Stanley passed his handwritten notice to the clerks. 'Madam Speaker, the opposition is moving this motion today...'

'I move the speaker no longer be heard.' Meredith Bruce was quick to respond.

'The question is that the speaker be no longer heard. All those of that opinion say aye, to the contrary no, I think the ayes have it. Resume your seat,' Bagshaw demanded of Stanley, who complied. 'Is the motion seconded?'

'I second the motion. Madam Speaker, this motion is important to debate today—' Messenger didn't have much time to get his first sentence out.

'I move the speaker no longer be heard.' Bruce was again quickly at the despatch box.

'The question is that the speaker be no longer heard. All those of that opinion say aye, to the contrary no, I think the ayes have it. Resume your seat.'

'The question is that the motion moved by the opposition leader be agreed to. All those of that opinion say aye, to the contrary no. I think the noes have it.' It was over in a few short minutes and the opposition had nothing left. 'Clerk.'

'Order of the day, resumption of debate on the third reading of Appropriation Bill Seven.'

'I call the prime minister.'

Gerrard came to the despatch box, jostled a few papers – just a twenty-minute speech to wind up the debate, a quick vote on the voices and the job would be done. He would then seek indulgence from the speaker and make a statement to the parliament resigning his commission as prime minister, immediately retiring from the parliament. Then it was Paris for Christmas.

'Madam Speaker, the legislation before us is a reward. A reward to the many hard-working Australians who have had a difficult year and deserve a good Christmas. We have seen the opposition attempt to oppose these payments and deny the electorate a good Christmas. Australian taxpayers will punish them at the next election for their callous behaviour, and the total disregard for their needs. Let the Australian people know that the opposition is now focused on an exercise of rejection and rebuff, and reduced to muckraking and nitpicking, pursuing matters of no substance so that they can stop Australians getting their Christmas bonus.'

As Gerrard continued his speech, Messenger ignored it and fidgeted with his phone, hoping for another message.

# CHAPTER 22

## THURSDAY 1.35 PM

'What's wrong, Gordon, are you okay? You look very pale. I'll get you some water.'

As Marjorie dashed off to get a glass of water from the cooler in her office, Gordon sank into his lounge, uncertain what to do next. Should he take the initiative to restore the integrity of the parliament? Would anyone care if he did, or not? He was a servant of the parliament, not the guardian – the politicians were the sentinels, not him. The politicians determined standards, putting their careers on the line every election to be judged by the people; he didn't. Democracy: for the people, by the people. It was not the job of a servant of the parliament to restore propriety to the institution and protect it – it was the politicians who had that responsibility, not him.

'Here you are, Gordon, is there anything else I can get you?'

'Yes please, Marjorie, could you get the chief justice on the phone, please?'

'Certainly, will that be all?'

Gordon looked at her, gnawing at his bottom lip, 'There is much I must do, Marjorie, and I'm a little scared by it all. If I don't act, then potentially a fraud could be committed and the Australian people will be the victims, but if I do act, then the even greater crime of trashing the parliament's history – its practice and its protocols, which I have proudly defended for many years – will have been committed against the parliament.'

'I don't understand.'

'And that, Marjorie, is the crux of my dilemma. Neither do I.'

She left Gordon in peace to get the chief justice, stepping aside as George Nikolaos entered carrying a large orange envelope. 'I have the final report for you, Gordon.'

'What have you got for me?'

'I have been able to confirm that Bagshaw did visit Gerrard on Sunday evening, staying a few hours and leaving her car waiting for her. I have pictures of her arriving and timed pictures of her leaving through a secluded entrance, looking a little dishevelled, I must say.' Nikolaos was a little reluctant to talk about his report. 'I also have evidence of her visiting the prime minister on further occasions for what seems in most cases to be inappropriate behaviour.'

'What do you suggest in your report?'

'The photographs I have been able to take on these occasions don't leave too much to the imagination, I'm afraid.'

'Are these all you have?'

'I have images within the PM's suite that are a little too grainy because of the infrared, but what you can see is not complimentary of the speaker.'

'What else?'

'As I said, I have her at the prime minister's suite on a further three occasions during the last few days, perhaps indicating that she is not as independent as she would have you believe.'

'Were you able to find the clerk from the drafting office?'

'Columbia is the latest recorded contact.'

'Mrs Gerrard?'

'Will leave on an Emirates flight to Dubai this afternoon, with a connection to Milan.'

'Not Zurich?' Gordon was disappointed.

'A late change of schedule, apparently.'

'Strange, I could have sworn she was off to Switzerland – I approved it.'

'She is.' George referred to his notes. 'She has booked an overnight train ticket to Zurich, under her maiden name Swanson, returning to Milan next Tuesday, using her personal passport, the one she uses when travelling unofficially. She has a hotel booking in Milan until next Thursday.'

'Nice one, George. Well done.'

'Will that be all, sir?'

'How graphic are the photographs from the PM's office?'

'Enough to leave nothing to the imagination.'

'Thanks, George, you have been fantastic this week. I appreciate the work you have done.'

'It was a pleasure, sir. I haven't done that sort of thing for quite a while.'

Gordon took the envelope from him – the weight surprised him – and led his confederate to the door. 'Drop by later for a farewell drink if you like.'

'That would be a pleasure, sir. If you need me further, sir, please call.'

Gordon tossed the envelope on the coffee table after quickly checking the contents. His face fell into lines of distress as he walked to his desk to answer the phone. He had hoped others in the parliament would have been able to take the initiative and leave him out of the mess in which he was now embroiled. It seemed the opposition were powerless to stand up to Gerrard and Bagshaw.

'O'Brien, speaking.'

'Gordon, it's Ben Hopetoun. Have you made a decision?'

'Hello, Ben. Yes, I'm afraid to say I have.'

'Did the speaker resign?'

'No, it was awful.' Gordon flopped into his chair. 'The media had been advised the opposition would be calling for her resignation and she bluntly told them to go away.'

'Do you have your evidence of collusion?'

'Yes, I just got a report from my man adding to the preliminary photographic evidence, which I am sorry to say is much more graphic, and it confirms what I regrettably suspected to be true. There is a crime being perpetrated on the Australian people as we speak.'

'Then you must act quickly, and with certainty. There is no time to waste.'

'You're right. When can you both get here?'

'We'll be there by 1.50 at the latest. Is that enough time?'

'Gerrard has only fifteen minutes of his speech to go so that will make it 1.55. Make sure you do not delay otherwise we are sunk.'

'Let's meet at the chamber foyer to save time. Take care.'

'See you soon then, Ben.' Gordon replaced the receiver, and noted the time in his diary: 1.40 pm. As he closed the leather-bound book for possibly the last time, Gordon began writing a proclamation that he had hoped he would never have to deliver.

---

Anita Devlin heard the bells for the resumption of parliament and began to hurry, scooting along in her sneakers. She guessed there was about to be action in the house and wanted to watch it in her office. She hoped Peter Cleaver would welcome her analysis of the Indonesian funding dispersal, and the possibly fraudulent act that was about to take place in the chamber. She had nothing solid, just circumstantial evidence, but she knew a politically sensitive allegation like this would run hard in the media and gain enough publicity to warrant further investigation, possibly through a parliamentary inquiry, or even a judicial inquiry, like a royal commission.

'What have you got?' Cleaver asked, as Anita hurried into his office, having dropped files and papers on her desk.

'It was hard to find, but within the antiquated Indonesian company registrations, I found the president is a director of a company that is a shareholder of the construction company ... no wait ... a major silent shareholder of a construction company, owned and managed by a childhood friend from central Java.' Anita paced the floor numbering off her points on her left hand.

'Big deal, what politician in Asia doesn't have a construction company?'

'Two. This construction company, Yogyakarta, won the tender for all the immigration centres funded by the Australian government.' Anita smiled. 'Plus, you are going to love this, the original budget estimates from the government were four billion, and the actual funding is now forty million extra.' Anita sat and kicked her feet on to the desk.

'So what?'

'Failed arithmetic at school, did we?'

'Stop playing with me, Anita.'

'It just happens to be exactly one per cent of the total deal.'

'Exactly?' Cleaver scratched his head roughly.

'Sounds like it could be a clip to me,' he said.

'And me. The question is, who is taking the clip?'

'How strong is the relationship between Surriento and Gerrard? Is it stronger than just heads of state?'

'I couldn't find much, but his wife went to Melbourne University and studied the same science degree as one Margaret Swanson, now Gerrard.'

'You're kidding me. Seriously?'

'You know those old-school connection sites on the web?

Well, if you put in a name, you can get a lot of information. I went searching for the president and found a link, then I also noticed his wife went to Melbourne University.'

'This is the reason I don't use social media.'

'You are a dinosaur, Cleave.'

'What else have you got?'

Anita was once more counting on her fingers. 'I have Margaret Gerrard, a dear friend of the president's wife.'

'Assumed.'

'All right, assumed friend.' Anita scribbled in her notes. 'I have a story about the prime minister resigning and, incomprehensibly, no response from his press officer. I have Margaret Gerrard flying to Zurich. I have forty million dollars added within the last few days to the original tender price, which is unaccounted for and for which no explanation is given, which could be a secret commission.'

'That is the most interesting so far.'

'I have amended legislation approved by the senate late at night, breaching all previous parliamentary conventions. I have a house of reps about to agree to this shonky Indonesian money deal ...'

'Alleged shonky deal.'

'Okay, alleged shonky deal without any proper parliamentary scrutiny, which I think is the most controversial.'

'It does seem strange.'

'Plus, I have a parliament seemingly out of control, because the speaker is refusing to take a formal vote.'

'Which all adds up to what?' Cleaver asked.

'The prime minister is about to rip off the taxpayers with a forty- million-dollar superannuation retirement gift.' Anita smiled broadly.

'You're only guessing. You can't confirm anything.'

'That's true, but I get the feeling Gerrard is up to something shonky, and I would like to run with it.'

'I think I could be persuaded to agree with you.' Cleaver stood at his desk and Anita jumped to her feet. 'It's flimsy and very risky but write it. I'll get the legal boys in Sydney to check it over before we publish. Try and emphasise the deliberate lack of parliamentary scrutiny. Good work.'

'Thanks, Cleave.'

'Will it get front page?'

'Maybe, but I can't promise it because parliament is out of control. Just get it done as quick as you can.'

---

'Marjorie, I just sent you an email with a document that needs to be printed on parchment. Can you get it done as quickly as possible for me, please?' Gordon called to his assistant.

'We don't have any. Will any paper do?'

'We what?' Gordon gasped. 'Why don't we have any? Christ, it needs to be on parchment, the governor-general is required to sign it.'

'We've been waiting for some, but they are yet to deliver. We can expect some tomorrow.'

'But I need it now. Jeezus!' Gordon rushed into Marjorie's office. 'What can we do? I'm running out of time.'

'The speaker may have some. I'll go and check.' Paige Alexander bolted from the room.

'You are kidding me, the speaker?' Gordon suddenly bent over, his hands on his knees, panting and shaking his head. 'What's the time? This is unbelievable?'

'It's 1.45,' said Marjorie, reading the proclamation. 'This is serious ... and we're using her parchment?'

'What a day. It's killing me.' Gordon straightened up and walked back into his office to put on his gown and pick up the security report and photographs in the yellow envelope. 'I need it within five minutes, no more.'

'Relax, Gordon, it'll be okay,' Marjorie said as she moved to the printer to ensure it was working.

'No, I can't wait any longer,' said Gordon, striding briskly to the door. 'Bring it to the chamber foyer as soon as it is done and bring George Nikolaos with you.' Paige was almost bowled over as they passed each other at the door, dropping the parchment, stepping on it and crumpling a corner.

As Gordon fled to the stairwell, his gown billowing as he searched for the other armhole, he tapped into his phone a text to Messenger.

> We need to talk urgently. No time left.
> Meet me in the opp rep courtyard in
> exactly 2 mins.

Messenger stood, bowed to the speaker, and immediately left

the chamber. To avoid scrutiny, he walked up the stairs by the adviser boxes, and left the chamber by the door leading to the whip's office. He saw no-one in the outside corridor, or the lobby to the chamber, and quickly made his way to the representatives' courtyard. He pushed hard on the heavy glass door and stepped out into the warmth of the day. Seeing no-one, he kept walking toward the corner of the opposition leader's office. As he rounded the corner of the building, he was startled to see Gordon O'Brien coming straight at him in a rush.

'You're the one sending me those texts?' Messenger asked. 'Why are you doing that? What are you up to?'

'We have just a few moments, so listen to me very carefully. I can't tell you what is about to happen, but when you have the nod from me in the chamber, and you will know exactly when that is, move a motion for the house to adjourn.'

'Why? Isn't that the job of the government?'

'Don't ask questions, just do it!' Gordon hissed. 'Then once the vote has been taken on voices, have Stanley read this motion exactly as it is typed, do you understand?'

'Are you sure? No, I don't understand. What is going on?

'As I have just told you, I can't tell you what is about to happen, so you must trust me.'

'Doesn't the government always adjourn the house?'

'Not on this occasion, so please do what I ask. The stakes are enormous, and if this venture is to work as planned, what we are about to do needs to be done correctly, so please do exactly as I ask.'

'I am not sure about this, Gordon. You want Peter to read this?'

'There will only one be chance, Mr Messenger. If you want transparent government and you want to defer this Indonesian funding, then move quickly when I give you the sign and have Stanley immediately read it at the despatch box, exactly as it is written, otherwise we are buggered.'

'All right, I'll try and do as you ask, but the speaker will never allow it. Why are you doing this?'

'No time to explain.' Having said all he could, Gordon scurried off back to his meeting with the chief justice.

Messenger returned to the chamber and called Stanley over for a quiet conference in the unused seats, right up the back, behind the Country Party, away from distractions and Gerrard's gaze.

The prime minister was fifteen minutes into his allocated twenty, and yet to speak on the amended legislation in any substantial way. His primary message was about him leading a fine and honest government, and how he had enjoyed the confidence of the electorate for almost twenty good years.

'Peter, I have just met with the clerk.'

'O'Brien? What did he have to say?'

'He gave me specific instructions and asked me to ensure you move this motion at the appropriate time when he indicates, and I move for the house to adjourn.' Messenger handed over the letter he had received from O'Brien, and Stanley quickly scanned it.

'Fuck!'

'Exactly. This is now a very serious game we are playing,' Messenger said.

'How does he expect this to get up if we're not taking divisions? The speaker will shut us done, surely?'

'I don't know, he didn't tell me.' Messenger was as confused as Stanley. 'He just said I should move the house to adjourn at the appropriate time, and that I will know when that will be.'

'This can't be true?' Hopetoun shoved the photographs and the security report back into the envelope and kept it at his side, along with a thin, red manila folder with a single document inside. 'Surely there must be another explanation?'

'There isn't one that I can think of I'm afraid, Ben,' Gordon replied.

'Then we must act, and we must do so right now. We must also ensure the process of the parliament is followed because if we don't, it would almost amount to an illegal coup d'état.' The chief justice started pacing back and forward. 'A coup d'état – is there no other way? You are sure, aren't you, Gordon?'

'I know one thing, if we release the Indonesian money today, and not in February, then a terrible crime will have been committed against the parliament, and Australia.'

'What do you think, your excellency?' Hopetoun asked the governor-general.

'Having seen the evidence, I trust Gordon, and if he thinks we must act, then we must.'

'This will end all our careers and probably send us to jail if we don't get it right,' Hopetoun said, still pacing, as Gordon scribbled a quick note onto a desk pad beside the chamber door and pushed the call button for an attendant in the chamber to come to the vestibule. 'We must avoid any challenge from the prime minister, and we must avoid anarchy at any cost.'

'I have tried to resolve the issue by other means, but they have failed.' Gordon said sadly. 'Regrettably, I considered this action for some time, and it is the only way that I can think of to protect the parliament. I have called extra security if we need it.'

'Are you sure, Gordon?' asked the governor-general.

'I am, absolutely.'

'You are a brave man, my friend.'

'I am not brave, Your Excellency, far from it. I'm the opposite, to be perfectly honest.' Gordon said nervously. 'I just need to do a brave thing.'

The attendant opened the door slightly and Gordon slipped the note to her, as Marjorie arrived with George Nikolaos and three burly security officers and five attendants. 'Sorry I'm late, we had trouble getting it through the printer.'

'Thanks, Marjorie.' Gordon took the document from her and passed it to the chief justice to read, who then passed it to the governor-general.

'Please sign it, Your Excellency,' said Hopetoun. 'Do you have the writs, Gordon?'

'Yes, they are here,' said Marjorie stepping forward and passing a manila file to Hopetoun.

In the chamber, Prime Minister Gerrard was into the last minutes of his oration as Speaker Bagshaw received the note calling on her to attend the vestibule as the governor-general wanted to convey important and vital instructions to her. Bagshaw immediately indicated to Charlie Edmunds, the chair of committees, that he should take the chair. Edmunds promptly replaced Speaker Bagshaw in the chair as she passed through the door into the vestibule.

Gerrard was momentarily distracted by the sudden withdrawal of the speaker, and stopped talking, turning quickly to refer to Meredith Bruce, who sat behind him on the bench. Twenty seconds remained on the speaker's clock. Once the prime minister had finished his speech, the speaker would normally announce the legislation had been read a third time and call for the motion to be agreed to, but now an opposition member was in the chair. Just a few more seconds until the vote was to be taken to approve the legislation funding the immigration detention centres and providing punters with a celebratory Christmas bonus and sending the Gerrards to a very comfortable French retirement, but the speaker wasn't in the chair. The opposition had the numbers – and now control of the chamber.

Gerrard leaned into Bruce, hissing in her ear. 'What the hell is she up to? We need her in here. We can't take a vote yet with them in the chair.'

'I'll extend your time, relax. She'll be back.' Bruce was quick to the despatch box and Gerrard stood, a little bewildered, beside her.

'I move that the speaker's time be extended five minutes.'

'The question is that the speaker's time be extended by five minutes. All those in favour say aye, the contrary no, I think the ayes have it. The prime minister's time is extended five minutes.'

Stanley and Messenger, who had resumed their seats at the table in readiness, sat a little perplexed as they watched the speaker leave and Gerrard request extra time. Stanley again, nervously, glanced through his intended statement to the house.

Speaker Bagshaw anxiously entered the vestibule to find the governor-general, the chief justice, the clerk, three security officers and attendants, and George Nikolaos lurking by the door to stop anyone from the chamber joining them.

'Your Excellency, this note said you needed to see me urgently, how can I help?'

'The chief justice would like a word.'

Hopetoun stood rigid, arms by his sides, hands held stiffly like a military officer at attention, the envelope gripped in his left hand. 'Madam Speaker, I have strong and overwhelming evidence that your recent behaviour in the house, and elsewhere, has brought the parliament into disrepute.' He raised the envelope above his head as if shading himself from the sun. 'It is my considered view – and I have the concurrence of the governor-general – that you should immediately resign your elected position and revoke your commission. Should you not resign forthwith, I will instruct these security officers to take you into custody to await federal law officers to attend and lay serious charges of fraud and conspiracy upon you.'

'What's going on?' Bagshaw's knees buckled slightly, but she steadied herself, looking to Gordon for support and getting none. 'What evidence?' she said hoarsely, forcing the words out.

'I have compromising photographic evidence of you allegedly acting inappropriately in the discharge of your duties with the prime minister.' Hopetoun began opening the envelope, and fanning photographs as he partially pulled them out, before pushing them back. 'These photographs, along with a deeply concerning security report, add weight to these alleged conspiracy charges against you. That you, jointly with the prime minister, hope to defraud the Commonwealth of Australia of significant money, specifically in the appropriation legislation currently before the house.'

'What?' Bagshaw laughingly stammered, her mouth agape.

'Furthermore, I am of the strong view that you have failed to discharge your duties as an impartial officer of the parliament.'

'This can't be right.' Bagshaw shook her head as tears welled in her eyes. 'Gordon, what's going on?'

Hopetoun continued, as Gordon avoided her pleading eyes. 'You also failed to alter your behaviour when challenged by an aggrieved opposition leadership group earlier today. You have had total disregard for the processes of the parliament and applied biased interpretations on your rulings. You have failed to interpret the parliamentary standing orders correctly, and you have neglected the rights, and privileges, of elected members of the parliament.'

'I was just doing what I was asked to do by the prime minister,' Bagshaw said softly. 'I was doing my job.'

'We understand that Zara, but this is what you now must do.' The governor-general stepped forward and laid a hand on her arm. 'You must resign or be charged with these offences. It is one or the other; there are no other options. My preference is that you resign, immediately.'

'I just wanted to do my job, for my people.'

The chief justice held a red folder before Bagshaw, pulling from it a stark white document with the seal of the chief justice emblazoned upon it. 'I present you with a formal letter of resignation under the seal of the chief justice. I wish you now to sign it, otherwise these commissioned officers will act to take you into custody and hold you until the federal police formally charge you with fraud and conspiracy.'

She hesitated only a moment, but all the fight had gone out of her. She took the proffered pen and signed the paper.

'What happens to the current sitting?' Bagshaw asked.

'That is no longer your concern, Ms Bagshaw.' Hopetoun snapped back the folder. 'I'll have your robe also.' Bagshaw took off her robe and passed it to him and was led off to her office by a security officer and a parliamentary attendant.

Hopetoun passed the robe to Gordon, who tentatively put it on. The chief justice also passed him the resignation letter and the proclamation delivered by a breathless Marjorie a few minutes earlier, now signed by the governor-general, and opened the manila file with the prepared writs for signing at the appropriate time. As Gordon steadied himself at the door, sucking two deep breaths into his lungs, Hopetoun said, 'Good luck, Gordon. We will be here when you get back.'

As Gerrard began his concluding remarks about his wonderfully generous government, Gordon entered the chamber and stepped up into the chair. 'Make way, please, Mr Edmunds.'

A stunned silence settled over the chamber as Edmunds made his way back to his seat and the clerk stood before the parliament. Members did not know how to respond. The instinct of some of them might have been to object loudly and query why there was a stranger in the chair. But someone wearing the formal robes of the speaker was seeking silence, which meant the house should continue to be quiet.

'The prime minister will resume his seat. Members...' Gordon cleared his throat and started again. 'Members, it is my melancholy duty to inform you of the immediate resignation of Speaker Bagshaw. I table her formally signed resignation for the consideration of the house.'

Richard Barker reached up and took from Gordon the emblazoned resignation paper and placed it on the parliamentary practice books beside the government despatch box. Gerrard snatched it up and resumed his seat to read it, Meredith Bruce standing and reading over his shoulder.

'According to parliamentary practice and procedure, if the speaker resigns there is required to be an immediate election for a new speaker, forthwith. I have assumed the chair in accordance with parliamentary practice to allow for the election of a new speaker,' Gordon continued.

Bruce resumed her seat, leaning forward to quietly discuss the incident with Gerrard, in a huddle with Menzies. She didn't know what to do, and sought advice from her boss, who appeared to be as perplexed as she. There was an immediate general commotion from members of the parliament as they discussed with nearby colleagues the unusual circumstance they now faced.

'Order, the house will come to order. As there has been no deputy speaker formally elected in the parliamentary period since the tragic death of Ms Kennedy last week, parliamentary practice directs the clerk to hold such an election for the speaker.' Gordon was reading from his prepared script. 'I table the governor-general's proclamation giving me the authority to act to elect a speaker.'

Gordon passed the proclamation to Richard Barker, and glanced at Messenger and locked eyes, raising one eyebrow to ensure he understood that now was the time to act. 'Once the immediate business of the house is concluded, we shall move to such an election.'

Before Meredith Bruce could respond from her strategic conversation huddle with Gerrard and Menzies, Messenger was at the despatch box.

'I move that the house do now adjourn.'

Bruce looked up from the discussion, distracted by her prime minister's pleas for the legislation to be voted on that day, and didn't think about the motion put to the house. She considered it was the right thing to do, in the context of getting a new speaker elected. Bruce questioned Gerrard on how to finalise the third reading of the legislation if the opposition were to have one of their own as speaker. She advised Gerrard they would now need to negotiate with the opposition after the election of the new speaker, and the following question time was possibly irrelevant and not required. Bruce reassured Gerrard, with the support of the attorney-general Menzies, that there was still time to get the legislation approved that sitting day.

Gordon continued, 'The question is that the house does now adjourn. All those of that opinion say aye, to the contrary no, I think the ayes have it.'

Stanley immediately stood at the despatch box, seeking the call from the speaker, taking government members by surprise.

'I call the leader of the opposition.'

'Speaker, before you adjourn the house for the election of a new speaker,' Stanley now read from the paper. 'I move that, given the government has just lost the confidence of the house through a motion moved by the opposition to adjourn the house, I now advise the house, that having been moved, and then won by a vote of the opposition, under long-standing parliamentary practice, I am now the new formally elected leader of the house of representatives and by this action the prime minister. Therefore, I direct you to immediately advise the governor-general to dissolve this parliament, so that a general election can be held at the earliest possible time.'

'The question is that this house now be dissolved,' stated Gordon.

Members of parliament could not have known the implications of the question. Who could understand such an obscure ruling, that the house be dissolved for an immediate federal election? The government leaders were not paying attention to the parliamentary proceedings and were unsure of the political significance of the events unfolding before them, still expecting a move by the parliament to elect a new speaker. 'All those of that opinion say aye, the contrary no, the ayes have it.'

'The noes have it.' Gerrard shouted, scrambling to the despatch box, suddenly realising that the parliament, and therefore his government, was about to be dismissed, and that his retirement plans had collapsed due to parliamentary process.

'The member for Melbourne will resume his seat. In accordance with the formal agreement between the previous government and the opposition, signed four days ago, confirmed today by a statement to this house by Speaker Bagshaw, there are to be no divisions. The ayes have it.'

Gordon ignored the howling protests from the government benches, led by Gerrard, as members suddenly became aware of the implications of the vote. 'I now formally prorogue the house of representatives. I will visit the governor-general with writs to be issued for a general election.'

Gerrard jumped to the despatch box. 'My government will formally advise the governor-general to ignore this vote. Convention says the governor-general must act on the advice of the prime minister.'

'You are no longer prime minister, I am,' shouted Stanley. 'And I have just advised the governor-general to dismiss the house. Who is the rabble now, cupcake?'

Gordon jumped from the chair, knowing he needed to move faster than Gerrard to get to the governor-general. But the governor-general was waiting, as arranged, in the vestibule to sign the election writs once Gordon could advise her that the house had been prorogued. As she signed the documents, Gerrard crashed through the door.

'What the hell do you think you're doing?' he shouted.

'I am signing writs for a general election, Mr Gerrard,' the governor-general calmly responded.

'I am your prime minister, and you are constitutionally bound to follow my advice.' Gerrard tried hard to remain calm. 'I advise you, that you should not sign those writs.' He took a deep breath. 'Let's all settle down, and work this issue out calmly, please folks. Where is Speaker Bagshaw?'

'Mr Gerrard, you are no longer prime minister. You have lost a confidence vote on the floor of the house,' the governor-general explained.

'It was just an adjournment motion,' Gerrard retorted.

'Yes, it was, and moved by the opposition.' The governor-general finished signing the documents and passed them to Hopetoun. 'I am advised by the chief justice that such an adjournment vote moved and won by the opposition of the day is identical to a vote of no confidence in the government taken by the house.' The governor- general stepped back, looked at Gerrard and smiled. 'And as I am advised by the clerk of the parliament, just now, you lost the vote. Therefore, you have lost government, Mr Gerrard, and therefore I have signed the writs so that the nation will immediately move to a general election.'

'She is right, Andrew,' Hopetoun added.

'Oh, shut up!' Gerrard snapped. 'What the hell are you doing here, anyway.'

'I was asked to attend,' Hopetoun said.

'By whom?' Gerrard replied incredulously.

'By the senior officer of the parliament.'

'*You*!' Gerrard turned on Gordon, 'This is your idea?' Gerrard's sudden thrust was quickly and deftly intercepted by security officers who held him back as he struggled against their grip until he slowly regained some composure.

'Mr Gerrard, please calm down,' the governor-general implored. 'The parliament is greater than all of us standing here, and we are just servants of the people. It has managed serious issues of constitutional disagreements like this before during its history, and no doubt it will do so again. We shall have a general election and the matters currently before the parliament can be revisited when the parliament resumes.'

Hopetoun added, 'By my calculation, this will be a few days prior to Christmas. Should you win the election, you can bring forward any legislation you see fit. So, your funding, which seems so important to you, can be approved by the parliament at that time, and the punters can get their money on time, if you win the election.'

'And the Indonesian detention centre funding will be sent, as originally planned, in February,' said Gordon. 'It's called proper parliamentary process – and that's why we call it a democracy.' He couldn't help himself.

Gerrard stood back from the security guards, calmed himself, straightened his jacket and adjusted his tie. 'When I return as prime minister, I will have all of your jobs, all of you,' Gerrard said, as he pointed at each of them individually, then stormed off. 'I will have you *all* for doing this to me, you will not survive this, none of you!'

'It seems the former prime minister is a little upset,' the governor- general offered.

'Yes, Your Excellency,' Gordon replied smiling broadly. 'It would appear so.'

# CHAPTER 23

## THURSDAY 3.48 PM

'It's over.' Gerrard sat at his desk, pinching his forehead as he gave the news to his friend in Indonesia. 'The earliest we can get it to you will be February.'

'That is not good for me.'

'There is nothing I can do about it now; I'm no longer prime minister.'

'That is a sad news, my friend. I will now have to withdraw the order for clemency for your citizens.'

'Amir, come on, you can't execute them because you won't get your money until next year.'

'There is no guarantee of that. You may not win the election.'

'I will win the fucking election and I will get you your money.'

'Andrew, I cannot be sure of it, so I will stop all works on the detention centres, withhold the clemency order and recall my ambassador, and you can forget any deal we may have had.'

'What? Why?'

'My people cannot trust you to keep your word, so if you want to regain our confidence, I suggest you win the election.'

---

Zara Bagshaw had returned to her office, drawn the curtains, and stretched out on her leather lounge. The darkened room held back the events of the day until a quiet tap on her door preceded the entrance of a staff member who whispered, 'Zara, your father is on the phone insisting he speak with you.'

'I can't speak to anyone at the moment.'

'He is refusing to take no for an answer, I'm afraid. He is becoming abusive.'

'All right, put him through.' Zara sat up, grasping the back of the lounge to steady herself, one hand gripping a bundle of tissues. She walked slowly to her desk, burdened with the weight of failure, and sat as the phone rang.

'Hello?'

'Honey, what's happened? Are you okay?'

'I'm fine. I have a migraine, but I am fine.'

'That's crap, you sound dreadful. I just heard the news about the election and your resignation, what happened?'

She sighed. 'The parliament thought I should resign because they basically thought I was biased against the opposition, so I agreed and resigned. The parliament was then prorogued, and now we are to have a general election. Simple really.'

'How are you feeling?'

Zara bit her bottom lip and wiped her eyes, dropping the hand with the receiver into her lap and letting her head fall back as she stared at the ceiling.

'Honey, are you there?'

'Daddy, I've done a bad thing.'

'Come home, darling, come home today.'

---

'I blame you really,' Anita said as she sipped her champagne from a plastic cup.

'For what, exactly?' Messenger had bought a bottle to celebrate the events of the day.

'I had the chance to get a front-page by-line, and now your mob will be plastered all over the first eight pages.'

'You can still run with the story.'

'It's only wild speculation now that the legislation wasn't passed; the story is in the bin.' Anita proffered her flimsy cup for more sparkling wine. Messenger obliged with a splash that sent a foam rinse over her hand. 'What happens now?'

'We go to a general election, and hopefully we come back as the government in a month.'

'Would you still send the money to the Indonesians?'

'Probably, since it's part of our policy, ironically.' Messenger pushed back on the legs of his chair, putting a foot on Anita's desk. 'We will guarantee to pay the stimulus package before Christmas to nullify it as an election issue, and when we come back to the parliament, we will scrutinise the funds going offshore a little more rigorously than we did this time.'

'So, you could be deputy prime minister in a month?'

'Seems that I could be, yes. Would that be a problem for you?'

'Not at all.' Anita smiled. 'The question really is, will I be a problem for you?'

'You already are.'

'So, no exclusives then?' Anita teased.

'I can absolutely guarantee to be exclusive,' Messenger laughed. 'If you're interested.'

---

The sun was warm on Gordon's face as he sat on a bench outside the staff cafeteria. The sound of children squealing and laughing in the nearby parliamentary childcare centre, oblivious to the fact that history had just been made, didn't disturb him. He was enjoying his moment of solitude. His phone buzzed incessantly with calls and text messages that he had ignored for the almost two hours he had been peacefully sitting there.

'Gordon?' A hesitant Paige Alexander approached. 'Are you okay?'

'Come and sit with me, Paige,' Gordon beckoned her closer. 'Did you know the Regent Honeyeater is almost extinct from the Canberra region?'

Paige sat tentatively, slightly concerned for her boss. 'No, I didn't know that.'

'Yes, it has a distinctive call.' Gordon was staring off into the distance. 'And there is one right there in that tree down the hill, do you see it?

Paige followed his pointing arm but could see nothing. 'No.'

'*Anthochaera phrygia* is a rare one, critically endangered as it happens.' Gordon still gazed off into the distance. 'It feeds on nectar and insects within eucalyptus forests, so I wonder what it is doing here?'

Paige tried harder to find it. 'That yellow bird, in the tree?'

'Well, it is only yellow tipped, but yes, that's it.'

'And it's endangered?'

'Around here it is. Just like me, I suppose.'

'Gordon, I've come to get you. There are heaps of messages for you. There are a lot of people waiting to see you in the office.'

'No doubt there are, young Paige.' Gordon stood slowly, stretching as he did to ease his stiff legs and shoulders. 'No doubt there are.'

'So, come on. Let's go face the music.' Paige, cheery as ever, wanted her boss to attend the office, as he always did, to administer the business of the parliament.

'I think I shall go home now; there's nothing left for me to do here.' Gordon smiled and began walking down the grassed hill, toward the tree with the Regent Honeyeater. 'My work is done.'

'Gordon?' Paige called after him. 'Gordon? Tell me what to do.'

But O'Brien had already left – and there was nothing more he wanted to do.

# DID YOU ENJOY THE READ?

Authors thrive and rely on the opinion of readers, and I wonder if you could help?

I would be extremely grateful if you let other readers know what you thought of *Duplicity* by considering leaving an honest review on Amazon or Goodreads or posting a review on your social media including the tag, @852press.

If you would like to communicate with me then please do.

I always respond to emails and enjoy chatting about future projects and seeking opinion about some of the issues raised with my writing.

If you would like to be added to my Advanced Readers list, then please let me know.

readers@richardevans-author.com

Best wishes
Richard Evans

# DUPLICITY

THE SECOND EPISODE OF THE DEMOCRACY TRILOGY.

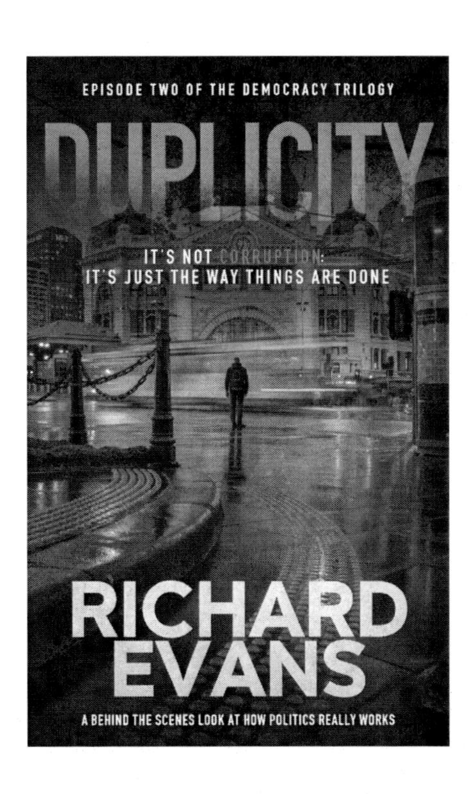

# CHAPTER 1

## DAY ONE – THURSDAY

Robert Wong knocked respectfully on his professor's wood-panelled office door. Finding it slightly ajar, he peered into the gloom and saw her concentrating on student papers. 'Professor Rukhmani? Have you got a few moments?'

The professor looked up and smiled as she recognised the student, pushing her marking pen into her tied-back hair. 'Sure Robert, come in. I've been meaning to contact you about your last paper.'

Wong tentatively ventured into the overstuffed office, wondering where he could sit.

'Grab a seat. Here, pass me that pile of papers.'

He removed the large stack of student work from the chair and the professor slapped them onto another pile behind her.

There seemed no order to the paper chaos surrounding the walls of the office, even the floor seemed to overflow with it.

'You seem really busy, sorry to interrupt.'

'No, not at all. I welcome the break. Don't worry about the mess—' The professor laughed, a little embarrassed by the state of her office. 'It's always like this. I seem to know where everything is though,' she said dreamily, perhaps thinking she should be more organised.

Wong sat on the edge of the chair, a little nervous about talking to his politics professor about his grand idea. Leaning slightly right so as to see around a high stack of papers on her desk, he asked apprehensively, 'What did you want to discuss with me about my paper?'

'This interesting idea you have about the legacy of Obama being a reason the Republicans eventually lost Congress and the presidency.' The professor reached up behind her toward another stack of papers, flicked up two assignments and with a quick flourish, withdrew Wong's paper with her attached notes. 'We haven't studied Saul Alinsky and his doctrine for community organising, so I wanted to ask why you referred to him so much in your paper. In particular, his nineteen-seventies ideas of collective community action to achieve political outcomes. Don't you think these ideas might be a little dated?'

'Just like everyone else in the United States, President Obama never accepted the legitimacy of Donald Trump as president, becoming, I think, very protective of his own legacy. It seems to me he encouraged his supporters to resist Trump by strategically initiating a targeted campaign against the president during the first term. It is highly unusual for a retiring president to remain politically active – even more so during the next election campaign. Bush, for instance, never campaigned against Obama.'

Wong opened his canvas satchel and fleshed around, pulling out a tattered book. 'I found Alinsky's handbook in a second-hand bookstore a few weeks back. The campaign methods correlate with how Obama ran his entire administration for eight years – and his community activism after he left office.'

The professor took the dog-eared book and carefully flicked through it. 'Alinsky was considered radical—' The professor paused as she flicked the pages. Without looking at her student she asked, 'Do you think Obama was a radical socialist?'

'Not really. Actually, I don't really know. Probably not, not strictly, but there is strong evidence that Obama was subtly using Alinsky's suggestions to incite division in the community.'

The professor smiled as she leaned back in her chair. 'That's a big claim. Can you cite any examples?'

'Well, in my view, there are plenty.' Wong sat forward, shifting the stack of papers aside to lean on the desk. 'During his time as president, Obama was consistent in blaming wealthy Americans for the social problems that beset the United States, especially after the financial crisis. He often suggested low-income earners were the victims of the greed of the wealthy and was always quick to support accusations of racism against police when black or brown Americans were involved – even when there was little evidence of actual racism.

In other words, he rubbed raw the resentment toward the police and the political system with his rhetoric – which mostly focused on the black community – and agitated almost to the point of inciting conflict. This could be interpreted as classic Alinsky teachings. His rules for radicals basically says: look for ways to increase insecurity, anxiety, and uncertainty in the community. No-one could deny the increased community demonstrations after Trump won.'

'Oh sure, who could forget. Everyone came out to demonstrate and many didn't even know why. They were angry with the result of the election and hate was stoked – it didn't help that Trump was an obnoxious dud either.'

'In my view, a lot of that disorder was driven by one of Obama's supporter groups, Organizing for America,' suggested Wong, pushing his glasses back up his nose.

'What makes you think Obama was instrumental in Trump's ultimate defeat?'

'The OFA started campaigning immediately after Trump won office. Every time Obama spoke, he incited community action to reclaim America. Remember he was out in the hustings on a regular basis asking citizens to resist and reclaim? And he hardly ever mentioned Trump by name; he just referred to the many challenges and lies from the administration.

'Like everyone else, he didn't think Trump was worthy of high office, framing him as an enemy of American values. Everyone spoke against the president, community action groups mobilised, and it virtually became a community revolution, which is classic Alinsky.

'In 2018 there were many congresswomen and men elected for the Democrats who came from a community movement. I found out the OFA recruited over fifty thousand community organisers to be disruptive against the administration by organising anti-Trump events.' Wong paused for a moment. 'They then drove the mail ballot vote and got out and secured those ballots for Biden in 2020.'

Wong reached back for his book, admiringly flicking through the pages before putting it back into his satchel. 'When you think about it, Obama was a little more politically covert than historians give him credit for. In my view, he was very manipulative and massaged his image extremely well. Obama is still loved the world over in lots of ways, but the truth is, he didn't achieve much as president – yet history has been very kind toward him, recording him as one of the best.'

'Interesting. I hadn't thought to link any influence of Alinsky on Obama. I probably wouldn't share your view – there are a lot of differing thoughts when it comes to politics – but you have made a good case for it in your paper, so well done.'

'Don't get me wrong. Sometimes these organised community tactics get things done – it is used a lot more by the major parties in a lot of western democratic countries at the moment.'

'Create division in the community and force the government to provide a solution.'

'Exactly.' Wong leaned back into his chair with a big smile, enjoying the moment with his favourite professor. 'The Democrats in the States, especially in places like Chicago, have been influenced by this kind of community organisation strategy for years – we now see it in action at most elections.

'This is the new power, I imagine. Community groups are

getting organised and campaigning on single issues impacting elections. They are usually well organised too, just like these so-called progressive parties emerging in Australia. And it's the reason, I think, Andrew Gerrard has been prime minister for so long.'

'Not because of his policies?'

'I think he's a populist prime minister who speaks directly to the have-nots in the community in order to maintain his power. He wedges policy all the time, but I finally sense a mood for change.'

'You think the electorate is in the mood to change the government?'

'Gerrard has made some really provocative procedural reforms to the parliament over recent years yet remains popular because he subtly drives community division on other policy. He is silent on his parliamentary reforms, which suggests to the electorate there's nothing to see. His party is better organised, using a whole raft of causes to get people out supporting him. Gerrard does exactly what Alinsky suggests – he picks a target, frames it to his advantage then personalises it, polarising the community to get active.'

Professor Rukhmani squeezed a slight admiring smile as she listened to her A-grade student.

'Get discontented voters who believe society is fundamentally unjust to take their lead from community organisers speaking about unfairness and suddenly you have a revolution.'

'One Nation and the other conservative groups?' she asked.

'Exactly. They're growing because the conservatives are not

strategically geared to organise the community. They seem too pompous to do anything other than act ethically, which is probably why they have remained in opposition for nearly twenty years. They don't want anything to do with the socially and economically handicapped, which leaves a gap in their policy for One Nation and others to fill.'

Rukhmani's chair squeaked as she leaned back. 'Are you going to use your study to advance a political career?'

Wong chortled a little, then said, 'That's exactly what I want to talk to you about.' The student leaned forward again with a broad, excited smile. 'Why don't you seek preselection for the federal election? I could be your campaign manager.'

The professor raised her eyebrows, flinging her arms out as if on a cross and looking to the ceiling in mock shock.

'You're kidding me, right?' the professor scoffed as she straightened to address Wong. 'And anyway, the election is too far into the future to even contemplate such a preposterous idea.'

'Haven't you been listening to the news?' Wong said, tossing his hands into the air in bogus exasperation as he sat back.

'If I could find my radio within this mess—' the professor looked glumly about her office. 'I'd be listening to music.'

'Haven't you heard about using technology, Professor?' The student sassed her. 'The government has been sacked by the governor-general.'

'What?' Rukhmani bolted upright in her chair. 'When?'

'About an hour ago. Apparently, the speaker resigned, and the clerk prorogued the parliament, or something like that.'

'You're kidding me?' Rukhmani fell back into her chair.

Bewildered by the news, she ran her fingers absent-mindedly through her tied thick hair.

'There's a federal election called for the ninth of December, and it's anyone's guess what will happen. I hope Gerrard loses.'

'They say a week is a long time in politics, and this week has been awful.' The professor slowly shook her head before slapping her hands to her thighs. 'This is unbelievable. First, we lose politicians in a tragic plane crash, and now this – unbelievable.'

'But with every misfortune comes opportunity,' Wong smiled, nodding excitedly with eyes wide. 'So, are you going to run in the election?'

'Me? No! Why?'

'You teach this stuff. Why not get real-life experience from an election campaign?' Wong was almost bouncing in the chair, his tongue squeezed between his teeth. 'We could treat it as a case study and film it for further academic analysis and research. We can have a website with our own social-media feed, and you could publish a daily diary linking back to theory.'

'Hmm, I'm not so sure it's a good idea,' said Rukhmani, screwing up her face as she considered the idea. 'For starters, the university would never allow it ethically and secondly, which party would I even stand for?'

'Does it matter? We could only do this in a seat where you couldn't win.'

'The conservatives would never endorse me, and the socialists challenge me with their extreme liberalism. The Greens, well? Yeah, nah. Not a good idea.'

'Either major party could select you in a seat that no-one cares about – and they think they will lose.'

'Such as?'

Wong laughed like a young child wanting to blurt out a secret. 'Why not run against Gerrard in Melbourne,' he announced triumphantly. 'It would be a fantastic story for the media, and we could have some really great fun.' He was speaking staccato-like, his tone rising and quickening.

'You'll get preselected easily if you make an application, I'm positive. But we'll need to move today. I'll run your campaign for you, and you'll get an applied political experience from the campaigning. This has got to be a great case study for you. We run the daily diary online and as I say link it to political theory. Plenty of your students would be willing to help. We may even get a documentary out of it.'

'What about constitutional issues?'

Wong's eyebrows raised, 'Which ones?'

'Citizenship, and perhaps office of profit.'

Wong considered the question for a moment, pinching his chin between his forefinger and thumb. 'We renounce any citizenship duality immediately just to make sure, and you apply for extended leave from the university, just for a month, before you submit your application.'

'That's a ridiculous idea,' said Rukhmani, punching a pointed finger at Wong. 'Anyway, the conservatives would never select anyone like me to run against Gerrard.' The professor placed her elbow on the desk clutter, tapping her fingers to her mouth and reflecting on the idea. 'It took them years and years to have Italians and Greeks elected who weren't born in Australia – they would never preselect an Indian woman federally.'

'You wouldn't be expected to win Melbourne against Gerrard. And there's always a first time for selecting an Indian woman. Think of the media you would generate.'

'I'm the wrong skin colour for Australians.'

'We've had plenty of people with colour elected. Remember the Kenyan senator from South Australia? There's still a Koori man in the Senate, and Speaker Bagshaw is Indigenous.'

'Yes, but they're not as black as me.'

---

'It's over.' Prime Minister Gerrard sat at his parliamentary office desk, pinching the bridge of his nose as he gave the news to his friend the president of Indonesia. 'The earliest we can get the money to you will be February.'

'That is not good for me.'

'There is nothing I can do about it now. I'm officially not prime minister for now.'

'That is a sad news, my friend. I will now have to withdraw the order for clemency on your citizens.'

'Amir, come on. You can't execute them now just because you won't get your money until next year. It's only a few months, for fuck's sake.'

'There is no guarantee that the money will be transferred next year. You may not win the election.'

'I will win the fucking election and I'll get you your money!'

Gerrard barked into the phone.

'Andrew, I cannot be sure, so I will stop all site works for the immigration detention centre on Ambon, withhold the clemency order on your drug-trafficking citizens, and recall my ambassador. You can forget any deal we may have had.'

'What! Why?'

'My country cannot trust you to maintain your word. If you want to regain our confidence, I suggest you win the election.'

---

'I blame you actually,' Anita Devlin said as she sipped sparkling wine from a plastic disposable cup.

'For what, exactly?' Barton Messenger had brought a bottle to the second-floor newsroom in the Federal Parliamentary Press Gallery to celebrate the events of the day. An allegedly corrupt prime minister being sacked was definitely something to celebrate.

'I had the chance to get a front-page byline in the national newspaper and now your mob will be plastered all over the first eight pages.'

'You can still run with your story.'

'It's only wild speculation now that Gerrard's funding legislation wasn't passed. The story about him ripping off the government is literally in the bin.' Anita proffered her flimsy cup for more. Messenger obliged with a splash that sent a foam rinse over her hand. She quickly swapped hands, flicking her wet hand dry. 'What happens now?'

'We go to a general election, and hopefully we come back as the elected government.'

'Would you still fund Gerrard's detention centres in Indonesia?'

'Probably, since ironically it remains part of our policy.' Messenger pushed back on the legs of his chair, putting a foot on Anita's desk. 'We'll guarantee to pay the stimulus package to the electorate before Christmas to nullify it as an election issue for the punters, and when we come back to the parliament, we'll scrutinise the Indonesian funding going offshore a little more rigorously than we did this week.'

Anita took a sip and contemplated Barton, a curious smile lingering as she watched him. 'So, you could be deputy prime minister in a month?'

'Seems I could be, yes. Would that create a problem for you?'

'Not at all.' Anita smiled as she gulped down her cup and proffered it for more celebratory bubbles. 'The question is, will I be a problem for you?'

'You already are,' Messenger joked.

'So, no exclusives from you then?' Anita teased.

'I can absolutely guarantee you to be exclusive,' Messenger laughed, as he looked at her. 'If you're interested.'

Anita also laughed, comfortable with the thought of having Barton Messenger in her life. 'Can I get an invitation to Yarralumla sometime?'

'Would you like to live there?' Messenger slyly smiled.

She suddenly sat upright, almost out of her chair. Anita chortled, 'Did you just propose?'

'No.' Barton responded gruffly. 'I'm only teasing. We're yet to even have that first dinner date you promised me.'

'What are you doing tonight?'

'I have a very early flight tomorrow for an emergency campaign meeting in Melbourne, so if it's not a late one, let's go Chinese.'

'Good idea. Let me pack up and have a chat to Cleave. I can either meet you downstairs at the Reps entrance or at the restaurant, you choose.'

'I'll see you downstairs. In about thirty minutes?'

'Sure, sounds great.'

Messenger crushed his cup and flicked it into the bin. He kicked himself out of the chair, saying goodbye as he left Anita.

She began by tidying her desk, filing scraps of paper into her various resource boxes and trays. Anita assumed she would be assigned to cover major policy announcements during the election campaign and provide political profiles of the leaders for the weekend editions. This would mean crisscrossing the country, living out of a suitcase for over a month, probably from the coming weekend, with little time for a social life. She mused her dinner with Barton might be the last opportunity to enjoy herself before Christmas.

Peter Cleaver was sitting at his desk when she knocked and entered. He looked up and motioned for her to sit as he finished reading what seemed to be an article ready for publication. The experienced political editor supported Anita in her recent pursuit of the prime minister, but parliamentary events overtook the potential exclusive. He pulled out a bent cigarette from a soft pack and lit it, sucking hard and breathing deeply – and ignoring the convention of a no-smoking workplace – before billowing smoke above her head.

'Your story raises an interesting connection between Gerrard and Indonesia and is very good. I can't run it now given today's events, but I think we should file it to use if Gerrard wins the election.'

'There's not much point now. The scrutiny of the legislation will be much better when it goes before parliament again. This alleged secret commission we identified will either be taken out or much better explained by the government.'

Cleaver pulled off his glasses and rubbed his face, cigarette dangling from his lips. 'Even so, I think we might be able to use it, so I sent it off to the boss.'

'Who? Your boss?'

'No, Hancock. I was pretty sure he would be interested, given he's a mate of Gerrard's.'

'Was he?'

'He liked it and asked if you would write more like it for the campaign.'

'Like what?' Anita waved an uncomfortable hand in front of her face to clear the smoke. 'Does he think a conspiracy lies behind every campaign sign?'

'No. What he wants you to do is write special interest stories during the campaign, sketches of the remarkable political things that happen every day. Providing a sort of human element to the lying morons if that is possible.'

'You're kidding me. I'm not a social diarist, we have those in Sydney.'

'Hancock has requested you to do it.' Cleaver replaced his glasses and drew heavily on his cigarette, provoking a rasping cough. He roughly stubbed it out in an over-full saucer. 'Fairly insistent, actually.'

'I'm an investigative journalist, Cleave. I don't write crap, you know that.'

'We're not asking you to write crap, Anita. We want the hard stories from the campaign.'

'You don't want policy analysis?'

'Nope, I've assigned two others to do that.'

'Hard news?' Anita said, sarcastically. 'You want me to write hard news?'

'Yes.'

'Where the hell do you think these stories lie if I don't analyse policy?'

Cleaver leaned back with his hands behind his head and a broad smile. 'That's for you to find out. You're the investigative journalist, are you not?'

'Don't patronise me.' Anita stood. 'I won't accept crap like that.' She stared at Cleaver, angrily gnawing her upper lip. 'Where do you want me to go?'

'Start with the opposition, work your contacts,' Cleaver smirked. 'How is Messenger?'

'Don't shit me, Cleave,' snapped Anita, shaking her head. She looked to the ceiling. 'How many words do you expect?'

'I want something every day. Your pieces can range from a

gossip tidbit to a substantial feature – that's up to you.'

'You're serious, aren't you?' Anita began prowling slowly in front of her editor's desk. 'You have no idea how this will work out. It's just a damn demotion. Why?' she whined loudly. 'You know the work I put into the last election. I even got a Walkley for it. This is crap.'

'As I said, Anita, this has come from Hancock himself, so I suggest you get focused on the campaign.'

'Hard news?' Anita chided, a little sceptical. 'You just want puff pieces, that's what they'll turn out to be.'

'That'll be your call.'

'I'm so sick to death of this business and the dark art of mate's politics. This misogynistic crap lies everywhere and nowhere more so than in this fucking office.'

'How do you mean?'

'You've shafted me, just like Gerrard was shafted today, and you have no answer as to why.' Anita stopped pacing and stood before Cleaver with both hands on her hips. 'Gerrard was about to commit a fraud and I broke the story,' she thumbed her chest. 'Now I've been relegated to the backbench as election campaign social commentator because he's a mate of Hancock's.'

'That's not the case.'

'Then explain why this is happening to me if it's not mates looking after mates.'

'We want a different tone and perspective from the campaign, rather than having to compete with social media. We want you to write stories with a bit of grunt.'

'So, no social crap?' Anita aggressively stood before him, now with both hands clenched on her hips.

'Not as far as I'm concerned,' Cleaver nonchalantly replied, pulling another bent cigarette from his pack.

'Will I be free to travel to either campaign?'

'Yes, but can you concentrate on Stanley's first, before looking at Gerrard.'

'I can't believe this.' Anita looked to the ceiling, tapping her right foot slightly. 'How do you want me to handle the sacking of the government?'

'Not actually a sacking, was it?'

She sighed heavily and asked, 'What would you call it, a resignation?'

'Politics is only ever about power, Anita. You either have it or you don't.'

'So obviously, as a woman, I don't have any power in this fucking men's cave. Journalistic ethics have little to do with it either.'

'Just do as we ask, please, Anita.' Cleaver implored her, torching his cigarette with a flame, and drawing in the smoke deeply. He managed to get out, 'Then everyone'll be happy,' before rasping a cough.

'Except for me,' said Anita. She turned on her heel and stomped from the office. 'Those things will kill you, by the way.' She slammed the glass door, rattling the entire office partitioning, kicked a nearby bin creating a storm of papers, grabbed her bag and left knowing she would eventually calm down.

'Fucking men shit me!' she barked as she marched toward the stairwell.

# CHAPTER 2

## DAY TWO – FRIDAY

The opposition leadership group agreed to convene urgently to discuss strategy for the unanticipated federal election at its party headquarters in Melbourne. Delays with Barton Messenger's early commuter flight from Canberra persuaded him to go straight to the meeting, rather than change and refresh at home in Williamstown, a coastal community twenty minutes by train from the CBD.

It was an opportunity for a latte at his favourite city cafe in Bourke Street, just around the corner from the Exhibition Street headquarters. A longtime coffee snob, Barton was looking forward to resuming his love of good coffee missing in most other cities, even more so in Parliament House in Canberra.

. . .

Settling at a footpath table, reviewing the lead stories of the national newspaper about the chaos and crisis in Canberra, a latte arrived, and the warming sun began to filter through the trees. It was his favourite time of day to enjoy a good coffee. As he took his first sip, Messenger's phone pinged a message.

Thanks for last night, it was great spending time with u. Let's do more of it once the campaign is over

Messenger grinned and quickly tapped a response on the screen.

Looking forward to seeing more of you hopefully before Xmas.

If you need to know anything about the campaign be sure NOT to call me.

Messenger smiled as he dropped his phone back into his jacket. He trusted his attempt at humour was a subtle reminder to Anita about the restrictions his role as deputy leader might bring during the campaign. Anita had agreed over dinner that communication between them should be scant, and if they had time for a social catch- up, they both agreed not to talk politics. Barton welcomed Anita's ethics and didn't want to compromise their budding friendship by denying her the opportunity of doing her job. It could also very well mean negative press for him.

Messenger settled back into his newspaper, flicking it open, then reading the coverage of the prorogued parliament. He tried to steer clear of articles about himself but couldn't help reading the editorial that supported his promotion to deputy leader, encouraging the party to further promote younger MPs and clear out the stodgy frontbench. Its coverage of the parliamentary crisis was extensive, highlighting the resignation of the speaker that led the parliament to abruptly prorogue and force the nation to an unexpected federal election.

Prime Minister Gerrard was plastered across the front page with menacing headlines that promised political retribution to those who caused the crisis. His fierce look, snapped by a parliamentary photographer as he brushed past the media, would drive fear into anyone with him and his statement made a veiled threat to the governor-general. He claimed she failed to act on his advice, which constitutionally she was required to do.

Gerrard didn't hold back his vitriol, vilifying parliamentary officers, including the Chief Justice, promising there would be changes when he was re-elected. A small assortment of brave commentators implied this crisis may be the end of the Gerrard era, suggesting it was time for the electorate to make a change to the leadership of the country.

Messenger's favourite section of the paper was always the cartoon, which today had Gerrard lounging like an opulent Greek senator from long ago asking, 'What is democracy? Freedom to elect your own dictator.' This brought him a small chuckle. As he sipped his coffee, his phone rang displaying a number he didn't recognise.

'Hello, Barton Messenger.'

'Barton, it's Jaya Rukhmani.'

Barton crushed his newspaper and sat straighter. 'Hello Professor, how are you?'

'I'm terrific. Very enthusiastic about the events in Canberra yesterday. You must be very proud of your election as deputy leader?'

'It's an honour, and to tell you the truth, totally unexpected. I didn't go to Canberra this week thinking I would be voted as deputy opposition leader, that's for sure. But I'll take it.' Messenger scoffed as a tram trundled loudly past and he placed a finger in his other ear.

'Who would have thought a scholar of mine could possibly be prime minister?'

'Not there yet, Professor, and I doubt I'll get the nod for the top job any time soon.'

'Oh Bart, you've always shown potential, and you have the ability, it's just a matter of time now.' The professor sounded authentic with her praise. 'Perhaps you should think about getting married, we like our prime ministers tall and good looking – and married.'

'I probably would be elected prime minister before ever getting married. At this time in my life, at least.'

'What's wrong with you? You're handsome and young, there should be girls falling all over you. I'd even put my hand up for that enjoyable task,' Rukhmani joked.

'Hmm, well the idea of marital bliss is not on my radar at the moment.' Barton was beginning to feel a little uncomfortable with the conversation. 'What can I put the pleasure of this call down to, would you like me to speak at the university again?'

'Hey, that would be great if you could, especially if you win government.' Messenger immediately regretted making the quip, remembering the last time he visited the campus was fraught with student dissidence during his speech. 'Actually, I wanted your advice – and perhaps a little help.'

'Happy to, what are you seeking?'

'I want to run at the federal election.' Messenger didn't respond, screwed his face, and gazed at his paper. 'Are you there?'

'Yes, I'm still here,' Messenger dithered a little. 'Can I ask which party?'

'Yours, of course,' Rukhmani clarified, a little irritated with her former student's indifferent response. 'My colleagues think it would be a terrific case study about the many challenges running an election campaign. It could possibly allow us to develop a teaching unit in the politics program on applied campaign techniques, which we would hope to offer from second semester next year.'

'Sounds interesting,' Messenger replied cagily, engaging the benign political speak he, like most politicians, was skilled at. 'Do you know which seat you might stand for?'

'We want to challenge Gerrard.'

Messenger pursed his lips and breathed out slowly, thinking through the information. It might be a proposition worthy of further discussion. 'He normally stands without many candidates running against him. I think his primary vote is something ridiculous like seventy-two per cent. We have a hell of a time trying to convince anyone to stand against him, and more often than not, we don't spend any money on campaign materials. We haven't stood a candidate for the last two elections. Why Melbourne?'

'A number of reasons. We think it would be a great experience because of the small number of independents. Plus, we think national exposure might create interest for our project, and we could get media footage to use in the unit. Of course, the university is in the electorate too.'

'Who is we?'

'A number of post-grad students and a couple of tutors from the university.'

'Are you serious about this?' Barton looked about him. 'I mean, it would require an enormous effort. You'll need plenty of people – and money.'

'People won't be a problem. We'll call upon our alumni students and their networks. The money could be problematic, but we're thinking of using crowdfunding websites.'

'Will they let you do that?'

'Not sure, but if we can and we do it well, it may resolve this ongoing issue about fraudulent campaign donors. In any event, it will allow us to include possible funding alternatives in the unit we are hoping to design. We really need to start addressing the many allegations of political favours being given for campaign donations that so many politicians are accused of. You haven't been accused, have you?'

'I had some trouble when I first started out with a property developer wanting to donate to my campaign, but we sent his money back. He then unscrupulously got it to us via another company, which our accounting missed. Caused a bit of pain for me that did.'

'What happened?'

'I was forced to provide an explanation to the federal police. Nothing came of it, but the media hounded me for months and they still raise it occasionally.'

'What happened to the money?'

'I donated all of it to charity under the moron's name.'

'I suppose what we can learn from your experience is that we need to be careful to weed out those who may want to manipulate us.'

'Exactly, and if you do, you will be a rare political candidate,' said Messenger as he lifted his coffee, pausing before sipping. 'Tell me, why do you want to run against Gerrard?'

'I suppose if I genuinely think about it and consider the true reasons, then I would have to concede it's about profile. Gerrard will bring us profile, and with that we will generate more media material to use. If we impact Gerrard's margin in some small way, that would be a huge plus for the development of the unit.'

'So why not run as an independent?'

'We want to include the preselection process in the study and the campaign structures of a major party. We think there are some valid ethical and moral constructs about the distribution of power within politics, especially the major parties, and we want to take a look at it.'

'I'm not sure how the party will react to your application.'

'Am I not qualified? I have been a citizen for almost twenty years now.'

'No, it's not that,' Messenger hesitated, gnawing at his bottom lip.

'Please tell me it's not because I'm a woman?'

'You know our party prefers to promote good women, and you are definitely one of them.'

'And yet you have none in your leadership team?'

Messenger squirmed a little at the retort. 'Not for lack of trying, I can tell you.'

'Yes, I know your position, Bart, so why are you hesitant?'

'We've never preselected an Indian migrant for a federal seat before.'

'Your party has had plenty of mixed Asian diaspora elected to various parliaments and you've had candidates with Indian backgrounds in state elections.' Rukhmani lowered her tone, 'What aren't you telling me?'

Messenger hesitated a little. 'Frankly, I'm concerned about the media and how they will treat you, and how the electorate will respond ...'

'To a woman of colour?'

'No,' Messenger protested. 'That's not it. I mean to a woman with your background. Please don't misunderstand me, I'm only thinking about the consequences should there be a red-neck campaign against you. You must know Twitter haters will go crazy.'

'That is precisely one of the reasons why we want to stand for this election. We want to expose any unethical bullying we may encounter and show how social messages can be misused and manipulated, for example by trolls on Twitter.' Rukhmani was suddenly upbeat. 'This is what I actually love about politics. Democracy is hard work, and we must fight to keep it. And we have to fight for ethical and moral equality.'

'I have to say, you're a brave woman, Jaya.'

'Rubbish, Barton, this isn't about me. It's about our political system and how the community must actively stop post-truth theory overrunning us. We need to constrain the power of propaganda from populist leaders like Gerrard.'

'I can't promise anything but let me talk to a few contacts and I'll get back to you.'

'Today?'

'I'm scheduled for a campaign strategy meeting shortly,' Messenger checked his watch. 'It should take a few hours, but maybe I can get back to you before the end of the day?'

'This is why you will be a great prime minister, Barton.'

'Why?'

'You're unafraid to make a promise, which I'm confident you will no doubt keep.'

'I had a good teacher, Professor. Talk to you later. This is good news, very exciting.'

'Thanks, Bart, chat soon.'

Messenger was somewhat taken aback by the call and slowly placed his phone on the table, thinking how best to manage the request. The professor would be a terrific candidate for the party, and frankly would be well suited to a safe seat, but to throw her to the political wolves against Gerrard could be a challenge for his party, and indeed, the electorate of Melbourne.

He wondered why he remained overly concerned about a

potential backlash against her. Was it a fear for her safety, as he had suggested, or did he harbour a subtle bias against her? The thought troubled him. And if it transpired there was no backlash against her, what did that say about his relationship with multiculturalism? If he earnestly believed in equality of diversity, why was he hesitant to endorse her candidacy? Perhaps he wasn't a strong believer in cultural tolerance after all.

Messenger folded his paper, collected his leather satchel, paid the bill, and walked quickly to Exhibition Street, the centre of state government offices. He waited for the green walk sign before crossing Bourke Street toward the location of the federal opposition's Victorian headquarters, now likely to be the base for the national campaign.

The meeting rooms were on the fifth floor. He swiped his security pass to gain access to the boardroom, dimly lit like a military bunker complete with projector, whiteboard, and flip charts at the ready to flesh out campaign strategy. A solitary colleague waited in the gloom, working his smartphone.

'Hi Jim, when did you get in?' Messenger was surprised to see him.

'Morning Bart,' Harper slipped his phone into his jacket. 'I came down last night for a meeting and thought I would stay.'

'Did the leader ask you to come along?'

James Harper didn't seem too pleased with the challenge. 'You might recall I was the leader just two days ago.'

Messenger sat opposite and considered his colleague. 'I'm not sure the leadership team would appreciate you being here today – the optics wouldn't be good.'

'Like the optics when I was dumped on Wednesday night, you mean?'

Messenger grimaced. 'Jim, that was an unfortunate political decision made by you to move to a vote. You were warned not to do it; you can't blame anyone else for what happened.'

'You certainly didn't help with your shenanigans during question time,' jibed Harper.

'We needed to chase down Gerrard and defer the funding for the immigration centre. You were blocking us.'

'Bart, I was set up by Gerrard to comply in the parliament, you know that.' Harper said it matter-of-factly, confidently leaning back in his chair. 'What happened in the party room subsequently shouldn't disqualify me from strategically assisting in the campaign. I was leader for eight years, for heaven's sake.'

'It's an opportunity for change.'

'What's going to change? My policies? My work in getting us into a winning position? None of that will change. Do I get to keep any of my legacy?'

'Jim, it's not about shunning you, it's the optics of having the former leader driving party strategy. In other words, are the punters voting for Stanley, or Harper?'

'Stop with the fucking optics, will you please,' Harper barked, sitting forward.

'We have promised you a ministry if we win.'

'So, what?'

'We just need clear air around the new leadership group so we can provide a positive message. You must know that?'

'I've had enough of this babble.' Harper abruptly jumped up

and moved to the door. 'I'll have a chat to Peter and see what he has to say.'

'Jim, it's for the best. You'll see.' Messenger attempted to placate Harper as he left the room, but he was already gone.

At that moment, Christopher Hughes strolled through another door. Messenger repositioned himself to where Harper had been sitting, by the leader's assigned chair.

'That was truly bizarre.'

'What was?' asked Hughes as he pulled a chair from the table opposite.

'Jim was just here expecting to be on the campaign strategy team, suggesting that as former leader he should be.'

'What did you tell him?'

'I told him to expect a ministry if we win, but to leave the campaign to the current leadership group.'

'Good lad,' said Hughes, the shadow minister for Industry and Member for Warringah in Sydney. 'Strategically it's for the best, and he can play a low profile in his electorate. We don't want Gerrard playing the leadership instability card during the campaign.'

Messenger smiled and cited a previous campaign slogan: 'If you can't run your party, how do you expect to run the country?'

'Exactly. The perfect cliché – I knew you would have one.' Hughes moved to the sideboard to pour a coffee. 'Would you like a cup?'

'No thanks, I don't drink that muck.'

'Coffee snobs you folk in Melbourne, aren't you?'

'Well, when you have the best baristas in the most livable city in the world then you tend to steer clear of the instant and percolated muck.'

'Who else is coming this morning, do you know?'

'Harry is down from the Federal Secretariat. The polling guru, Andres, will no doubt be coming.' Messenger laughed at the thought. 'I've asked Julia Laretsky from the women's division and sequestered Sussan Neilson from Pete's office to handle comms.'

'So just six of us?'

'Seven if you count the leader.' Messenger waved an acknowledgement as Laretsky entered the room. 'I don't see any need to have it any bigger, unless you think we should have a representative from each state. If we did want a national structure then there would be no reason not to have Jim on the team, given he is our best man in Queensland.'

'What, you don't think Tilley is capable?'

'Of course, he is – at a rodeo,' laughed Messenger. 'Hello Julia, thanks for coming.'

'Hi Bart, Chris. Nice day for it.' Laretsky pulled files from her oversized soft leather rose-pink bag and took a place at the table. 'You guys must have had some fun over the last few days.'

'Not much fun dumping a leader, I'm afraid, Jules, but enormous gratification having Gerrard sacked by the parliament and seeing his reaction. We just have to win now,' replied Messenger.

'This is our best opportunity for snatching power from Gerrard, and those unfortunate deaths last week makes it game on as far as I'm concerned,' Laretsky said as she flicked through her paperwork.

'Yes indeed, truly unfortunate for the families and a great tragedy for the parliament. I suppose Andres will apprise us if we benefit from it.'

'Andres can tell you what?' The pollster had just walked into the room, dumped his computer and thick folders at the end of the table and walked to the coffee station.

'We were just talking about the death of our colleagues in the plane crash,' Hughes said as he checked his phone.

'I'll wait until we get into the meeting, but I can tell you there is good news. Is there anything to eat other than these crappy biscuits?'

'Good news about people dying?' Messenger queried, looking askew at Hughes.

'The king is dead, long live the king,' Hughes glumly offered in response.

'And so, the political caravan moves on,' Messenger cynically added.

'Right let's get on with it.' The charismatic voice of Peter Stanley silenced everyone as he strode in with Harry Lester and Sussan Neilson trailing behind. 'We have an election to win.'

# CHAPTER
# 3

## DAY FOUR – SUNDAY

'Remind me why we're here, again?'

'You know why,' sighed Miles Fisher, the prime minister's steadfast adviser, a little frustrated with the impatient pacing of his boss.

'Do we really need them?' Gerrard walked to the other end of the overstated corporate lobby, with sweeping views over Sydney harbour, the enormous sails from the racing yachts cutting through the breeze. 'Is that a Whiteley, do you reckon?' Gerrard was now distracted by a painting by the floor to ceiling window.

'It's called Balcony 2 and I believe he did it around 1975.'

'It's crap,' Gerrard turned away. 'He's so overrated.'

An elegant woman entered through a large silent door and sat at an open desk with only a telephone on the glass top. 'They won't be long, Prime Minister.'

'What's the hold up, luv? I was advised this was supposed to be a 10 am meeting and now it's ten past. I have things to do.'

The woman smiled, 'They won't be long. Would you like a drink? There is water in the boardroom, a tea perhaps?'

'If they aren't ready for me by ten fifteen, we are out of here.'

The woman gave a calm toothy smile in response, saying nothing and referring to a few pieces of paper in front of her.

'Boss, they won't be long, this is important, so let's just stay calm,' placated Miles.

'I am calm. I just don't like these people. Who the hell do these morons think they are?'

'They run Australia, that's who they are.'

'I run Australia you dickhead, not some pampered, precious, privileged group of business owners,' Gerrard spat the words.

'Stay calm boss and choke them with cream.'

'I am calm, Miles, for chrissakes,' Gerrard quietly snarled.

The telephone softly hummed, and the woman immediately answered, softly responding before replacing the handpiece. She then stood and walked to Gerrard. 'The board will see you now, Prime Minister.' She turned to lead him through the access to the boardroom.

'More like a cabal than a board,' sneered Gerrard to Fisher. 'I'll see you soon, young man.'

'Cream, boss, choke them with cream.'

Gerrard tailed the woman as she opened another nearby door and announced him to the room. No-one stood to greet him as

Gerrard waited by the door surveying what was before him. Twelve chairs were occupied with a solitary one left empty and alone on one side of the enormous heavy timber table. Gerrard scoffed silently to himself as he took the seat, leaned back confidently in his chair, and waited for someone to speak. He perused those opposite and the image of a bottle of cream came to mind as he smiled.

'Prime Minister, thank you for coming to see us,' Kerry Jameson softly said.

'Pardon?' Gerrard decided he should take control before shoving handfuls of cream down resisting throats. 'Sorry, I didn't hear you.' Gerrard cupped his ear.

The frail owner of five casinos cleared his throat with a phlegmy cough and projected, 'Prime Minister, thank you for coming to see us.'

'No problem, how can I help?'

'You know our group and our interests, so we don't need your help, rather, we would like to help you get re-elected.'

'That's very kind of you, I appreciate it.' Gerrard smiled like a toothy used car salesman welcoming a new client onto the lot.

Tony Hancock, a friend, and confidante of the prime minister chipped in. 'Andrew, we just want to get confirmation directly from you today that a number of our issues will be handled by your government during the next term of parliament.'

'Oh, hello Tony,' Gerrard squinted through an overstated grimace. 'I didn't see you there squirrelled away in the dark, it's a long way down to the end and my eyes aren't as good as they used to be.' Gerrard smiled and then turned away. 'I must say, I'm not very happy with the editorials your mob have been running since Friday. I hope they're not your words.'

Hancock sat back in his chair preferring not to engage his friend.

'Prime Minister, we are concerned about a number of policies you have been promoting in the media over the last few years and we would like reassurances.' Felicity Osman, the respected finance sector executive joined the conversation.

Gerrard begrudgingly turned to look at Osman, pursed his lips as if sucking on a lemon and ran his tongue over his front teeth. 'What policies might they be?'

'Well for one, the refusal of your government to recognise coal seam gas exploration as a legitimate resource investment.'

'Fracking?' Gerrard sat forward leaning on his elbows on the table. 'You want a change in the government's resources policy to allow fracking in Australia?'

'Yes.'

'Breaching every promise and policy we have developed over the years to reduce atmospheric carbon. Ignoring all our international obligations.'

'Yes,' repeated Osman, sternly.

'Like a good fracking, do you?' Gerrard stared at Osman, paused for a moment, fighting the need to add another comment, slightly nodding his head. 'What else?'

'We want you to loosen access to international workers.' The familiar voice of property guru Frank Lowsonne brought a smile to Gerrard's face.

'Good morning, Frank,' Gerrard nodded. 'Expensive penalty rates worrying you, are they?'

'It's not me, Prime Minister, the labour market needs competition.'

'Nothing to do with hospitality workers or casinos then?' Gerrard sassed them, seeming to have misplaced his cream bottle. 'Anything else?'

'We want a repeal of the Native Title Act,' Allan Connell, the mining magnate offered. 'It's too costly as it currently stands, and we have already paid way too much for rights to dig. The compliance requirements and the need to employ Aboriginals are extreme. This new Act is killing us internationally.'

'So, you think it's fair to rip off our Indigenous brothers and sisters?'

'You suddenly get a heart, Andrew?' snapped Connell.

Gerrard looked down the table with scorn. 'Is that it?' There was silence. 'So, if I agree to do what you have asked then you will support the government?'

'Pretty much,' Osman responded.

'What's in it for me?'

'What?' Jameson asked, cupping his ear. 'What did you say?'

'I said ... what's in it for me?' Gerrard barked turning to Jameson, then added quietly. 'You deaf bastard.'

'Good media, campaign funds, plus we can provide you people on the ground, and any additional resources you may need,' Hancock smiled as he listed off the benefits.

'I didn't say what's in it for us, Tony boy, that goes without saying. I said, what's in it for me?' Gerrard glanced at Jameson, the leader of the group. 'I want to know what you are prepared to do for me if I do what you want?'

'What do you need?' Jameson hoarsely whispered, his voice beginning to strain.

'No, that's not what I asked.' Gerrard had no cream left. 'I want to know what you will do for me?' Their silence was instructive to Gerrard. The collective tension from the wealthiest, most influential, independent business owners in the nation was palpable as some sat quietly while others fidgeted avoiding engagement.

Gerrard let his request linger for a moment then repeated his demand a little louder. 'What's in it for me, my friends?' Each owner remained silent, preferring not to move nor respond to each other, apparently knowing Jameson would speak on their behalf.

Jameson coughed a wheeze like a smoker before saying, 'We will consider your request and let you know later today.'

Gerrard said nothing as he gawked at the old man, a slight smirk moving his lips. Finally, he said, 'You think I'm going to let a bunch of overstated nobodies who have abused their privileged position in Australia to grow obnoxious wealth, tell me, your prime minister for over seventeen years, what he can and can't do?' The leader stood and politely pushed his chair back into the table and leaned forward, resting his forearms on the high back. 'You folks are crazy brave to think you can seduce me to your will like that. You want action on your policies? Well then, you'll just have to do what everyone else in this country does, and that's grovel at my office – not my house in Canberra anymore, but my office across the bridge. You can stick your sad little offer up your collective arse and get behind my re-election campaign if you know what's good for you.' Gerrard began to walk to the door. 'Hancock knows how things work with me, so I'd suggest you listen to him. And I can tell you this ...' he stopped and turned, pointing back at the group. 'Things don't work with me when I have to wait ten fucking minutes for an audience with you pompous pricks.' He walked through the double door and slammed it as hard as he could, rattling its partner.

'So that went well?' suggested Miles, smiling as he jumped up to meet the striding Gerrard.

'The dairy is fucking closed today.'

'Whenever self-interest is running in a political race, always back it, because you know it's trying its hardest,' Tony Hancock finally said to the quiet group after the door stopped rattling.

'What's his self-interest?' Felicity Osman asked.

'Winning another term, then retiring to Paris.'

'So, if we get him elected and buy him an apartment in Paris, he will do what we want?' Lowsonne asked.

'No,' Hancock sceptically replied. 'We just offended him, and he has no reason to do us any favours. Quite the opposite, I'd reckon.'

'So maybe we should back the other side. Surely, they will finally run a strong campaign,' suggested Kerry Jameson, as he struggled to stand. 'Let's get rid of the prick once and for all and go to work on Stanley. It's time for his mob to be back in government anyway.'

'Agreed,' said Lowsonne.

'What's the first step?' Osman asked.

'I'll initiate media support and perhaps Kerry can contact Wolff?' Hancock asked.

'Sounds like a plan, let's hook up in a few days after the Cup on Tuesday, I'll be in Melbourne trying to win a few dollars.' Jameson began shuffling off to his office. 'Have a great day everyone, sorry it didn't turn out as we expected – and speaking of the races, put some money on the English stayer, Gorgeous Girl, she'll win by a length.'

Felicity Osman hung back to talk with Hancock as the others began strolling out chatting among themselves about tips and plans for their Melbourne Cup holiday.

'I'm not sure that went very well at all. Gerrard seems to be way too cocky for my liking,' Osman suggested. 'I'd have thought he'd have been dead keen to listen to our policy plans.'

Hancock smiled and rubbed a hand against his face, 'Welcome to the world of Andrew Gerrard, prime minister extraordinaire.'

'Will he win?'

'He should, but I don't think he'll stay for the entire term. He is sixty-seven and I reckon he'll pull the pin early, so it may not matter who actually wins, we get what we want no matter the result.'

'It's way better for us to back the winner, I would have thought,' Osman said as she slowly made her way from the room.

'One of my journalists discovered his wife left for Switzerland the other day and is not due back until the new year.' Hancock slowly walked out with her. 'It may mean nothing, but knowing those two, as I do very well, then something is going down. So, if we back Stanley and he loses then it may not make any difference if Gerrard retires soon after the election.'

'I didn't realise politics was this hard.'

'Trust me, Felicity, politics is easy. It's only ever about numbers and simple arithmetic.' Hancock stepped back and let Osman walk through the door. 'Whoever has the numbers has the power. We just strip Gerrard's numbers off him and we get what we want?'

---

Anita was at her desk in Canberra filing her first campaign story when her phone buzzed. 'Hello, this is Anita.'

'Anita, this is Tony Hancock, have I caught you at a bad time?'

'Mr Hancock, hi. Sorry—' Anita startled, dropped her phone as she sat upright and quickly picked it up again. 'It's fine, I was just filing a story.'

'You work way too hard,' Hancock said politely. 'Say listen, I just wanted to say how much I thought your Gerrard piece the other day developed into a tremendous conspiracy. I must say though, I remain a little sceptical about the notion a prime minister was about to rip off the government with some secret deal with the president of Indonesia, but I liked it.

'Are you ever going to run it?'

'Nope. But this leads me to why I called. I had a chat to Pete Cleaver just a few minutes ago, and he told me you are a little annoyed by the campaign role I want you to do.'

'Mr Hancock, I'll do whatever I'm asked to do – I just thought it was a waste of resources.'

'Maybe you're right,' Hancock waited for just a moment. 'Look, the media group are going to support Stanley. We're going to give him the full five-star treatment and promote him to win government. So, this becomes a vital strategy of the group for you to lead. I want you to begin running the editorial on his campaign.'

Anita couldn't speak.

'I want you flying with him and staying at his hotel, so I've arranged that with his team. They will bill me directly. Just make sure you also get good background and profile pieces from the campaign. He's only been opposition leader for a few days and Australians are never going to elect a stranger. So, make sure you bring him into the homes of voters for me. Can you do that for me?'

'I don't know what to say.'

'You'll be okay, Anita; just do the job I want you to do. Write strong editorials and get the human-interest pieces that will sell Stanley's team. If he wins, we can then talk about you moving up from the Canberra bureau to Sydney, and maybe into television.'

Anita's hand was shaking as she cupped her mouth. She was a little startled, mixed with the enthusiasm of the responsibility she was being handed. 'Thank you, Mr Hancock.'

'Don't underestimate how much value you provide us, Anita, just do this job well for me, please. Will you do that?'

'I'll do my best, sir.'

'I want more than your best, young lady. Call me directly if you need anything.'

Hancock clicked off and Anita dropped her phone on her desk, then knowing she was alone jumped up excitedly screaming as loud as she could. Her first instinct was to call Cleave, but she had someone more important to speak to.

'Hi Barton, guess what?' Anita could not control her excitement.

'What gorgeous?'

'I'm travelling with Stanley, and no doubt you, for the campaign. I've been assigned to promote the hell out of your lot and get you elected.'

'I'd heard on the grapevine Hancock was going to support us,' chortled Messenger. 'That's great, we can see more of each other.'

'This is the start of something big, Barton Messenger, for you, and for me. This is crazy.'

'I always thought you would be recognised for your hard work. I suppose we can catch up when I link up with the leader.'

'Hancock told me if I get you elected then I could get promoted to television.'

'Fantastic.'

'You don't sound terribly convincing.'

'Melbourne or Sydney?' asked Messenger, a little nervous about what such a promotion might mean.

'Way too early to say. Hey, don't worry, we'll work our way through it. You'll be a heartbeat away from being prime minister by the time I make the move.'

'I had better be on my best behaviour then.'

Anita smiled as she curled a strand of hair. 'It's never personal the things I write about you, Bart, you know that don't you? It's just politics.'

# CHAPTER 4

## DAY SIX – CUP DAY (TUESDAY)

The sun quickly broke the ocean horizon, filling the bedroom with light. The increasing warmth aroused Jonathan Wolff from his slumber.

A sharp ache in his head attracted his fingers and he gently rubbed the scar of an old wound to relieve his discomfort. Opening his eyes to gaze into the mirror above the bed, he realised his friend from last night was still with him. He slid from the bed without disturbing her to prepare his usual breakfast and plan his day.

Wolff's Gold Coast apartment was only ever used by him as a holiday residence when he wasn't overseeing an election or a political campaign somewhere in the world. The demand for his special services was high and kept him from his favourite place for too long. Covert campaign strategy and assistance was the specialty he offered generous benefactors wanting to win an election or influence government policy, but he never took money from politicians, considering it a conflict of interest.

He padded naked across the marble tiles of the open concept living room to a modern galley-style kitchen and began to prepare a pot of French Earl Grey tea and a bowl of strawberries, toasted oats, and vanilla yogurt. He enjoyed living on the coast, and especially his sub-penthouse that provided commanding views along the famous beaches.

The apartment was full of glass. Bright, airy, and secure, the perfect place for his much-needed breaks from the demands of dealing with people. Gnashing on his oats, he thought about hitting the waves. As he watched keen surfers in the early morning swell, he realised he would first have to rid himself of last night's guest.

Turning his mind to his phone, he found it in his strewn leather jacket and checked his messages. Sitting on a high wooden stool at his marble kitchen island, he scrolled through various messages, spotting notifications from six missed calls. He recognised the number and pushed the redial button, waiting for Kerry Jameson to answer.

'Wolff!'

'Mr Jameson, how are you? How can I help?'

'Always straight to the point, never any chit-chat.'

'Nothing to talk about, Mr Jameson.'

'Can you get to Melbourne today? Where are you?'

'I arrived back from Zimbabwe on Saturday. I was expecting your call sometime this week.'

'Zimbabwe? Did our boys win?'

'Yes, the opposition leader is – shall we say – no longer relevant.'

'Don't tell me anymore. I would prefer not to know,' Jameson said quickly. 'Are you able to get a flight?'

'I'll check, but it should be okay. Who are you backing?'

'Self-interest.'

Wolff chuckled. 'No, not in the cup, I meant in the election.' He walked to the boiling kettle and poured steaming water into his white teapot. 'Are we supporting Gerrard again?'

'No. As I said, self-interest.'

'No surprise. I think he's overrated now. Perhaps it's time for someone new.'

'Someone from his party – or would you recommend the opposition? What are your thoughts on Stanley?'

'Doesn't really matter. In a lot of ways, both parties are mirror images. We don't have the robust politics they do in Africa.'

'We're supporting Stanley, although we retain reservations.'

'Which are?'

'Well, he was only elected leader last week, for one thing.'

'That could be problematic in getting his message out. Most folks in the electorate wouldn't know who he is from a bar of soap.'

'That is why we need you to manage the campaign.'

'I'll do my best. What service do you need?'

'Strategy, and probably recruiting boots on the ground. We're sending funds to them.'

'Any other services?'

'Like what?'

'Like the ones I supplied to your friends in Zimbabwe?'

'Different country, different politics, needing different outcomes.'

'I still have your credit card from the recent job in Taiwan, shall I use that?'

'That should be okay. Have your rates changed?'

'I have a bonus on positive election outcomes now, but we can talk about that when I see you later today.'

'That'll be fine, I'll get a ten per cent, $200 000 advance to you tomorrow.'

'I'll get down to Melbourne this afternoon, depending on flights, and we can go through it. Is Hancock active?'

'He and Gerrard are mates, but he supports us getting rid of the government.'

'Other than the obvious issues, why do you want to get rid of him?' Wolff jumped as he suddenly felt a hand slip around his waist, caressing his naked stomach before moving lower while another clasped his chest, then warm lips on his back. 'Mr Jameson, I have to go. I'll be in touch later today.'

'Righto.'

Wolff turned and the nude girl warmly kissed him. 'Good morning. How did you sleep?' he finally asked, stepping back. 'Would you like tea?'

'That would be nice,' she said dreamily, straddling a stool. 'You look sharp this morning, no headache?'

'I don't drink. How's your head?'

'The champagne you opened was sensational. Was it local?'

'No, French. Would you like milk?'

'No thanks.' A freshly poured mug of tea was passed to her. 'You must work out a lot, you look in good shape for an old bloke.'

'Couple of times a week.' Wolff climbed on the stool next to her. 'You live nearby?'

'I live in Sydney. I'm up here for a conference. Do you know where my bag is?'

'To be honest, I don't even remember your name.'

'Well, Mr Wolff. Does that mean I didn't leave an impression?' she said demurely from behind her shoulder, eyes smiling.

'Nice one.' Wolff smiled. 'Can I drop you somewhere this morning?'

'That would be great. I'm staying at the Hilton.'

'I'll have to leave in around an hour, so if you want a shower or something, I have plenty of towels and girly things in the bathroom.'

'Well, I do want something. Shall we do it here?' She tapped the marble bench then ran her hand between Wolff's thighs, lingering.

Wolff knew the decision he was about to make might cost him valuable time, but he took her hand and led her to the bedroom.

---

'Barton? It's Jaya. Please tell me, what's going on?'

Messenger was enjoying a coffee after lunch at a cafe around the corner from campaign headquarters. He walked off from the table to take the call.

'Hi Professor, what do you mean?'

'You said you would get back to me, and you haven't.' Messenger scrunched his face, remembering she was right. 'You promised me, in fact.'

'I'm deeply sorry, Professor, but I've been a little distracted with the leadership group.'

'Can I seek endorsement? What do I have to do?'

'Yes, is the short answer. The nominations close tomorrow and preselection for all vacant seats is Saturday.'

'Tomorrow?' yelled Rukhmani. 'Today is a public holiday and you expect me to have this done by tomorrow?'

'I'm sorry, Professor, I can't explain it, I just forgot to get back to you.'

'No other reason?'

'No,' Messenger paused for a moment. 'Like what?'

'Racism is revealed in many subtle forms, Barton, and God knows I've experienced a lot of it throughout my life.'

'I forgot, I'm sorry,' Messenger was a little befuddled. 'That doesn't mean I'm a racist.'

'Barton, you come from a position of privilege, and you wouldn't know racism if it bit you. It's always subtle – the person never thinks they're racist, but deep down in their heart, they are.'

The professor paused, Messenger waited, not wanting to respond. 'I'm surprised by your behaviour, but I won't have it influence my judgement. Can I use you as a reference?'

'Of course, you can, and I'll speak to our president about your endorsement and the project you're planning.'

'Is that another one of your promises, or just political spin?'

Messenger squirmed a little. 'I'm truly sorry for letting you down, I didn't mean it.' He rubbed the back of his head. 'I'll talk to the president immediately. If you have issues getting your application in by the deadline, let me know as early as possible.'

'I'll do my hardest to get it in; one of my students will help me. Thank you for your enthusiasm.'

'Professor, I'm deeply embarrassed not keeping my promise, please forgive me.'

'No issue, Bart, as I said, when it comes to these sorts of selection processes, I'm used to the covert nature of bias against me. I get it at the university all the time. Bye for now.'

The phone went dead. Messenger tried to dismiss the points made to him, but the lingering thought of unconscious bias and his commitment to equality was challenged by her. Did he believe the professor – was he really a racist?

'Bad news?' asked Sussan Neilson as Messenger returned to the table a little absent-mindedly to finish his coffee.

'No, I failed to do something for a colleague, and she accused me of being racist.'

'That's a little harsh. Anything I should be concerned about?'

'My politics professor at university wants to run against Gerrard as our candidate. She is planning to use it as an academic case study so she can design a teaching unit on applied campaigning. They want to blog it and film it. Should be fun.'

'What's the problem?

'She isn't preselected yet, which is scheduled for Saturday.'

'Is she suitable?'

'She has a PhD in politics, she's an immigrant, a child bride from an arranged marriage, a single mother, although I think her adult son lived with his father when he was younger, not sure about that. She's a long-term Australian citizen and she is the perfect candidate.'

'What's the problem?'

'She is Siddi.'

'Where is that, I've never heard of it.'

'It's the cultural group in India that originated from Africa.'

'So?'

'They're very dark skinned.'

'Oh.'

'That's what I thought.' Messenger raised his eyebrows and shook his head slightly. 'It seems that even thinking that thought means I might be racist. I'm also worried the party might not accept her, and if that happens, perhaps we are indeed sending xenophobic messages out into the community.'

'Leave it to me. If you think she'll be a good candidate, and if we put her up against Gerrard, and she's doing it as a university case study, it's a win-win for everyone.'

'That's a bit cynical, isn't it?' Messenger gnawed his bottom lip.

'To use your oft clichéd phrase – it's the optics. We'll be seen as inclusive and close Gerrard down from hitting us with immigration as an election issue. Pretty hard to argue politically that we have a discriminatory policy when we are inclusive with our candidates, wouldn't you think?'

'So, we use her for publicity as much as she uses us?'

'Yes, of course. It's politics, Bart. You know that,' said Nelson as she finished her coffee. 'I'll pull in a few favours and get the media ready, just make sure she gets her application in.'

---

'You travel light.' Wolff dropped his leather backpack on a chair and sunk into a soft leather couch at Jameson's swanky Melbourne office high above the casino.

'When I'm working, I like to move fast, so if it doesn't fit in the bag it doesn't come,' Wolff smiled. 'Did you pick a winner today?'

'I never bet; I just collect.'

'Nice philosophy.'

'It pays the bills.' Jameson presented Wolff with soda water and took his whiskey to collapse in the lounge chair. 'Thanks for coming down, we are keen to make this change of government happen and you're just the guy to do it for us.'

'Always willing to support you, Mr Jameson.'

'And you did a great job for us in Queensland.'

'Beautiful one day, perfect the next.'

'Especially with a change of government,' Jameson smiled broadly. 'What do you know about Stanley and his mob?'

'Not much. I would have thought James Harper had the best chance of winning an election, but this Stanley bloke and his new leadership cronies are hard to get an angle on at the moment. I suspect there isn't much government experience in their team?'

'You're right about that. They have a major headline speech on domestic violence tomorrow at a sporting club out at Mulgrave, here in Melbourne, so let's hope they get traction. Hancock is already primed to promote them,' Jameson said softly. Coughing a little, he took a swig of his whiskey.

'I'll observe their strategy over the next few days and give you a report on what we'll need. I've already spoken to several community contacts to begin to get feet on the street. So, we'll be ready to go probably Monday if you give us the green light.'

'How will that look?'

'We'll begin with community rallies – town hall–type meetings, in the most winnable electorates. Each with the same message, saying the same things every day in every electorate.'

'Every day, that'll be tough.'

'This election against a headline act like Gerrard can only be won at the grassroots. Using Twitter and other social channels will help generate momentum, but it's talking to the masses in the suburbs that will change votes. Our people will be in the audience at meetings, providing vocal support and encouragement to give the perception of a growing community movement. Social media coverage of the rallies will rapidly create a political movement, potentially influencing voting patterns across Australia. But it needs community organisers, and we will need at least one hundred and fifty-five, one for every seat.'

'Do you have those sorts of resources?'

'I can recruit both agitators and organisers, who are easy to mobilise, especially if there's money involved. It'll be up to them to get their own volunteers. By election day we should have a reasonable movement at the voting booths, which will influence voters as they arrive.'

'How much will this cost us?'

'Plenty, but it's not the money, it's the positive outcome we want. We all want good government, don't we?' Wolff smiled.

Jameson took another swig of whiskey, declining an immediate response.

'Do we need any muscle?'

'I wouldn't have thought so, but it's a little too early to say. Let me assess the campaign before I give you an answer. Just make sure Stanley's mob keep any stuff-ups out of the media. I can only do so much – if they're useless campaigners, I can't do anything to help them.'

'We want Gerrard gone – do what you have to do.'

'I haven't let you down yet – or for that matter your international colleagues – have I?'

Jameson smiled and slightly shook his head.

'Trust me, Mr Jameson,' Wolff leaned forward and engaged Jameson deeply in the eyes. 'I'll ensure Gerrard won't be prime minister of this country after the election,' said Wolff menacingly.

# READER REWARD

As the author of this work, I offer you, the reader, the opportunity to redeem a cash award for introducing this work to any literary agent, publisher or producer that offers an acceptable contract Richard Evans for this work. The reward offered is 10% of any initial book advance or option contract for film up to a maximum of AUD $10,000.

Why am I offering a cash reward to readers?

- **Odds:** 98%+ of all works published today initially found their way to a publisher by introduction as opposed to arriving via "the slush pile" so the odds are better doing it this way.
- **Volume:** Writing is an inherently solitary endeavour and as an author I struggle (off the page) to network, mingle, and promote my own work. Offering readers, a reward to do it not only augments my inability but also multiplies the effort as each volume in the hands of reader starts diverse chains of discussion and introduction, one of which will lead to success.
- **Collaboration:** Reading is unique among all entertainment vehicles in that it requires effort from the reader: the author and reader collaborate to tell the story. Hearing what readers enjoy is exciting to any author and the collaboration of this reward program offers the reader a chance to help jump start the career of an author he/she

enjoys. Besides, publishers are much more interested in readers' likes vs. authors' offerings.

**Suggestions:**

Via this reward, our mutual goal is to introduce this work to literary and publishing professionals or producers. Many are likely familiar with the term *"six degrees of separation,"* the theory that anyone on the planet can be connected to any other person on the planet through a chain of acquaintances that has no more than five intermediaries. This is what I aim to accomplish here with your help.

- Think about who you know in publishing (literary agents, editors, readers, executives, etc.) and pass this volume on to them*.
- Think about who you know and who they might know in publishing.
- Think about who you know that reads and would enjoy this book.

Send any leads, or opportunities, or introductions via the email link below.

rewards@richardevans-author.com

Thank you in advance for your help.

# ACKNOWLEDGMENTS

The challenge in completing a project like this can be a lonely life riddled with self-renunciation and doubt, but I am indebted to a team of terrific folks who helped me overcome this anguish.

Nick Brown is the author of the Agent of Rome series and is based in England; we workshopped the story and he recommended various structural changes, including additional chapters. I appreciated his advice and confidence and his learned guidance helped enormously.

As a storyteller, I need an editorial partner to help me turn written passion into absorbing sentences, so my collaboration with the brilliant Nan McNab has provided me immense assurance and I remain truly grateful for her work on the manuscript. As it happens, we crossed paths at primary school, such is the small world in which we live, and I have enjoyed her advice and recommendations.

I am indebted to my team of beta readers who provided feedback with enthusiasm and in some cases incisive criticism. Patty Kavadias, Jayden James, Denise Klemm, Phil Barrasi, and my brother Peter Evans, have contributed greatly to the project. I especially acknowledge Ann and Michael Keaney for their wholesome enthusiasm, advice, and friendship.

Writers Victoria have also helped me with manuscript assessment, and I encourage anyone considering the writing journey to join your local or national association, as they provide excellent services. I also appreciated being recommended for their patron support program in 2017.

The team at 852 Press have been enthusiastic for a second edition and I thank them.

It is vital to have strong family support when working on writing projects and I wish to acknowledge mine for their insight, humour, and advice during this project. Julia, Anthony, Kaitlyn, and Taylor have all said they would read it once published, so please contact your local bookshop, and place an order.

Finally, let me acknowledge the many folks I have met during my political and business career who have all helped shape my imagination, my creativity and in some cases the stories I draw upon when writing about politics. The journey has been a pleasure to share with you.

As a political insider, Richard Evans served as a federal member of parliament for Cowan in Western Australia during the turbulent 1990s. He now specialises in writing political thrillers, writing about the exotic characters in the mysterious world of the Australian Parliament. He lives in the coastal village of Airlie Beach, the gateway to the Whitsunday islands, with a view from his writing desk overlooking the Coral Sea.

For more information about his other books,
or to contact Richard please visit:

**www.richardevans-author.com**

Visit Instagram for updates on
Plots, Publishing, Politics and Personal news.

instagram.com/richardevans_author

**Episode two of the Democracy Trilogy**

The Mercantiles, a long-established, clandestine group of high-taxpaying business owners have grown frustrated by Prime Minister Andrew Gerrard's failure to meet promises, and decide the nation needs a change of government at the upcoming election. They call upon experienced and ruthless political operative Jonathan Wolff to organise their election campaign and defeat the prime minister.

Realising he cannot win the election his way, Wolff initiates an explosive campaign designed to remove the prime minister by defeating him in his own electorate using an independent candidate.

Investigative journalist Anita Devlin is appointed by her editor to promote the Stanley campaign as the publishing owner, unknown to her, is a member of the Mercantiles. She discovers the nefarious Wolff strategically working the campaign, and endeavours to expose his influence and manipulation.

**Episode three of the Democracy Trilogy**

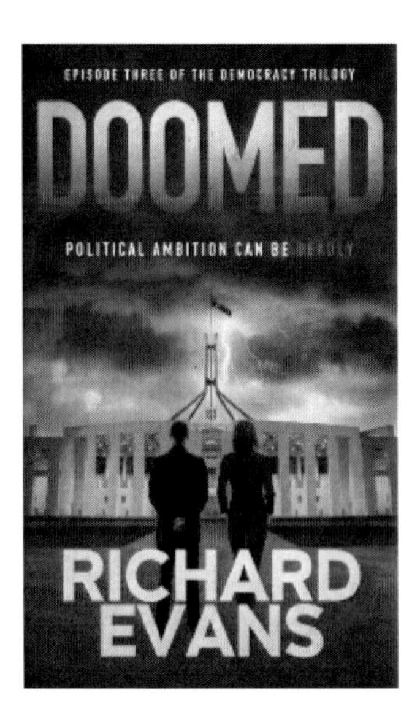


Three years after a change of government, the nation is facing huge social, policy, and environmental-related disasters yet the Australian government seems paralyzed on how to proceed. Two senior ministers resolve that a change of prime minister is essential for Australia's future and begin to lay the foundations for his dismissal.

Meanwhile, the parliament is held in a balance of power by the independent, Jaya Rukhmani, who can decide at any time if government legislation will be approved. Upon hearing the news that former prime minister Andrew Gerrard wishes to re-enter parliament, Jaya turns to Barton Messenger as an ally.

*Doomed* takes us behind the scenes of a parliament unaware of how ambition and political manipulation affect the everyday Australian. When the environment and economy are brought into the mix, which will be the one to flourish, and which one is doomed?

**For more information and purchasing options visit**
**852 Press.com.au**

She wants her culture and country back. Independence was never ceded, and she will do whatever it takes to get it back, including the ultimate sacrifice. When government peace talks stop, revolution begins.

Revolutionary leader, Nellie Millergoorra, campaigns for an aboriginal homeland to preserve indigenous culture by advocating the prohibition of mining in Arnhem Land using a United Nations declaration to convince a disrespectful government to sign a treaty. Nellie will do whatever it takes to finally gain independence and end government regulation over her people.

When there is no agreement, she recruits mercenary special forces to inflame community chaos establishing an explosive aboriginal revolutionary movement.

In a surprising confrontation with a reluctant prime minister, who is threatened with an ultimatum he can't ignore, Millergoorra negotiates a treaty whilst facing her own battle for survival.

*Forgotten People* is gripping political thriller featuring surprising plot twists, compelling characters, and a kick-arse female heroine.

**For more information and purchasing options visit**
**852 Press.com.au**

He's the nation's chief law maker. His daughter is fighting for her life in intensive care, a victim of a terrible crime. Will he ignore the prime minister's demands and his own laws to save her? Or will politics and the Catholic Church prevent him from doing his job?

Treasurer, Parker Osborne, initiates a covert plan, in partnership with Vatican emissary, Cardinal Rosseau, to guarantee proposed euthanasia legislation is destined for failure in the national parliament triggering a leadership challenge.

In a surprising development, the prime minister makes a decision which changes everything.

The Kill Bill is a gripping political thriller featuring emotional and surprising plot twists, convincing characters, and exposes the black-art of politics that will have you questioning the ethics of assisted dying. If you like fast-paced, page-turning thrillers that draw you into the story then Richard Evans' fourth book will not disappoint you.

Buy The Kill Bill today and learn how the black arts of politics really works.

**For more information and purchasing options visit**
**852 Press.com.au**

**She changes her name but not her attitude.**

A streetwise opportunist escapes despair and abuse in the big city by seeking opportunities in the mallee. She changes her name but not her attitude when she discovers wealth and privilege ripe for the taking from the influential Dowerin family of the mallee.

Rose Dowerin replaces her husband as the local federal politician. The subsequent trappings of influence and power as a minister in the federal government suit her ambitions. It's a privileged life, a life very different from the abusive streets of Melbourne from where she escaped and the dry dusty heat of the mallee.

Under threat Rose falls back into her malevolent ways to overcome the forces against her until an unexpected family twist changes everything.

THE MALLEE is an action-packed thriller with a strong female lead featuring emotional and surprising plot twists, convincing characters, and exposes the dark-arts of politics that will have you questioning the system.

If you like fast-paced, page-turning thrillers that draw you into the story then Richard Evans' seventh book will not disappoint you.

**For more information and purchasing options visit**
**852 Press.com.au**

852

PRESS

## ABOUT THE PUBLISHER

We are an independent publisher, helping Australians tell their story.

We are keen to share our experiences and processes with Australian writers so they can self-publish their own works. We will be launching a range of resources, services, and events for those with a story to tell.

**Visit our website for more information.**

**www.852Press.com.au**

Made in United States
North Haven, CT
06 August 2024